Waiting For Moonlight

Clive Jefferys

A Battle Of Britain Drama

McCormick Vigar

Cover design and production by
© Emer Jefferys
Instagram: @thecleverpoppet

First published as an eBook in 2020
ASIN: B08HY7XVZ1
McCormick Vigar

First print edition 2021
ISBN-13: 9798589719024
McCormick Vigar
Typeset in Garamond 12/16pt

This novel is dedicated to Gwyn Samuel.
He inspired me to stop just talking about it, and actually
write it down.

Acknowledgements

Whilst this tale is fiction, its historical background owes much to the tremendous efforts of many researchers, historical societies and authors. Family anecdotes and local historians also provided a wealth of insights into life in Sidcup during this period. They helped make a bygone world become real again, often in ways far more surprising than even my own imagination.

I have drawn from far too many online and printed sources to name them concisely, but I would like to express my particular thanks for the published works of The Battle of Britain Historical Society, John Mercer, Alfred Price, Len Deighton, John Ray, Michael Glover and Patrick Bishop.

I am especially grateful for the support and encouragement given by my good friend, Heather Byrne, who showed tremendous patience and dedication in working on my final manuscript.

Sidcup re-imagined

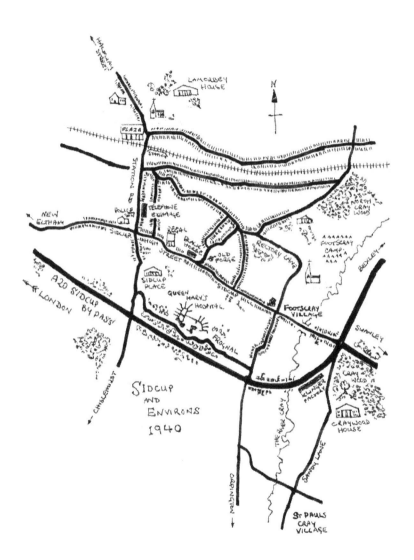

SIDCUP AND ENVIRONS 1940

Prologue

Under a cloudless night sky, a welcome chill was settling gently upon the land. Yet here and there, in sheltered places, the heat of the day lingered just a little longer.

The stars cast their light across the expanse of the universe and from the southern sky, the full moon shone with stark intensity across the landscape below. The moonlight held it all in sharp contrast, casting out across a patchwork of fields to a wooded hilltop, where the most ancient of trees stood sentinel to the slow passage of time. As seasons passed, as the cycle of life turned, all as it had since the beginning of earthly days… the trees stood witness. On this late summer night, a gentle breeze lifted their branches and rustled their leaves from time to time and all that dwelt there slept, except one.

Mother Fox stirred from her slumber, as the first ray of moonlight reached into the secret place in which she laid. After a short while, she turned towards its glow and welcomed the cheer of its illumination within her underground home. She looked towards her daughters; curled up, snug, nestled safely together and watched as one yawned and still half-asleep, pawed gently at her sister. Mother Fox thought of her husband, gone already to the night hunt, she thought proudly of her two sons, now departed from their den forever. They had long since heard destiny's call and went out into the world to seek their fortunes, alone.

Mother heard the screeching bark of her mate, far away, a summons to join him. She huffed to herself with satisfaction, prodded her daughters awake and with sleepy eyes, the two young vixens followed her up the burrow towards the light. With instinctive caution, Mother looked around the clearing and with ears held high, crept out into the moonlight. She stared deep into the woods, savoured the last scent of summer upon the wind and perceiving no danger, called her daughters to her side. Whilst they bickered as sisters often do, Mother looked up at the great tree above them, towering high into the night sky. She gazed in adoration at its great, shimmering ivy-clad form, at the heavy, careworn branches and gave thanks for its protection. This ancient oak was her god and deep amongst its gnarled roots was her home... for her family, her forebears and back through the ages, beyond imagination.

Father Fox barked again.

Mother answered his call and led their daughters onwards, scampering quickly through the undergrowth, until they came to the limit of their woodland sanctuary. There they found him, looking out towards the flat, treeless place where the two-legged creatures had built their great dens of rock.

Since her first cub days, she had watched those selfish destroyers creep ever closer, laying waste to her once beautiful forest with their merciless new order. Mother had watched them build their stone dwellings higher and higher, in envy of her towering oak god. She lamented the demise of her once-great domain, by now reduced to just this little hilltop, surrounded by a perverted, invaded world.

Father gruffed for attention and she followed his gaze towards the moon, now hanging low in the sky. She saw clouds approaching, coming to smother its brilliance and behind them came something, darker, enormous and menacing.

In the distance, a momentary flicker of intense light struck the earth and the foxes watched it in awe and wonder. They looked at each other with trepidation and then, a vicious, ripping crackle of sound raced across the landscape. The young vixens flinched with fright and shrank behind Mother, whilst Father continued to stare at this new, unfamiliar threat.

Another lightning strike shot earthwards and its brutal, tearing report came quicker, as the thunderstorm advanced towards their tiny realm. Mother's senses sharpened, as all around, the air charged with electric anticipation. She warbled a warning to Father and then, as one, the family fled back into the heart of the wood.

Helter-skelter they ran and jumped through the nettles and briars, until they reached the great oak and scurried below. There they cowered, deep underground, as the hideous, deafening crackles and booms drew close overhead. With wide-eyed, twitching fright, the foxes looked anxiously towards their shelter's threshold. The vixens mewed with fear and Mother drew them into her embrace, as she looked to Father and prayed to the great tree spirit for protection.

Suddenly, the burrow was filled with a blinding flash of pure, white light. A stupefying crash of thunder, the loudest noise that they had heard, shook their world.

Mother Fox, Father Fox and their daughters screeched in terror, as from high above, the dreadful deluge plummeted down.

Chapter 1

The first soldiers walked into view at the far end of Court Yard. Their arrival had been expected since first light and after hours of anticipation, the moment had finally come.

Three hundred yards away at the palace gate, two sentries watched the men approach for a few seconds more, to be certain of what they saw.

'Go on then lad... you had better tell the others that they're here,' the old sergeant ordered. The youth ran back across a short stone bridge towards the Great Hall of Eltham Palace, to spread the news of the approaching procession.

The sergeant looked back up the road, past the clap-boarded Lord Chancellor's House. In the bright morning sunshine, he squinted his eyes to see through the glare as hundreds more men came into view. The great oak trees that lined Court Yard cast deep, dark pools of shade beneath their summer-laden branches and the men flickered in and out of view, ghostlike, as they traversed each burst of bright sunlight. They looked weary, dishevelled, filthy and in most cases, lacking in any weapons that would usually set them apart as fighting men.

They look completely done in, the sergeant thought.

Just a few months earlier, they had set off for battle in France with such confidence in their ability to serve King and Country. However, the events of the last few weeks had shocked the entire nation. Instead of securing a great victory, the army had been routed and ran for the sea. Now, all eyes cast to their leaders to explain how such a calamity had befallen them.

The sergeant heard a shout from behind him.

He turned and saw his young counterpart returning, accompanied by their commander. Looking anxious to set to work, the pair hurried across the moat bridge, then paused to take in the scene.

The full impact of the moment wrote large across their commander's face.

'Sergeant Culpepper, tell them to muster on the lawns,' he instructed. 'Any injured men should step forward so they can be attended to first.'

'Very good Mister Courtauld, as you wish sir.' Culpepper replied awkwardly.

'The rest can wait on the grass,' Courtauld concluded. 'Until we are ready to feed them.' Without waiting for a response, he turned and walked briskly back across the bridge and a further hundred yards across the green, past well-tended flower beds, towards the towering stone building.

Alerted by all the commotion, many of the townsfolk had come out of their houses along the road. Small groups of women, children and older men stood blinking in the dazzling sunlight. They watched in silence at first, not sure how to react to the sorry spectacle.

One of the women called out.

'Come on everyone… let's give our boys three cheers!'

The response was instinctive and hearty on the first hip-hip, but quickly fizzled away. They settled for a muted applause, which in turn, soon evaporated. A few soldiers gave a few half-hearted cheers in polite response, but their exhaustion and miserable demeanour made it quite obvious that this wasn't a time for celebration.

Today, their future focussed only as far as getting something to eat and to sleep. Some were barefoot and others had hardly any clothes on their back, let alone their full uniforms.

'Why haven't those men got boots, Mr Culpepper?' young Bob Taylor asked.

'It's because they had to wait in the water before they were picked up,' Culpepper explained, before dropping all notion of military formality. 'You can't swim far in army boots, Bob.'

He'd seen this before, at the evacuation of Gallipoli in 1916. Back then he'd been like one of these poor blighters, waiting to get off a beach, to escape an advancing enemy.

In reality, the young men filing past on the bridge were the real soldiers today. Albert Culpepper didn't feel much like a proper sergeant; he was just a middle-aged man with an armband that his sister had sewn only yesterday. Its black cloth displayed the white letters LDV, *Local Defence Volunteer.* This was his only sign of authority alongside a civilian trilby hat and careworn tweed jacket, atop a tradesman's blue dungarees. His platoon had been formed only a few weeks before, in answer to a wireless broadcast by Anthony Eden, the Secretary of State for War. The young men and veteran soldiers of Britain had been asked to step forward and be counted in this time of national crisis.

This day was Tuesday 4th June 1940 and the British Army had suffered its worst defeat in history, at the hands of Nazi Germany. For the second time in just over twenty years, Western Europe was at war.

France had been dissected and Belgium, the Netherlands, Denmark, even as far as Norway, had all fallen to invasion. Now the majority of the British Expeditionary Force, outwitted and defeated, had been evacuated in what would become known as *The Miracle of Dunkirk.* From there and other ports of Western France, Royal Navy ships and hundreds of civilian vessels had rescued over 300,000 Allied soldiers, before the German armies closed a trap set in motion just three weeks earlier. Ramming home their advantage, the Germans were now pushing south towards Paris. No-one knew whether the French could resist this new offensive for long.

Over the last three days, the coast of South East England had taken tens of thousands ashore from boats of all sizes, every hour, in varying disorder. The railways were disrupted by trainload after trainload of survivors, brought to ad-hoc concentration points set up across the Southern Counties. Half a mile from a railway station on the outskirts of London; Eltham Palace was just such a place where a few thousand men could be gathered, clothed and fed. Their presence would be registered with the War Office and then they would be sent back to their regiments, as the army worked to regain its composure.

Now began the mammoth task of bringing order to this chaos, whilst the people of Britain struggled to comprehend the scale of defeat.

Albert watched as hundreds of men dispersed across the pristine lawn in front of the Great Hall. They lay on the grass, eagerly lighting cigarettes handed out alongside tin mugs of tea. The relief on their faces was so palpable that it could have passed for a great party, if only the reason for their invitation had not been so tragic. Conversation and nervous laughter rang out here and there. Many just sat in silence, staring into the far distance where their thoughts might be found. Some were already fast asleep. A gentle breeze ruffled the trees around the tranquil setting and Albert listened to the rustle of their leaves for a few moments.

He shook his head slightly, as he struggled to grasp the ramifications of this day. He turned to look back down Court Yard, at the growing number of men approaching and, in particular, some whose appearance was quite surreal. One large group drew near, with faces, arms and legs blackened by naval fuel oil and seawater. Nine of them were dressed in red Victorian ladies bloomers with blue and white striped pyjama shirts, presenting an utterly bizarre ensemble. Wherever they had landed, the good people there must have turned out their jumble as a means to clothe them.

As they passed by Albert, one called out.

'What's the matter guvnor, ain't you never seen French tarts out on a beano before?'

A peal of raucous laughter rang out.

Albert smiled, pleased that they had some spirit left to show.

'It's been twenty years since I could last afford you,' he replied.

The young men laughed again in appreciation.

Surveying this fancy dress parade, Albert noticed a few blue-grey French uniforms amongst the mass of khaki, their owners looking even more displaced than their British counterparts.

He looked at the sorry spectacle and simply felt... *numb*.

Albert had spent the last nine months telling himself that everything was normal. He had chosen to believe the newspapers and the wireless, persuading himself that it would all work itself out well in the end. Poland's war would prove an unfortunate, but isolated event, the great armies of Britain and France would stand together just as in 1914 and the Germans would baulk at the prospect of another great war. It was all bluff and bluster; there was no substance behind that strange man with an even stranger moustache.

Yes, it had been far better for Albert to carry on with his respectable life as a timber merchant, still grieving the death of his darling wife. By carrying on as normal, nothing would change, just like everyone else said.

Unfortunately, it had all gone wrong. By last week, it was obvious that the British Army was in full scale retreat.

Now, everything is lost! Look at these poor sods... dressed like clowns, he thought.

Albert felt angry, but more than that, he was frightened too.

He told himself to get a grip.

'I doubt those lads expected to find themselves here today,' he murmured out loud.

Bob looked puzzled, unsure how to reply.

'You stand here,' Albert instructed. 'Keep telling them to come on through, head for the grass and that someone will come to them. I'll go back inside to see how we're doing in there.'

'Yes Sir!' Bob replied enthusiastically. He gave an eager salute and marched towards the next group of men, with what he hoped was an air of great authority.

Albert walked back towards the Great Hall. There seemed to be a bit of a commotion around one of the tables set up outside for refreshments. Three men were exchanging cross words with two others, a matter of queue jumping it seemed. Large mugs of tea and piles of doorstep sandwiches were on offer and as he passed by, a great mountain of a man grabbed Albert's arm.

'Tea n' Wad?' he exclaimed in a broad Scottish accent. 'Is that th'best yae cin do? Efter what we've bin throo...it's cunny and whisky w'need!'

Albert felt his face flush.

'I don't think that is quite on the menu today,' he replied politely. 'But I'll see what can be done.'

He carried on, annoyed by his own embarrassment on hearing such coarse language, and into the great building, where he encountered a scene of barely-organised chaos. Hundreds more men sat or stood in ragged queues to collect blankets, a plate of hot stew, a mug of tea, or were just milling around waiting for someone to tell them what to do.

Albert looked up and admired the beautifully restored wooden trusses fifty feet above him, one of the finest examples of a medieval hammerbeam roof to be found anywhere in Britain today. There was plenty of his own timber up there now he considered with pride. From the 13th Century, this great hall had been at the heart of one of the most important royal palaces, the epicentre of English politics for nearly two hundred years. The legendary Henry VIII changed all that when, in later life, he switched his favour to his palaces at Hampton Court and Greenwich. This once-great bastion gradually fell into disrepair and by the 18th Century, was fit for no better use than as a cow shed.

He had last been here four years ago, when it became the private domain of the fabulously wealthy Courtauld family. They had taken the lease of the derelict palace to build their family home, intent on restoring this historic hall to its former grandeur. Ruined buildings were demolished, the moat dammed again and new gardens laid out with a fabulous, modernist Art Deco mansion built as its centrepiece. A year later, Country Life Magazine lauded the Courtauld's creation as one of the finest, most fashionable houses in Britain. Albert pondered that instead of hosting upper class dance parties; this great building now set the stage for a drama far more in keeping with its ancient origins.

Like a scene from Shakespeare, he thought, sensing that a tragic new history was being played out in front of him.

His thoughts began to wander yet again, an ever more frequent habit as the loneliness of bereavement took root over recent few years.

Born and raised in Hackney, Albert had escaped poverty by joining the army as a boy soldier and by the time of his discharge in 1919, he was a fully trained carpenter. At first, he took whatever odd jobs he could find during the difficult times that followed the First World War. One day in 1921, he saw a newspaper advertisement for skilled tradesmen that would change his life forever. On a winter's morning, he took the No 21 trolley bus out to Eltham in Kent and presented himself for interview.

Exciting times lay ahead for the towns and villages nearest to London, as a new building boom promised transformation of these hitherto quiet rural communities. In this respect, Albert had correctly chosen a lifetime's employment, providing he could overcome the first hurdle posed by Mr Brunton, the Joinery Foreman of Suburban Homesteads Ltd.

Having satisfactorily answered questions about his experience, all was going well until he was taken down to the workshop to demonstrate his skills. At this point he had to remove his gloves to ready himself for work, thereby revealing what had hindered his progress since leaving the army.

He was missing the last finger on his left hand, the forefinger and little finger on his right.

Mr Brunton raised his eyebrows.

'You seem to have lost something, Mr Culpepper?'

'I didn't mislay them sir... Johnny Turk took them from me,' replied Albert. 'But it doesn't stop me in my work, if you'll let me show you.'

Over the next half hour, Albert cut example tenon and mortise joints of varying complexity, admirable for their perfection.

The men of the workshop gathered around to watch his frenzy of activity, an inspiring demonstration of how to overcome injuries generally considered an absolute bar to such work in those days.

'Mr Culpepper, we've seen quite enough thank you,' Mr Brunton declared, with a smile. 'You can start on Monday, if you've a mind to?'

Albert readily accepted his offer with thanks and made to leave, when one of the other joiners called out cheekily.

'Oi *Fingers!* See you next week!'

That nickname stuck with him for the rest of his life. He didn't mind at all, not even when from time to time, his workmates teased him by making a V sign. It all made for a good story to tell for years to come, about how he got into the trade.

Besides, if you had to have something shot off… there were far worse appendages for a man to lose.

The clatter of dropped tin plates broke the thread of Albert's nostalgia and he looked around the huge space of the hall again. The ladies of the Women's Institute were busy with their stew and potatoes and generally speaking, everyone seemed to have something useful to do.

His gaze fell upon one young man sitting huddled in the middle of the hall.

He was an unremarkable, average sort of chap in his early twenties perhaps, with a shock of unruly brown hair. He wore a blue woollen blazer, too short in the sleeves and a pair of grey flannel trousers, easily two sizes too large.

He bore the vacant expression of someone deeply in shock.

With his arms wrapped tightly around his legs, he seemed to be trying to contain shakes running through his body as he stared at his plimsoll shoes. His left hand was covered by a crude blood-stained bandage and with his dirt-encrusted, unshaven face and tousled hair; he presented a sorry-looking sight indeed.

Albert picked his way through the throng towards him.

'Soldier… is there anything I can do to help you?' he announced, trying to reprise past confidence.

The young man didn't respond at first, but after a short while, looked up.

'Please could I make a telephone call… to let my father know that I'm alright? He's probably not heard anything 'bout me for weeks, not since I wrote him… from France,' he explained. 'My letters are probably sitting in a ditch…. somewhere over there… with everything else… for all I bloody know.'

Albert had found his purpose.

'Come with me then lad. My office is just down the road and you can use the telephone there.'

'Thank you sir,' the young man responded. 'I'll ring Mr Hardcastle at the haberdasher's, next door.'

He quickly rose to his feet, his composure briefly restored.

Ten minutes later, they stood at the telephone in Albert's timber yard and asked the operator to connect his call. After a few minutes waiting for the connection, evidently Mr Hardcastle accepted the phone call and gabbled back with excitement.

There was silence for a few minutes, presumably whilst the soldier's father was brought to the telephone.

Not wishing to impose, Albert left the office and waited outside on the iron staircase. After ten minutes or so, the young man walked out with tears in his eyes.

'Thank you sir, that was very kind of you. I'm George Kendrick,' he revealed. 'But my friends all call me Ken.'

His face broke into a wide, happy grin.

Albert felt the glow of his youthful optimism and quite suddenly, his own spirits lifted too.

'My name is Culpepper… Albert Culpepper,' he announced.

With a chuckle, he had held up his right hand and displayed it proudly.

'My friends call me Fingers!'

Chapter 2

Although ten months had passed since Germany had invaded Poland in September 1939, the so-called *Phoney War* of inactivity that followed had largely been an anti-climax for the people of Britain. Children evacuated from the cities returned home within a few months as thankfully, mass bombing and poison gas attacks did not materialise.

So whilst the nations of Europe girded their military loins in preparation for war on the continent, the civilian population of the British Isles felt itself largely abstracted from the impending conflict. Apart from a small offensive into the Saar in September, the French missed the opportunity to strike deep into Nazi Germany, whose military strength was mostly engaged in Poland. Expecting another long and bitter conflict like The Great War, the allied armies instead wanted more time to establish their defences in France.

In truth, most French and British politicians had hoped that diplomacy might still prevail. Over the first wartime winter, British Prime Minister, Neville Chamberlain, had continued in much the same spirit of appeasement that had only served to embolden the Nazi regime in preceding years. The RAF was told to drop propaganda leaflets, not bombs, on Germany. To Chamberlain, considerations of avoiding damage to private property took precedence over actually striking hard at the enemy. It would be some time before the naivety of this stance would be exposed, in stark contrast to the utter ruthlessness already deployed by Nazi Germany elsewhere.

Despite every augur of Hitler's intent, Chamberlain fantasised about a rebellion within the German state to depose its dictator. He hoped that a last minute miracle of international diplomacy might yet avert the outbreak of a full-blown war like that of 1914.

Whilst the armies of France and Britain mobilised and settled down to a long, boring winter at the frontline, the newspapers had struggled to serve up much that was really newsworthy. With the exception of the sinking of the German battleship, Graf Spee, in December, the German war machine was left largely unchallenged by the faint-hearted allies of Poland.

Everything changed in the spring of 1940, when Britain and Germany finally faced each other in Norway. The Nazi forces quickly prevailed and soon after, launched an invasion of the Low Countries.

The German army, the *Wehrmacht*, overran the Dutch and Belgian armies and lured the best of the British and French forces northwards. Then it launched a second, audacious attack through the Ardennes forest of Luxembourg, far to the south. An avalanche of German tanks and motorised troops thrust westward with unprecedented speed. Supported by overwhelming airpower, the Germans reached the French Channel coast only seven days later. The speed of war had accelerated far beyond the walking pace of The Great War.

Under the pressure exerted by this new, devastating form of warfare, the Allied armies in Belgium reeled from blow after blow and were forced into a fighting retreat towards the port of Dunkirk. As the Wehrmacht closed in and prepared for the kill, the Allied cause appeared to be lost.

Yet as utter defeat seemed imminent, salvation came from the desk of the German Supreme Commander himself.

Hitler had become increasingly fearful of his generals and the threat that their success might pose to his own authority. Mindful of how the great First World War generals,

Hindenburg and Ludendorf, had seized power from their Kaiser, Hitler turned to his most trusted political allies to exert his will. Instead of allowing the Wehrmacht to crush the Dunkirk pocket, he called it to a halt. The generals of the German High Command were incredulous, but their political master would not be swayed. Instead, he called upon the Luftwaffe, led by his faithful follower, Reichsmarschall Herman Goering, to deliver the coup de grâce to the allied troops trapped on the seashore.

This proved to be a major miscalculation, as British fighter aircraft arrived in force around the beachhead and frustrated the Luftwaffe's efforts to bomb the evacuation to a halt. Both air forces suffered grievous losses over the following days, but this bought time for the Royal Navy and an improvised fleet of small vessels, to shepherd the majority of troops to safety.

Nonetheless, just a few hours after the last British ships retired from the French coast, Wehrmacht soldiers stood on the deserted embarkation beaches to survey the carnage. The cameras of German war reporters filmed their pick of over 50,000 abandoned British vehicles, tanks, artillery guns and their supplies, stretching back for fifty miles in every direction. It presented a previously unimaginable, almost fantastical, image of the total and utter defeat of one the most respected armies in modern history.

Nevertheless, the bulk of the British army and many of their allies had escaped to England. To pluck a little success from the mire of such utter defeat was a miracle in itself, but virtually all of their equipment of war and thereby, the means of Britain's future defence, now lay abandoned in France.

The German army turned southwards to complete its victory and the French military and political establishment fell into total chaos.

Paris was gripped by panic, as rumour and counter rumour of French resolve, or capitulation, rebounded around the world.

It seemed only a matter of days before the German leviathan would seize absolute control of Western Europe.

Ken and Albert walked back up Eltham Hill towards the assembly point, each one lost in his own thoughts.

Albert looked at the young man by his side and recalled the fear he experienced when standing in water up to his neck, off a foreign shore twenty five years before. He reflected how this foolish world was repeating the same mistakes of the past.

Ever since the Spanish Civil War had been played out on cinema newsreels, the potential for death dealt by huge aircraft formations bombing civilians en masse would change how wars were conducted forever. The tales of glory and derring-do on a distant battlefield, that had proved false to Albert's generation, would this time reap a bitter harvest at home as well. This new conflict in 1940 would truly become a war of entire peoples. The Nazis had rained destruction from the skies above continental Europe and it seemed that no matter what defences were put in place; it was held certain *that the bomber will always get through.*

Albert pondered that the young man walking next to him may have lived to fight another day, but for how much longer? For that matter, he wondered what lay in store for everyone as the forces of destruction gathered on Britain's threshold. He wanted to say something encouraging, but no words felt adequate and they walked on in silence.

As they turned the corner into Court Yard, Ken faltered in his stride.

'Oh God... not already,' he gasped, recapturing Albert's attention.

During their absence, a dozen army lorries had arrived and were parked nose to tail before the narrow moat bridge. Several officers in barracks-clean uniforms were ordering men around, evidently preparing to load them aboard the vehicles.

Military discipline was seeking to assert its rule again.

Albert felt the tension rising in his young companion and he quickened his own step, as they attempted to work their way through the crowd.

Their progress was halted by a corporal standing stiffly in their way.

'Are you a London regiment?' he asked of Ken, as his odd civilian garb gave no clue.

'No Corp, I'm Service Corps, at Buller, Aldershot,' replied Ken.

'Well, you better get inside,' the corporal barked. 'You need to register and wait for a rail warrant. Then you can get properly on your way soldier.'

Softening his stance, he concluded with more empathy.

'Well done on getting home… good luck.'

Albert sensed that Ken had lied, but he could not blame him.

Let him have a little longer before he is drawn back, he thought.

They quickly walked on and inside the palace.

It was now late in the afternoon and the sunlight cast its light less vertically through the tall, high windows of the Great Hall.

Dark shadows lurked beneath their casements.

Order had superceded chaos and the men now sat or lay on blankets, in neat rows up and down the hall. An odd sense of calm had settled, as many slept in exhaustion after the ordeal of the last few days. A thick pall of cigarette smoke hung above them, catching the sun's rays and gently swirling about as the few people on their feet moved around, disturbing the air.

'Well… this is where we part our ways.' Albert said with forced exuberance.

Ken smiled.

'I guess I should thank you again Mr Culpepper. Thanks for not saying anything contrary in front of that corporal.'

'Look after yourself young man and get yourself back to your unit soon. You don't want to be declared absent without leave, that wouldn't serve you well, would it?' replied Albert.

Albert turned to go, but paused for a moment.

'Look me up if you are ever this way again, you know where my office is. It would be good to see you again,' he offered. 'You know, smartened up, in happier times?'

They shook hands and parted.

Ken found a spot to sit down, resting his back against the cool stone wall with his legs stretched out in front of him. He lit a cigarette, savoured its smoke and exhaled with satisfaction, watching it billow in the air.

It had been the longest, most awful few weeks of his life and he was glad to be home.

He fell fast asleep.

Stephen Courtauld stood at one of the heavy oak tables at the head of the hall. The steam from two large tea urns gently rose around him, catching the sunlight with meandering indifference.

Courtauld had served with distinction during the First World War, rising to the rank of Major, awarded the Military Cross for valour. Now in his late fifties, having enjoyed a playboy's life of luxury and adventure around the world, he was determined to give practical support to his country again.

Today he began modestly, breaking open packets of small postcards that had been brought in earlier.

Each one carried a hurriedly printed, but simple message. *I am well and will be in contact with you soon.*

There was space enough to write a name and a loved one's address under the War Office stamp. These would be given to each man, with strict instructions not to make any other comment that might disclose military information or spread alarm; otherwise the message would destroyed.

A shortage of pencils had been solved by snapping them in half and re-sharpening a point for use.

He felt pleased with his own ingenuity.

He saw Mr Culpepper approaching and called out.

'Mr... *Sergeant*... Culpepper...over here if you will?' he said, the return to military convention still a novelty to him. 'I've been looking for you everywhere.'

'Yes sir, I've been keeping myself busy. What can I do for you sir?' Albert replied.

'Oh hang all this ranks business Albert,' said Courtauld. 'I want to ask your advice. Your brother-in-law is an air warden over in Sidcup, isn't he? Perhaps he can give us a little help?'

'I'm sure Ted would be happy to oblige, but it depends what you have in mind Mr Courtauld?' Albert replied.

Happier now that he had broached the subject, Stephen Courtauld proceeded quickly.

'I want to take you up to the roof, as I have an idea to discuss,' he revealed.

Five minutes later, the two of them stood atop the Great Hall and without doubt, it was the tallest building for miles around. This vantage point delivered a commanding view of the suburban sprawl of housing into London to the west,

Shooter's Hill and Woolwich to the north, south to Chislehurst and eastwards to Sidcup, five miles away.

It would make for an excellent air raid observation post, Courtauld proposed and there was no denying it. The question to answer was how it should be made available to the authorities.

Albert agreed to talk to his brother-in-law, who as Chief ARP Warden in Sidcup, was their closest source of expertise at this time.

They gazed out across the panorama of housing, fields and woodlands and contemplated what the future might bring.

If instead, they had looked directly upwards, at the object glinting in the sunlight high above… they would have seen just how close this war had already come.

Chapter 3

From an altitude of 39,000 feet, the view across Kent and South East London was absolutely breath-taking on this clear summer afternoon.

The pilot and observer of the twin-engine Junkers 86 reconnaissance aircraft were members of an elite club of airmen that flew so high, that the world below curved away from view. In an era when most flying was done below 15,000 feet, these two men felt truly privileged to be taking part in such a daring enterprise that day. Peering upwards to the stratosphere, the sky turned a darker, inky blue, marking the upper limits of the atmosphere. Speeding through the thin air, the Junkers left only the faintest whisper of a contrail to betray its presence to the world below.

This aircraft's design was first taken from the drawing board in the early 1930's, as the fledgling Luftwaffe started to prosper under the Nazi government that came to power in 1933. Still observing the limitations of the Versailles Treaty, Germany's aircraft had to carry the pretence of civilian purpose. The design of the Ju86 was a compromise; ostensibly a passenger plane, but capable of being remodelled as a medium bomber. However, its military shortcomings came to light when first used in anger by the Condor Legion in the Spanish Civil War. Nonetheless, the Ju86 played its part in helping develop the design and doctrine for the Luftwaffe's next generation of combat aircraft, with which it would unleash a new, devastating form of warfare in 1939.

Considered obsolete in its original form, Junkers designers saw the potential for redeveloping its airframe to fulfil the new concept of high altitude reconnaissance.

Since 1936, Germany had equipped its civilian airliners with secret cameras to systematically map Europe from the air. With the utmost irony, the first ever aerial photo mosaic of the British Isles was created by Nazi Germany within just two years. The essential foundation of Germany's forthcoming Lightning War, *Blitzkrieg*, would be up-to-date information about where to strike its enemies' industrial and military resources. With this directive in mind, German designers set about the development of specialist aircraft to supply such intelligence under wartime conditions.

The aircraft flying high above Eltham that day was the prototype P2 model, with a crew of just two men in a streamlined, pressurised flight cabin. Fitted with high performance engines and greatly increased wingspan, the P2's maximum altitude had increased by an incredible 40%. Most importantly, its bomb bay had been replaced by additional fuel tanks and an array of precision cameras. Flying way above the combat ceiling of any contemporary fighter plane, the aircraft was virtually immune to attack.

Taking advantage of the British disarray prevalent over the last few days, it had flown in from the North Sea and over the Thames Estuary to avoid detection. The aircraft had arrived over North Kent just as the sun sank lower in the sky, casting shadows across the landscape. Luftwaffe intelligence staff would utilise observed shadow lengths, in conjunction with the known height of landmarks, to provide accurate scale and relief when interpreting the photographs that spied on Britain that day.

This afternoon's objectives were the Royal Arsenal munitions factories at Woolwich, the great Port of London, then north to the Royal Ordnance Factory at Enfield and finally, eastwards to Essex and back across the North Sea. Satisfied with the aircraft's position for the start of the photo run, the observer activated the cameras in the aircraft's belly and began their automatic exposure sequence.

Not that they would ever know it, but Albert Culpepper and Stephen Courtauld were immortalised as tiny, tiny dots on photographs 8 and 9 of the 300 that would be taken over the next forty five minutes.

The Junkers flew on... recording buildings, roads, railways, factories, shipping on the Thames and three aerodromes, RAF Debden, North Weald and Hornchurch.

Then homeward-bound, the spy plane flew towards the North Sea and slipped into the twilight of dusk.

Chapter 4

The sun had almost set and Ken Kendrick slept fitfully. Sometimes he murmured out loud, occasionally his left leg twitched awkwardly as he lay there, lost in a dream.

He felt like he was flying, soaring high above the world. He looked down upon a chaotic sight of hundreds of vehicles, each one creeping slowly in column along a road straddled by tall trees. For as far as he could see, a teeming masse of thousands of people, soldiers and civilians all mixed together. Some were on foot, some with horses and farm carts, others travelled in motor cars and army lorries, all piled high with baggage. He could hear the snorting of huge artillery horses as they strained to pull large howitzer guns up the long, slow-rising hill ahead. In the intense heat and billowing clouds of dust, everything had slowed to a snail's pace behind the artillery train.

Ken heard shouting, screaming, panic.

From the abstract vantage point of his dream, he could see himself looking out of the canvass tilt at the back of a lorry. He saw German fighter planes approaching, skimming above the fields at breakneck speed as they closed the distance to their target. Ken heard the dreadful rattle of their machine guns, the slow sickening thump of their cannons, pandemonium, women screaming, children wailing, explosions, deafening noise.

Ken was in his body again, running, running, running.

The attack was over.

Silence.

He stood in the middle of the road.

Smoke from burning vehicles stung his eyes, bodies lay strewn about and his gaze was drawn towards a young

French artillery officer. The elegantly dressed figure walked towards him, stopping at each horse lying in the road still harnessed to the gun limbers. Most were dead, but a few were thrashing about and whinnying in agony with broken legs, savage wounds, bellies ripped open. The officer held a revolver, firing one shot, then another and another, to put the animals out of their misery.

The officer continued to approach Ken.

The Frenchman was crying. Tears cut wide streaks through the filth on his harrowed face and Ken stared at the muzzle of the revolver. Slowly the gun moved upwards, it was rising, pointing, taking aim.

Ken heard laughter, dreadful laughter and then he awoke with a scream.

The other people in the hall looked at Ken in momentary alarm. He felt hot-drenched in sweat and his wounded hand nagged painfully.

He stared at the ceiling pendant lamps, casting their light with a stark, artificial yellow glare. Looking down, he drew his legs up and hugged them tightly. Now that all was quiet again, everyone got on with their business and Ken avoided their gaze by closing his eyes for a while. Having collected his senses, he looked for his cigarettes, drew one out and lit it, trembling, between his lips. Ken remembered where he was and looked around, feeling a little calmer now.

Someone had brought in a wireless set and the huge room echoed to faint music from a Home Service radio broadcast. He strained to hear it better and finally picked up on an old melody, as the last verse drew the song to a close.

The music reassured him, a familiar sound in an unfamiliar setting.

Looking across the hall, he saw Albert talking to two young women. The taller one, with her auburn hair mostly tied up in a scarf was an especially pretty young woman, the like of which Ken had not seen for ten months whilst he sat at the front line waiting for something to happen. Just five weeks ago, that something, worse than he could ever have imagined, did happen. By some miracle, he had escaped the Nazis, was back home in England, sitting in this strange old castle hall looking at pretty girls.

A shadow of his nightmare crossed his mind for an instant. He forced it away, locked in a tiny secret corner, never to come out again, he hoped.

The other woman, a younger, shorter brunette, was laughing now.

She was nice too, but more demure somehow, less expressive, less attention-seeking than the other.

Well, that was his impression, but what did he know about women?

Not much.

Ken could tell the girls were excited about visiting the spectacle of this place tonight.

Easy for them, he thought. *They've come here to gawp at all this commotion, but they didn't know what it was like over there.*

He felt deeply troubled by confusing feelings of relief, anger, guilt, all mixed up.

So many of his mates were gone, lost, captured, some dead for certain, because he had seen it happen. Like many a soldier before him; he resolved to forget it all, to live for the moment, to embrace what he could see and hold in his hand right now.

No yesterday, no tomorrow, just today.

The group of people caught his attention again. Mr Culpepper carried the large wireless set and the girls were trying to move a heavy table.

Ken saw his chance, stood up and walked briskly across the room.

'Ladies, let me help you…what can I do?'

The confident one seized the moment.

'Well young sir, we need to move this into the middle so that everyone can hear it. I bet you've got the muscles for the job.'

'I reckon I have Miss, let me take this end.' Ken responded. 'Do you think you two could manage the other end alright?'

The taller girl giggled.

The other looked serious and quite put-out.

'We can manage it fine ourselves, actually,' she replied curtly.

'Oh Betty, stop getting so het up, let's all do it together,' the taller girl interrupted and gave Ken a flirtatious wink. 'Don't you mind my little sister, she takes things far too seriously at times.'

They all gave a good heave to the table and dragged it across the floor, with Albert Culpepper peering over the top of the radio set as he followed them. Once they were satisfied with the table's position, the wireless was placed down and switched back on, taking a lot less time to warm up than it had before.

'Thank you Ken,' said Albert. 'Good to see you looking a lot better. Let me introduce my nieces, Elizabeth and Virginia. Girls, this is Ken Kendrick.'

The taller girl spoke first.

'Charmed I'm sure,' she said, offering her hand in grand fashion to Ken.

'Oh Ginny will you behave?' Betty cut in. 'You're not Scarlet O'Hara and you're certainly not Vivian Leigh either!'

'Oh fiddle-de-dee, don't listen to her, I'm sure.' Ginny continued, in her best American accent.

Ken had to admit it was rather good and rather funny.

They all laughed, even their uncle.

Introductions complete, Albert took charge.

'Everyone, let's just settle down. This is a serious business… the Prime Minister's speech is due soon.'

Reality had returned.

Word had got around that the BBC would be broadcasting the text of an important speech given in parliament earlier that afternoon. Everyone gathered around to listen, as new clouds of cigarette smoke bloomed above them in the yellow light. It was one of those rare moments in history when a news bulletin had been written by the Prime Minister, Winston Churchill, himself. The nation was waiting to be told of the true scale of events of the last few days.

Churchill had only taken office four weeks before. The failure of the British landings in Norway had led to a vote of No Confidence in Neville Chamberlain's leadership. Whilst he won by the slimmest of margins, it became obvious that he could no longer continue. Perversely, the Norwegian Campaign had been the responsibility of the Admiralty, under the command of the then First Sea Lord, Winston Churchill. Yet despite the failure of his department, he was propelled towards the premiership as one of only two acceptable candidates. The other contender, Lord Halifax, demurred. Churchill became the country's leader and only a few hours later, Germany launched its invasion of the Low Countries.

Churchill's appointment was not widely popular, as his maverick reputation was long-established in the minds of most British people. Many felt that Halifax was simply waiting for the new prime minister to fail, ready to take the title for himself at a more favourable moment. Certainly, every single day that followed heaped successive defeat and disaster upon Churchill's shoulders. Paradoxically, he seemed to grow in stature with every setback. He was a man unlike any other that had preceded him in recent years and with every personal appearance and broadcast, the people of Britain were beginning to hang upon his every word.

Soon the clipped, upper-class voice of the BBC newsreader could be heard from the radio set, reading out the Prime Minister's account of events of the last few days. Evidently, Churchill had not minced his words about the challenges now facing the country and there was little immediate succour for his audience.

Churchill knew that the people needed to hear the truth in order to earn their trust. His words echoed around the hall for over ten minutes, concluding with a warning of the very real threat of invasion they all now faced. He declared that the British nation would continue to stand against Nazi tyranny and would never surrender.

The broadcast ended and the hall was silent.

Everyone looked to each other and inwardly, many strengthened their resolve. The future was bleak, frightening and uncertain, but conversation turned to consent and collective support.

Ken stood there taking it all in, gathering his thoughts and feelings. The exertions with that table had really hurt his injured hand and feeling increasingly unwell, he decided he needed some air.

He walked through the arched doorway and out onto the grass.

Outside the air was cooler, the chill of night had descended and he looked up at the moon and shivered.

A dark thing, hiding in a tiny corner of his mind, stirred again.

Something was wrong, disturbing, something that Ken didn't want to acknowledge.

Chapter 5

Sunday 11th August 1940 was an unusually dull, overcast afternoon in Northern France.

At a bleak, windswept military aerodrome, a group of men had gathered beneath a gloomy sky to await the arrival of their new commanding officer. His landing request had only been received ten minutes earlier, prompting a flurry of activity across this corner of the airfield. Word travelled quickly from the radio room, to roofless hangars where the mechanics laboured, to the array of tents where men tumbled from their camp beds. It even went as far as the huge new mess tent that was being erected alongside the main airfield buildings.

The appointment of a new commander had raised disquiet amongst the men of the 10th squadron, *staffel*, of bomber group Kampfgeschwader 1. They'd heard he was a direct appointment from the Air Ministry in Berlin, the *Reichsluftfahrtministerium,* conjuring an image of a pen-pushing, bureaucratic zealot, intent on making everyone's life hell from hereon. The staffel had been on non-stop operations since early May and had moved to this bombed-out former RAF airfield, along with ninety more aircraft of KG1, only two weeks earlier. With little respite from continuous combat, half their original number in aircraft and aircrews had already fallen casualty. The most recent blow had been to lose their commander, Oberst Heinrich Von Schrader. He died not in combat, but, of all things, a burst appendix.

Overworked, thrust into battle again and again, Von Schrader had ignored the recurring pain in his belly, thinking it was the return of a long-felt stomach ulcer. Seven days ago, his appendix ruptured and 48 hours later, he died of septic shock in a hospital in nearby Amiens. Greatly respected by his men, it was a sadly unsoldierly way to die. He had been an officer of the old school, a veteran of 1918, formal, aristocratic, but always fair.

His would be a tough act to follow.

The sound of the approaching aircraft signalled the arrival of the new man in charge. Thirty or so men decided they would go out to the runway perimeter to take a first look at their new leader. To their surprise, instead of a Junkers 52 transport plane, a twin-engine Heinkel 111 bomber emerged from the low cloud base and circled the airfield. It appeared to be brand new, still in base factory paint and delivery markings, a much-needed replacement for aircraft recently lost in combat.

The Heinkel came in to land in perfect, textbook fashion. With only a single bounce on touchdown, it gently decelerated, taxied over towards the group of men, pulled up and its engines idled to a halt. The pilot disappeared from inside the flight cabin and this prompted several onlookers to run over and open the main hatch underneath the fuselage. Two legs dropped down and one of the crew swung himself out, stood fully upright and looked around. He was quickly joined by three more of his comrades. With all four dressed in standard khaki flight suits, it was impossible to tell who was in command.

After exchanging a few conspiratorial smirks between them, one stepped forward. He was an average looking man in height and looks, but rather stockily built. He pulled off his flying helmet to reveal a crop of dark hair, closely shaved at the sides and back. He was young, probably not even thirty years of age and already a major. Yet, by his casual appearance, he could easily have been mistaken for one of the mechanics toiling away in the hangars.

The most senior of the airfield staff present stepped forward and gave the requisite Nazi salute.

'I am Stabsfeldwebel Freund. Welcome to Rosières-en-Santerre, Herr Major.'

The new arrival returned his salute in kind.

'It's good to meet you, Freund.'

He reached out and shook the sergeant's hand with surprising informality.

'I'm Muller… *Horst* Muller,' he revealed.

His face broke into a wide grin.

'Now then Freund, where can we get a beer?'

He was a very different fellow to his predecessor.

Ever since Ken Kendrick arrived at Eltham Palace that day in early June, the whole of Europe had gone through truly seismic political change.

The French had fought fiercely against the second German offensive but the Wehrmacht broke through, precipitating the collapse of the entire French army. Paris became a ghost town almost overnight as the government and much of its population fled, joining millions of refugees on the trains and roads that led south. In envy of Hitler's success, Italy's fascist dictator, Bernito Mussolini rejected calls for neutrality and instead, declared war on Britain and France on the 10th June.

The next day, Prime Minister Churchill took a British delegation to meet the French Government, once he had found it hiding in a chateau in the Loire Valley. He tried to persuade the French to continue the fight, but the impromptu conference was overshadowed by defeatism and recrimination against Britain for evacuating its troops from Belgium. Churchill returned to England, knowing that his pleas had been in vain. The Third Republic of France writhed in its final death throes, riven by confusion, despair and an air of betrayal.

The evacuation from Dunkirk had not been the end of Churchill's travails in France. A further 190,000 British troops were still there, caught to the west of the second German offensive advancing on Paris. Another evacuation began, extracting soldiers from ports all along the south western coast. The military catastrophe was aptly concluded on the 17th June, when one of the last departing ships, *Lancastria*, was sunk off the port of St Nazaire. The passenger liner capsized and drowned six thousand people on-board. Accounting for a third of all of British fatalities suffered during the ill-fated campaign, news of this final disaster was suppressed for a long time afterwards.

On the 22nd June, Adolf Hitler sat in the same railway carriage used for the signing of the Armistice of 1918. As he savoured the abject humiliation of the French surrender delegation of 1940, he dubbed that moment as *the greatest German victory of all time.* Church bells rang in celebration throughout the Reich for three days, while he toured newly-occupied Paris and then rushed back to Berlin, to bask in a hero's welcome.

Instead of a protracted war that left millions dead, Nazi Germany had conquered virtually the whole of Western Europe in barely six weeks. With Britain seemingly on the brink of defeat, the German people were euphoric with relief and believed the war had been won. It seemed utterly illogical that the English would keep on fighting and Hitler, and most of the world, waited for the British government to seek terms for peace.

Europe's new Führer was looking forward to inflicting a second Treaty of Versailles, to make Britain and France squirm under an avalanche of outrageous economic demands. This expectation was not without foundation.

During the 1930's, a minority of extreme and eccentric British aristocrats had tried to court Nazi favour. They had unintentionally convinced Hitler of the decadence of the British ruling classes and that, like the French, they would be extremely vulnerable to *violent* persuasion. To hurry them up to this obvious conclusion, Hitler decided to apply the maximum military pressure and the mighty Luftwaffe was instructed to grind down British defences and morale. An invasion fleet was ordered to gather on the Channel coast, to add further substance to the threat.

Whether Hitler was actually prepared to risk launching such an invasion was the great question of the summer of 1940. Germany may have had the greatest army in Europe, but the sea around Britain was a barrier without equal.

Even if a crossing was successful, Hitler feared the terrific cost to his armed forces in such a precarious operation. Furthermore, he was wary of a world without the British Empire, in which the USA and Japan would rush to fill any vacuum. So he waited for the offer of a political compromise, but nothing came.

The obstacle to Hitler's strategy was the sheer strength of will of Winston Churchill, a man with an unusual combination of qualities to lead his country out of its present predicament.

Born into one of the great families of the British Empire, Churchill had been raised with privileged access to many of the most important people of his era. Before starting his political career, he had been an adventurous news reporter during the Boer War, then a serving officer in the British Army. Elected to parliament in 1900, in time he rose to high office in the last great Liberal government. As First Sea Lord during the First World War, he was blamed for the failure of the Gallipoli landings in the Turkish Dardanelles. Stripped of office, he served as an infantry officer on the Western Front, placing experience of the army back under his belt. He returned to political prominence in the 1920's, but as Chancellor of the Exchequer presided over economic failure and his political career seemed finished. Yet in one respect, the growing threat of Nazi Germany, he had been proven to be absolutely correct.

By the time he came to be Britain's leader, Churchill had amassed forty years' experience of the politics and the mechanisms of the British Empire. Alongside many terrible mistakes in a thoroughly chequered political career, he had also garnered an almost unparalleled global perspective, far broader than that possessed by the lowly-born Hitler. Churchill understood that the sea was both Britain's best defence and also its absolute lifeline to ensure his country's long term survival. He had learnt the perils of seaborne invasions, but also the strength of the Royal Navy, recently demonstrated again at Dunkirk. He reasoned that the immense resources of the empire would ultimately deliver strategic advantage over the German and Italian dictatorships.

Even so, his premiership had begun with a different battle, within his own cabinet of ministers.

The one day on which Britain nearly gave up the fight was the 27th May 1940. With half of the army surrounded at Dunkirk and yet to be rescued, political opinion was bitterly divided between seeking an armistice or fighting on. Churchill only just won the argument and from the frail foundation of that moment, he began to build a *No Surrender* consensus across British politics.

After June's calamities, his political turning point came mercifully quickly in early July. Churchill ordered the Royal Navy to confront a large part of the French fleet at Oran, gathered off the coast of Algeria. If taken under German command, these mighty French warships could tip the balance of naval power against Britain during a Channel invasion. The French battleships refused to surrender and came under withering fire; many were sunk or heavily damaged with great loss of life. Whipped up by Nazi propaganda, French public opinion soured against the same British who had deserted them at Dunkirk.

Nonetheless, Churchill had shown the world that Britain still had the means and the spirit to defy Hitler.

On assuming command of the 10th Staffel, it had not taken Major Muller long to reorganise the most able of his men, but that had been the easy part.

He soon discovered a poor state of affairs in the kampfgeschwader and across the entire Luftwaffe in the West. Having moved into captured airfields along the French, Belgian and Dutch coasts in such a hurry, logistical support was stretched to the limit. There were hundreds of unserviceable aircraft, erratic supplies of fuel and spare parts, even a chronic shortage of suitable munitions to bomb up his aircraft for operations.

Even with the new Heinkel he had delivered, Muller's staffel was forty percent below its proper establishment in aircraft and manpower. He had only 73 flight crew and 46 service mechanics, to operate at best, twelve aircraft in various states of repair. Fortunately, Muller also possessed a good instinct for organisation and improvisation. After days of shouting down the telephone to Air Support District officials and bartering with other units, he began to secure the means to bring his unit back to readiness. Such disregard for procedure almost brought the straitlaced Stabsfeldwebel Freund close to a nervous breakdown, under relentless pressure of his commander's increasingly strident demands.

In contrast, Muller seemed to have no fear of getting his own hands dirty as he bartered for supplies with neighbouring units. Looking to trade fuel for machine gun ammunition, he visited fighter wing Jagdgeschwader 54 at its airfield on the coast at Campagne. There he witnessed something that would have a profound effect on the battle ahead, as the unit's mechanics attempted to attach external fuel tanks to the fighters to extend their combat range over Britain. The *drop tank*, as it came to be known, consisted of a simple, disposable fuel cylinder fixed beneath an aircraft to extend its flight duration, whilst conserving normal internal fuel reserves. Crucially, the pilot could jettison the external tank before entering into combat, to fully regain his aerodynamic speed advantage.

The latest production model of the Messerschmitt 109, the E-7, was designed to couple to a 300 litre drop tank with a standard mounting point. This would almost double flight range to 1300 kilometres, but none of the precious new aircraft had arrived at the frontline yet. So, several mechanics at Campagne had offered to make an improvised fitting for the geschwader's current aircraft instead. They had tried their best for three days, but as Muller witnessed, their makeshift solution just led to ominous pools of leaked fuel beneath each trial aircraft.

Clearly, their efforts had been in vain.

Muller noticed the dismay of one of the fighter staffel commanders, a Prussian aristocrat, Oberleutnant Von Gehlenburg. Without drop tanks, his pilots would have to continue to fret about their fuel gauges as soon as they crossed the English coast. Many a dogfight over Britain would be cut ridiculously short, because the German pilot had to go home before he ran out of fuel. Muller returned to Rosières, deeply concerned about the effect this would have on protecting his bombers.

Nonetheless, the 10th Staffel's recuperation had proved to be blessing; exempting it from joining *Adlertag,* the first

major Luftwaffe assault on mainland Britain on the 13th
August. On this *Day of The Eagles*, the Luftwaffe had tried to
throw its full force against English airfields. Hampered by
bad weather, poor radio communications and an
unexpectedly fierce response from the RAF, the attack was
an utter failure. German airmen quickly nicknamed it *Black
Thursday,* in commemoration of their heavy losses and failure
to meet hardly any of their objectives.

Insulated from this poor start to the main assault,
Muller's men responded well to the new man in charge and
morale quickly improved. Whilst he had brought superb
personal flying skills, the same could not be said of all the
new aircrew sent to refill the ranks of his unit. They were
mostly good-hearted lads, keen to do their duty for the
Fatherland, but they clearly lacked adequate training for the
challenge ahead. Nonetheless, he injected a spirit of urgency
into his command and within just eight days they were ready
to resume operations. Most importantly, he listened to his
most combat-experienced men. He wanted to know exactly
how British airmen fought.

Prior to his arrival, Muller learnt that the staffel's first
sorties against Britain had been part of *Kanalkampf,* the
Channel War. The Luftwaffe attacked convoys in the
Channel and probed coastal defences, trying to bring the
RAF into combat over the sea. The British had refused to be
drawn in any great strength over this watery No Man's Land.

The Luftwaffe's leader, Herman Goering, misread this as
a sign of British weakness and ordered more attacks inland,
expecting to quickly overwhelm his opponents. Although
victory in mainland Europe had cost the Luftwaffe nearly
half of its pre-war strength, Goering still had 1300 bombers
and 1000 fighter aircraft, outnumbering Britain's fighter
planes four to one. To him and the outside world, German
mastery seemed inevitable, just as he had promised his

Führer. However, his Luftwaffe was being asked to cower its opponent in a manner that it had never been designed to do.

The founding purpose of Germany's airforce was to provide low-altitude battlefield support to the army. Its Junkers, Heinkel and Dornier bombers were lightly armed, designed for fast, reactive intervention, not strategic bombing in its true sense. They did not carry heavy enough bombloads to deliver permanently damaging attacks, the *Knockout Blow* that the British public feared. Both sides were affected by poor understanding of their opponent's true strength. The nominal size of an RAF squadron was twenty operational aircraft, but a Luftwaffe staffel fielded an average of only twelve and both sides overlooked the arithmetic implication. Consequently, when British Intelligence counted Luftwaffe units, they overestimated the number of aircraft by 40%. By the same principle, the Germans counted RAF squadrons and underestimated their strength by the same factor.

Simply put, RAF Fighter Command was far larger than the Germans realised, misguiding Luftwaffe strategy right from the start of the campaign.

To further compound his problems, Goering lacked decisive instruction from his supreme leader. Hitler listened to argument and counter-argument by each of his armed forces, but avoided giving any clear directives. Germany's navy, the *Kriegsmarine*, was dwarfed by its opponent. After suffering considerable losses during the Norwegian campaign, its commanders were consistently conservative about their ability to protect German forces during a channel crossing. The Italians were evasive about committing any significant naval contribution and after Oran, the French Fleet had little to offer either.

Those close to the Führer suspected that he had little confidence in the situation and Goering was starting to have his doubts too. As a master of Nazi pomp and bluster, he resorted to using sheer weight of numbers to try to grind the British down.

So as Major Muller led his men back into combat, the RAF was putting up a good fight and Luftwaffe losses were accelerating. With August drawing to a close, airmen on both sides sensed that the battle was approaching its climax.

Chapter 6

Betty Vigar pedalled her bicycle furiously as she swerved around potholes on her way home to Sidcup. After completing a lunchtime errand in Eltham, she had stayed just a little too long at Uncle Albert's office and now, she was late returning to work. She glanced at the sky every few seconds, just as everyone had learnt to do since the war came to Kent. As she careered along, she watched swirling tresses of vapour trails high in the sky and listened to the roar of aircraft engines some way beyond.

On this hot sunny afternoon of the last Friday in August, Betty considered how much closer the aerial conflict had crept over the last two weeks. At first, it had been exciting to hear of formations of German aircraft attacking aerodromes down at the South Coast and the brave boys of the RAF shooting them from the sky. By now, the novelty had worn off as the stark reality of war arrived above her home town.

Just a few nights ago, London was bombed, albeit briefly, and the Germans were now regular visitors overhead, forcing people to run for cover several times a day. The streets were littered with broken roof tiles, smashed by falling debris from the battle taking place above. Spent bullet cases fell to the ground in immeasurable thousands, shrapnel and pieces of aircraft came crashing down without warning, making it hazardous to walk outside sometimes.

Last week, a low level dogfight took place over nearby Chislehurst village. Stray bullets spattered down the parade and shoppers ran for their lives, as a twin-engine Messerschmitt 110 fighter roared overhead, trying to escape a pursuing Spitfire. Clipping the tree tops, the German cartwheeled into the woods and exploded into a thousand pieces. A month ago, the crash site would have attracted hundreds of sightseers, by now it hardly warranted any attention at all.

Events like this were now all too common.

Betty rounded a corner in the road and saw Sidcup Police Station up ahead at the cross-roads, just where the high street began. To her dismay, the electric siren on its roof started to wail and people began to clear from the pavements.

She pedalled even harder, whizzed past neat Victorian shop fronts, straight over the junction and past Burton's shopping parade. She swerved around a double decker bus outside the Regal Cinema and shot down the street, towards Sidcup Hill. She pulled hard on the brakes and came screeching to halt outside Harrop's Chemist, to be greeted by her boss himself.

He was standing anxiously in the doorway with his ARP Helmet strapped on his head.

'There you are,' said Mr Harrop. 'Get inside quickly Betty, didn't you hear the siren? There's a raid coming. Now hurry up and get under the stairs with Mabel.'

His eyes looked ridiculously small behind the thick lenses of his wire frame spectacles.

Without saying a word, Betty quickly took her bicycle inside. She wheeled it straight towards the back of the shop, behind the counter to the back room. There sat Mabel Smith on an old sofa beneath the staircase, wide-eyed, as sick as a pig.

'Betty, where have you been? I've been worried silly. Honestly, we were fretting about you, we really were,' she exclaimed, in a nervous torrent of words. 'You've been gone over two hours. I thought you'd been machine gunned by those awful Narzies.'

'I took the back order to Boots and popped in to see Uncle Albert, I was perfectly safe.' Betty replied. Looking towards Mr Harrop at the shop front, she shouted out, *'unlike you...* now get indoors or you'll end up like Mr Farrell.'

Mr Harrop didn't take kindly to the comparison and hurried inside.

Mabel looked queasily at Betty.

'Is it true they only found a finger?' she whispered.

'Yes, nothing but a great big splodge of jam and one finger!' Betty replied, with morbid relish.

Mabel looked even queasier.

She was glad that she hadn't been there to see it herself. She decided to put her head in her hands and not think about it too much.

Mr Farrell's demise really wasn't something to joke about. A week ago, on an afternoon much like this, he'd been standing outside his barbershop watching a frantic dogfight high above. A stray German cannon shell came plummeting down and blew him into pieces. Whilst Betty might tease Mabel with her lurid description, like everyone she avoided mention of his baby daughter, Mary, cradled in his arms at that dreadful moment.

Two lives snuffed out, just like that.

Betty, Mabel and Mr Harrop sat on the sofa like Three Wise Monkeys, wondering if anything was going to happen.

'It's terrible for business... all this coming and going. We seem to be in and out of the shop half a dozen times a day of late,' said Mr Harrop, nervously.

'I wish they would just go away,' Mabel groaned.

She lifted her head out of her hands for a moment then buried it again, with a whimper and a belch.

Betty stared at the wall that divided them from the shop and listened.

Now she could hear the bombers coming, the pulsating, low frequency droom-droom-droom of their engines. No-one said a word as the tension mounted, except for the occasional groan from Mabel. The droning got louder, its vibrations penetrated the building to rattle and tinkle hundreds of glass bottles on display out front.

As the chorus of chinking bottles rose higher, Betty considered by how much her world had changed in recent months. A year ago she was little more than a schoolgirl, but now she truly believed herself to be a woman. She was certainly doing a woman's work and wondered how she was going to broach the subject with Mum and Dad, about doing something more *important*. She might join the Women's Auxiliary Air Force to work with the fighter boys, or go on the buses and learn to drive a double decker now that all the men had gone. Betty's generation of women was finding out that wartime brought new possibilities and she wanted to do her bit for her country too.

The sound of the bombers' engines began to fade.

Although not immediately overhead… they still weren't too far away.

'I'm going out to have a look,' Betty announced and before anyone could stop her, she was up and out into the shop.

She approached the front door cautiously.

Mr Harrop had locked it earlier, so she reached up to slide back the large bolt.

'Get back here Betty,' Mr Harrop shouted from the back. 'With all that glass out there, you'll be cut to shreds if a bomb falls.'

Ignoring his advice, she cautiously slipped out onto the street.

Looking up into the sky, there was absolutely nothing to see at all. The engine noises were far more distant, somewhere to the south, maybe as far as the aerodromes at Biggin Hill or Kenley over ten miles away. The heavy, deep base boom of distant explosions pulsed across the air and disconcertingly, against her chest too.

'Someone's copping it,' a voice called out.

Betty was a little startled.

She looked round to her right and standing just a few feet away, was a young soldier with his forage cap cocked jauntily to one side.

He gave her a big grin.

'You should be in your shelter until the All Clear sounds,' he cautioned.

His face looked suddenly familiar.

Given the limited selection of young men hereabouts these days, Betty recalled where they had met before.

'Oh… you're the soldier that helped us with the wireless that night at Eltham Palace, aren't you?' she said, whilst thinking how smart he looked in uniform.

'I certainly am,' Ken Kendrick replied, recognising her too. 'I'm sorry I don't recall your name… I was a bit queer that day.'

He paused a moment. 'I think your sister was called… Ginny… wasn't she?'

Absolutely typical. Ginny this, Ginny that, Ginny la-di-da. Betty thought to herself angrily.

'Yes, Virginia is my sister, my name is *Elizabeth*. So what brings you here today? Mr….?'

'Oh, please call me Ken,' he cut in. 'I never went far away actually. After I got back to my regiment… I was posted to the camp at Foots Cray.'

He paused for a moment.

'Now I've got six days leave, so I thought I'd start with the wonders of Sidcup town.'

He looked up and down the deserted street.

Before Betty could properly judge whether he was being sarcastic, the siren sounded again, its constant tone announcing that all was safe for the moment.

Mr Harrop appeared behind her, without his helmet, a chemist again.

'That's that then,' he said, 'come on in my girl, we have work to do.'

Betty looked at Ken.

'I hope you enjoy your afternoon. Nice to meet you again.'

Ken wanted to delay her a moment.

'I remember your… uncle…wasn't he? I'd like to go and see him, wasn't his office in Eltham? I can't remember where it was though?'

Betty hesitated before replying.

'Uncle runs the timber merchants on Eltham Hill. It's almost opposite the swimming baths. Its only three miles, I was over there at lunchtime.'

'Thank you *Betty*,' Ken continued, smiling again. 'Perhaps I'll see you around?'

'Perhaps…' she replied and walked back inside.

It dawned on her that he had a lovely smile.

Ken looked up and down the high street again.

A few people had reappeared on the pavements, resuming their daily routine.

He picked up his kitbag, slung it across his shoulder and with new purpose, walked up the road to look for a bus stop.

Mabel had regained her composure and busied herself by making Betty busier.

All the shelves and their wares needed dusting, whilst she sorted out customers' prescriptions for this afternoon. Mr Harrop went back to his potions and lotions, as he called them, and everything was as it should be in his world again. He thought about Mr Farrell, his poor family and what a tragedy it was. Mrs Farrell was an attractive lady with two young boys to look after and a barbershop without a husband or a barber. He resolved to pop by later and see how she was coping, as she could probably do with a little help. Not for the first time in his life, he considered his options for a second Mrs Harrop some way down the line. Hopefully, better than the first, who had run off with a smarmy man with a spivvy moustache, fifteen years earlier.

Ernest Harrop was the wrong side of fifty, short, round, balding and rather short-sighted. Nonetheless, he thought of himself as a decent fellow, with a good business and considerable standing in the community. He could still be a good catch for a fine lady of Sidcup, providing he could ever find his wife and divorce her.

With a shudder, he recalled last Tuesday.

Screaming onlookers, that ghastly, gory mess splattered up the pavement and shop fronts, for yards in every direction. Every bit as bad as his worst memories as a soldier on the Western Front, but now right here on his own doorstep, literally. He reconsidered that his plan was perhaps inappropriate, given the circumstances. Gwendolyn Farrell was a nice lady indeed, wracked by terrible grief for her dead husband and daughter. He resolved to stand by her as a friend first and foremost, for the moment.

Mind you, a barbershop would fit quite nicely with a chemist, he mused and *she does have a very lovely figure.*

Ernest savoured the thought of her full, milky breasts for a brief moment, but was interrupted by an acrid smell filling his nostrils.

He wrinkled his face in disgust at the bitter fumes rising from the bowl in front of him. Realising that he had incorrectly mixed this medicinal compound, he started again.

Busying himself afresh, he was completely oblivious to the metaphor that the chemical stench had just served to his most recent prescription for life.

Harrop's had been the town's main chemist since Ernest's grandfather set up shop in a then sleepy country village, way back in 1869.

Over the next seventy years, Sidcup had grown to become a splendid town of over 10,000 inhabitants. Its rise began in the 1840's, when wealthy people arrived from London to build large stately houses, followed by artisans and shopkeepers needed to serve the growing community. In those days Sidcup was overshadowed both by Lamorbey, a village to the north where a railway station opened in 1866 and to the east, by the small town of Foots Cray.

Yet Sidcup's growth accelerated, driven by land sold to retail speculators to build smart parades of modern shops in abundance. Within just a few years there were over 200 premises plying a tremendous variety of trade. Gas lighting for streets and houses arrived in 1882, a cottage hospital, proper sewers and the crowning glory was the provision of the first mains electricity in 1902. Old Lamorbey and Foots Cray were cast into the shadow of a bright, upstart neighbour, as Sidcup became the principle town of the area.

A second building boom began after The Great War, creating a sprawling suburbia that consumed almost every village for miles around. In Sidcup's high street, the grand old houses along the southern side were demolished and replaced by even more commercial developments. The world's largest chain of men's outfitters, *Montague Burton The Tailor*, arrived in 1937. It built a huge three storey parade with its own retail premises as the centrepiece. With glamourous modern flats, a snooker parlour and splendid dance hall above, Burton's clever sales formula found many ways to draw people to its cash registers.

Ernest had been born in the house behind the shop and inherited the business after his father's death in 1923. He married, but enjoyed only brief happiness, until his wife decided a travelling salesman was far more exciting than a sensible country town apothecary. Her departure had stolen Ernest's personal contentment ever since. In a town like Sidcup, he had absolutely no chance of attracting respectable female companionship, until he was free to marry again. To fill his spare time, Ernest involved himself with church matters and enjoyed his work with the local Boy's Brigade. The approach of war had brought new opportunities for civic duty and he had helped set up the local Air Raid Patrol. Not that there had been much to do until recently, apart from nosing around late at night, which suited his personality rather well. Like most people hereabouts, Ernest sensed his quiet life was going to change dramatically, given how badly the war was progressing.

His thoughts were interrupted when Mabel appeared in front him.

'Mr Harrop, Madame Delafort is out front and wants to speak to you,' she announced with obvious anxiety.

Oh God… what does that old bat want? Ernest thought to himself.

Assuming a professional smile, he adjusted his white coat and walked out to greet one of the Grande Dames of Sidcup, the fearsome Maude Delafort.

There she stood; aged, diminutive and inscrutable, much like old Queen Victoria re-incarnated, dressed in black from head to toe, as if in mourning like her role model. In her sombre garb she looked as if she was a hundred years old, but was more probably only in her sixties. An archetypal *spinster of this parish* as she had never married, as far as Ernest knew, there was also nothing in the least bit French about her either.

Nonetheless, no-one argued with Maude Delafort.

'*Madame*... how very lovely to see you,' he greeted her, with well-practiced shopkeeper's charm.

'Yes, yes, indeed,' she barked in response. 'I am seeking my stomach powders. I have had to come in person... as your delivery boy has failed to bring them to Craywood... yet again.'

'I'm sorry about that, but Peter was called up to the Navy last Friday, our deliveries are somewhat behind,' Ernest offered in explanation. 'The girls are doing their best to catch up.'

The lady looked unimpressed.

To reinforce his point with more authority, Ernest picked up his ARP helmet from under the counter and concluded, more officiously.

'There is a war on, you know...'

Madame Delafort looked even more unimpressed.

Chapter 7

Ginny Vigar stood at the crossroads in Foots Cray village alongside a dozen other factory girls, as she waited for the No.21 bus to arrive. She was hot, tired and glad that the weekend had begun.

She wasn't in the best of moods that Saturday lunchtime, as her supervisor had just revealed that her days in the management offices were over. Everyone that could be spared from clerical duties was needed down on the production lines now.

However, Ginny didn't want her hands dirtied with oil and grime, not after working so hard to acquire her secretarial qualifications. Her employer, the Austrian-owned Klinger Engineering Company had opened a large factory in Foots Cray in 1937, on a sprawling industrial estate founded by the Crittall Window factory nine years earlier. They and many other companies were drawn here by the opening of the A20 dual carriageway that greatly reduced journey times to London, plus a rapidly growing local population to provide a good source of workers. Consequently, Klinger decided this was an ideal site for its manufacture of engine gaskets, valves and gauge glasses in England. The company name was rather hilarious to English ears, but the works provided good, steady employment for over a thousand people.

Since the outbreak of war, most factories had undergone a rapid transformation, as hundreds of women were recruited to replace male workers conscripted into the armed forces. A year ago, the end of the Saturday morning shift would have been signalled by a mass exodus to the pubs of Foots Cray. Unfortunately for the landlords of The Barley

Mow, The Seven Stars and The Red Lion today, the newly emancipated females still felt obliged to head straight home to resume their household chores. Within minutes, all was quiet hereabouts as the factory was locked up for the weekend.

It had all been tremendously exciting for Ginny when she first walked through the factory gates in 1939. Trembling with nerves, she had been taken upstairs to the management offices with their modern steel furniture, posh bosses and exotic foreign visitors from head office. The Austrians, who were officially Germans since Hitler's annexation of their country in 1938, but were always the same thing really in her view, had stopped coming last summer. She thought it funny that, in principle, she and the other Klinger employees were all now working for the enemy. The office girls would often joke that a Fifth Columnist spy was still hiding in the company flat on the top floor, waiting for the right moment to jump out and sabotage the war effort. Despite these tales of intrigue, this English base of Klinger was quickly commandeered for the British wartime economy. Its production targets were dramatically increased, hence the need to recruit even more workers downstairs.

So as Ginny whiled away her time waiting at the bus stop, she thought over her options. Maybe it was time to look for a new employer; one that would make more appropriate use of her hard-earned shorthand and typing skills. There was plenty of talk lately that even young women like her would soon be conscripted into war service. Ginny wondered how she could avoid such an unpleasant outcome.

Looking again for the bus, she saw a man astride a big black motorbike speed over the crossroads. She instantly recognised the distinctive features of the most eligible bachelor in town. Quickly pulling at her stockings, she licked her lips and flicked her hair, ready to greet the utterly handsome Raymond Delafort, one of the most dashing, and poshest, men she knew. Everyone knew him by sight hereabouts as his family had lived around here… forever.

Not that she appreciated it; her *Vigar* surname also had a Norman-French origin much like the Delaforts, sharing a longstanding association with this part of Kent. Yet the contrast between the two families could not have been greater, as the Delaforts were gold-plated, copper-bottomed, famously rich. Raymond was the sole heir to his family's fortune and considered to be the local playboy, the finest of catches for one lucky woman one day. He was tall, well-built and had the blackest hair she could wish for. He sported a perfect moustache to complete a more than passing resemblance to dashing movie star Errol Flynn, with a little bit of brooding Gary Cooper thrown in as well.

Raymond pulled up his motorbike alongside Ginny and with its engine idling gruffly; he took out a gold cigarette case and lit a Pall Mall. He savoured the first draw for a moment before turning off the motor, then paused for effect, before speaking. As silence descended, all the girls at the bus stop strained to hear what he would say.

'Hello Virginia, what a fabulous day. How lovely to see you here… in the *sunshine*.' Raymond greeted her, with subtle emphasis on the last word.

Ginny blushed.

Several of the girls behind her exchanged whispers, one giggled.

Ignoring them, Ginny pushed out her chest.

'I'm feeling just divine, Raymond. You do look fine on your motorcycle,' she replied.

Ginny had first met him properly at Burton's dance hall a month ago, when he came over to talk to Mabel Smith with whom Ginny was paired for the evening. Yet Mabel had looked distinctly uncomfortable and took herself away with an excuse, leaving them to chat. Raymond certainly could talk when it came to making a girl feel special, underscoring his reputation as a Ladies' Man. Of course, he had the pick of the bunch these days and it seemed that Mabel was well out of her depth. Ginny considered herself no fool and she also knew that she held considerable advantage over most girls. She was a veritable English Rose. Tall, like her father, she shared the same striking auburn hair as her mother and was blessed with full, but pert breasts. Altogether, she had a perfect figure with long legs *that went all the way up to yer bum,* as Mabel often told her with envy.

Ginny had matured early; discovering the notion of sex whilst most of her peers still dwelt in childhood's innocence. Whilst she had never actually *gone all the way*, she had come pretty close with a couple of the older lads at the Lamorbey Children's Home. Those boys were mostly from London, given a better chance in life at this country orphanage, but they were rougher, wilder, worldly-wise types compared to local lads. They had revealed the word *fuck* to her and what it really meant, as well as its use as an insult between coarser people. More by chance than design, Ginny had learnt how to please men and rather liked what they could do for her in return. She understood she was considered a beauty and with her flirtatious nature, she was altogether graced with the feminine wiles required to get what she wanted. She always looked her very best, whatever the occasion and you might ask if she was vain, or insecure. That was a hard question to answer... as it's often only a fine line that separates the two.

Ginny had met up with Raymond three times more since the Burton's dance. With every date, their clandestine relationship progressed just a little bit further and each time perhaps, a little more than expected. Nonetheless, she knew she had to be more subtle than most girls to realise her ultimate goal.

He was witty, charming and rich.

One day, who knows… she might be Mrs Delafort!

The only problem was that whenever she was in his company, they seemed to go just a little bit too far. She couldn't help herself, he was simply so lovely, he just had that entrancing, almost hypnotic, effect on her. He was stunningly attractive to her, the sort of man that would make you want to do *anything*.

Ginny kept asking herself… is this really love?

As yet, she didn't know the answer.

Now she found herself simply admiring his handsome features.

'Why don't you just hop on the back and I'll give you a lift? Where are you heading to?' Raymond asked.

'Ooh I'm not sure I should… you'll go far too fast for me, I'm sure.' Ginny replied, perhaps a little too openly.

'I can go as fast as you want me to,' he replied with a dashing smile.

Ginny rose to the challenge.

'Go on then… but just up to the high street! I'm meeting my sister and don't want to look too windswept, or she'll sneak on me to Father.'

Raymond stood up and kick-started the motorbike's engine and adjusted the throttle a little, until the engine exhaust note settled down to a slow, barking heartbeat. He reached out and took her hand to help her onto the pillion seat.

'You'll have to lift your dress a little… just put your legs alongside mine,' he instructed. 'Your feet go on those pegs down there, then put your arms around my middle and hang on tight.'

Ginny followed his advice carefully and enjoyed this new, intimate experience. The heat and vibration of the engine beneath her felt strange, unfamiliar, intoxicating. She slid her legs against his and put her arms around him, just a little lower than he had probably expected.

He looked over his shoulder at her.

She looked back into his eyes and squeezed her legs a little harder against his.

'Don't let me fall off, will you?' she asked, not completely joking.

The girls giggled again.

Raymond revved the engine, released the clutch and with a booming roar from the exhaust, the motorbike launched itself forwards. He gunned the engine harder and harder, up through the gears and despite the steep hill, within a few hundred yards they were travelling at well over 60 miles an hour.

This was Ginny's first time on a motorbike, not that she would want to admit it and she hung on tightly, thrilled and scared all at once. The sensation of wild speed, the noise of the exhaust pipe growling behind her, the wind rushing through her hair was altogether one of the most exciting experiences she had ever had. Her heart was almost pounding out of her chest as they sped past the newspaper offices at the crest of Sidcup Hill. Then they were into the high street proper and Raymond slowed down, bringing them to a sudden halt opposite The Black Horse Hotel, the exact place where Sidcup was founded in ancient times.

He looked back over his right shoulder to judge her reaction and their eyes met again.

Their faces were very close now.

Neither spoke.

After a few seconds, Ginny moved her right hand lower, between his legs.

Her hand lingered and squeezed him there.

Then she stood up on the foot pegs.

She swung her right leg behind and over the machine with surprising grace and skipped onto the pavement. She straightened her dress and adjusted her hair. She felt over-excited, her heart was racing, but outwardly she presented an air of perfect composure.

'That's quite enough for today,' she announced firmly.

'I can take you for a longer spin, if you fancy it?' Raymond asked. 'Do you really have to meet your sister now?'

'She'll be wondering where I am, I'd better go.' Ginny replied and keeping his eyes firmly in her gaze, she lowered her voice.

'But you might want to take me tomorrow?'

Raymond was firmly on the hook.

He knew it and she knew it.

'Why don't you meet me after church tomorrow morning and we'll see where we can go from there?' Ginny continued, her voice laden with suggestion.

'You attend St Mildred's don't you? Just opposite the Plaza?' he asked.

'Yes we do and remember to look your best,' she replied. 'We are respectable people remember… *Fiddle-dee–dee!*' And with that, Sidcup's Scarlet O'Hara walked off and disappeared amongst the crowd of Saturday shoppers.

Raymond mulled over the implications of their conversation. He slipped his motorbike back into gear, turned across the road and headed back down the hill towards Craywood House, his ancestral home.

With a wide smile on his face, he hurtled down the road.

Raymond considered how well his plan for the not-so-innocent Ginny Vigar was shaping up and relished the prospect of his next conquest with amusement. His carefully crafted reputation as the rich country squire continued to work its charm.

Yet in truth, these days the Delaforts were not at all as grand as most people thought. Fortune's rollercoaster may have gifted them with a fine reputation, a grand house and a few landholdings, but yet again... the family found itself with little actual money.

Raymond's family association with this quiet corner of Kent spanned nine hundred years, all the way back to the Norman Conquest.

The village of Footescraye took its name from a Saxon thane, Godwin Foote and the Cray river, but in 1067 the land was seized by Odo, the half-brother of William the Conqueror, the new Norman king of England. The earliest documents in the Delafort family archive bore the mark of both nobles, testament to an early association with these new overlords. Raymond's ancestors quickly discarded their Saxon heritage. Sometime after the *Domesday Book* of 1085, they took on a Norman-styled surname, *De La Forêt*, meaning Of The Forest, in which they lived.

Further towards London, on top of a large flat-topped hill sat the hamlet of Cettecopp, which had grown around a smithy and a hostelry, the first Black Horse Inn. This was a resting place for travellers and their horses on the Maidstone Road, once they had forded the river at Footescraye and toiled up the steep road towards London. Both communities jostled for the attention of city-bound merchant trade with the rival village of Wellyng, four miles to the north. That settlement sat on the famous Watling Street, one of the most important wayfares of England, predating the Roman conquest. This great road started at the sea port of Dover, struck out across Kent past the great cathedral city of Canterbury, crossed the River Thames at London and reached out westwards, all the way up to the Roman city of Wroxeter on the Welsh border.

Over the following centuries, this locale grew in importance with the foundation of a royal palace at Eltham. Now with the anglicised name of *Delafort*, the family prospered from feeding the court entourage that burgeoned around the royal site. If anybody had ever bothered to write a detailed family history, it would have described a long process of diligent self-advancement. They gained influence and affluence, long before Henry VIII deserted medieval Eltham in the 16th century. Once the monarchy departed, the redundant Eltham Palace and its surrounding villages quickly slipped back into quiet rural anonymity.

Nonetheless, local farmland served to feed the ever-growing city of London and as the area known as Sidcup and Foots Cray quietly prospered, so did the Delaforts. Yet as commoners, they never warranted any mention in history books per se.

By the late 17th Century, they had enlarged their manor house at the Cray Wood and farmed many smallholdings. Socially, they positioned themselves well; close to titled families and their great estates at Scadbury, Foot Cray Place and the domain of Viscount Sydney at Frognal. Yet, like many old families, as fortunes wax, they can also wane. The turning point came in Regency times, when the Delaforts embarked upon a series of disastrous investments, unfettered gambling and a love of drink, far stronger than what was served in City coffee houses beloved by the financial speculators. In just one generation, the Delaforts lost a fortune that had taken several hundred years to build and all was mortgaged to the hilt.

Fortunately, Raymond's grandfather, Josiah Delafort, proved to be a dramatic break from the recent past. He had the advantage of becoming a well-educated man, the product of a father who wanted to parade a son schooled in London. The totally unplanned outcome was that Josiah was an uncommonly clever man in such a country backwater. His father died in his seventieth year in 1860 and at just 25 years of age, Josiah inherited all the Delafort possessions. He immediately set to the pursuit of modernity with truly Victorian zeal.

Josiah sold enough land to settle the most pressing debts and embraced the new wave of learning and science that cascaded across 19th century Britain. He invested in new-fangled farm machinery, modern seed stocks, new animal breeds and scientific land husbandry. In just a few years, the yields of Delafort farms increased fourfold and his miraculous achievements became quite the local sensation.

With the arrival of the railway at Lamorbey in 1865, Josiah's farms also profited from the greater speed that their produce could be carried, still fresh, to new markets. In return, the railway brought a new type of person to the area; middle class London professionals seeking to build a wealthy suburb of grand houses and land prices soared. Josiah sold plots in newly fashionable Sidcup for building developments, at a much higher price than that for tillage. All in all, he played a key part in moving this part of Kent from quiet countryside, to genteel London suburb and market garden.

With his future set, Josiah married well to Caroline Bridger, a prosperous landowner's daughter from Welling and in due course, four children were brought into the world. Their first child, James, was born in 1875 followed by twins, Hannah and Thomas two years later. However, disaster struck just six months later when on a hot September night, the rambling, old Craywood House caught fire.

The flames took a rapid hold of the Medieval and Elizabethan wooden structure and within minutes, the whole building was fully ablaze. Four servants died in their attic stalls and the Delafort twins perished in their cots.

Numbed by this great tragedy, Josiah and Caroline took their surviving son and rented a house in Chislehurst until eventually, they overcame their grief. With their determination restored, they built a grand new Delafort house at Cray Wood in thoroughly modern style. It was as much a declaration that they would not be cowered by fate, as it was to declare their rising social status. In 1880, they were blessed by the birth of another daughter, Maude, and alongside James, she became the next of the Delaforts to reach maturity.

The family had restored its fortunes without venturing out to the British Empire in search of fantastical fortune and avoiding any form of service to the Crown. None of them ever served in anything more than a local militia, keeping far away from the adventures that underpinned the success of the empire. Whilst farming remained Josiah's foremost passion, he became famous for taking up any chance to buy even the smallest parcel of land that ever came to auction. Many of his peers thought him foolish for such indulgences, but with great foresight, he sensed that the great metropolis had an endless appetite for expansion. *London is approaching*, he once confided to his young daughter and she never forgot his advice.

The 20th Century dawned upon the Delaforts recumbent in Edwardian splendour in a grand house with a fashionable ornamental garden, set at the foot of Cray Wood overlooking the valley. Caroline passed from this world in 1902 at the relatively young age of fifty five and Josiah died four years later, having equalled his father's seventy years. Many said of a broken heart, a troubled man, but at least he could be confident that his family's future was secure. However, James Delafort shared much of his character with the gamblers of past generations and the new master of Craywood House saw his future in politics. Yet, no matter how much he manoeuvred, he wasted the best years of his life on never gaining a seat in Parliament, or any civic position of great note. Nonetheless, on the way he did successfully acquire Daphne, a beautiful, much younger and energetic socialite as his wife and they produced two children, Evangeline and Raymond. James had turned his back on the countryside, preferring a fashionable London residence and glittering social life that he could ill afford.

All of this was watched with much distaste by his sister, Maude.

However, old Josiah must have had some inkling that James might not follow the path chosen for him. Josiah's bequest had granted Maude a lifetime's enjoyment of Craywood House and considerable influence over family matters. Quite contrary to contemporary attitudes about women, by various legal ploys, he had ensured that she had a de facto say in all matters pertaining to the family's principle assets. This brake on James' wilder schemes meant that for the time being, the farms and properties could not be liquidated without Maude's consent.

To James' immense frustration, he found that even the most useless parcel of land, the hilltop Cray Wood itself, could not be sold. Its title was wrapped up in a kind of ancient legal claptrap that made the Delafort family its custodian, but not its outright owner in a conventional sense. It was simultaneously Crown land, but in possession of the Delaforts, for immutable benefit of one to the other. However, the cash proceeds from the farms were a different matter and James helped himself to the profits as much as he liked. The farms fell into a gradual decline, due to lack of investment and the negligence of poorly chosen, ineffective managers left in place by an absent James. Very much her father's daughter, god fearing and diligent, Maude preferred a life close to Delafort estate affairs. Yet, as an Edwardian woman with few legal powers, at best she could only seek ways to subtly work around James' poorest decisions. She lamented their ever-declining fortune and prayed for a miracle to deliver them from inevitable impoverishment.

Maude's call was indirectly answered by the outbreak of war in 1914, as James found that he had to answer the country's call to arms. His politicking for social gain had led him to join the reserves of the Royal West Kent Regiment a number of years before, with little thought that he would ever actually have to go into battle one day.

Now as Major Delafort, James had acquired a title of sorts, after all.

He departed for France in 1916 at the head of his company, waved off by Maude, his darling Daphne, two year old Evangeline and infant Raymond. The lease on their London residence lapsed and Daphne and the children returned to Craywood House, to live under the scrutiny of Maude. They all waited for James' safe return, but he disappeared into No Man's Land at the battle of Arras a year later. With her husband reported as Missing In Action, Daphne was shaken into a new appreciation of the realities of life.

This manifested itself in two ways.

She poured her love into her two young children, but also chose to step outside her cossetted life by volunteering for nursing duties at the newly opened Queens Hospital at nearby Frognal House. Working on the wards of Dr Harold Gillies, the pioneering reconstructive surgeon, she worked with diligence and compassion with soldiers suffering the most horrific disfigurements. It was an occupation previously unthinkable for a lady of such high social standing as Daphne Delafort, yet she cast perceptions of gentility aside. Like millions of women at this time of national crisis, she found the resolve and emotional strength necessary to meet the challenges of a suddenly brutal world. She held a hope to find James amongst the hundreds of mutilated soldiers that passed through her care, but it was not to be. Cruelly, her charity brought tragedy yet again. Daphne fell victim to the Spanish Influenza Epidemic of 1918, leaving two young orphans and their aunt to look towards an uncertain future.

With The Great War over, James was legally pronounced dead so that his last will and testament could be fulfilled. His entire estate reverted to a trust under the control of Maude and Godfrey Burridge, the family solicitor, until Raymond reached his twenty fifth birthday. Then he would inherit everything, whilst endowments provided for Evangeline and Maude.

As legal guardian, Maude ensured the children were brought up in accordance with her notions of reserved Victorian frugality. The hard years of the First World War had brought farming to its knees and now cheap imports from the Americas undercut home-produced foodstuffs. The British farming economy staggered, already enfeebled by the loss of so much manpower to the war. The Delaforts should have fared better given their heritage, however with no Josiah at the helm, profits dwindled even further. It was simply beyond Maude to manage the family's farming affairs properly. With great irony, the loss of nearly a million war dead had raised the value of those that survived and working men's incomes rose rapidly. The upper classes that provided the officer corps at the forefront of battle, had suffered casualty rates five times higher than lesser ranks. The landed rich reeled from the loss of husbands, sons and heirs and death duties threatened to bankrupt them. As the wealth of Britain started to move from the top towards the bottom of society, Maude's financial salvation came from an unexpected source.

Town and country planning laws were relaxed to encourage a building boom of suburban homes, fit for those heroes that had actually returned from war. Under the pressure of taxes to pay, Maude realised her only option was to sell much of the family's land assets to speculators. These property developers were acquiring agricultural land all around London to build housing estates of smart modern homes in the tens of thousands. To her surprise, she soon found a flair for such matters. She auctioned land in penny packets and gained a reputation as a tough negotiator, well able to play one bidder against another. With Mr Burridge's help, she often withheld small parcels of land in key places to frustrate developers' wider ambitions, until they were prepared to pay the higher prices she sought. Despite the Wall Street Crash of 1929 and the depression that followed, large swathes of the pastures, tillage and orchards of old Eltham, Sidcup and Welling were put to tarmac, concrete and brick.

Maude's share of this suburban transformation reasonably restored the Delafort bank balance. She knew that selling assets was a once-only solution, so her wards were brought up with a modest financial security. True to her values, they lived reasonably, but sensibly, and kept up appearances for all and sundry to observe. The children were taught that they were better than people hereabouts, quite simply because they were Delaforts. No local school could ever be good enough for them and they were educated at home by tutors.

Raymond's childhood was predominantly an unhappy one, devoid of contact with the outside world, lacking in friendship with other children. His misery was compounded by his aunt's obvious preference for his sister. Evangeline could do no wrong it seemed and thrived as the focus of their aunt's love. Conversely *Ray-Monde*, as Maude usually emphasised a second syllable, could do little right. She rarely let him venture far from Craywood and seemed to carry an air of perpetual disappointment in him. Yet no matter how much Raymond despised his aunt, there was one thing he now had to be grateful to her for. This was her determination to keep a small part of their farming heritage intact... by retaining Bridger's Farm.

It was a sizeable holding of thirty acres, inherited from Maude's maternal grandmother, situated at the foot of Shooter's Hill on the Great Dover Road. By 1940, its cottages and disused manor house found themselves surrounded by the new housing developments of Welling, the odd one out amongst sprawling suburbia. As the man of the family, it was Raymond's responsibility to farm Bridger's. Whilst he utterly detested agricultural work, it had the immense advantage of being a reserved occupation, preventing his conscription into the armed forces.

Wartime Britain needed every bit of land put to crops as well as every available man to fight for it. As an agricultural worker, Raymond had been granted a way to avoid getting directly involved in this wretched conflict. Aged twenty four, with his inheritance imminent, he had big plans for the future. These certainly didn't include getting his hands dirty on that farm forever, or having his head blown off on a battlefield either. With a bit of luck, he hoped that the government would see sense and end the war as fast as possible. Then he would be able to do what he wanted... with no-one to tell him what to do anymore.

Such were the limitations of his appreciation, or interest, in what would soon become a second world war of truly horrific proportions. As far as he could see, France was beaten, Germany was triumphant and Britain should seek peace with Hitler on any terms. In Raymond's world it made far more sense to join the bully's gang, rather than keep getting punched in the face by him. Even more importantly today, the other significant benefit of Raymond's circumstances was that he was now one of the few young men left in Sidcup.

This gave him the pick of the female population... something he was already taking considerable advantage of.

Chapter 8

As the Vigar family prepared for church that bright Sunday morning of the 1st September 1940, exactly a year had passed since Germany's invasion of Poland.

Despite the calm of those early hours, this would be anything but a day of rest for people across much of Southern England.

While Ginny and Betty fought over the bathroom and their mother readied breakfast, the Luftwaffe was already well advanced with its own preparations for the day ahead. Bombing targets along the coast, the Germans were pounding on Britain's front door, getting ready to barge their way in.

At this stage of the campaign, Luftwaffe commander-in-chief, Herman Goering, presided over a threefold strategy for victory.

Firstly, sending large formations of aircraft to draw English fighters into combat, leaving airfields and factories unprotected from repeated bombing raids. Secondly, launching hundreds of small nuisance attacks, often at low altitude to confuse and divide British defences. By repeatedly cutting and bleeding the RAF, Goering believed he could force his opponent to the point that it must withdraw its remaining fighters from the key battle area. To add even more pressure, the third and newest element of the strategy was to send bombers further afield by night. They flew to Liverpool, Belfast, Bristol, Hull and many more cities, to strike at the industry that supported Britain's war effort.

In 1940, neither side could offer much in defence against aircraft attacking in darkness. Fighter pilots and anti-aircraft guns could not see their quarry and the probability of hitting their targets was ridiculously low. What losses the Luftwaffe did suffer at night were mostly due to bad weather, mechanical failure or pilot error.

Even so, German airmen were able to demonstrate remarkable accuracy in their nocturnal missions. The success of their raids was beyond adequate explanation, uncomfortably highlighting Britain's inability to match them in kind. RAF Bomber Command was trying to reciprocate by attacking the Nazi heartland, but results were piecemeal in comparison. Yet they served an unforeseen purpose, as repeated air raid alerts sent workers into their shelters, causing more interruption to Nazi war production than the meagre weight of bombs actually dropped on target.

Having been told that the war was as good as won, the German people were becoming angry at their government's inability to stop these apparently free-roaming English *terrorfliegen*.

So for increasingly political, as much as military reasons, the Nazi leadership needed a decisive and quick solution to the problem of continued British resistance.

As the summer of 1940 drew to a close, over two thousand combat aircraft would continue to grapple for air supremacy above England, with each side seeking a way to break the other.

It was a spectacle watched by millions of ordinary people from their gardens, streets, factories and farms. They witnessed the unfolding drama with grim fascination, as machine attacked machine in a surreal, twisting spectacle of noise, fire and smoke.

Only when a parachute blossomed or a body fell to earth, were they reminded that this was man fighting man, in the worst, oldest habit of humanity.

Ginny bounded into the kitchen, victorious from her forty minute beauty barricade in the bathroom. She had left her little sister with barely fifteen minutes to get ready before they all set off for church.

'Oh Mother, you are a wonder. Sausages!' she exclaimed, as she plucked a fork from the table and headed for the frying pan.

'Go away young lady,' Patricia scolded. 'We've got one each and an extra one for Father. They're especially good; I got them from Price's. There's plenty of bread, we will sit down and eat properly at the table… all together.'

Edward Vigar walked in the back door, took off his cap and headed straight for the teapot. He was a tall straight-backed man in his early fifties, strong and lean from a lifetime of hard physical work and still sported a shock of thick brown hair.

'Got a brew on love?' he asked.

He began to pour himself a mug of tea, but stopped.

'Hmm, better let it stand a little longer.' Edward decided, observing the thinly flavoured water.

Patricia looked at him expectantly.

In response, he produced two neat newspaper parcels from his canvas haversack. He opened them carefully, to reveal half a dozen eggs and a good-sized leg of mutton. Of late, the Vigar larder generally stood testament to the worsening food supply across the nation. So these parcels demonstrated how life near the country had its advantages, when it came to procuring a little bit extra.

'That looks lovely,' Patricia declared, picking over the meat with diligent inspection. 'Wherever did you get it from?'

'Raymond Delafort came up trumps, Love,' he revealed. 'He needs new fences at Bridger's, so…. I said I'd get it sorted for him next week. *Fingers* will sort me out some rough timber… good enough for the job.'

Ginny's face blushed bright with embarrassment.

Patricia shook her head, as she took four of the eggs to the frying pan.

She was always a little bit peeved when Edward called her brother that in front of the girls.

Yet Patricia knew that if it wasn't for Fingers, she would never have met her husband. She recalled that afternoon long ago, when she first ventured south of London to see how her brother was settling into his new job and new life. That evening, she met his best friend from the joinery shop, a tall cheeky chap called Ted. He brought along his old army comrade, a studious little chemist called Ernie who seemed to have a hundred jokes for every topic. After a hilarious Saturday night spent in a pub, full of japes and fun, a firm friendship grew between these new pals. Eltham became a regular weekend haunt for Patricia and of course, there was an underlying incentive. One thing led to another and she became Mrs Edward Vigar a year later. The newlyweds rented a two-up-two-down cottage near Sidcup Station and settled down to start their family.

Several years and two babies later, Edward took his chance to set up his own small building firm and likewise, Albert opened a timber merchant in Eltham. With Ernest's local connections and plenty of hard work, they scratched each other's backs for favours and their businesses prospered. Always keeping their ears open for gossip, they often joked that they mostly knew what was going on hereabouts… before it had even happened.

With its mix of industry, farming and proximity to London's wealth, the area withstood the austerity of the depression years and then Edward's building business really took off. At its peak, he had fifteen men working on private and commercial builds. The crowning glory had been to win contracts on building the luxurious new Plaza cinema. Its opening night in 1935 was one of the happiest and proudest events in their family story.

The profits from helping to build *Dad's Palace,* as the Vigars named it, allowed them to pay cash for a brand new, semi-detached house in Hazelmead Road. Patricia loved its chic modern chalet style, forming an impressive triangular frontage with its neighbour. With two large bedrooms upstairs, a third downstairs next to the living room, an inside bathroom, dining room and kitchen at the back, it was light and airy compared to their narrow, gloomy old Victorian home. With a brand new Morris 12 saloon car on the drive, standing behind wooden sunrise pattern gates, their life quickly became the epitome of middle class prosperity.

Edward was proud of the town that he had helped build and even before this new war broke out, he founded the local Air Raid Patrol.

With Ernest at his side, they walked the streets of Sidcup most nights on the lookout for bombs, saboteurs and to tick off anyone that broke blackout rules. Over in Eltham, Albert joined the LDV, now called the Home Guard, completing their commitment to national service. Patricia announced that once again they were *The Three Musketeers*, reprising the nickname she had bestowed upon them nearly twenty years earlier.

Her nostalgia was interrupted by a sudden noise.

'Oh Mum. She hasn't had my sausage has she?' Betty shouted from the bathroom.

'We've scoffed the lot.' Ginny screamed back.

Betty rushed into the kitchen, spoiling for another fight.

Patricia looked at the eggs in the pan, just perfect.

'Will you all be QUIET!' she ordered.

With her reign restored, they all sat down to a civilised breakfast, just as she wanted. However, within a few seconds, the air raid siren added to conversation by wailing its own morning call.

The Vigars looked at each other with resignation.

They picked up their plates and mugs of tea and headed off to their Anderson shelter in the garden.

Meanwhile, the Luftwaffe was raising the stakes on the day by attacking docks, airfields, aircraft factories and railway junctions across the Home Counties. Represented by wooden markers on plotting tables in dimly-lit RAF control rooms, the aircraft they represented fought to the death in brilliant sunshine above. By mid-morning, the funeral pyres of scores of crashed aircraft pointed their black fingers to heaven whilst the battle raged on.

As terrible as the carnage on the ground was, the arithmetic of war was taking its toll on the Germans too. Travelling four times as far to meet their adversary, their fighter planes did not have the range to roam freely over the combat area. Whereas an RAF airman could parachute to safety over England, his German counterpart would certainly be captured instead. The Luftwaffe needed five times as many men to crew its bombers and the loss of every plane represented a grave blow. Having already lost 900 aircraft since July, many units now struggled to muster more than 60% of their original strength. Flying repeatedly to cover rising manpower shortages, German flyers were caught in a vicious circle of exhaustion and declining effectiveness.

Even though the home advantage was strong for the RAF, it was under enormous pressure too and had lost 150 aircraft in just the last week. Mounting casualties, disruption to supplies and communications, repeated bombing of its aerodromes, all conspired to accelerate the decline of its fighting capability. Whilst new aircraft deliveries were keeping pace with losses, many of Fighter Command's most experienced pilots had already been lost in combat. As the conflict escalated, their newly-trained replacements were being killed three times faster than their veteran counterparts.

Even worse, major divisions had grown between Fighter Command's key leaders. Air Vice Marshal Keith Park commanded 11 Group in Kent, Surrey and Sussex and his peer, Trafford Leigh-Mallory led 12 Group, covering the counties immediately to the north and east of London. They held identical ranks and led similar forces, but completely disagreed over strategy.

Park supported the orders of their commander-in-chief, Air Chief Marshal Hugh Dowding, frugally deploying individual squadrons into hit-and-run combat, whereas Leigh-Mallory sought a complete change of strategy to use what he called a *Big Wing*. He wanted to employ huge formations of RAF fighters all at once, in the hope of destroying the Luftwaffe in a succession of mammoth aerial battles. Whilst maintaining a calm exterior, privately Dowding was horrified by the enormous risks inherent in Leigh-Mallory's proposition.

Only Dowding knew the complete picture across the whole of Fighter Command, reading daily squadron casualty reports with increasing dismay. Just yesterday, out of seven hundred fighters sent into combat, forty had been destroyed with half of their pilots killed or seriously wounded. Even worse, the tallies of German aircraft wrecks collected at dumps revealed that his pilots' victory reports were considerably over-optimistic. Whilst he could only guess at how many damaged Luftwaffe aircraft crashed after leaving British airspace, the current loss ratio was firmly stacked against the much smaller RAF. The arithmetic was simple. If

Fighter Command's losses continued at this pace, it would cease to exist within just three weeks.

Faced with such a dreadful prospect, Dowding might soon have to abandon the battleground to conserve enough aircraft and pilots to resist the imminent German invasion. He knew that such a withdrawal would embolden the Germans still further. Politically, it would signal yet another major British defeat that might precipitate the collapse of Churchill's government. He resolved to carry on with his current strategy for just a few more days, before making such a momentous decision.

Not that Goering knew it… his war of attrition was finally bringing Fighter Command close to crisis point.

Chapter 9

With their breakfast eaten from their laps, the Vigar family sat in their tiny tin shelter for an hour or so, whiling away the time. Apart from the sound of distant thunder at about 10am, not a lot happened.

Of course, they all knew it wasn't really thunder.

Someone's copping it, Betty thought to herself, remembering her encounter with that nice looking soldier. She smiled to herself in a moment of whimsy and then shook her head, back to more sensible thoughts.

The All Clear siren sounded and they made their way back to the house. They grabbed their hats and coats and hurried along to St Mildred's Church to commence worship slightly later than usual. The highlight of the service was a christening and afterwards everyone lingered outside in the late morning sun, to exchange pleasantries and gossip a little before returning home to prepare their Sunday dinners. As the congregation stood around chatting, a young man dressed in elegant country tweeds strolled up to the Vigar family.

'Good morning, Mr Delafort,' said Edward, acting as if they had not met already that day. 'You didn't fancy some contrition then,' he joked.

'I wouldn't know what you mean Mr Vigar.' Raymond replied with a look of innocence. 'I was just passing by and saw you all here… a bit later than usual?'

Edward knew that he wasn't the reason for Raymond's arrival and glanced over at Ginny. Raymond took his cue and went over to talk to her. Pouring on the charm… she was soon laughing and giggling at his banter.

Patricia walked over to her husband.

'I wish you wouldn't encourage that, Ted,' she said. 'He must be five years older than her and far too racy for our girl. I don't want her getting involved with anything too serious at her age. Not now… even if he is a Delafort.'

'Oh don't fret Patsy, there's no harm in it,' replied Edward, rubbing his belly for a moment. 'Besides he's a handy chap to know these days.'

'Will you behave,' Patricia replied, laughing. 'I'm not having you sell off our daughter for a few joints of hooky meat!'

Betty stood by half-listening, feeling invisible yet again, such was the wondrous attraction of her ever-popular sister. She looked across at Ernest Harrop who had only just arrived, red-faced and quite out of breath. A large bruise on his forehead, that she first noticed yesterday afternoon, had taken on a darker hue. It intrigued her again. She caught his lingering glance at Ginny in her light summer dress, the profile of her legs immodestly revealed by the sunshine behind her.

Betty had always been the one to watch and listen.

She knew well enough that Ernest wasn't quite as decent as he made out. Mabel Smith had quite a few little troubles with him in the shop, always seemingly innocent, accidental, a hand that slipped to where it shouldn't on occasion. When Betty first started work there, Mabel had said she should watch herself when she was up the ladder to the top shelves. It was only recently that Betty realised Mabel wasn't referring to the danger of falling. As much as she knew it was wrong, she couldn't tell on Ernest. He was one of her father's best friends and despite her more recently adjusted opinion… he had always been a wonderful pretend uncle, ever since she could remember.

Like most seventeen year old girls, Betty often thought about boys and the secrets of womanhood that lay ahead for her. Unfortunately, this wretched war removed almost all potential suitors from her reach. Anyway, what with Ginny fluttering her eyelashes and showing a bit of leg at every possible opportunity, Betty knew that she would be hard done by in competition. She did love her sister very much, but they were complete opposites in almost every way. Whilst she was thoughtful, considerate and careful, Ginny seemed to care only about herself and strove to be the centre of attention at all times. For all that though, they were a tight-knit family and Betty felt that Dad loved his little girl maybe just a bit more.

Ernest looked over to Edward anxiously and indicated they should have a word or two in private, so they stood to one side.

'Ted, I had a telephone call from Area Control ten minutes ago. The balloon's gone up, it sounds really bad,' Ernest revealed.

They walked off and discussed this news in their official capacity, both of them looking skywards with a serious expression.

Ginny broke away from the crowd at the church gate and walked up to the two men, seeking to interrupt them. She thought she had picked her moment well, as her mother was fully engaged in conversation with other ladies of the parish and was well out of earshot.

'Oh Daddy…' she said, employing her practiced get her-own-way tone of voice. 'Raymond has said he'll take me for a spin on his motorbike…it'll be such fun. You don't mind do you?'

Edward and Ernest carried on talking, ignoring Ginny's presence.

So she took her father's hand and asked him again.

'Oh please Daddy… can I go for a spin on Raymond's motorbike before dinner… Daddy?'

For once, Edward did not give in to her wishes.

He turned and replied matter-of-factly.

'No Virginia. You need to go home with Mother and Elizabeth and get the dinner on the go. You should all go straight home and listen out for the siren, in case you need to take shelter.'

Ginny thought to argue for a moment, but recognised the look on her father's face that signified his word, on this occasion, was final. With her ploy defeated, she returned to Raymond and with a carefree air, pretended that she had thought better of his invitation.

'Oh Raymond darling, I think you'll just have to wait for another day. I think you'd drive far too fast for me and I shall positively *swoon* with too much excitement.'

'My steed is always ready for you, My Lady,' he replied. 'Your wish is always my command.'

Ginny blushed a little.

Delighted by his double entendre, she whispered her response in his ear.

Raymond was pleased with her secret proposal.

Ernest had been watching the young couple's exchange and confided to Edward.

'You really ought to keep your eye on the Delafort boy you know.'

'Oh don't you start, Patsy is always giving out as well.' Edward snapped back. 'She's nineteen now and we have to let her grow up. She's a sensible girl and Raymond Delafort is a straight sort of fellow.'

'It's not him I'd worry about,' Ernest explained. 'She's headstrong and no-one wants to see her get into trouble.'

'What do you mean? She's not going to *get into trouble,*' Edward replied angrily.

'I didn't mean *that* way,' Ernest clarified. 'I just mean, well, she's young and perhaps… she doesn't realise the effect she has on men sometimes? I just wish the best for her, like you. Like we all do… you know that.'

'Oh I'm sorry, it's just that nothing is normal these days,' Edward apologised, then took a deep breath as he calmed down. 'We need to worry about much more serious matters now,' he continued. 'We should gather the patrol together for a meeting this afternoon. If the bombing is as bad as you say down at Biggin Hill… it really could spill over here soon.'

Adding emphasis to his statement, a loud boom echoed through the air.

Everyone flinched.

A ripple of a dozen more explosions quickly followed, bringing everyone's conversations to a halt.

'Don't worry,' Ernest declared loudly. 'It's just the Ack-Ack guns at Bexleyheath… they often fire off a few practice rounds.'

Standing a few yards away, Betty noted that the sound had come from quite the opposite direction. The crowd relaxed a little, but with their chatting interrupted, they took this as their cue to disperse and head for home.

Turning back to Edward, Ernest was expecting to continue with their planning. To his surprise, he realised that Albert Culpepper and a young soldier with a huge kitbag had arrived. Albert's little Austin 10, with its Home Guard sign on the front doors, was parked by the curb.

The three old friends greeted each other cheerfully.

Albert sought to answer Ernest's look of puzzlement at the new, fourth member of the group.

'This is Ken Kendrick… Ted and I have adopted him for a few days,' he said playfully.

Ernest turned to the soldier and was met by an altogether strange expression. The young man looked disconcerted, well…almost… *shocked.*

He hesitated, before offering the expected greeting.

'Er… very pleased to meet you again, it's a lovely day today, isn't it?' said Ken as he reached out and shook Ernest's hand.

'Yes, um…splendid, sorry… have we met before? Kenneth?' Ernest's confusion continued.

'Yes, on Friday,' Ken paused for a few seconds, before adding more detail.

'*Outside your shop*… don't you remember?'

Edward started laughing at Ernest's continuing bewilderment and decided he should explain Albert's adoption joke.

'Ken is the chap that Fingers helped out that day with a phone call. You know… when the boys came back from Dunkirk? I was over in Eltham yesterday, looking over Courtauld's observation post and I popped into the yard, when Ken turned up.'

He paused.

'The long and the short of it is that he's on leave and of no fixed abode. So he's come for Sunday dinner.'

Then the penny dropped.

Ernest had remembered the story about the wounded soldier and the phone call, and here he was in person.

'Excellent! Always keen to do our bit to help our brave soldiers,' said Ernest. He grabbed Ken's hand and shook it more heartily this time.

Ken had noticed Betty standing just a few yards away.

She saw him too, but then Ginny glided in front of him.

'Charmed I'm sure,' she giggled and held her hand out to him, assuming her grand movie star persona. Before anyone could interject, she linked Ken's arm and led him away as the new object of her fascination. He looked over to Betty and raised his eyebrows in apology,

Edward just waved his hand and indicated that he shouldn't be concerned.

Betty looked on with resignation.

'Bloody terrible what happened to him isn't it?' said Albert.

Not in on the secret, Ernest looked at the other two men for an explanation.

'He gets seven days leave before he's posted God Knows Where, goes home to his Dad and then… gets booted out by his wicked step-mother,' Albert explained.

'Look… we don't know the full ins and outs of it Bert, we shouldn't stand in judgement.' Edward cut in.

'I know, I know,' Albert replied. 'But it's a rum story from what he told us yesterday. I'm just glad he popped in to see me at the office like that, out of the blue. I had often wondered what happened to that lad.'

Ernest decided it was time to get the full story.

The three of them chatted away in their usual closed huddle, adding the full details of Ken Kendrick's tale to the annals of The Three Musketeers.

Meanwhile, Raymond had watched Ginny's attraction to the soldier with considerable annoyance. Whilst he was used to playing the game with girls like her, this new player upset his strategy.

Yesterday's motorbike ride was meant to be a masterstroke conclusion, to a carefully crafted plan of not-so-chance encounters over the last few weeks. On the back of buttering up her father this morning, Raymond had hoped to get Ginny away this afternoon to see a whole lot more of her again. Harrop hadn't helped of course, throwing him filthy looks and Raymond knew that just for the moment, he had to watch his step. Equally though, he knew plenty about Harrop from Mabel Smith and had recently discovered a whole lot more.

Just a few words to the right people and Harrop's fall from grace would be sudden and complete.

Those silly old fuckers. They think they are so clever, but I'll show them soon enough, Raymond thought angrily.

He didn't like the attention that Ginny was giving to that common soldier. Walking straight over, he interrupted their conversation.

'So what brings you here… to my town?' Raymond asked in haughty fashion, ignoring Ginny, launching straight at his opponent.

Ken was taken aback.

'Oh… just visiting, got a few day's leave and Ginny's father has invited me to Sunday dinner. My name's Ken, pleased to…'

'Well, *Virginia* has better things to do I'm sure,' Raymond interrupted disdainfully.

Ginny was not amused at this turn to the conversation. It was spoiling her fun with this handsome man in uniform.

She snapped back at Raymond.

'Yes. I have plenty of things to do and I will do them as and when I please, thank you!' To underscore her determination, she continued. 'We're going to the pictures tomorrow night and Ken will be my beau…. won't you Ken?'

Ken was bewildered by this rapidly developing situation and wasn't exactly sure what he'd got himself into. He knew one thing… that his first impression of this snooty-looking toff wasn't favourable.

'Well… yes… I think that would be nice,' Ken replied, prompted by Ginny squeezing his hand tightly. Emboldened, he continued, 'that'll be just the ticket.'

Ginny smiled sweetly at him and turning to Raymond, fluttered her eyelashes mischievously.

'You must come as well,' she announced, 'we can bring *Mabel* too.'

Now that was too close to the mark for Raymond, his plans were crashing down around him.

'I shall be in the balcony…' he continued, then sniped at Ken. 'Whereas, some people belong only in the s*talls*.'

Ginny was enjoying this contest and waited for the next jibe with anticipation.

'I believe they are showing *The Four Feathers?*' Ken rebutted. 'That should suit someone like you, perfectly.'

It was game, set and match to the soldier.

The film he named dramatised how a man accused of cowardice might yet redeem himself. This perfectly insulted Raymond Delafort, a healthy young man, conspicuously *not* in uniform.

Raymond was left speechless by the inference. He stormed off down the road towards his motorbike, with Ginny's laughter ringing in his ears.

'That was clever of you Ken, whatever made you think of that?' she exclaimed.

Ken chuckled with relief.

'Oh, it was the last flick I saw before I set off to France last year. What is on at the pictures these days anyway?'

'Look for yourself,' she said, pointing over Ken's shoulder.

He turned around and realised that they were standing right opposite a cinema.

Across the Plaza's grand façade large black letters spelt out that the main feature was *Busman's Honeymoon*, starring Robert Montgomery and Constance Cummings.

Ginny laughed again.

Taking stock of his good looks, she had an idea.

'Actually…why don't we go anyway? We can bring my sister and my friend Mabel along too… if you can handle the three of us?'

Ken considered the proposal for a few seconds.

'My leave isn't over until Wednesday, it would be good fun before I go. Oh…. why not? It'll be smashing.'

'Then it's agreed,' Ginny declared, sealing the deal. 'Come on… we had better be getting home.'

However, she wasn't to know that Ken's decision had actually hinged on the mention of her little sister. He looked around for Betty, but saw that she and her mother were already walking away.

Equally, Ken wasn't to know Ginny's true motive either.

She hadn't forsaken her plans for Raymond Delafort and tomorrow night, not one little bit. If her instincts were correct, he wouldn't give up the fight for her attention and a new challenger would raise the value of the prize.

Uncle Albert started his Austin and called out.

'All aboard that's going aboard!'

They all clambered inside. Ken squeezed alongside plump Ernest on the back seat, with the enormous army kitbag laid across their laps. Then the little car creaked and rattled and pot-potted along as it accelerated down the road.

'Last one home's a silly sausage!' Ginny shouted out the window towards her mother and sister.

Outwardly, that Sunday lunchtime seemed little different to any other of recent years. Yet if they had looked behind them, they would have seen columns of thick black smoke rising ominously above London's docks ten miles away.

Chapter 10

Today's Luftwaffe operations began with a handful of high altitude weather reconnaissance flights that chased sunrise across Southern England. Soon after, scores of Messerschmitt 110 twin engine fighter-bombers swooped through the early morning haze and bombed coastal airfields along Fighter Command's frontline.

At 9.52am, a hundred Messerschmitt 109 fighters were seen crossing the coast between Dungeness and Margate, no doubt sent to clear a path for a large bomber raid following behind. In response, one hundred and twenty RAF fighters were sent to intercept them and a chaotic dogfight quickly developed over Ashford, spilling eastwards to Canterbury and Margate. Away from this diversion, the main raid of eighty German bombers slipped through between Dymchurch and Folkestone. It split into four separate groups, making it even harder for RAF operations controllers to decide on the best response.

The airfields at Detling near Maidstone and Eastchurch on the Isle of Sheppey were struck first. By 10.30am, RAF Biggin Hill was under heavy bombardment too. The aerodrome had to close immediately for repairs to its landing fields and its squadrons were ordered to land elsewhere. At 11.15am, a second raid of more than a hundred bombers was spotted approaching the Thames Estuary, heading directly towards London.

The formation split onto separate target headings and by 11.45am, bombs were falling on London's docks. The other half of the raiding force struck north to hammer airfields at Hornchurch, North Weald and Rochford in Essex as well.

As the British fighters struggled to deflect German air raids, it was becoming clear that there had been a change in Luftwaffe tactics. From his headquarters at Bentley Priory in Middlesex, Dowding telephoned Park at RAF Uxbridge. He wanted to know why the raids were penetrating British airspace much more easily.

Park's answer was blunt.

His squadrons were reporting suddenly twice as many German fighters in the air, preventing them from getting to grips with the bombers.

Park abruptly finished the call.

The reason for this sudden tip in the balance was straightforward. To make best use of their limited range, the majority of German fighter units, the *jagdgeschwaden,* had been moved to coastal airfields in the Pas de Calais area of Northern France. The shorter distance to the battle area now gave them an extra ten minutes of fuel over South East England.

In addition, Goering had overridden his field commanders' tactical protocols. He demanded that they reduced their fighter reserves and sent far more Messerschmitts into the combat zone at once. Even more significantly, this morning's *free hunt* over Ashford would now become a rare event and the fighters would fly directly alongside the bombers instead. Drawing upon his experience as a First World War fighter ace, Goering believed his old instincts would prevail again in 1940. If he had been able to squeeze into a fighter cockpit himself, he would certainly have recognised the crazy, swirling mass of aircraft clashing above Kent…just like the frenetic air battles of the old Western Front of 1917.

However, by making his fighters fly close to the slower bombers, Goering had robbed his Messerschmitts of using their dogfighting advantages of surprise, greater height and speed. This put them in a far weaker position during the first, most crucial seconds of any engagement. Hoping to increase the survival rate of the bombers, his order now doubled the risk of Luftwaffe fighter pilots being killed or captured. These highly skilled, young flyers were utterly dismayed that their commander-in-chief so badly misunderstood modern air warfare.

Goering's direct intervention would have major consequences, as the attrition of Luftwaffe fighter strength began to accelerate.

Certainly, Horst Muller appreciated this closer fighter escort, as he piloted his Heinkel 111 bomber back from the morning raid on Biggin Hill.

When his staffel first crossed the English coast around 10am, British fighters had managed only one half–hearted attack before becoming embroiled with the Messerschmitts. This left two of his bombers sporting a few bullet holes and their crews somewhat shaken, but they carried on regardless.

Muller had flown in the Polish campaign, but entirely missed the Battle of France due to a posting to the Air Ministry in Berlin. Recalled to active duty three weeks ago, he took command of his staffel with immense pride, ready to take on the English. He soon came to respect the expertise and determination of RAF pilots, who had by now removed four aircraft from his command. The first suffered engine damage on their second mission, falling behind on the return flight and disappeared over the Channel. With only a small chance of being rescued if an aircraft ditched at sea, the so-called *Kanalkranheit*, Channel Sickness, was one of the greatest fears of German flyers in the summer of 1940. The crew of that missing plane was never seen again. The next two aircraft were shot down by English fighters a week ago and yesterday, the fourth had been hit by anti-aircraft fire and plummeted into the cloud base, trailing smoke.

Muller was pleased with today's operation. They had joined the other bomber groups, the *kampfgeschwaden,* over Abbeville at a height of 5000 metres and their fighter escorts met them right on schedule. After crossing the Channel, they proceeded in well-organised fashion towards their targets. The weather had been fairly clear to start with, but they encountered thicker cloud cover as they flew deeper into English airspace.

Nevertheless, Muller knew he could rely on his excellent navigator to place them accurately over the target. The bomber stream headed north-west at first and when they sighted the River Medway at Rochester, Muller led his staffel away from the main raiding force. He veered sharply west and whilst rapidly dropping height to gain speed, his Heinkels followed him towards Orpington.

This was becoming a familiar route over northern Kent, rich with many target options that kept the British guessing about their true purpose. North of Orpington, they turned sharply south and headed for Biggin Hill at an altitude of 2500 metres, approximately 8000 feet. Then they turned again, to approach the airfield from the north-west and Muller instructed his navigator to target the southernmost buildings. As seven Heinkels followed them towards the bomb run, the navigator left his seat and took up his second role, at the bomb-aiming position at the front of the cockpit. The other bombers would take their cue from him and launch their bomb releases behind, to hit the grass landing strips and other facilities.

Muller spotted British fighters on the left beam climbing up towards them, but they were being harried by several Messerschmitts. He calculated that he would be long-gone before these British planes could climb to this altitude. The airfield's anti-aircraft guns began firing and the Heinkel juddered and jumped, buffeted by black shell bursts looming large in its path. Although the streamlined, fully glazed nose of the aircraft gave excellent all round vision, it offered no protection whatsoever to its crew. The fuselage resounded to the crack and bang of cascading shrapnel, but the English gunners were off their mark today and the formation was already well into its final run.

The navigator peered through the bombsight and as the airfield came into view, he flicked a switch to arm the circuits in the bomb bay and activated the autopilot to take control of the aircraft. By making adjustments to the bombsight, the aircraft followed his command with gentle variations to speed, height and direction. With the target lined up, he reached across to his left and wound a handle to open the bomb bay doors. In front of him, two gauges showed him airspeed and altitude. He turned the bomb sight dials to the corresponding data and its mechanism calculated a recommended vector and release point to hit the target. Finally, he set the salvo timer to a close single-second interval between each bomb release.

The target crept into the centre of the bombsight.

However, this bomb aimer preferred to trust his own judgement.

Overriding the auto release, he waited a further second and a half until he sensed the moment was right. He calmly activated the manual bomb release, which also returned control of the aircraft back to Muller in the pilot's seat.

Standing within eight vertical silos at the centre of the plane were two giant 250kg and twenty four 50kg high explosive bombs. They dropped out of the bomb bay in rapid succession and tumbled for a few seconds in the slipstream. Gravity pulled them nose down and they hurtled towards the main buildings at the south of the airfield.

Each weapon carried a straightforward contact fuse, electrically armed a few seconds after it left its bomb rack, priming it to detonate upon impact. The aircraft behind Muller's each carried similar payloads, mostly the small SC50's and a few larger bombs, all together, between twenty four and thirty two per plane. Their salvos were set to release on a broader dispersal pattern, to create a wide crater field across the airfield.

The staffel dutifully followed their lead plane's cue.

Like a sudden downpour of bitter rain, a dense cloud of bombs fanned out across the target area.

The young man in the front of Muller's aircraft remained prone, peering out of the glazed nose at the world below.

As the formation passed over Biggin Hill, the gunner in the rear-facing belly sponson observed the fall of bombs all the way down. He roared in jubilation as the airfield was rent from end to end by hundreds of explosions, many amongst housing blocks around the aerodrome. Within just ninety seconds, RAF Biggin Hill was transformed into a lunar landscape of craters, rendering it impossible for any aircraft to take-off or land safely. The gunner had his Leica pocket camera ready in anticipation and from his lofty position, photographed the terrific spectacle for his scrapbook.

The navigator shouted out in surprise.

Looking far ahead, he glimpsed the familiar outline of a Heinkel 111 crash-landed several kilometres to the south of the airfield. He wondered if it was the aircraft lost during yesterday's raid here, but was too far below to see for certain. Nonetheless, the crew immediately exchanged optimistic banter. They hoped that maybe it was their own comrades who had survived a forced landing, to be sent to a British prison camp to munch on awful English sausages for a few weeks. As Muller steeply banked the aircraft, he craned his neck to look behind. Over his left shoulder, he could see that the last three of his aircraft had made a poor, ragged turn off the bomb run and were considerably out of position. He ordered the radio operator, in the top gun position, to tell them to close up tighter together for better mutual protection in the event of another British fighter attack.

Inwardly berating the poor piloting on display, Muller considered the many shortcomings he had encountered, during and after, his posting at the Air Ministry in Germany.

The spectacular string of victories across Europe, culminating in the defeat of France, had stunned everyone at home into a state of euphoria.

Yet again their *Führer*, Adolf Hitler, had proved unstoppable.

He had taken the Rhineland back from France in 1936, created a union with Austria in 1938 and annexed the Sudetenland of Czechoslovakia shortly after. All without a single shot being fired, as Britain and France chose appeasement over armed conflict. With the greatest historical irony, Hitler was dubbed *General Bloodless* at home. Then he turned to military aggression and the invasion of Poland in 1939 returned a connection with the land of Prussia and more to Germany. Soviet Russia invaded from the east, to create a secretly agreed partition of Poland. The might of Germany's armed forces turned in the opposite direction and now, almost all of Western Europe lay prostrate before a new Germanic overlord.

Muller had witnessed Hitler's triumphal return to the Reich Capital on the 6th July, fêted like a latter-day Alexander by 500,000 cheering Berliners. Instead of millions dead on the Western Front, Hitler had delivered incomparable victory within just 8 weeks. It felt like a miracle. The people threw flowers and kisses at the conquering soldiers parading through their city, in a joyous outburst of relief. If they had known of the genocidal horrors already being inflicted upon the people of Poland, their gratitude would have been far less rapturous. Only a few years would pass before the full shame of Nazi barbarism fell upon the conscience of a complicit German nation.

With the glorious, victorious, summer drawing to a close, everyone was in holiday mood. Although demand for munitions was growing beyond all expectation, German businessmen chased profits instead of production quotas and military output actually fell. While Britain's aircraft factories built two hundred new Spitfires and Hurricanes each week, German industry dawdled. In Hitler's medieval court, self-advancement was the biggest priority.

Raised in preparation for the struggle against his country's perceived enemies, Muller had been taught to repudiate the morals of his parents, to embrace the cruel dogma of National Socialism. Like most of Germany's youth, he became enthralled by a Führer who made anything seem possible. Providing work for millions of people with a grand modernisation of the nation and its armed forces, Nazi bankers secretly printed vast sums of money to fund new autobahns and industry. The ballooning inflationary weakness of the economy was hidden from sight. Few people realised this miraculous recovery was built upon sand, and that the only solution would be to seize the wealth of neighbouring states by military conquest.

In 1936 at just twenty one years of age, Horst walked away from a comfortable middle class life to join the rapidly-expanding Luftwaffe. He excelled in pilot training and with a personality well suited for *der Angriff*, the attack, he was selected for bomber school. He progressed rapidly and in 1938, joined the elite Condor Legion to fly in support of fascist General Franco during the Spanish Civil War. With this invaluable combat experience, Horst was rapidly elevated to a status way beyond anything possible before the Nazi era.

Just two years later, he was now a major, the youngest in the entire Luftwaffe. His dedication was rewarded with command of one of the most powerful weapons systems in the world; his own staffel of Heinkel twin-engine bombers.

Muller was proud of the thirty nine brave men he had led into battle today.

They had invaded British airspace to within 20 kilometres of London itself, to drop 16 metric tonnes of high explosive bombs on a well-protected airfield, for the third time in as many days. Faster without their bomb loads, the bombers sped along at 350 kilometres per hour over the fields of East Sussex, towards the safety of home territory. He looked to his left to see smoke rising again over Dover. Then he spotted a fresh raid of a hundred or more Dornier 17's and Heinkel 111's approaching with close fighter protection. A swarm of English fighters were bearing down on them. To his right, he saw yet another formation; this time of twenty Dornier 17's pelting into England at low level.

Despite his fatigue and the stress of ever-present danger, Muller was exhilarated by the spectacle presented before him. He felt truly privileged to be part of something much bigger than himself, a witness to the birth of a glorious new epoch in world history.

He called out over the intercom to his four comrades on-board; instructing them to keep a lookout for British fighters for just a few more minutes.

They flew past Hastings and entered thick cloud cover rolling in along the Channel. Muller wondered if this might curtail operations that afternoon. As the crew relaxed a little, the upper gunner started singing the Luftwaffe song *Bomben Auf Engeland*. When he got to the chorus… his improvised, ribald version of what the Maidens of Germany would do for their returning heroes, plunged his comrades into roars of laughter.

Muller laughed as well and told them he would write to their mothers, to warn them about their filthy-minded boys. With the tension of the mission subsiding, the crew chatted away over the intercom as the coast of France crept into view.

Their commander had been on duty since 4am and now eight hours later, he was weary. He was looking forward to a good lunch, celebratory banter with his men and a good sleep back at Rosières-en-Santerre.

Chapter 11

The Vigars' set about their lunchtime preparations, spurred on by the prospect of the illicit joint of meat sizzling away in the oven. The women busied themselves with preparing the vegetables and the potatoes were put in to roast too. The menfolk sat in the garden around a crate of brown ale and as they supped away, conversation moved back and forth between gossip and wider events.

Morning sunshine had been replaced by passing clouds that cast drifting shadows across the garden, but it was turning into a hot day, underscoring the prospect of an Indian Summer for the week ahead. Whilst that was good for recreation, this continued fine weather would extend the German opportunity to launch an invasion. For Britain's sake, cloud and rain would have been far more welcome.

Ken Kendrick looked around the garden. More than half of it had been turned over to growing basic vegetables and the trickiest of all to grow well, the runner beans, looked particularly promising. He walked up to the gate in the back fence, turned, looked back towards the house and was lost in thought. He decided to take a peek out of the gate, towards the open space that separated the houses from a railway line.

All was tranquil and familiar there. Half a dozen young boys were casually kicking a football around, still in their Sunday Best clothes. One of their mothers called out from a few houses down, scolding them against getting dirty.

In the house, Edward Vigar had finished his phone calls to his fellow air raid wardens. Satisfied with the arrangements for their meeting later on, he walked through the dining room and out through the French Doors, to join the men in the garden.

'Where's the beer lads? I've got a good thirst on,' he announced. He looked towards the open kitchen window and called out to Patricia. 'When's noshing time, My Queen?'

'It'll be about 45 minutes,' she replied and with more than a hint of irony added. 'Are you *sure* you are all quite comfortable out there?'

'Oh don't you worry,' he replied. 'We'll do all the washing up and you can put your feet up and have a nice rest later. You deserve it Love.'

He seemed oblivious to her gentle sarcasm, a frequent habit before Sunday lunchtimes. All four men were standing now, beer bottles in hand, staring over the right-hand fence at the huge column of smoke that had risen above London, ten miles away to the northwest.

'I'd say that's somewhere near the docks they've done this morning,' Ken suggested.

'And they've been bombing the airfields too,' Ernest contributed. 'but I'm sure we're getting the blighters back, good and proper.'

The truth was, of course, that nobody really knew what was going on, such was the surreal existence they all shared these days. It was all a pretence of ordinary life, amidst truly extraordinary events.

Nowadays, people hung on the words of BBC radio newsreaders every evening, to glean any understanding of the progress of the war. As hopeful as the daily tally of theirs and ours lost in combat sounded, it was pretty obvious that these macabre scores didn't quite match the evidence presented to most people. Although the RAF was allegedly shooting down many hundreds of Nazi aircraft, a sky constantly full of vapour trails and the sound of distant explosions confirmed that the Germans were back again and again. There seemed to be no end in sight. The only glimpse you could get into the heart of the matter was through the camera lens of optimistic, government-censored newsreels at the cinema. With such great air battles taking place all around Sidcup, the town found itself in the calm eye of a man-made storm. Consequently, Edward and Ernest's group of volunteer wardens had had little real work to do so far.

Their foremost responsibility was to operate the local air raid sirens day and night, ready for whenever a Warning Alert or All Clear was rung through from Observer Corps Area Control. They were nominally in charge of two large electric sirens for Sidcup and Lamorbey. One sat atop a 30 foot pole outside their tiny office at St Mildred's Church School, the other on the roof of the police station up at the high street. The latter was often a bone of contention, as the police constabulary held sway over its operation and there had been many disputes regarding use of its circuit breaker.

In compensation, Edward was allocated a portable siren that he kept in the boot of his car, making sure it was always on hand for emergencies. He often cranked away at the handle to add to the roar of its electrically powered brothers, mostly because it gave him something to do. In addition, the wardens practised snuffing out incendiary bombs with buckets of sand, rehearsed the rescue of people from bombed-out buildings and clearing danger areas after a raid. Their final duty was to officially record damage to people and property caused by enemy action.

Fortunately for Sidcup during the last twelve months, the patrol's activities had been confined to enforcing the blackout, endless training and nothing more. Many of their wives regarded the Sidcup ARP as a coincidental excuse for a social club and it was true that their meetings often took place in The Carpenters Arms pub, just around the corner from the Plaza cinema. They had originally convened at The Railway Tavern in Alma Road, but it proved to be just a little too close to home to avoid surprise inspections from their spouses. The war had hardly touched Sidcup and most people felt they were safe, as to them it seemed there was nothing round here worth bombing anyway. Whether the wardens' efforts were appreciated or not, one thing was for sure, they all cared about their community, their country and to coin a popular saying, *they wanted to do their bit.*

Whilst in many respects they were itching for a small opportunity to put their training into practice, they wisely feared the price that would be paid if they were ever called to action in earnest.

Like many people at this time, a cheerful veneer of normal life thinly covered their concerns about the future.

After staring at the distant smoke cloud for a minute or so, Edward put voice to everyone's likely thoughts.

'It's hard to believe what's really happening sometimes, isn't it?' he piped up. Then he felt a little foolish, as the young soldier beside him had obviously seen a great deal of what was really happening already.

One of the girls had turned on the radio in the dining room, the sound of dance music wafted out of the open French Doors into the garden.

The men stood without talking for a minute or two, before the ice was broken again by Ernest.

'So Kenneth, what part of town do you hail from?'

'It's just *Ken* actually Mr Harrop, a nickname... because of my surname. I'm from Bermondsey, Grange Road, just behind the market.'

'Oh I see, have you much family…er… brothers…sisters?' asked Ernest.

Ken did not speak for a few seconds, as he contemplated his response.

'Just my Dad. Then there's his wife, my step brother and step sister,' he replied. 'My mum died just after I was born.'

He paused, revealing the real reason for his hesitancy.

'I had a twin brother… but he went with her.'

Ernest decided he had better change the subject.

'Your father, what does he do for a living?'

'He runs a dairy business, he's a milkman and Bertha runs the family restaurant.' Ken hesitated, 'well… it's a dining hall really… they cater mostly for workers at the Alaska Fur Factory, breakfasts, lunches, teas… you know.'

'Your step brother and sister… do you see much of them?' Ernest continued.

'Not really, Lily and Dick were both put in the Temperance Children's Home. I do try and see them when I can.'

Ernest looked confused by that last statement, so Ken felt obliged to explain a little further.

'After Mum died, to start with I was brought up in Chatham by my aunt. I was five when Dad remarried, he came and got me, but Bertha left her two in the Temperance,' Ken revealed awkwardly. 'She thought that was best for them… um… how about you Mr Harrop, do you have a family?'

'Unfortunately not, but I live in hope,' Ernest replied uncomfortably and changed topic again. 'So tell me about life in the army… you're Royal Engineers are you?'

Ken glanced at the regimental flash on his shoulder.

'That's a new addition. I've only just joined them. I was training as a draughtsman for a plumbing firm before all this. Last month I was transferred to the RE's.'

'A draughtsman eh?' Edward chimed in. 'We could do with your help in the firm reading building plans from time to time.'

Now that he had started talking, Ken felt obliged to carry on.

'I originally joined the cavalry territorials in '38, but there's not much call for that these days. I fancied the uniform if I'm honest, but me and horses didn't get on.' Ken laughed for a moment and continued, 'I was called up for full service just before war was declared and I ended up with mules instead. We left them all in France of course...I'm bloody glad to leave them buggers behind!'

All three of them laughed in appreciation and Albert joined in the conversation.

'Ernie and I have plenty of experience with those grumpy sods from the last lot, haven't we Ernie?'

The older men recounted experiences from the trenches twenty years before and their anecdotes flowed forth. Some sad, some funny, the four men spanned two generations yet shared a common bond of service, given to their country in times past and present.

Betty looked on from the kitchen sink whilst she scrubbed carrots. Ginny stood behind her a moment, following her gaze out of the window.

'You like him, don't you Sis?' Ginny whispered.

Betty blushed.

'I don't know what you mean...but he's alright I suppose,' she declared.

'I'd say he's more than alright Betty, you've got a fancy on him I think.'

'No I haven't. Are the parsnips ready yet?' Betty replied.

Ignoring her question, Ginny persisted. 'I've asked him out to the flicks tomorrow, why don't you come along? It's Robert Montgomery as Lord Whimsy... you like a bit of a murder mystery.'

'Two's company, three's a crowd Ginny,' said Betty, knowing full well she'd end up on her own.

It wasn't the first time that had happened.

'No, don't you worry, get Mabel to come along too,' Ginny suggested. 'Come on… it'll be a hoot. We haven't been to the pictures together in ages and we all need to forget our worries for a few hours.'

She paused, waiting for a reaction.

'Go on, say yes, go on… say you will...' she badgered.

Betty knew full well that her big sister's persistence was not something to battle. Ginny could keep on and on like a stuck record, for days if necessary, to get her own way. So Betty agreed to the proposal and to ask Mabel along as well, when she was back at work in the morning. Satisfied with her sister's agreement, Ginny went into the dining room to lay the table and Patricia followed her to supervise.

Betty couldn't help but wonder what Ginny's ulterior motive might be, as there generally was one somewhere. She decided that it was probably just to get Dad's consent to go to the cinema, as he wasn't keen, of late, on Ginny going out at night without a chaperone.

Last Thursday, Ginny had come home sounding considerably worse for wear. She had been up Burton's to go dancing with Mabel and returned very late. Betty was already in bed downstairs and didn't really know the full ins and outs of it, but she'd heard Dad talking sternly to Ginny in the dining room. He must have raised his voice to have woken Betty up. Once she'd gathered her senses, she went straight to her bedroom door to eavesdrop on the hullabaloo in progress across the hall.

Mum was involved too and Betty heard the odd snippet to the effect that *nice girls don't behave like this* and that *ladies should be more modest in what they wear*. Betty didn't consider herself a prude by any means, but she knew how young women should conduct themselves and her sister didn't always conform to such standards. She heard Ginny run upstairs in floods of tears and slam the door to her bedroom.

The next day there was a wall of silence on the matter.

Betty asked Mum what had happened and as usual, was told not to bother herself about such things.

The subject was closed.

Ginny wouldn't say anything either, but Betty instinctively knew that a man was involved somewhere in the middle of it all. At the time, she couldn't for the life of her work out who it might be. This was particularly annoying, as there weren't exactly many suspects around here these days. Eventually, she had settled on the notion of a mystery soldier, as there were plenty of those to choose from.

Generally speaking, it was like living in two parallel versions of life in Sidcup of late. There were the local inhabitants, who carried on as normally as they could manage and at the same time, there were always soldiers passing through or army lorries towing big guns from somewhere to another. Military things happened in the same time and place as local life, but rarely connected. It was a strange experience to be living in a community you'd known all your life and not understand much of what was going on about you anymore. However, Betty knew that *Careless Talk Costs Lives*, she minded her own business and didn't ask too many questions. However, this didn't stop her watching the upheaval of life in Sidcup to draw her own conclusions.

She had been weighing up her most recent observations and decided that The Riddle of Ginny's Latest Suitor was solved by Raymond Delafort's appearance outside church this morning. That wasn't a chance encounter by any means and even Dad seemed unsurprised. Admittedly, they had always had varying degrees of contact with the Delaforts as there was often work to be done around their various properties. Dad often said that *he had made quite a few quid* out of their custom over the years, but usually added, *but he had to have the patience of a saint when it came to collecting payment.*

Also there was the question as to why Mabel was so upset last Friday morning? When Betty arrived for work, she had been in a terrible state, in floods of tears. Apparently she and Ginny had fallen out over something the night before.

Was it about something or… someone?

The evidence was mounting and in this particular mystery, the arrival of that hooky meat this morning further supported Betty's hypothesis. Knowing her sister as she did, it would be entirely typical for Ginny to set her sights so high, but even so…. on Raymond Delafort?

Apart from all the obvious class differences, there would be the enormous challenge of getting past Old Madame Maude on the way to the altar, not a battle that anyone should invite.

Betty looked out to the garden again and thought about Ginny's more immediate proposal and Ken Kendrick. He seemed like a nice man and maybe for once she should take a leaf out of her sister's book?

Just a leaf, mind you.

Betty shuddered to think what would happen if she ever took a whole chapter.

She laughed to herself… whatever was she thinking?

At that moment, Patricia tugged her youngest daughter out of her daydreaming. It was time to get the carrots on the go as everything else was nearly ready.

There was a distant, thunderous rumble again.

It continued for about five minutes and everyone carried on, as if nothing unusual was happening.

Fifteen miles away to the north, at RAF Hornchurch in Essex, people were running for their lives as yet more bombs cascaded down.

On the other side of Sidcup, Maude Delafort was already finishing her solitary luncheon at Craywood House, contemplating parish matters of great importance. She was a woman who had lived her life by the clock and it annoyed her considerably that the air raid alert had delayed the morning service at All Saints.

Of course, she took no notice whatsoever of the siren and was exasperated that her gardener-driver-handy man, Mr Fellowes, had not readied the car for 9.50am. She had stood at the front door for over twenty minutes before he eventually made an appearance. Without any apology, Fellowes went straight to the stables and brought the car around the front to meet her. While she sat in the back of the old Rolls Royce limousine during the short journey through Foots Cray village, Maude had mulled over that *you just can't get the staff these days*. Actually, it would have been more accurate to admit that she couldn't afford them.

It was a far cry from her youth, when Papa was at his peak and there were a dozen people running the house for the family. Over the last twenty years, the rise in general living standards and profound social change had conspired to make a servant's life an increasingly unattractive vocation. Though her family's fortunes improved in recent years, Maude had been forced to make do with just Mr Fellowes and a part-time cook general, Mrs Tedbury. She was a grumpy woman who came in from the village, to clean the house and prepare the main meals of the day as Maude required.

Once at All Saints Church, Maude's annoyance escalated when Mr Fellowes attempted to sit next to her on the front pew, before she sent him off to his proper place at the back of the church. She sat alone until the All Clear sounded just after 11am and at long last, the Tedburys and Mrs Fellowes arrived, along with the rest of the congregation.

After the service, Reverend Johnstone was unsympathetic to Maude's anguish, citing national emergency and the importance of taking heed of air raid alerts. At that moment, as if to underscore his point, the whole neighbourhood reverberated to the crashing boom of big guns being fired, he presumed, at nearby Foots Cray Army Camp.

He concluded with Maude's least favourite phrase… *There is a war on…* which seemed to be the universal excuse for poor standards these days.

A hundred and seventy miles away in Northern France, Horst Muller was thinking much the same thing. He was surveying the sorry sight of one of his Heinkels, perched nose down in a ditch at the south eastern perimeter of the airfield.

Built in 1938 by the RAF, this modern aerodrome had been occupied by the Luftwaffe shortly after the French surrender and taken over by the headquarters staff of bomber group Kampfgeschwader 1. Whilst the main buildings and hangars had been extensively damaged by the same Luftwaffe now in residence, it offered a good arrangement of taxiways and hardstanding dispersal areas. Covering several square kilometres, the airfield boasted three excellent concrete runways. Two formed a cross, whilst the third ran east-west just beside the main Amiens railway line. Rosières was an excellent facility for the 3rd Gruppe of KG1, even if its personnel presently had to live under canvass until the buildings were made habitable again. The 1st and 2nd Gruppe were stationed under much the same conditions, at the even larger Montdidier airfield, twenty kilometres to the south. All in all, the bomber group comprised of thirteen staffeln, nominally a mighty force of 200 aircraft, but less than half remained in service after three months of heavy combat.

A little earlier, Muller had brought his kette of three aircraft in to land on Runway No1, taxied to a halt about 300 metres from the main hangars, dismounted and watched the remaining five of his aircraft come in.

The last plane was flown by one of the new pilots.

He misjudged his final approach, came in far too fast and nearly overshot the main landing strip. The bomber had bounced along the last stretch of runway, straight over the rough grass at its end, dug its wheels into softer ground and pivoted forward, crashing the glassed flight cabin into the ground. It stood there pathetically, with its tailplane pointing high in the air.

Muller observed the sorry scene through a pair of binoculars and sighed deeply with disappointment.

A team of ground crew were struggling to work out how to right the aircraft and get it back to the workshops. The plane didn't look too badly damaged, but would certainly be out of service for a day, while the mechanics replaced its twisted propellers and repaired the smashed canopy.

Its hapless pilot stood by, looking aghast.

Two of his men were being stretchered away with grievous injuries, having been thrown the length of the plane by the final impact. One young man had a broken leg, the other was drenched in blood from a terrible head injury. The other two crew members looked on with deep concern for their unconscious comrade. This cameo stood against a backdrop of manic activity across the large Luftwaffe airbase. The volume of noise generated by dozens of returning aircraft overhead and touching down, was deafening.

On the northern perimeter by Runway No3, the remaining dozen Heinkel 111's of the 12th and 13th staffel stood alongside nine Junkers 88's, visiting from KG76 at Creil. As their ground crews worked around them, the

Junkers' engines started with raucous coughs of black exhaust smoke and would soon be ready for take-off. Six ex-civilian lorries, heavily laden with crates of bombs, had driven out to the still silent Heinkels to begin loading up their payloads.

Muller adjusted his binoculars to read messages that the armourers had chalked on several of the newly unpacked bombs. A flight crew were having their picture taken alongside one large bomb, displaying an amusing cartoon of a drunken Winston Churchill. Several fitters stood nearby, clearly impatient to start fusing and hauling the bombs into the aircraft.

Scanning around the airbase, Muller saw that Runway No2 was closed after a Dornier 17 from KG 2 crash-landed there twenty minutes ago.

The badly shot-up aircraft had made it all the way back from England, but unable to reach its base at Cambrai, it came straight into Rosières. Just a few hundred metres before landing, its left engine had burst into flames.

Muller had watched with dread as the pilot struggled to keep control. The aircraft touched down, but then its undercarriage collapsed under the burning engine. Still moving at 120 kilometres per hour, the plane twisted violently, wrenching the left wing around, flipping the aircraft onto its back.

The contorted wreck came to a violent halt, not even halfway down the runway and its almost instantaneous deceleration probably killed all of the crew outright. Even if any of them had survived that, there would have been no chance of escape from the burning fuel that ignited the wreckage. A fire crew had finally doused the flames and were waiting for the arrival of a tractor to pull the wreck out of the way. Afterwards, they would have the gruesome task of retrieving what was left of the crew.

Muller's gaze left this terrible scene and returned to the up-ended bomber and its sorry-looking pilot. Letting his binoculars hang from his neck, he turned to the operations staff sergeant, Stabsfeldwebel Rüdiger Freund, who had joined him on the hardstanding.

He wearily made only one comment.

'Tell that fuckhead to report to my office in twenty minutes.'

Muller walked back to the service buildings.

As he approached the hangars and office block, he passed an ambulance with its rear doors wide open. Inside, two tiers of stretchers held six corpses, each one fully covered by a blanket. Muller thought about Freund's impending crew casualty report and wondered who would be listed.

He walked into the office and Gefreiter Fischer, their office administrator and general dogsbody jumped up from his chair and stood to attention.

Without saying a word, Muller walked past him, sat down at his own desk and reached into the bottom drawer. He took out a bottle of schnapps, poured a large glass for himself and knocked it back in one gulp.

Since his staffel was declared operational two weeks ago, it had flown continuously, often two sorties a day. He had lost four aircraft to enemy action, at least thirty men and now a fifth plane was out of service.

With only seven serviceable aircraft, he wondered how he was going to meet his next mission requirement.

Muller was tired.

It was barely lunchtime and he still had to deal with a novice pilot who couldn't fly properly.

Chapter 12

Maude Delafort had just taken the lunchtime crockery down into her basement kitchen and was standing ready at the sink, when she heard the roar of Raymond's motorbike outside. She watched him through the scullery window as he pulled up on the gravel drive, dismounted and walked off towards the front of the house.

Raymond had missed Sunday lunch yet again and it was becoming a habit.

She didn't expect much from him, she never had, but it was not unreasonable that, in her opinion, they should meet at least once a week to discuss family matters.

It was already a highly frustrating day.

After the debacle at church, Mrs Tedbury had departed straight after serving lunch and now here Maude was, like a common housemaid, about to wash the dishes herself. Most people would have gone upstairs immediately to seek the person they had been awaiting, but Maude was not most people.

She listened to Raymond walking about impatiently in the grand hall above and considering that he had been late for her, she saw no reason to hurry. She ran the taps, added washing soda and set about scrubbing the pots and pans.

Maude smiled as she served a *soupçon* of revenge for her infuriating day.

Raymond could wait.

Contrary to appearances, Maude was not a cold-hearted person. Although she mostly presented a stern exterior and chastised everyone about this and that, the truth was that she was just lonely. Now that Evangeline and Raymond had grown up and pursued their own lives, for the good and the bad, the last few years had left her alone in this big house full of memories. She certainly had time enough to contemplate just how very different her life could have been.

Her greatest failing had been to love the family and what it stood for, far too much for her own good. Maude had enjoyed an idyllic childhood raised in luxury and status, but the gentle pastimes offered to an Edwardian lady held no interest for her. As a young woman, she held no enthusiasm for romance or marriage, preferring a more energetic role alongside her father as he conducted his business. By the time Mother and then, Papa, passed, she had already settled upon life as a spinster. While her brother showed little regard for the wellbeing of family finances, Maude had been well-schooled to fill the gap. James was entirely free to pursue his London life and she did her best to oversee the farms and other Delafort affairs in his absence. In this respect, she would have done quite a good job, had it not been for James constantly draining their profits. In consolation, she had enjoyed a level of independence that was entirely uncommon for most women of that era, but at the cost of solitude while the world passed her by.

So it was especially ironic that James' disappearance in battle precipitated the most dramatic and singularly happiest period in Maude's life. When Daphne brought her children to Craywood House in the summer of 1917, the house was transformed into a family home again. She proved to be a warm, fun-filled person with a great resolve that had underpinned her husband's endeavours, to a much further extent than anyone could have supposed. She didn't sit about waiting for her husband's return like the shallow, simpering creature that Maude had expected.

Instead, this vivacious, beautiful, twenty nine year old woman put her time to good use; caring for her young children, helping Maude with estate matters and even volunteering for nursing service at the local hospital. This last action had particularly impressed Maude. She came to imagine her sister-in-law as a latter day Florence Nightingale, walking by lamplight amongst the wounded men under her care. In many subtle ways, it turned out that Daphne and Maude were like-minded souls after all and their friendship grew spontaneously.

They were both practical and energetic people and although ten years apart in age and born of two different eras, they shared many views about how the world might be made a better place. The house rang to laughter and happiness, as the two women and two little children built a new kind of family together. Despite the troubles of war, Craywood House became a good place to be again, however, this was not to say that Daphne was without sadness. As the months passed by after James' disappearance, the hope of his return became progressively more forlorn. When each day was done, Maude would often hear Daphne sobbing in her bedroom late into the night and sometimes, would go to comfort her. Maude gave her solace and hope, underscored by a strong faith in God to return James to them one day.

The Ladies of Cray Wood, as they came to be known, became a force to be reckoned with and in return, Daphne taught Maude how to enjoy the more frivolous side of life too. She had brought enough of her London socialite nature to lighten Maude's dark old-fashioned world and led her towards a liberation of spirit that on occasion, quite literally, swept her off her feet.

Every night, the house resounded to the sound of the gramophone; introducing Maude to the wild abandon of American ragtime music and most shockingly, the delights of alcohol. They laughed, they danced and they drank the nights away as the summer of 1918 became truly the happiest time of Maude's life.

Yet the Great War would strike one last terrible blow to humanity, as if the millions of lives lost in the trenches weren't a large enough price already.

American soldiers inadvertently brought a deadly new influenza virus to Europe and in May 1918, it broke free from a crowded military hospital in France. The illness spread like wildfire amongst troops of all nations mired in the squalid conditions at the front line. The disease wrought such havoc in the Imperial German Army in particular, that it directly contributed to its military collapse later that year. To protect morale at home, the news was suppressed at first by British wartime censors, but in countries outside the conflict, the pandemic was freely reported. By the end of that year, the grave condition of King Alfonso of Spain gave rise to the incorrect naming of *Spanish Flu*. It spread out from Western Europe to reach every place on earth, killing almost 50 million people over the following two years.

On a late October afternoon in 1918, two year and a half year old Raymond developed a high fever and within hours, he lay floppily in his cot, as if close to death. The family and staff of Craywood House feared for the worst, but prayed for the best. Daphne tended to her son in isolation, believing that only she should risk contact with this highly contagious disease. Maude wanted to help too, but Daphne insisted that she kept her distance whilst mother tended to son alone.

However with terrible irony, Spanish Flu did its worst amongst adults, whilst children and older people would often recover quickly. The cause of this perverse outcome was the way the virus encouraged a profound overreaction of the body's immune system, in effect turning it back against itself. Often, the fitter you were; the worse the reaction and subsequent decline. Rapid onset of pneumonia would suffocate most victims and any that survived this, would fall prey to secondary bacterial infection and gruesome haemorrhaging of the lungs. In an era before penicillin, this led to a 20% mortality rate, appallingly fifty times greater than normal influenza. The pandemic caused suffering and loss of life on a scale not seen since the great plagues of medieval times. After a week in Daphne's care, young Raymond was fully recovered and playing in the garden once more. The crisis seemed over and Daphne returned to her work at the hospital.

Whether she caught the virus from her son or one of her patients, no one would ever know. Four days later, she became convulsed with fever and took to her bed.

Her face turned scarlet as she gasped for air, the bed sheets were stained with specks of blood that flew from her mouth with each agonising breath. Maude stayed at her beloved Daphne's bedside through the short days and the long hours of night, she beseeched God to save her, but to no avail. On the third morning, Daphne was released from her torment and passed away from this world, held in the arms of her devoted Maude.

As the sad, weak autumn sunlight crept warily past the bedroom curtains, Maude's world collapsed around her.

She had lost her greatest friend… and her lover too.

What started as companionship had blossomed into an overwhelming, intoxicating love affair during that brief summer of 1918. Loneliness and grief had given vent to desires that neither woman would have ever dared acknowledge until Cray Wood gifted them the opportunity. They had kissed, caressed and made love, little knowing how fate would damn them both so quickly. Maude would be forever haunted by the retribution she believed God had dealt for the mortal sins that they had committed.

When Daphne's coffin was lowered into the grave at All Saints three days later, the grief stricken, funereally-dressed Maude Delafort walked all the way home, alone, in her new role as the de facto Widow Of Craywood House. Maude owed everything to her beautiful Daphne, for giving her a brief intoxicating love of life that she would never, nor want to, emulate again without her. So she set herself to self-inflicted penance punctuated by anger, loss and remorse.

Mired in grief, she retreated from the world at first, but eventually she found a new purpose to her life. Maude resolved that her lover's children, her brother's heirs, this next generation of the Delaforts, would find true happiness and good fortune again.

Maude had just finished putting the washed dinner crockery into the wooden drying rack, when she heard the telephone ring upstairs. She trotted up the stone stairs from the kitchen and out through the screened door, bringing her into the grand entrance hall.

Raymond had beaten her to it and lifted the receiver.

'Good afternoon, Craywood House,' he answered with a butler's tone.

Evidently, it was his sister on the other end of the phone and she gabbled back at him, in her usual frenzy of excited chatter.

Maude stood by, impatient to take the call and contemplated, with mixed emotions, just how much Raymond looked like his father these days. In many ways it reminded her of happier times, but equally it brought home how much James in absentia, alive or dead, had shaped her life so profoundly.

'I don't know who you mean, but if you are looking to talk to our Aunt, she is here… as ever.' Raymond said sarcastically, always repudiating the warmth his sister expressed for Maude. He passed the handset over, whilst announcing that he was famished and would go down to the kitchen to look for his dinner.

'Hello Moomie, how are you?' Evangeline shouted down the line.

Her pet name for Maude was an affection that Raymond had denied all of his life.

'I'm all the better for hearing from you, my darling Evie,' Maude replied. 'Heavens, this line is terrible, I can hardly hear you. Now tell me all your news from London my dear.'

They set to their weekly conversation about her exciting young life, working at the Admiralty.

Raymond walked downstairs in search of the remains of the luncheon that he had deliberately missed. This was a necessary strategy to avoid the purgatory of cross-examination that dining together generally invoked. Now that he mostly lived his life at Bridger's Farm, he was nicely away from Maude's prying eyes, but the grandeur of Craywood House did still offer some advantages. He planned to use its splendour in the days ahead, hence his desire to get into Maude's good books this afternoon.

If it wasn't for this, not even wild horses would have dragged him anywhere near her by choice.

Conversely, the family meal at the Vigar house couldn't have been more convivial.

The mutton had been a splendid treat, with lots of potatoes, vegetables and of course, Mother's special gravy, it made a fine feast for everyone crowded around the dining table. The finale should have been the mock apricot flan. However, the grated carrot, almond essence and plum jam concoction had been more of a triumph of ration-motivated optimism, than reality.

Ken had proven to be quite the chatterbox once he got going. He had them all in stitches of laughter with his army stories and impersonations of the characters involved. Patricia sat in-between the older and younger generations, enjoying the sight of her family all gathered together. Ken was the obvious novelty of the day and it was nice to see Betty so animated for once, but Ginny as ever, was not one to lose the limelight for long. She drove the conversation onto her favourite films, her likes and dislikes of different movie stars.

On Patricia's right-hand side, Ernest and Edward discussed their plans for a new warden rota. She revelled in the sight of her husband and his best friend engaged in conversation, with all the excitement and sense of purpose that usually belonged to much younger men.

However, sitting opposite, Albert was quiet.

She observed her brother's faltering attempts to join in with conversation and sensed the cause of his sudden sadness.

'She would have loved a day like today, wouldn't she Bert?' Patricia ventured, instinctively.

'Lillian loved a good family dinner… that she did,' he replied nodding his head, his lips suddenly thin with sadness.

'I think of her every day you know,' Patricia whispered. 'She'll always be here… in our hearts… that's what matters.'

She reflected on the genuine love she had held for her sister-in-law.

'I know, I know, you've all been very good to me since she passed,' Albert replied hoarsely. 'At least she didn't see this awful war… that much is a mercy… I suppose.'

Patricia decided to change the subject away from Albert's wife who had died of cancer of the womb two years previously. Picking up on her husband's conversation about his ARP shift; she butted-in to poke a little fun at Ernest, always an easy target.

'Well, that suits your lurking about… late at night… doesn't it Ernie?'

'What do you mean?' he croaked defensively.

'Oh come on, there's nothing better you like to do, than creeping around trying to catch out people with their blackouts,' she said, laughing. 'I've seen you loitering around here with your little torch and warning notes at the ready.'

More than usual, Ernest was taking it all far too seriously and went red in the face.

'I'm just doing my duty Patricia,' he declared defensively. 'You know full well that a Nazi bomber can see a light bulb from 20,000 feet, if someone doesn't have their blackout up properly.'

'You had better write me a few of your little *chitties* in advance and be done with it,' she replied, to a chorus of laughter.

'That would be highly improper for the good lady wife of the Chief Warden, I'll have you know,' Edward interrupted, aping the accent of a posh BBC newsreader.

They all laughed again.

Except Ernest of course...he didn't see the joke at all.

In fact, he looked pretty put out.

'I've got a chitty for you Mr Vigar, Mr Culpepper and you... Mr Harrop,' Patricia instructed. 'Report for duty at the kitchen sink, there's plenty for you to do in there.'

The three men arose sharply.

Edward gave his wife a Nazi salute.

They disappeared next door, to begin clattering and banging with the pots and pans in the sink.

Ken made to get up too, but Patricia stopped him.

'Not you Ken, you're our guest,' she said in a motherly fashion.

'Honestly, I don't mind, please...' Ken responded.

'No. I have spoken... and you don't want to upset a lady do you?' Patricia continued. 'Now sit down, I want to ask you something.'

This got the girls' attention too and they stopped arguing about Robert Donat and Errol Flynn and looked at their mother.

'Well, I've been talking to Ted and as we understand it, you are planning on going back to the camp this afternoon?'

'Well, yes I am,' Ken confirmed.

'But your leave doesn't end until Wednesday lunchtime, does it?' Patricia asked. 'Well... we don't think you should spend the rest of your leave in the barracks, especially when there's a perfectly nice home for you *here*,' she concluded with a big, kindly smile.

Ken was flabbergasted.

It was true that he had no wish to return to Bermondsey and didn't have anywhere else to go, except back to the army camp in Foots Cray.

Nonetheless, Patricia's offer was too generous.

The girls looked on expectantly, as they certainly hadn't seen this coming either.

'I ...um... really shouldn't impose on you like this,' Ken replied with embarrassment. 'You have been so generous...I feel that I shouldn't...'

'Don't be silly,' she declared. 'We would love to have you stay with us, it's what you deserve and... it's already been decided.'

Patricia would suffer no argument on the matter. 'Your kitbag is in the front room and the camp bed is set up there, already made up for you.'

She paused and smiled again. 'Mind you, it won't be totally free board and lodging. Ted and Bert have plenty of work that needs doing. So a helping hand won't go unwanted.'

Before Ken could make any reply, Edward appeared behind him from the kitchen and draped a tea towel neatly over the young man's face.

'Good... that's all decided then. No argument,' Edward continued. 'And your first and most important duty.... is the drying up.'

From under the tea towel, Ken conceded defeat.

'Righty-Ho. I accept your kind invitation Mrs Vigar, but can I take this off first?'

Ginny leant across the table and lifted the veil.

'See... you can't get rid of us that easily General Kendrick,' she said and pinched his nose hard.

Everyone burst out laughing.

So the soldier was here to stay.

Ken caught Betty looking at him and she blushed.

Without saying a word, she stacked up all the dinner plates, laid the cutlery neatly upon them and handed it all to Ken.

She nodded towards the kitchen.

He took her offering, rose from his chair and walked into the kitchen to commence his first family duty. Albert bustled past him and headed for the bathroom, situated opposite Betty's downstairs bedroom. He looked slightly flustered and returned a few minutes later with his hat, coat, ARP helmet and satchel in hand.

'I'm going to head down to the warden office, I'm on duty soon and it's gone two o'clock already,' he said.

'What, no rounders Ernie?' Edward called out from the kitchen.

'Oh Dad!' the girls exclaimed in unison.

'Aren't we a bit too old for that now?' Betty protested.

'We are *never* too old for rounders, it's the Vigar way,' Edward replied. 'Are you shirking PE, Ernie?'

'I really must be going, sorry everyone...' Ernest replied, walking to the hallway.

The house door slammed shut behind him.

'Was it something I said?' Patricia ventured.

'Oh God knows Pat. I'll be seeing him later, I'll find out what's what…silly old sod that he is,' Edward responded.

Patricia sighed and shook her head gently.

She felt sorry for Ernest these days, a pale shadow of the happy-go-lucky man of his youth. She considered how much that awful Doris had ruined his life, carrying on with all manner of men, seeking attention all the time, humiliating him until, eventually, she did the decent thing and ran away completely. Selfish people like that give no thought for the impact of their actions on the people around them, Patricia considered.

A sudden loud popping, fizzing noise made her jump.

Ginny had turned on the wireless, at full volume.

The crackle of static electricity filled the air for a few more moments, until Ginny stopped laughing at her own prank and took notice of Patricia's disapproving glare.

She turned off the radio set.

'Come on, let's clear up,' Patricia instructed.

The ladies finished tidying the dinner table.

A feeling of domestic calm settled upon the Vigar home. Ginny went upstairs to her bedroom to check her make-up, leaving Patricia and Betty alone in the dining room.

Mother and daughter smiled at each other with satisfaction, for entirely different reasons.

Chapter 13

The atmosphere inside the giant mess tent at Rosières-en-Santerre airfield was absolutely electric, as two hundred and fifty airmen talked excitedly about that morning's adventures over England. Most were still in their flying fatigues, having been ushered straight here as soon as they disembarked from their aircraft. Some recounted close encounters with British fighters whilst others mourned comrades lost, the thrills and successes of their missions.

There was a palpable sense of relief in the air.

White-jacketed orderlies came in to start clearing the long dining tables, anxious to prepare for the next sitting. They were conscious of the increasing noise of aircraft overhead that heralded the arrival of their next customers. Now with a good meal in their bellies, the flyers were elated, relieved, but tired and many were already thinking of heading to their camp beds.

Despite the noise of conversation, the sudden shout of the Kampfgruppe Commander's adjutant bellowed across the din, as he called the men to attention. As one, everyone stood to attention as Majorgeneral Karl Angerstein walked in to join them.

At one end of the tent, several wooden crates had been fashioned into a simple stage and Angerstein stepped upon them, in order to address the men. The 3rd Gruppe's commander, Oberst Willibald Fanelsa, had been shot down just a few days before and Angerstein was here to bolster morale, until a replacement was appointed. After a short speech applauding their efforts and sacrifice of comrades fallen in battle, he gave the order to stand down. As the flyers began to leave, Angerstein worked his way through the crowd. He held conversations with all ranks, strengthening the bond of comradeship between senior commander and his men.

Horst Muller stood with the pilots of his staffel at the other end of the tent and they were just about to leave, when Angerstein walked towards them. They saluted and in return, he gave them particular praise for their raid on Biggin Hill that morning. Reports confirmed they had bombed precisely and achieved their objective, much to the satisfaction of High Command.

He asked Muller to step outside with him, so they could talk privately.

'You did well today, I hear that your staffel performed excellently.' Angerstein announced. 'It has been noticed, once again Major.'

'Thank you Herr Generalmajor, thank you indeed.' Muller replied.

'You've had quite a task Muller, your staffel was in a poor state when you arrived.' Angestein continued. 'You are our highest achiever. It seems your reputation is well deserved.'

'We all strive towards Final Victory sir.' Muller responded.

'I've been looking at the reports of your last three missions and you achieve good bomb patterns on target. Is there any particular reason for this accuracy?' Angerstein asked. 'Have you made any changes to your aircraft or tactics that we should know about?'

Field modifications to aircraft were a key component in the continued development of military technology on all sides of the conflict.

As with the RAF, the Luftwaffe had an active system of collating the results of such experimentation and where appropriate, propagating the most successful ideas between units.

'My navigator-bomb aimer, Hartmann, has an uncommonly good eye for hitting target.' Muller revealed. 'When I first arrived here I used a little trick I learnt from my commander in Spain. I held a shooting competition for the men and that soon determined who the best shots were.'

He paused to add emphasis.

'Hartmann stood out easily, he's got a quick mind and phenomenal eye sight, I swear he can judge distances better than any bombsight. With him in my aircraft and good discipline in the rest of my staffel, we can fulfil our objectives sir.'

'This is interesting. We must talk to your man with the magic eyes.' Angerstein concluded. 'Such people often have talents that can be shared amongst many.'

He moved onto the real point of the conversation.

'I want you to go over again later this afternoon. We have a particular mission that needs a good leader... to strike a difficult target. Can you be ready by five o'clock?'

'Of course, Herr Generalmajor.' Muller responded, knowing he had no choice in the matter.

So there it was.

There would be little rest for Muller and his men this afternoon. Their second operation of the day was already pinned on the map tables of High Command.

Muller presumed their discussion had reached its conclusion, but then Angerstein hesitated, as if making a decision.

'Let us walk some more, on this wonderful afternoon,' he declared and led them further away, out of earshot from the men around the mess tent.

After a few minutes awkward silence, he turned to face Muller directly.

'You flew in Poland, Major?'

'Indeed I did, now that was quite a show.' Muller responded.

He sensed that his superior officer was seeking a more informal dialogue.

'So how do the English compare to those wretched Poles?' Angerstein asked. 'Tell me frankly... not the horse crap I hear spouted out in strategy conferences.'

Muller realised that the Generalmajor wanted to hear the truth, a bird's eye view from over Britain.

'The English are well organised, that is certain,' replied Muller, then continued cautiously. 'They only send small formations of fighters against us, just enough to pick off our bombers, just a little, on every sortie.'

'Ah... they want to avoid a major confrontation?' Angerstein asked. 'Where are our fighters when this happens?'

'They are there, mostly. However, the English wait for them to withdraw... when they are running low on fuel, I would guess, Herr Generalmajor.'

Angerstein contemplated this supposition for a moment, before he asked another prepared question.

'Have you seen the English radio towers?'

'You cannot miss them sir, they are spaced out every thirty kilometres or so, right along the coastline.' Muller continued, feeling bolder. 'If they are listening stations... perhaps they have greater bearing on the matter?'

'They are crude devices, not important.' Angerstein countered. 'Besides their control rooms are in deep bunkers, quite impossible to assault.'

He paused for a few seconds, before moving to a new topic.

'But when you do reach their airfields, why are they hard to neutralise?'

Muller could feel the approach of criticism, but he was not a man to shy away from giving an honest opinion.

'Unlike the Poles and French, the English do not lay out their aircraft in neat rows for us to destroy. They are well-spaced out, protected within special earthworks or… already in the air.'

'As if they know we are coming?' Angerstein asked.

'That would be one interpretation.' Muller replied, now wondering if espionage or betrayal was at the root of the matter.

'And the English fighter pilots, how do they perform?'

'With great discipline, they choose their moment to dart in and out of our formations. They never attack in large groups and do not stay for long.'

The Generalmajor laughed.

'Are they afraid of our jagdgeschwader?'

'They do not lack courage sir… perhaps they are conserving their strength?'

'How so?' Angerstein asked, with genuine interest.

'Maybe the English find replacing pilots as hard as we do sir?' Muller replied.

Angerstein nodded.

'You're sounding like our fighter flyers now Muller,' he responded. 'They say they should be free to hunt the skies… not escorting our bombers. It slows them down, puts them at a disadvantage, they claim.'

Muller decided to keep his opinion to himself.

They walked on further.

By now they were several hundred metres from the mess tent. Standing side-by-side, they watched mechanics at work on aircraft over by the eastern perimeter of the airfield.

Looking at the wide, clear bright sky above them, Muller felt he had the perfect opportunity to highlight a far more pressing issue.

'There is another problem Herr Generalmajor… one that is *impossible* to resolve,' he declared boldly.

Angerstein turned to face him again, surprised by the sudden negativity in this expert Staffelkapitän's manner.

'We rarely have what you see here.' Muller revealed. 'Over Southern England, there is generally thick cloud cover and it's low… mostly forcing us down to 2000 metres… '

'Before you can see the target,' Angerstein interjected, 'and this increases our losses from ground-fire?'

'Yes, on many occasions all is well as we commence the bomb run, but then the target is obscured on the final few kilometres,' Muller replied.

'So it's like trying to throw stones into a barrel…?'

'Yes sir, very much so and…'

Angerstein raised his eyebrows, encouraging Muller to be more forthright.

'There are too many barrels and not enough rats in them," said Muller. 'We rarely see aircraft on the ground… we are mostly bombarding grass and buildings.'

'I see…. the English have an enormous number of airfields, are you saying their aircraft are widely dispersed?'

'Yes, Sir. It's not like Poland… there is nowhere for us to land the heavy, decisive blow,' Muller concluded.

This was a thorny, inconvenient truth.

'Perhaps the jagdflieger are correct… they must hunt the English in the air?' Angerstein pondered. He corrected himself, in line with official diktat. 'But the Reichsmarschall has instructed they will fly close to our bombers,' he stated firmly. 'That is the policy.'

Formality had sharply returned.

'Remember Muller… *we are the fist of the Luftwaffe*. Without bombers there is no attack, the jagdflieger will do as they are told!'

'Until… Final Victory, Herr Generalmajor.' Muller declared.

'Yes. Until Final Victory!' Angerstein responded, dutifully reaffirming their well-practiced maxim.

As they walked back to the operations office, conversation focussed on the new raid. Within ten minutes, the briefing was complete and Angerstein left for his next meeting.

The schedule was tight.

Muller's raiding force had to meet other units assembling over the Channel by 5.30pm, to meet their fighter cover before entering British airspace. Muller knew he worked best under pressure, but this was going to really test him, right under the gaze of Angerstein. Muller had been promoted for the raid, leading not only his own seven aircraft, but also the remaining Heinkels of the 11th and 12th staffeln that he had watched earlier. He hoped this operation was a test of his suitability for the position of Gruppe Commander, as Fanelsa's replacement. So this could be Muller's next chance for promotion. Maybe not for the long term, but at least until a more senior officer was selected.

On the other side of the operations office, Freund and Fischer had already set to work preparing the logistical requirements of the raid. They were busily organising maps, orders for fuel, munitions, ground crew, armourers and airmen. Satisfied that all was properly underway, Muller decided to make the best use of the three hours left to him before take-off.

He walked out to his staff car and told the driver, Gefreiter Amacher, to take him back to his billet in Meharicourt, a small village to the west of the airfield. He wanted to grab an hour's sleep and then return in time for the briefing he had set for his men.

As the car sped around the perimeter road on its short journey, Muller thought over the plan of attack. He reconsidered the moment when Angerstein produced a set of remarkable reconnaissance photos, taken over north-west Kent a few months earlier.

The crux of the matter was that they had to find the start of an autobahn at a peculiar-sounding little town called *Sidcup*, on the south eastern outskirts of London.

Chapter 14

Ernest Harrop bustled down Hazelmead Road, glad to have escaped the stifling atmosphere of the Vigars' home.

At one stage during lunch, he had been drawn so strongly, repeatedly, to the curve of Ginny's fulsome breasts, that for a moment, he was convinced that their soldier guest had noticed his lurid gaze. By the time Patricia commented about his nocturnal patrols, Ernie's paranoia had become almost unbearable. Although he knew that she couldn't have been referring to his sordid activities, it was more than his nerves could stand any longer. As he strode towards the warden office, he told himself to calm down and the greater the distance he put between him and the Vigars... the better he felt.

Ernest had considered himself a perfectly normal person until the years of solitude, to which Doris had sentenced him, finally started to take their toll. Middle age only seemed to highlight his own paucity of sexual fulfilment, ever more sharply in comparison to the freedoms enjoyed by the younger generation around him.

In a manner, all this changed two years ago when he chanced upon a courting couple, one night in an alleyway. As he spied upon their fumbling fornication, he was gripped by an intense sexual excitement that inspired a whole new, secret and undoubtedly perverted pastime. Since then, he had perfected his knowledge of every local place favoured by young couples and from where he could observe them without discovery. The advent of war and his enrolment with the ARP provided a perfect alibi, to wander around without suspicion and fulfil his voyeuristic desires to his heart's content.

However, all this changed last Friday night.

He had stumbled upon what first appeared to be his wildest fantasy come true, but nearly became his undoing.

It still could yet, for that matter.

Ernest had hardly slept since.

As he walked down the road, his mind was in turmoil as he relived it all over again for the umpteenth time.

That night had started much like any other blackout patrol. Ernest walked down from the high street and began his beat with the shopping parades, opposite the railway station.

He looked quickly behind the Plaza and checked the rear windows of the flats above the shops next door. Unfortunately, the occupants' blackouts were too good, offering not a single glimpse of their private lives for him to savour. So he walked back out across the road junction, called in briefly at the wardens office, then set off down Hazelmead Road.

The streetlamps that heralded modernity when these estates were first built had been extinguished since the onset of war, returning the country to a medieval darkness. Once again, the night hours became the realm of accidents, injury and death, as on the very darkest, you could barely see the ground before you.

So most sensible people now chose to retreat indoors after sunset.

It was a quiet enough summer's night, the quarter moon shone through indifferent clouds to provide scant illumination of the deserted streets. It had rained, briefly, about an hour before and now the air carried the humid, cloying smell of damp summer scents. Apart from the occasional hum-drop-roar of a vehicle changing gear as it drove along somewhere nearby, there was little to note.

At 20 Hazelmead Road, the Johnsons had let a chink of light show through their front curtains, but a quick rap on the window and a shouted warning had the desired effect. Within a few seconds, a muffled apology came from inside and the blackout was restored.

Ernest took out his torch, pencilled a note in his Watch Book and with the indiscretion duly recorded at 11.54pm, he resumed his patrol. He listened to the drumming warble of an aircraft's engines high above in the black sky. If it was a German raider, he wondered just how it could see anything on a dark night like this. Accepting his lack of knowledge in such military matters, Ernest's thoughts returned to his immediate duties and he carried on his way.

As usual, he took a right at Augustine Avenue and walked through the gates into Chaucer Park. This was a grassed recreational area, formed in-between the Sidcup railway line and the back gardens of houses along the southern side of Hazelmead Road. About six hundred yards long and a hundred wide at this end, it tapered to a point in a triangular fashion back in the direction of the shops and cinema. Ernest always gave this little park a quick walk through, as it allowed him to observe the back windows of these houses. This increased his potential to levy fines on repeated blackout offenders and occasionally, glimpse some titillating sights too.

He had started to walk down along the fence line when, just for a moment, he thought he saw a tiny flicker of light, like you would see from someone lighting a cigarette.

There was a flash of bright light from the back of one of the houses.

To his dismay the light stayed on, casting a bright rectangle of illumination, fifty yards long down a garden, all the more vivid for the inky darkness of its surroundings. Chinks in curtains were one thing, but an entire window full of blazing electric light, beckoning every Nazi bomber was tantamount to treason in Ernest's mind.

He ran as fast as he could towards it.

As he huffed and puffed towards his goal, it was perhaps inevitable that he would misplace his footing.

Just a few yards short, he tripped and fell head first in the wet grass. Cursing his clumsiness, he regained his feet and made the mistake of staring directly into the blazing light. Then it was extinguished and all around was plunged into even inkier blackness.

With his night vision temporarily stolen, he squinted through his spectacles and saw that one of the gates in the fence line was wide open. This seemed especially queer in the circumstances, so he cautiously worked his way forward and slipped into the garden.

Looking at the back of the house, he could see just enough to suggest an upper bedroom window had been the source of the offence. Unlike the others, the curtains were half-drawn apart to leave a dark gap perhaps four feet wide in the centre, whilst the moon dimly lit the material hanging on either side.

Ernest drew stock for a few seconds, deliberating as to what to do, when a figure appeared at the window. To his utter amazement, it was a young woman dressed only in her underwear, with long dark hair cascading over her shoulders.

She started to move gently, emphasising the curves of her almost naked body. Ernest was so utterly transfixed by this vision of erotic beauty; that he walked further into the garden.

With eyes screwed up, he tried to focus on the delicious spectacle.

She had turned her back to him now and started to slowly caress her scantily-clad buttocks with her right hand, whilst the angle of her left arm suggested that she was performing the same motion upon her breasts. The woman swayed from side to side, as if to the beat of a sensual rhythm, accentuating the softness of her beautiful young physique. Her skin shone blue-white in the moonlight.

Ernest walked even closer, until his instinct for clandestine observation asserted itself and he slipped behind a large ornamental bush to hide. He was utterly entranced by the striptease taking place before him, better than anything he had ever seen before. Even when he had watched the couples in the woods, he had rarely seen much more than a flash of breast or thigh as a man arched his back between a woman's open legs.

However, tonight's erotic exhibition was the best ever. Better even than the mucky postcards he bought from the landlord of The Black Horse, of French whores exposing themselves with perverted method.

Better than a photograph, this was moving… *this was real.*

Ernest felt his manhood grow hard and insistent. He opened his flies and started pulling himself quickly towards pleasure.

Momentarily, the woman disappeared behind the curtain as if to check something, then she returned, this time staring beyond Ernest, out into the garden. Her silken slip had fallen so low on her right breast, that its nipple was almost revealed. Ernest's excitement gathered pace and as the drifting clouds high above parted, he eagerly waited for the moonlight to fully reveal her beauty. Suddenly, the full intensity of the ethereal light shone down upon her and she smiled, as if revelling in the experience.

Ernest was just at the point of sexual release, when he registered that her hair was not dark at all.

It was a trick of the cold light and just for a moment, his eyes picked out a reddish hue. As his lust expelled upon the ground in front of him, he realised who was providing his sexual entertainment.

Looking down and around him, the clarity of his night vision had returned and now this garden was all too familiar. He recognised the wooden deck chairs stacked neatly against the kitchen wall, the small wrought iron table and chairs on the crazy paving in front of the French Doors.

This was Edward Vigar's house.

Ernest realised he was looking at his best friend's eldest daughter.

With a swish of the curtains, Ginny was gone.

Sheer panic brought Ernest to his senses. He didn't understand what was happening here, or why she was behaving like this.

He bolted for the back gate.

Within just a few more strides he would have escaped, when a tall figure loomed out of the darkness.

Before Ernest knew what was happening, he had been pushed to the ground. Then his right arm was twisted so painfully behind his back that he thought it would snap.

'You fucking, dirty old bastard. You dirty, dirty cunt.' A voice growled in his ear.

Ernest squirmed in agony, pinned to the ground by terrific force. A gloved hand clamped firmly over his mouth, stifling his attempts to scream.

'I'm going to take my knee off your back and we are going to get up, slowly. Don't make a fucking sound,' the assailant commanded. 'If you try anything, I'll break your miserable fucking arm. Do you understand?'

The assailant twisted Ernest's arm even further upwards, to give agonising emphasis to the threat.

'Understand?'

'Yes, yes, oh please don't hurt me... please don't,' Ernest wailed through the gloved hand in terror.

'Right, up we get… slowly… slowly….' the attacker growled. 'That's it, you old fucker. Now walk slowly towards the gate.'

Ernest was in no position to argue.

The force exerted on his twisted arm ensured that.

They shuffled up the garden, past a wooden shed on the right and the tall stack of runner bean canes on the left. Then he was cast onto the ground again and lay face down, paralysed with fear, expecting a fearsome assault at any second.

Nothing happened.

Ernest lay there whimpering and with his right arm now freed, he slowly brought it back round to relieve the pain a little. With his left hand, he pushed down on the ground to turn himself over onto his back.

The figure stood above him, silhouetted against the starry sky.

He was all powerful, a black, menacing devil of the night that held Ernest's fate in the balance.

'So this is what you do is it Harrop? You creep around spying on young women to fulfil your filthy, dirty, perverted ways?' the man accused.

What could Ernest say in his defence?

Absolutely nothing.

'I'm so sorry, I didn't mean to. It's a mistake, I'm so sorry,' he whimpered.

'Don't give me that claptrap, you nonce! I saw what you were doing in there. What would her father have to say?'

The man paused and then continued with sarcastic relish. 'Shall we go and see him? Let's wake the whole house up, we can show them what you did… I bet it's spread all over the place like custard!'

'Please, please don't hurt me, let me go please,' Ernest pleaded, his voice shrill with fear.

A few seconds passed, inexorably slowly.

Suddenly, the stranger lunged towards him.

Instinctively, Ernest put his good, left hand in front of his face in feeble defence to the blow he expected.

Instead, he felt a sharp tug at his clothing.

'I'll be having this, just as a little keepsake of this evening. *Insurance* shall we say?' the attacker announced.

Ernest didn't understand what the dark figure was referring to. Then he felt the full force of the man's foot stamp hard into his groin. He howled in agony and curled up into a ball, his knees almost under his chin, his face contorted with pain.

His attacker retreated into the darkness and Ernest lay trembling in terror.

He heard him call out one more time.

'Remember Harrop, I've got insurance... *I'll call on you again one day.*'

After a short while, Ernest gained enough courage to get to his feet.

With his head clearing, he knew he had to get away in case someone came to investigate the commotion. He quickly hobbled into the park, then back towards the relative safety of Augustine Avenue.

Once in the street, he tried to stand properly upright. His right arm was terribly sore, but this was nothing compared to the intense pain emanating from his groin. As shock set in, he felt light headed, nauseous and knew he was about to be sick. He slid down to the ground and crawled behind some bushes to vomit, then waited in the darkness until he was absolutely sure he was safe.

After about ten minutes, he dared to feel in his coat pocket for his packet of Sweet Afton. With no care for the blackout anymore, his trembling fingers found his matches, lit and smoked a crushed cigarette.

Then another, lit from the first.

With his nerves sufficiently calmed, his arm now felt a little less painful and he decided he needed to get home as soon as possible. He was drenched with cold sweat. It dripped down from his armpits inside his shirt, ran off his bruised face, his feet were cold-soaked in his shoes.

This had been the most terrifying experience of his life since his army days. Whilst he had always feared discovery during his sordid adventures, he was now felt entirely cured of the frisson of excitement this had previously added.

The pulsating, puffing sound of a steam engine met his ears.

Looking towards the station, he could see a goods train approaching, outward-bound from London. Showers of sparks spat through the dense black smoke pumping out of its funnel. As the locomotive drew parallel to him, he could see the driver illuminated by the devilish glow from the open firebox. Then they were gone, as the long procession of tarpaulined trucks squealed and trundled by. It was unusual to see a train at this hour and Ernest realised he had no idea what time it was.

He reached for his pocket watch on his waistcoat and found it was no longer there, the chain was missing too. His father's expensive, solid silver timepiece, his pride and joy for which he was famed hereabouts… was gone.

With dismay, he realised what his assailant had taken from him.

Ernest stood outside the school opposite St Mildred's and forced the dreadful memory of Friday night from his head.

He tried to forget his near indiscretion at dinner with the Vigars.

Ernest told himself, as he had done a hundred times over the last two days, to get a grip on his nerves. He resolved to keep away from Edward's family for the time being, hoping that everything would blow over so that normality would soon return.

Even so, he didn't really believe his own advice.

Ginny had walked into the shop yesterday lunchtime to meet her sister and Ernest had nearly yelped in fear. She did no more than exchange pleasantries with him and the two girls quickly left. From this he was greatly reassured that she hadn't seen him in the darkness and was none the wiser about Friday night's events.

At first he was wracked with guilt at what had happened outside her bedroom window. By last night, his rationality had returned enough to reason that Ginny's behaviour was hardly acceptable, whether he had been invited to observe it or not. Of far greater concern was the identity of his attacker and why he had been there, in anticipation of Ginny's lurid entertainment.

So it must be someone linked to her.

Keeping away from Ginny would presumably distance Ernest from that awful man too, whoever he was. He recalled the aggression of the attacker's crude speech. Set against the starry sky, he had appeared tall and was clearly a strong and violent person. The fact that he knew Ernest by name was no great surprise, given his place in the community, but the fact that he had stolen his watch worried him greatly.

What could he mean by *insurance*?

What did this imply?

It seemed an inescapable conclusion that this man had not finished with him and all Ernest could think of doing was hiding away. It wasn't much of a strategy, but it was his only option in defence against an unknown adversary.

Yes, keeping his head down was the best thing he could do.

With his thoughts a little cleared by the walk down Hazelmead Road, Ernest felt calmer now. He went round the back of the school, passed the sandbag blast wall and entered the small office that was now Lamorbey's ARP warden station.

Sixteen year old Roger Deacon was sitting at the desk.

The tall, willowy youth stood up to welcome his superior to duty.

'Hello Mr Harrop, you're a bit early aren't you? I didn't expect you until 3 o'clock?' he said cheerily.

'Er… well… I thought I'd come down and keep you company for a bit Roger,' Ernest replied. 'Anything much happened this afternoon?'

'No, it's been as quiet as the grave, not a single call or nothing… not for hours Mr Harrop. Jerry must be licking his wounds I reckon,' he revealed.

'Oh go on home Roger. I expect you want a bit of dinner don't you? Remember we've got a parade here at 6 o'clock.' Ernest suggested amiably. 'You buzz off…. I'll cover for you.'

'I don't mind if I do, Mr Harrop, cheers for that!' Roger replied and was out of the door like a shot.

Ernest bolted the door, sat back down at the desk and held his head in his hands. He'd had quite enough of this weekend and was looking forward to opening the shop tomorrow morning.

He just wanted some peace, quiet and normality.

So he sat back in the chair and looked at the Aircraft Recognition signboard on the opposite wall. On the corner of the poster, some wag had drawn a cartoon Hitler that stared back menacingly.

Ernest felt a bead of sweat run down his right cheek and he nervously wiped it away.

Then he glanced at the door to double check that the bolt was properly drawn across.

He lit a cigarette and just for once… he felt perfectly happy being all alone.

Chapter 15

Just as always, the telephone conversation with Evangeline was the highlight of Maude's week. They chatted away about this and that, day to day life at the Admiralty Office in Greenwich, goings on in Sidcup, gossip about work friends that Maude had never met and the hurly burly of life in London.

Maude took in only half of what Evie said, but she wasn't really too bothered. She was simply glad to hear the sound of her voice. Maude was happy that her surrogate daughter was moving forward in life and making something of herself, but she missed her terribly too. Evangeline took strongly after Daphne both in appearance and character. With raven-black hair and a tall, statuesque physique, she was single-minded, confident and definitely wasn't shy of having fun. Maude was utterly devoted to her and wished she saw more of her at Craywood House, but understood that it was hard for her to get away from her important work in these troubled times.

They had been talking for about twenty minutes when suddenly the connection was cut, as often happened of late. Maude was left standing alone again in the hall. She put down and picked up the handset a couple of times, but the operator remained disappointingly absent. She waited for a few more minutes, in the hope that the phone would ring again. No call came and on final inspection, the line remained stubbornly silent.

She walked into the sitting room, sat down on the sofa and stared into the garden. Maude considered that if the phone line was cut here, there really was nothing to worry about at Evangeline's end of the line.

Maude didn't have much to do that Sunday afternoon. She looked through Friday's copy of The Times newspaper, which Mrs Tedbury had placed on the coffee table next to the fruit bowl. She returned to staring aimlessly out of the window. The room was hot and she dozed a little, her head bobbed as she awoke several times.

After a while she woke properly from her nap. She watched Raymond appear at the far end of the garden and walk towards the house. As he strolled past the rose beds, Maude steeled herself for her next encounter with her nephew. He ascended the steps to the patio, the look on his face suggesting he reciprocated the same emotion.

'Good afternoon Aunt Maude,' he said with a weak smile, as he walked inside.

'Indeed it is Ray-Monde, did you find yourself something to eat downstairs?' Maude replied.

Their conversation had made its usual, awkward start.

'Yes, there was beef left in the cold press, I made myself a sandwich.'

He sat down in the armchair next to her and continued.

'How are you feeling today, how is your stomach?'

'It has been causing me discomfort I will confess,' Maude revealed. 'My dyspepsia seems to be aggravated by our wartime diet, but we all have our own cross to bear Ray-Monde.'

'I do worry about you Aunt.' Raymond replied, with barely concealed hypocrisy.

Maude knew that when Raymond gained his inheritance in five months' time, she would be the only remaining obstacle to the wilder excesses of his ambition. Come what may though, she was confident that she would still be able to discretely pull the strings that controlled Delafort affairs, just as when her brother was alive. She and Godfrey Burridge, the family solicitor, had been in cahoots for many, many years.

Nonetheless, the day that she had dreaded for so long was approaching.

Whilst the war continued there was little that Raymond could actually do to wreck family affairs. No-one was buying or selling property, as people didn't know if what they had today would even exist tomorrow, or even if they would still be alive. All mortgages and lending had been suspended for the duration of the war, because banking was now in the grip of the state, printing vast amounts of money to fund the war effort.

Maude suspected that if he could, Raymond would throw her out onto the street in the blink of an eye. Nonetheless, her right of abode at Craywood House was sacrosanct. As long as she still had breath in her body, she would protect their domain… *and protect the world from Raymond too.*

She decided it was high time to deliver news that she knew would displease him.

'There are three letters from the Agricultural Ministry for you in the study. They arrived on Thursday afternoon.' Maude announced.

'Really? More dull paperwork and yet more forms and nonsense I suppose?' Raymond replied, trying to hide his discomfort.

'They are more than that Ray-Monde… there seem to be discrepancies regarding the livestock at Bridger's.' Maude revealed. 'They're also asking why you haven't taken up any of the orchards and put them to tillage yet. What exactly is going on over there?'

'Nothing for you to worry about, it's all in hand,' he replied condescendingly.

Maude got straight to the point.

'You are going to get yourself in hot water young man, I'm not a fool you know!' She said firmly.

Raymond squirmed under her sudden interrogation.

'It's none of your business Aunt. Everything is going like clockwork at Bridger's and...'

'Well that's not what I hear,' she interrupted. 'Apparently you are hardly ever there, gadding about somewhere no doubt. In fact, from what I'm told, all the work is being done by Mr Cameron and his youngest son.'

'Who have you been talking to? This is utter nonsense. I'm there every day, working away.' Raymond countered.

Maude said nothing, continuing to hold him in her stare.

The tick-tock of the grandfather clock in the hall marked the passage of their awkward silence.

Four chimes rang out.

Maude relented a little and tried a different tack.

Moving to the edge of the sofa, she bent forward and took hold of his hands and turned their palms upward.

'Look... these are *not* farmer's hands Ray-Monde, there are no callouses or cuts. They are the clean, soft hands of a gentleman.'

He pulled them from her grasp and crossed his arms defensively.

Before he could form a response, Maude cut in again. 'I'm trying to help you... if the men from the Ministry arrive to inspect the farm... they will catch you out, no mistake. You have to *do* something.'

'What do you mean what do I *have* to do?' he replied, rapidly retreating.

'One of two things,' said Maude. 'Get that farm working properly and productively or, commit yourself to something more worthy... before they make you.'

'I'm not joining up... if that's what you mean? I have a reserved occupation, they can't make me.'

Maude would not be swayed from her attack.

'They will take the farm from us if it doesn't meet their quotas, you know that. You'll be conscripted just like your father was,' she stated firmly. Then she tried a kinder suggestion, 'your grandfather would know what to do if he was still alive… can't you take a leaf from his book?'

Raymond said nothing.

They sat in silence again, at an impasse.

She waited patiently for his reply. He avoided her gaze by looking glumly at his feet. To him it felt like the same old story, Maude dictating, expecting him to do what he was told. She had a well-honed ability to strip away his defences and leave him with nothing.

He hated her for it.

Yet, there was no denying the logic of her argument. In fact, if she knew what was really going on with the local black market chaps, she would have been disgusted. Ironically though, he'd almost enjoy such a revelation, just to see the look on her face when she comprehended the shame it would bring on the family.

Raymond reached across the table and took an apple from the fruit bowl. He took a huge, heavy penknife from his jacket pocket and proceeded to carefully peel the fruit.

Maude looked at his deliberations and a shiver ran up her spine.

He always carried that knife, with its razor sharp blade, far sharper than you would expect for such a crude implement. It was a heavy military issue tool, grotesquely large, about eight inches long with a foldout blade at one end and an evil-looking hinged spike running down its body. It had belonged to her brother, mislaid before he departed for France in 1916 and was the one of the few things left to mark his final, military career. Raymond's love of sharp knives stemmed from his discovery of this keepsake, but just where he found it was completely inexplicable to Maude. It became his dearest possession, perhaps, she wondered, because it provided a connection to the father that he could not remember. However, she was repulsed by the sight it. To her, it served as a repeated reminder of a truly shocking event in his childhood, one that revealed the true, dark, nature of his character.

Raymond finished peeling the fruit and casting the skin on the table, held the apple in the palm of his left hand. He carefully sliced three neat segments on the uppermost side and held them out to Maude, like a peace offering.

'I shouldn't… it'll be too acid on my stomach after luncheon,' she said.

He gestured again, knowing her weakness for fruit.

This time, Maude accepted and took the slices for herself. The apple was deliciously sweet and she savoured the flavour, disregarding the consequences for her digestion. He took a large bite out of the remainder of the apple and with two more bites, it was gone.

'I have a nice surprise for you Aunt Maude.'

Now this will be a novelty, she thought.

'I've been looking around the garden and it's looking pretty sorry for itself. So I suggest we tidy it up? We might as well enjoy the last few days of summer?' he proposed. Sensing that he was on the winning side this time, he continued. 'I'm going to clear out the summer house and smarten it up… *just for you, Dear Aunt.'*

This was guaranteed to please her, as everyone knew that Grandfather Josiah had built it especially for his daughter when the formal gardens were laid out in the late 1890's. It was a stone-built, Palladian folly, the size of a modern bungalow and sat at the far end of the gardens, set against the backdrop of the ancient Cray Wood. It was the focal point of the whole landscape design, with formal flower beds, lawns and pathways stretching out two hundred yards between it and the house.

It had been known as *Maude's House* ever since the day it was built, the epicentre of her childhood happiness, perfect for dolls tea parties, concerts and plays to delight her parents and friends. When she was nine, Papa had even allowed her to sleep a night there, but that had ended badly with nightmares and tears. Mother was furious and Maude was never allowed to stay the night there again. Nonetheless, nothing better embodied the joy of her early years more than her memories of the seemingly endless summer days spent in Maude's House. However, it had since become symbolic of the Delaforts' decline in fortune, a rather sad, dirty, forgotten place. It was filled with all manner of rubbish that had accumulated over twenty years of decline in the house and garden.

'I've had a good look over it and actually Aunt… it's not that bad. The roof is sound, it just needs clearing out and a spring clean.' He added triumphantly. 'I thought I'd do it myself… just for you.'

Maude was rendered speechless. Her face beamed with rare delight, as she thought how lovely it would be to see the summerhouse restored to former glory.

She thought of Daphne and their first, lingering kiss.

They had been walking in the woods collecting blackberries one afternoon, when a torrential downpour of rain forced them to run for shelter in the folly. Soaking wet, breathless, they stripped off their sodden clothes, and their laughter and happiness had prompted their first act of lovemaking.

Raymond looked at his smiling aunt and considered that he was finally learning how to manipulate her.

Hiding his sense of victory, he looked at her on the sofa.

'Shall we have some tea?' he asked innocently.

The cause of Maude's telephone problems were to be found a little over two miles away; in Sidcup's main telephone exchange, housed in an impressive modernist brick-built building at the top of Station Road.

Within a small, rather airless office, Chief Supervisor Cecil Barker, was becoming increasingly uneasy. Over the last four weeks, bombing had inflicted great damage to the telephone network of Southern England. Civilian GPO resources had been commandeered at an alarming rate, to patch up links between airfields and Home Defence services all around Kent.

Not that he was privy to such things, but this afternoon RAF Biggin Hill's sector command centre was out of action again, as its phone lines had been cut during heavy bombing. Right now, telephone engineers were swinging like monkeys from tree to tree, as they strung emergency phone lines between the aerodrome and an impromptu facility being set up in the village. The new operations room would be in a baker's shop, next door to the local post office with its small rural switchboard.

Methodical and diligent, Cecil was perfectly suited to his profession and, in his own modest way; he was a key part of the war effort. Like most of the men left in Sidcup, he was beyond call-up age and now had to do the job of three people, as more than half of his pre-war colleagues had already joined the armed forces.

This afternoon, he was *sitting in the hot seat*, as he'd heard American film stars call it, on guard against any further disruption to his local telephone network. Their link to the outside world was supplied by three thick underground cable bundles, each capable of relaying up to a hundred simultaneous calls on to the other major exchanges in the area.

However, the cable to Eltham had been damaged somewhere by enemy action three days ago and only a portion of its lines were still working.

To make matters worse, about an hour ago, the connection to the main exchange at Orpington had been cut without explanation. A German raider had jettisoned its bombs over the town and two of them hit its telephone exchange, severing all trunk calls through that area. With Orpington now out of service, Sidcup was reliant on the north cable to Bexleyheath and just twenty one remaining open lines in the westwards cable to Eltham, to relay any long distance calls. Competition for these lines rose steadily until a minute ago, when Cecil received an order to formally reserve every remaining trunk line exclusively for the defence services.

He walked into the operator room, where seven switchboard girls and three older female supervisors manually connected calls from nearly six thousand local subscribers within this densely telephoned area. He told them to only connect trunk calls of an official status until further notice. Then he sat down to watch the tall switchboards that covered the entire forty foot length of the high-ceilinged hall.

Small lights on the connector boards blinked here and there. Hidden electrical switches clattered away, to punctuate the electric hum of the machinery.

Instead of the usual polite greeting, the operators now asked… *Is this call of urgent national importance?*

Chapter 16

The telephone in the next office rang shrill and insistent. Yet Stabsfeldwebel Freund ignored its plea for attention, as he grappled with the complex matter of empty fuel drum returns.

Muller's raiding force had been fully loaded with fuel and ordnance and Freund's next task was to quantify how much had been taken from stores to do so. Counting bombs and ammunition was the easy part, but aviation spirit was always a challenge. Every aircraft's fuel tanks were topped up before each mission, yet the quantity used to do so varied greatly. It all depended on how far, how fast and how efficiently each aircraft had been flown previously. So the starting point to calculate consumption was always to count the empty cans returned from the dispersal area.

Freund knew that usage was higher than his official log tables predicted and his most urgent duty was to calculate the reserve left in the Rosières fuel dump. He had to anticipate future needs and order re-supply from the Air District, never an easy process without the correct mathematical justification to underpin the requisition order.

The telephone fell silent.

Each Heinkel 111 carried a maximum of 3,500 litres of aviation fuel and filling nineteen aircraft from empty would be 66,500 litres. Freund had a return to dump tally for two hundred and seventy eight, 200 litre fuel drums from both refuelling operations. Life would have been so much easier if they had a few bowser lorries with pumping gear, instead of man-handling thousands of fuel drums around the airfield every week. Sometimes their new deliveries came by lorry, other times by tankers brought on the railway line at the northern perimeter of the airfield. Even that brought problems, as transferring such vast quantities of fuel brought the airfield's activities to a halt while every man was mustered to help.

The telephone started ringing again.

Freund cursed its interruption and wondered where Fischer was when he needed him.

He concentrated on his calculations afresh. The number of empty fuel drums indicated that topping up had taken 55,600 litres, an average of 2,926 litres per plane. This was important to know, as the next refuelling of returning aircraft would give him average fuel consumption for this afternoon's target range, with a specific weight of bombs. This did assume that all aircraft had roughly the same amount in their tanks before fuelling, but in the absence of accurate data, his best guess figure would have to do.

This raid would be the gruppe's deepest penetration into English airspace so far, 270km away in a straight line. Yet combat missions were never flown in a straight line and looking at the mission plan, each plane would easily cover 650km today. With adverse weather, evasive action, or just getting lost, it could be as much 800km for some aircraft. Being in the Luftwaffe was not all about flying. Having a good head for mathematics and accurate paperwork was exactly why Freund had this job.

That telephone was really getting on his nerves now.

Freund shouted for Fischer's attention.

There was no reply and he shook his head with annoyance, determined not to lose his train of thought.

The thing that frustrated Freund's mathematical world was that not every aircraft returned from combat. So he wanted to know how much fuel was being lost from his topping up equation. At least he no longer had to provision them until more replacement aircraft arrived and these were few and far between over the last three weeks.

From the nominal strength of forty two aircraft, Muller's three staffeln had only been able to take nineteen aircraft into combat this afternoon, as four were currently unfit for service. Freund didn't need to be a mathematical genius to calculate that the 3rd Gruppe was currently at only 54% of full strength. That assumed that the four aircraft currently undergoing repair could be brought back to roster quickly. Considering they had received only eight replacement aircraft during their time at Rosières, this meant they had lost twenty seven aircraft since early June. The majority of these losses had happened in just the last four weeks. At this rate, he wouldn't have any aircraft to worry about at all by mid-October.

He decided to return to his more immediate task and considered the bomb loads being carried. By relating take-off weights, target ranges and past performance, he was convinced that he could devise a more accurate formula to forecast the fuel needs for each type of mission.

The phone stopped ringing, but then, started again.

Fed up by its insistent interruption, Freund decided he had better answer it himself and walked next door.

'Operations Office, KG1 Rosières. Stabsfeldwebel Freund speaking,' he announced into the receiver.

The caller was a staff officer with the kampfgruppe commander. Apparently, Angerstein was now over at Montdidier and had an urgent question.

'No… the last of them took off thirty minutes ago sir, right on schedule, at 5pm,' Freund replied.

The caller barked instructions to him and hung up, just as Gefreiter Fischer walked back into the office. He was carrying a wooden tray laden with coffee, bread and cheese, their reward for the last four hours of frenzied activity.

Freund stared blankly at his colleague as he considered the implications of the telephone call.

'Oh shit!' he exclaimed.

Given the enormity of what he had just heard, it was all Freund could manage to say.

He pushed past a startled-looking Fischer and ran down the corridor to the radio room, in search of the first flight operations officer he could find.

Chapter 17

The number of aircraft congregating over the coastal town of Boulogne-sur-Mer was truly an awe-inspiring sight.

The citizens of this ancient French port looked skyward at the fascinating, dreadful spectacle of hundreds of German aircraft converging from every direction. These Junkers, Dorniers and Heinkels had timed their journeys from airfields across Northern France, all to meet here in just the last few minutes. The sound of their engines combined into an oppressive, deafening roar that shook buildings and beat the ears of onlookers.

The first group to arrive led the next on a wide circuit above the town, as they waited for the last of their comrades to arrive. The fighter cover appeared from the north and within ten minutes, a total of sixty Messerschmitt 109 fighters had joined the aerial carousel.

To an old man watching from the streets below, they resembled a flock of noisy starlings swooping and darting above a monstrous throng of blackbirds methodically circumscribing the sky above his town.

The arrival of the last contingent prompted the circling formation to break out into a point and then, the conglomeration of aircraft streamed out to sea towards England.

The Frenchman looked at his pocket watch.

Les Boches sont en retard, he thought and went on his way.

Muller's nineteen Heinkels were already over the sea, in the centre of the huge raid at a height of 4500 metres.

In the lead aircraft, call sign V4+AJ, an additional crew member sat in the navigator's seat, Leutnant Kristian Bauer, the pilot that couldn't land properly. He checked over the flight chart on his lap and glanced nervously at this afternoon's gruppenkomandeur to his left.

'Remember, watch me closely and watch the sky even closer,' Muller responded.

'Yes Herr Major,' Bauer replied.

'In the air you can call me Horst, just keep an eye on our waypoints. I have every faith in you, Kristian.' Muller announced in a friendlier manner.

Lying prone at the front of the cabin, Werner Hartmann was not so sure. He was disgruntled enough that he had been excluded from his usual place alongside his commander, but even more so, that he would have to spend the entire flight lying uncomfortably in the nose of the aircraft. Admittedly, his usual seat offered no more protection in the unarmoured cabin, than where he was laying now. Nonetheless, with nothing but glass and perspex between him and the worst that the British could throw at him, Werner felt doubly exposed.

His stomach churned and he looked at his wristwatch, marking the time at 5.42pm as they approached the English coast. Of course, in British airspace it was now 4.42pm, as the British just had to have a different time zone to the rest of Europe.

An island nation, in thought and deed, he considered.

As he looked down on the coastline, he thought how different this was to the Tyrolean mountains and forests of his homeland. He craned his neck to the left, to the right, above and below… the phalanx of bombers was a reassuring sight as they took battle to the English.

Without realising it, Werner started to hum a song to pass the time, perhaps to calm his nerves a little. After a few seconds, Bauer picked up the refrain too and the two of them had hummed their way well into the second verse, when their commander's voice interrupted them.

'That's enough of that Hartmann… we are on a mission, not in kindergarten,' Muller chastised.

'Listen up boys… *Little Hänschen* misses his mummy!' Gerhard Metzger called out over the intercom from the belly gun sponson.

He had been listening to the childish tune, as had everyone else on board.

Snatches of laughter came through Werner's headset and he was embarrassed by the reference to the nursery rhyme he had been humming.

Just nineteen years old, it was only three years since Werner first experienced the thrill of flight, in a glider plane soaring like an eagle above the Tux valley where he had been born. From that moment on, he knew his destiny was to fly, to see the world as God did. Unlike most of his friends who followed family tradition and joined the mountain regiments of the Wehrmacht, Werner chose the Luftwaffe. Yet his ambitions as a pilot went unfulfilled. It soon became apparent that the hunter's skills imbued by his father, had prepared him better for navigation and gunnery.

Whilst he was a devout Catholic, like many a soldier, Werner assuaged his conscience by clinging to his sense of duty and comradeship. Ensnared by the trauma of war, he now lived in an almost perpetual dreamlike state as his mind stifled thoughts of the past and rejected any consideration of the future. He lived minute-by-minute and the only thing that mattered anymore was his place amongst his comrades. They were his family now, where loyalty, discipline and routine underpinned getting their job done and doing their best to keep each other alive.

Outside of this circle, it seemed that only death, destruction and brutality were the order of the day. Any concept of compassion, empathy or mercy towards the enemy had become an abnormal, dangerous aberration that might endanger him or his comrades.

War had turned normal Christian morality upon its head.

Werner looked upwards and watched the Messerschmitts criss-crossing at tangents to try to keep their speed higher, now they had been ordered to match the slower forward advance of the bomber formation. This constant zigzagging increased the distance they flew, negating the small fuel advantage they had won since moving to their coastal airfields. Today's hunters felt their prospects had travelled full circle in the last week.

Muller's voice crackled over the intercom to alert the crew for combat and Werner's stomach contracted into a tight knot.

His mouth felt dry.

The Tommies will come soon, he thought.

He concentrated on the haze across the horizon, searching for the inevitable fast-moving specks of English fighters. When they did come, those little specks would grow rapidly larger, with machine guns blazing, bringing death to many of his comrades before the day was spent. In counter balance, many people would be killed by Werner's work at the bombsight, but he no longer thought about the consequences of the destruction he cast behind him. Nonetheless, as he observed the ugly conglomeration of war machines all around him, he considered that *God's heart must be broken by the things that I can see.*

It was a rare moment of contemplation, as he had almost entirely lost his sense of self within military service.

Werner was not the only person considering his place within the scheme of life that day. If God was listening to the growing cacophony of voices rising to the heavens from this part of the world, he gave no acknowledgement. The mother and baby huddled in a shelter, the farmer watching the aerial armada cross his cliff-top fields, a young Scotsman fretting about the temperature of his Hawker Hurricane's straining engine, a German fighter pilot eager for another victory.

All prayed to see another day.

There were a lot of people calling out that afternoon… for success, for salvation, for their mother, father, brother, sister, wife, husband, children, their cause or their nation.

If God had a telephone exchange like Cecil Barker's that day, practically every light on the switchboard would have been blinking.

Chapter 18

Flushed with the apparent success of the conversation with his aunt, Raymond inspected the interior of the summerhouse for the second time in the last few days.

Admiring its colourful Romanesque frescos, he imagined how splendid it would look, once cleared of all the rubbish presently stacked high to the ceiling. He quickly found the rattan furniture he remembered from childhood and decided that with a good spring clean and furnishings taken from the house, it would all spruce up nicely.

Raymond looked at the old oak refectory table that stood, rather impressively, in the exact centre of the building. Ten foot long by four wide, its ancient jet black wood was crudely carved in the Tudor style, or perhaps even older. It was almost certainly one of the oldest of the Delafort family possessions.

He laughed out loud.

He had just recalled how as a small child he used to hide underneath it, whilst Aunt Maude paced around the garden in frustration at her inability to find him. Raymond remembered snuggling up beneath its protective shield, feeling safe, invisible and somehow, invincible. For hour upon hour, he would lay there and listen to the trees outside… as their branches creaked and whispered in the wind.

Surveying huge bundles of rotten picket fencing, dusty sacks full of god-knows-what, old tools and more piled high around him, Raymond initially thought that a jolly good bonfire would sort out the problem. He soon realised that would require an enormous effort, to move everything far enough away to safely set such a fire. The seed of an easier solution began to grow in his mind. Leaving via the front of the summerhouse, he walked around the corner and carefully trotted down the grass bank on which the rear of the building sat.

From down here, the garden was about fifteen feet higher; highlighting how much the Victorian landscapers had levelled the shallow valley that used to separate the house from the wooded hill. They had gradually built up the level of the garden until it culminated here, with a steep drop down to the edge of the woods. The abrupt end to this man-made plateau seemed to emphasise a clear demarcation between the modern world and the old.

The rear of the summerhouse was supported by tall brick-built foundation walls and in the centre of the wall that faced the woods; there was a sturdy wrought iron door. Raymond turned its ornate handle and the door opened stiffly, just a few inches. He gave it a good hard shove with his shoulder, the door yielded and he was able to step inside.

Once his eyes adjusted to the gloom, he could see a large void spanning the entire width of the building. This was subdivided by seven brick columns that reached up to thick arches spanning the roof, bearing the weight of the structure above. It struck Raymond as a little bit odd, as the scale of the architecture massively exceeded the requirements of supporting the modest building above. The diminutive bricks of the cellar's construction revealed their great antiquity, much the same as the great table above. He considered that this place felt more like the crypt of an ancient church, than the cellar of a rich man's folly.

Raymond decided that this would be a perfect place to hide all the rubbish out of sight.

Why make extra work for yourself, when you can shove it all under the carpet? He thought, in a manner totally in keeping with his character, and as ever, as if in conversation with another person.

It seemed that it had been a long time since anyone else had ventured inside this dark, obscure space. The air was cool but stale and musty, but more than that, there was a peculiar smell. It was a sort of fungal, vaguely rotten aroma. Yet the bare earth floor seemed perfectly dry underfoot. Only then did Raymond notice a large wooden trap door, just a few feet in front of him at the centre of the cavernous room. He walked forward, bent down and pulled at the hatch. The wood was very old and as he applied his strength, it cracked and splintered as it lifted.

The sunlight from behind him streamed in, to illuminate a deep pit.

He could only see down about eight or nine feet towards the bottom, but as far as he could judge, it all seemed as dry as a bone. It suddenly occurred to him that this might make an excellent hiding place for his ill-gotten gains from the black market, well away from Bridger's Farm.

Yes, *a secret place within a secret room* appealed strongly.

He tried to close the trapdoor, but as he lifted it again, the decayed wood broke under its own weight and disintegrated into several pieces. Looking into the pit again, he made a mental note to procure a ladder, by which he could safely descend below. Satisfied with his discovery, he walked back outside into sunshine.

Raymond looked into Cray Wood, something that he generally avoided doing. Certainly, Aunt Maude didn't like the woods much either, as he had never seen her venture into its heart. When he was about five years old, she had once been very angry with him, but he could no longer remember why she had warned him about wandering alone in there again. For a variety of reasons, mostly his own, he had followed this advice ever since.

Covering about a square mile, this wild coppice of old trees and dense undergrowth was all that remained of the great forest that had covered this land two thousand and more years ago.

At its centre, the land rose steeply to a round hilltop, standing at least a hundred feet above the river valley. Up there the trees were much older still and Raymond's attention was drawn to the largest and most ancient of them all. Its thick trunk was probably sixty feet in circumference but it seemed hardly possible that it was still alive. Most of its heavy, tired branches were bone-white, stripped of their bark and the two largest were supported by cock-eyed, timber trusses. Thick strands of ivy pulled at it from the ground, clothing the great tree in a shimmering green coat of triangular leaves. The various elements of this surreal tableau created an altogether sombre, depressing representation of extreme age. Raymond didn't like the woods and he didn't like that tree in particular.

Suddenly, he had the oddest of thoughts.

He imagined the tree as a decrepit old man astride crude crutches, a weary traveller, looking back at him from across the expanse of time. The tree seemed to cast an air of presence about it, an authority over anything or anyone that might draw near. Raymond noticed twenty or more jet-black crows perched upon its highest branches. His rational senses told him that they were the cause of this rather odd sensation of scrutiny. He waved his arms about and shouted, expecting the birds to take fright and fly away.

They remained at their station and kept a silent, unflinching vigil. Something unpleasant stirred in the tiniest corner of Raymond's mind.

Blood.

He recalled another, stranger, moment from his childhood.

He saw little fingers digging in the dark, stinking soil beneath that ancient tree, until they found the heavy, steel body of an army penknife. Raymond remembered the electric excitement of opening its blade for the first time. The metal had glinted brightly in the sunlight, casting a dazzling, blinding reflection in his eyes. Then he recalled something else… his sister's puppy.

So much blood.

He flinched, involuntarily, shaking the memory from his head.

For an instant, Raymond felt immeasurably cold.

He quickly turned and clambered back up the grass bank.

Looking at the welcoming vista of the rose garden and house, his mood lightened and his thoughts returned to his plans for the next day. He noticed the rising, urgent roar of approaching aircraft engines reverberating overhead and looking upwards, he saw nine fighter aircraft hurtling southwards. Their wings carried the red and blue roundels of the home side. Rather uncharacteristically, Raymond wondered what it would be like to be in service to his country.

Despite his strong instinct for self-preservation, he conceded, begrudgingly, that those chaps above him were intent on a far greater purpose than clearing up garden rubbish and hiding contraband.

In a rare mood of affection for her nephew, Maude had been downstairs in the kitchen preparing an afternoon tea for them to share.

She collected the tray of brisket sandwiches, jam, drop scones, teapot and cups from the dumbwaiter in the dining room and brought it into the sitting room. Just as she walked out onto the patio in search of Raymond, she saw the Hurricane fighters of 601 Squadron tear overhead, en route to battle from their airfield at RAF Debden in Essex. This squadron had previously operated from Tangmere in West Sussex, but after the onslaught of the 15th of August, moved up to Essex to help cover 11 Group's losses.

Not that Maude knew or cared about their identity as they flew over Craywood House. As far as she was concerned, they were all heroes acting in defence of her beloved country. As she watched Raymond walk up the garden for the second time today, Maude considered that the comparison could not have been more damning.

Sometimes Maude could see her own father in Raymond, for a fleeting moment, in the way that all children carry an echo of their forebears.

If Papa was still alive, he would know how to put things right, she thought to herself.

With his eclectic mix of the modern and the old, of science and nature, of the past and the future, Josiah Delafort had truly been a great man. She could almost hear him now, espousing the latest farming innovation or humming those old, old country songs of which he was so fond.

Maude laughed to herself about how he would often disappear on one of his *great walks* across the fields and woods, to ponder a particular challenge or opportunity. He might be gone for so long, for hours, even a whole day and night, that her mother would become frantic with worry. He would return, cheerful, but clear-headed, enthusing to all around him about a new stratagem and set to the task to see it done. She contemplated just how disappointed Daphne would be in her son today, in contrast to those brave young men flying high above.

Maude prayed that perhaps he might yet find a worthy purpose in life. However, she had good reason to know that her nephew would never be able, or could ever be trusted, to pursue what you might call a normal life.

The dark shadow over Raymond's soul had been shockingly revealed to her when he was just five years old.

She knew it was her burden of knowledge to carry, alone.

On the other side of Sidcup, the sporting afternoon had petered out once the young lads from the neighbours' built an unassailable lead over the Vigars.

After several games of rounders, the production of a cricket bat changed the match into one of Tip and Run. Within a madcap scoring system, Ken carried personal honours of four rounders, twelve runs and three wickets, followed by Ginny and Betty with a rounder and four runs each. Three Vigar howzats were disputed by the boys, but in return, all of theirs were upheld as also were three rounders and eight runs. Edward became one of The Three Stooges and kept falling over, much to the amusement of all the children. He went back into the house, returned with his beloved Ensign box camera and took a commemorative photograph of a glorious, carefree afternoon.

By then the scores had fallen into such a farce that Umpire Albert declared it was at first a draw, then in the lads' favour, because they were obviously better than *smelly girls*. It was, perhaps, inevitable that Player Of The Match was awarded to five year old Jimmy Marsden from three doors up. To resounding cheers, his face beamed with happiness and a sense of worth alongside the bigger boys.

Ginny took off in pursuit of three young lads, who screamed with laughter as she chased after them, while threatening kisses, hugs or cold baths, if she ever got hold of them. The rest of the Vigar team gladly conceded defeat and were already sunbathing on the grass, when fighter aircraft sped over them.

The remaining children looked skyward and argued back and forth.

'They're Spitfires!'

'No, they're not, them's Hurricanes!'

With arms spread wide, they all tore into battle, rampaging up and down the park to imitations of machine gun *Da-Da-Da's* and the cry of *Curse you Biggles, Aaraaaraaaagh!*

'Time for a brew... before I go on duty, Love?' Edward asked.

'You know where the kettle is Ted,' Patricia replied promptly, as she stretched out her legs in the warmth of the late afternoon sun.

'Yes *Mad-arm*, your wish is my command,' he replied, as he headed back through the gate towards the kitchen.

Ken and Betty sat side by side watching the fighter aircraft head towards the horizon. With other people around neither had a problem making conversation, but sitting together, just the two of them, neither knew quite what to say. It is one of the great ironies of life that those who are the most attracted to each other... often find themselves lost for words when alone together.

Betty broke the ice.

'I'm going to give up my job at Uncle Ernie's and do something more important.'

'What do you fancy doing then?' Ken responded with genuine interest.

'I was thinking of joining the WAAFS, I'll be old enough to enlist soon,' said Betty, 'or maybe learn to drive the buses. I like the idea of that.'

'I'm sure you'll do a good job, whatever you choose.' Ken replied. 'But I'd hate to think of you being in any danger at all.' He added awkwardly, 'well... I mean *all* of your family, any more than we are all in danger these days, I suppose.'

Betty blushed.

Not that she minded. She was pleased that maybe, just maybe, he was expressing a particular care about her.

'Well I'd hate for you to get in any danger too,' she replied without hesitation.

'Yes, well let's all do our best to keep safe and look forward to the day when this war is over,' Ken concluded shyly.

The moment had passed, but was replaced by a more comfortable silence.

They both stared ahead, over the railway line, to where the aircraft had become just tiny specks and then… were gone.

In the kitchen, Edward had filled the kettle and took a match to light a burner on the cooker. With the gas tap opened wide, a paltry flame ignited and he looked at it with disappointment.

The gas pressure is down again, he thought.

Looking up at the clock he saw that he had well over an hour before his 6pm parade. Yet at this rate, the kettle might only just boil in time. He emptied half of the water back down the sink, sat the kettle on top of the stuttering flame and hoped for the best.

He walked out into the hall and into the bathroom, to change into his blue boiler suit, ready for his patrol.

At the top of Station Road in the telephone exchange, Cecil Barker was dozing in his chair.

Mrs Price, today's senior switchboard supervisor, walked into his office and informed him that *all* their trunk lines were in constant use by the defence services. No–one in Sidcup could presently talk to, or receive a call from anyone in the outside world.

Cecil sat up, doing his best to look as if he had not been asleep. Whatever his private thoughts were on the matter, he chose to be outwardly optimistic.

'Nothing ever happens here,' he declared. 'I'm sure normal service will resume later tonight!'

Mrs Price frowned and returned to the switchboard hall.

At a height of 18,000 feet just south of Tonbridge, the fighters of 601 Squadron were bearing down on a group of bombers that had crossed the coast at Camber, just five minutes earlier. Thirty German aircraft had broken off from the main formation and already bombarded the coastal aerodromes of Hawkinge and Lympne, for the third time in as many days. With their work done, they were now homeward bound, no doubt thankful for their easy targets.

In the midst of 601's B flight, Pilot Officer Douglas McFadden was still worrying about engine temperature. The throttle mixture was probably too rich and his Hurricane's engine was running hot. Nineteen years old and only eleven months into his RAF service, he had been pushed through operational training in July and joined the squadron a fortnight ago, to be thrown straight into active duty. That most of his peers were only a year or so older underscored how months, even just weeks, now counted for so much in this daily life and death struggle.

His flight commander's voice crackled over the radio headset, 'Ignore the empties, we want full bottles of pop today Gentlemen.'

McFadden continued to fret about his engine, his height, his speed, as he struggled to keep his place in formation as they pelted towards battle.

'Keep your eyes peeled for those yellow-nosed bastards,' the voice came again. 'There'll be up there somewhere.'

McFadden scanned around the cockpit canopy, squinting into the sun over his right shoulder. He had been taught that the German fighters tended to keep the sun at their backs, to give them the opening advantage in combat.

He screwed his eyes tighter, staring into the dazzling sun.

It was too much to bear.

He closed his eyes tight shut for a few seconds, to try to clear his vision, and looked again. He tried a trick taught to him by one of the more experienced pilots.

As he looked westward, he banked to port for a split second, flipping his starboard wing up, so that the wing tip obscured the sun for a moment, to give him a less dazzling view.

It helped a little.

Satisfied with the result, he repeated the process over and again.

The German raid of a hundred and eighty bombers and fighters was now only five miles to the south east, slightly below them at 15,000 feet and almost over Maidstone.

Above and behind them another group of Hurricanes, from 85 Squadron at Croydon, was about to commence their attack.

McFadden's heart was pounding, at well over 160 beats per minute.

All he could think of at that moment, over the deafening roar of the Rolls Royce Merlin engine, was that he didn't want to let anyone down.

This was only his ninth day on operations and so far he had not achieved much; twisting and turning and finding himself alone in an empty sky. Each time he had returned to base with his tail between his legs.

Today, he was determined to put on a good show for the chaps, to prove that their investment had been worthwhile.

He did not want to court the shame of failure, when so many around him were giving and achieving, so much.

Above all else, he wanted to bag a Jerry in memory of Flying Officer Michael Doulton who had gone missing, presumed killed, whilst attacking Dorniers over Gravesend yesterday. At 31 years of age, Doulton had been an old man in fighter pilot terms; enlisting in 1931, into reserves in 1936 and back to active duty in 1939. He had taken the young McFadden under his wing, trusting him to be his lookout for enemy fighters. Doulton became an inspiration, showing him skills that might preserve his life and, perhaps, make him into an effective hunter.

McFadden's Hawker Hurricane was an older design, in many ways the poorer cousin of the Supermarine Spitfire in terms of dogfighting performance. It had been drilled into him that his duty was to destroy German bombers, while squadrons flying Spitfires grappled with the Messerschmitt 109 escort fighters. In one-to-one combat, the Messerschmitt possessed many excellent qualities including its small size and superior dive rate. Most importantly, it carried a radically different weapon system to the eight machine guns fitted in the wings of the Hurricane and Spitfire.

Pre-war RAF weaponry philosophy had focussed on firing as many bullets as rapidly as possible. In the early 1930's, when most nations' fighter aircraft were little different to their fabric-covered First World War predecessors, the idea of carrying so many machine guns seemed awe-inspiringly powerful. However by 1940, the destructive power of rifle calibre bullets fell far short of the German combination of two machine guns and two, or even three, large bore cannon guns per aircraft. Firing an explosive projectile ten times bigger than a British 0.303inch bullet, just one hit from a German 20mm FF cannon could rip even a modern metal-skinned aircraft apart. Messerschmitt pilots also had the choice of firing either weapon type separately or together, giving them up to 50 seconds of firepower compared to the meagre 16 seconds at a British pilot's disposal.

A recent discovery provided some hope of redressing this imbalance. Inspection of crashed Luftwaffe bombers revealed that the Germans hadn't armoured the rear of their engines.

Potentially, this made them highly vulnerable to stern attacks. However, this placed the attacker in clear sight of a bomber's rear-facing machine guns, as he tried to close the distance. Whilst a far easier tactic to undertake, a stern attack carried greater risk as German gunners sprayed a wave of bullets in defence. Another option was to attack from an intercepting tangent; from the side, above or below. This meant shooting at deflection against a fast moving target, dispersing bullets over a wide area and thereby, decreasing their destructive potential.

In recent weeks, a new and even more dangerous combat tactic was being tried out by the bravest fliers, the frontal attack. Hurtling head-on towards an approaching aircraft tested the attacking pilot's nerve and ability to the maximum. It was certainly not recommended for the novice pilot.

RAF fighter pilots had found a partial answer to these challenges; by synchronising their guns on a single focal point, about 300 yards ahead. Whilst creating a good concentration of fire, this required the pilot to have a phenomenal aim during the wild acrobatics of a dogfight.

If the target was too close, it was common for the two streams of fire from the wings of the British fighter to actually pass-by the skinny Messerschmitt, without scoring any hits at all. So the sum of these tactics offered only interim solutions, until British fighters could be fitted with heavier weaponry equivalent to the cannon guns of the Messerschmitts.

Doulton's disappearance had deeply upset McFadden, especially so as he had been introduced to his mentor's pregnant wife, Carol, only a few days beforehand. She now sat at home in the forlorn hope that her husband might yet miraculously return to see their child born. McFadden felt guilty that he never even saw his friend's plane go down.

By coincidence, these German bombers were using a radio frequency close to that being used by his squadron today. As McFadden drew closer, he could hear the chatter of German airmen.

For a moment, he even thought he could hear someone singing and laughing. Eavesdropping on their relaxed banter, it was apparent that they hadn't spotted 601 Squadron in the vast blue sky.

'Gentlemen, we're going in through the front door today,' the flight leader's voice crackled in his headset again. 'Head-on-attack. Break to starboard... Tally-Ho. Tally-Ho!'

The Hurricanes in front peeled off and dived straight towards the leading German aircraft.

'Oh dear God!' McFadden shouted to himself.

He pushed the flight stick forward and followed them into the dive.

Suddenly, his headset was filled with the whooping and shouting of his fellow pilots, as their adrenalin, their excitement and their fear was unleashed by the thrill of the hunt.

'Achtung, Spitfuer!' a voice cried out mistakenly over the RT. The German voices rose and coalesced into a babble of alarm.

McFadden was flying directly at the lead group of bombers; a dozen Dornier 17's. Despite the dangers of a head on attack, the front of these bombers was their least defended area with just a single machine gunner to fire back. At a closing speed of over 600 mph, the last thousand yards would close in the next 3 seconds, requiring nerves of steel and split-second reactions to avoid a collision. The Germans would literally fly into a wall of British bullets, yet their front gunners had virtually no time to shoot back with any accuracy. However, as tracer bullets reached out to meet McFadden, it was terrifying enough just the same.

The bomber formation loomed ever larger.

With just a moment to decide, McFadden selected his target. He turned the safety catch on his flight stick and pressed the gun trigger.

In each wing, four Browning machine guns commenced firing. The entire airframe shook under their recoil, causing his plane to buck and yaw. To his amazement, he saw his bullets shatter the glasshouse cockpit of a Dornier and rake savagely across its left wing.

McFadden pulled back on the stick and skimmed over the top of the enemy aircraft. He was confronted by another, much larger bomber flying straight towards him.

He instinctively pressed the trigger again, but his bullets skewed wide, as he jerked the stick down and right to avoid collision and plummeted into clear space below.

The entire engagement had lasted no more than eight seconds. In two, three second bursts he had fired a total of 765 rounds of ammunition, of which 224 had hit his first target.

The Dornier's cockpit was riddled by his gunfire, instantly killing all four of its crew. Many of the same bullets tore through the bomber's bomb-bay bulkhead and ricocheted off the steel bomb casings. Thirty two of these bullets deflected sideways and pierced the fuel tank in the Dornier's left wing. This released a spray of aviation spirit that caught the hot exhaust ports of the adjacent engine and ignited with a searing yellow flash.

As McFadden dived out of the formation, he looked behind and saw a German bomber plunging earthwards spewing fire and smoke.

He was pretty certain that this was his doing.

By pulling his aircraft upwards while rotating on its axis just like Doulton had taught him, he completed a reasonable Immelman climbing turn. The G-forces of this violent manoeuvre briefly dimmed his vision.

As his sight returned, he saw that he had gained a good position above the bombers. He watched the circus of British fighters darting around tracer fire from the German machine gunners.

Despite the intense noise around him, all he could hear was his own heartbeat and the sound of his lungs bellowing for breath.

A tremendous sense of achievement began to register in McFadden's mind. A moment later, a cannon shell exploded behind him... and tore off his Hurricane's tailfin.

It was one of several fired by the Messerschmitt that had stalked McFadden for the last fifteen seconds. Machine gun bullets peppered his right wing, engine cowling and tore away his cockpit canopy.

A wall of flame erupted before him.

It was just thirty three seconds since his attack began.

Now his aircraft was engulfed in fire, spinning towards the ground at 360 miles per hour.

Chapter 19

The next link in Britain's chain of defence could not have been more different to the high performance aircraft battling in the sky above Kent that day.

Two men stood by a circular wooden table at an Observer Corps position atop Detling Hill, just to the north west of Maidstone. Walter Camp was a plumber, Sidney Worsell a greengrocer. They were two middle-aged volunteers, who gave fifty hours of their week to underpin a unique warning system, created by Fighter Command over the previous four years.

Firstly, approaching enemy aircraft were detected by radio direction finding stations, paraphrased as *RDF*, comprising of huge radio masts strung out along 300 miles of the southern and eastern coastlines. Looking far out to sea, this new technology could detect large formations of aircraft approaching from the continent and operated in any weather, day or night. As soon as invading aircraft crossed the RDF belt and travelled inland, the second element of the so-called *Dowding System* came into play.

Thousands of volunteers like Walter and Sidney manned a huge network of watch stations across the country, using what Winston Churchill would later dub as the *Mark One Eyeball*. Working together, RDF stations and Observer Corps volunteers reported the size, position and heading of enemy aircraft formations to 32 regional headquarters. They, in turn, reported to Anti-Aircraft Command and RAF control rooms, empowering Britain's military leaders with vital, current information about the enemy's movements. In the Battle of France, ninety percent of RAF sorties had been squandered on fruitless searches for the enemy over a huge geographical area. In densely populated Southern England, the reverse now held true. Without wasting time and effort on standing patrols, Fighter Command could take decisions that increased its results threefold. In theory, RAF fighters could be given enough warning to take-off and climb to combat altitudes, ready to meet their attackers in exactly the right place.

Even if the Luftwaffe had understood the implications of this immense intelligence system, it would have been impossible to counter. It was a huge, interlaced network of thousands of people, in hundreds of places, all connected by telephone. If any links were cut, the flow of information quickly found a myriad of ways to reconnect and maintain Britain's control of its defences.

Sidney Worsell was the spotter this afternoon, sighting a simple theodolite-like device, a *pantograph*, towards the masse of German bombers traversing the horizon. As the teller, Walter looked at the pointer tracing across a simple map pasted to the table top. He called out the grid reference and read off the height of the bomber formation, from a graduated scale on the side of the pantograph's sighting bar. Combined with an estimation of the aircraft type observed and their approximate heading they would report their observations by telephone to their area control officer within seconds. They rarely knew the context of what they saw; their job was simply to watch and report. Yet they did know that they were *doing their bit for England* in their own small way.

Whilst the controllers at Fighter Command were so enamoured by the information provided by RDF, the inaccuracies of this new technology often left a lot to be desired. Fighter squadron commanders in combat were regularly frustrated by RDF vector instructions that often led them amiss by ten miles or 10,000 feet in height. By now, many RAF fighter pilots put greater store in reports from humble men like Sidney and Walter, than those derived from the towering radio masts along the coast.

Satisfied that they had correctly tracked the raid, Walter spoke into a telephone speaker tube hanging from his neck.

'Detling OC here,' he called. 'German Raid. Ninety plus, at 10,000 feet, grid 24. Dorniers, Heinkels, Messerschmitts. Ninety plus. Heading north, repeat, north, at 250 mph.'

This placed the raid east of their position, moving towards the Medway towns and Thames Estuary. Walter was glad that the Germans were heading away, as smoke still hung over the nearby airfield after two raids in just the last 24 hours.

The Luftwaffe seemed to really hate little RAF Detling, attacking it again and again over the last few weeks. However, the first raid on the 13th August had been the worst. Observers on duty that day saw a bomber formation approaching and dutifully telephoned headquarters in Maidstone, but their warning wasn't passed on to the airfield in time. They stood by, powerless to intervene, as the airfield carried on as normal, unaware of the impending calamity. Caught out in the open, over a hundred and fifty personnel were killed or injured during that bombardment.

Whilst no-one could have stopped the raid, a Take Cover warning would have saved many lives. The bomb dumps blew up amongst the carnage and the damage was so great that fires burnt for two days. Consequently, policemen were put on local buses that passed by the aerodrome, to order passengers to look away from the terrible sight.

Some good did come of this though. The chain of command was relaxed a little. Wherever possible, OC stations were given a direct telephone line to local airfields so they could warn them directly of impending attack.

The reason for the Luftwaffe's obsession with RAF Detling was because reconnaissance flights had often photographed large numbers of Hurricanes and Spitfires within its perimeter. That they had only landed here when low on fuel, or when their own aerodromes had been under attack, was not understood by German strategists. Luftwaffe Intelligence believed it to be a key fighter station, when in reality it was just a minor airfield for bombers of Coastal Command. They continued to target Detling as a priority, unaware that this had no impact on Fighter Command's strength at all. The weak defences of this minor aerodrome, and others like it, only compounded Luftwaffe Intelligence's false belief that Germany was gaining supremacy over the RAF.

Walter took his pipe out of his pocket and filled its bowl with tobacco. He lit it, sucked a few puffs of smoke and savoured its sweet aroma as he gazed at the aftermath of the air battle they had just watched.

Across the landscape, nearly a dozen columns of smoke marked crashed aircraft. Over to the east, a large number of fighter aircraft were having their own private mêlée. The din of straining engines, the thump of cannon fire and the rat-a-tat-tat of machine gun fire accompanied their swoops and pirouettes in the sky.

Walter's eyes fixed on a long trail of thick black smoke that led to another falling, spinning aircraft.

There was no sign of a parachute as yet.

'Any tea left in the thermos, Sid?' he asked his colleague.

With that, their modest duty was done for the time being.

At Kent OC headquarters in Maidstone, Walter's report was analysed, then passed on to Anti-Aircraft Command. There it was cross-referenced with other observers tracking the passage of the raid.

This game of cat and mouse had unfolded ever since the formation crossed the coast at 4.47pm, as every turn in its route kept the British guessing about its real objectives. In many ways, the raid was being run like a naval convoy. The bombers were stewarded by their fighter escorts and, in turn, each unit peeled off to attack its designated target.

This raid's trajectory now threatened towns and airfields either side of the Thames Estuary. A warning was passed to Fighter Command and the Air Raid Patrol Office for North Kent, which would pass it down to local ARP stations. From Maidstone to Chatham, Gillingham and Sheerness, air raid sirens started to wail ahead of the expected path of the German bombers.

When the onslaught first began in July, these red alerts had been sent out several times a day, bringing daily life in factories, offices and homes to a halt. However, the disruption to the war economy had been so great, that the authorities adopted a far more dispassionate stance about the threat to civilian lives. By necessity, alerts were now only issued for major raids, whilst the myriad of small hit-and-run attacks sent by the Luftwaffe were mostly ignored… whatever the consequences.

However, this afternoon's large raid deserved every attention and the whole mechanism of Anti-Aircraft Command was swung into action yet again. A minute later, a young WAAF girl in the plotting room of 11 Group's command centre at RAF Uxbridge, received an instruction through her headset from her Controller in the gallery above.

She reached out across the large map table with her croupier's stick and pushed the wooden block representing the raid another eighteen inches to the north. It was one of fifteen such markers inching their way across the plotting table; attacks large and small, taking place right across Southern England.

The WAAF moved the block marked 90+ over the small village of Hollingbourne in Kent, then she stood back from the table and waited.

The last sixty seconds had been the most terrifying of Werner Hartmann's young life. Perched in the nose of the Heinkel, he had an almost uninterrupted view of the British fighters that hurtled head on into the Dorniers, just 500 metres in front of him. He had wished that he was absolutely anywhere else in the world, than here.

The flight cabin of a Dornier directly in front took the full force of a Hurricane's machine gun volley, virtually disintegrating into a cloud of debris… that hurtled back towards Hartmann's ashen face.

A ball of fire erupted from the stricken aircraft's left engine. The Dornier fell earthwards and a split second later, the same British fighter tried to ram their Heinkel head on.

Muller had instinctively banked their plane steeply right, to avoid the deranged British pilot. Then they nearly collided with another of the Dorniers.

Hartmann's part in this five second drama had been to be hurled against the perspex. He stared at the other aircraft's twin tailplanes come within just a few metres of their right propeller, before Muller pulled them back out of harm's way. Time had ground terrifyingly slowly as Hartmann watched both near misses happen just in front of his face, powerless to do anything to protect himself.

It was obvious that two more of the Dorniers in front were in trouble and, trailing smoke, they dropped away.

One levelled out momentarily, shedding its cockpit canopy and three of its crew bailed out, their parachutes blossoming in the sky.

The other bomber rolled over into an inverted, vertical dive. Its crew were pinned into their seats by overwhelming g-forces, as it plummeted out of control.

'Too many Schnapps, Herr Major?' their belly gunner joked on the intercom.

He was completely unaware of how their wild acrobatics had narrowly averted disaster.

'Shut up Metzger, concentrate on the fighters.' Muller replied.

'Two on port beam!' shouted Willi Seiler, from his gun position halfway down the back of the Heinkel. The last syllable of his warning was drowned out by the stuttering rasp of his machine gun.

Hartmann pulled himself back onto the bomb aiming platform and looking up, saw another British fighter about to roll over into an attack.

This galvanized him into action, cocking the machine gun with his left hand and with his right hand, he heaved the circular gun mount into position. He grabbed the pistol grip and opened fire, emptying the 50 round ammunition drum in two and a half seconds, filling the cockpit with acrid gun-smoke. He had no idea if it had done any good as the Hurricane flashed past, but it certainly made him feel a lot better.

Just as quickly as it started, the British fighter attack petered out.

'Go get 'em boys!' Seiler shouted jubilantly.

With a considerably better view than any of the other crew members, he could see that twenty Messerschmitts flying sun-up had pounced on the British fighters.

British hunters had become the hunted.

The bomber group ploughed ahead, leaving a frenzied, twisting dogfight in its wake. The remainder of the Messerschmitts, thirty or so, maintained their watchful position flying above, cruising at the same speed to conserve their fuel. Each fighter pilot was now watching his gauges closely, knowing that once drawn into a dogfight, fuel consumption would double. Already 150 kilometres from base, they had a maximum of five minutes at full combat speed before they had to break off and head for France.

'Willi, count up… how many have we lost?' Muller called over the intercom.

From his glass cupola, Seiler had a perfect 360 degree view around the Heinkel.

He was the eyes of the pilot, looking above and behind.

'DJ has gone down Herr Major, I saw it on fire. GJ is smoking from its port engine. I can see most of the others, let me check…'

'What about the 11th and 12th staffel?' asked Muller.

'I think they are two down, I can't really see,' Seiler replied. 'Wait… GJ is falling behind, they can't keep up. They're dropping back.'

Muller thought for a moment and gave him a new instruction.

As not only observer and machine gunner, Seiler also controlled the aircraft's main radio equipment.

'Tell Kalb to jettison his bombs and head for France. Tell the rest to close up tight behind us,' Muller ordered calmly.

With no time to think about the fate of their comrades, by necessity, his mind was fully focussed on the mission objective.

Gunter Kalb, the pilot of Heinkel call-sign V4+GJ, didn't actually need Muller's approval. He had already pulled the emergency release to drop his bomb load. Falling further and further behind the main raid, his plane banked steeply and headed south, while trailing smoke from both engines. As the stricken aircraft fled the battle with two of its crew seriously wounded, its discarded bombs were strewn across the countryside below. The resulting explosions pock-marked several fields; killing two cows, demolishing a four hundred year old cottage and leaving three craters in the A20 Ashford to Maidstone road.

Alone over hostile territory with damaged engines and losing height, the chances of a safe return were dwindling rapidly. Kalb's real decision was whether to even try to return to home, or instead, make a forced landing here in Kent. He could save their lives, at the cost of captivity in a British prison camp. It was for this reason that the south coast of England had become the focal point for so many German plane crashes, and airmen taking to their parachutes. Unlike the frontline of a land battle that can be crossed in a few seconds, the English Channel was a huge barrier. At least twenty five and often up to seventy miles of open sea, there was little chance of survival for an airman in the water.

Kalb looked at his altimeter and how much it had already dropped.

At this speed it would take fifteen minutes to reach the coast, the same again to France, providing his airspeed didn't fall any further.

Wrestling with increasingly sluggish flight controls, he looked anxiously at the engine temperature gauges on the overhead panel. Both 1100 horsepower Junkers Jumo powerplants were running hot, burning oil, which suggested their cooling systems had suffered damage. If either engine fully overheated and seized up, it would be impossible to keep his Heinkel in the air for long.

He throttled back a fraction, to try and reduce the engine strain.

The altimeter accelerated its fall and he was forced to throttle up immediately. This brief experiment had lost 200 metres of altitude in just five seconds… precious height that he could not regain.

With airspeed still falling towards stalling point, Kalb was struggling to maintain the aircraft's forward momentum.

Instinctively, he dropped the aircraft's nose to gain speed.

More height lost.

He glanced down at his navigator, who lay barely conscious on the blood-covered cabin floor.

Kalb knew he had to make a decision and quickly.

The sea not only kept the Wehrmacht out of England, it also trapped many Luftwaffe airmen inside it too.

Albert Culpepper was dozing in one of the deck chairs that Ken had brought out to the park earlier, when his sister gently shook his arm to waken him.

'Bertie, hadn't you better be going soon?' she reminded him.

Half-awake, he sat up, gathered his senses and checked his wristwatch.

'Oh blimey, it's nearly 5 already, you're right. I'm supposed to be on guard duty at 7,' he exclaimed. 'I had better get home and change into my uniform.'

'But you've got time for a cuppa before you go?' Patricia asked. 'Mind you, Ted's been gone ages. I don't know what he's doing in there?'

'If he's got the brew ready… I reckon I have time,' Albert replied. 'But I need to be off fairly sharpish, Patsy.'

He looked at Ginny, Betty and Ken as they lay out on picnic rugs a few yards away. They were basking in the late afternoon sunshine and he considered how idyllic a scene it presented. Albert was so proud of his nieces and, never having had children of his own, they had always been the centre of his world.

It seemed like only yesterday when they were born and he and Lillian had showered them with love, hoping that they too would be blessed. It wasn't to be, but it hadn't mattered that much in the end.

Of course, he would never get over Lillian's passing, but they had enjoyed a wonderful life together nonetheless. He had his Patsy, her children and his good friend Ted to give meaning to his days.

However, Albert knew this war was like no other before.

It was getting closer by the day, by the hour even and he worried about what was in store for the people he loved.

The German bombers were seven miles short of the Medway Estuary, when the remaining staffel in front took a sudden turn to the west.

Muller watched closely, as the Dorniers continued turning away to line up on RAF Detling, then he took his turn to steer the bomber group westwards. He was now in the vanguard, leading his Heinkels with twenty Dorniers from KG76 following closely behind. The afternoon sun was sinking lower in the sky and as they flew towards it, Bauer was nervously busy with his map and quadrant.

Muller looked to him for instruction.

'Where are we heading Kristian? Give me a bearing…'

Bauer was in a panic.

As a qualified pilot he should have been quick with his response, but on operations so far he had only ever followed, never led. His navigation skills were unpractised.

'A minute please, Herr Major… I need to calculate our position… after the turn...' he replied hesitantly.

'Bauer, give me a fucking landmark.' Muller barked. 'We are covering six kilometres a minute. I need a bearing and I need it NOW.'

'I'm sorry… please give me a moment… Herr Major…' Bauer replied feebly.

Werner Hartmann lay at the front of the flight cabin, listening to their tense exchange of words. He flipped open the bombsite cover in front of him and checked the target compass. Having flown this route many times already, he had understood the mission briefing at Rosières perfectly.

He turned his head towards Muller.

'Head 10 degrees to starboard Herr Major,' he shouted above the roar of the slipstream. 'This will take us to Sidcup. As we get closer, we'll be able to pick up the railway lines to London… they will guide us in.'

Without even a terse word of thanks, Muller banked the aircraft slightly right onto the new heading.

The latest twist to this raid's true intentions was revealed.

Whilst Muller was by common measure a decent man, he was above all else, a senior Luftwaffe officer and a dedicated instrument of the state. In this respect, he was a typical product of this era in Germany; cultured, well-educated and amiable on one hand, but on the other, utterly ruthless in the pursuit of his goals. Ever since he stood in the Nuremburg arena, alongside 40,000 fellow teenagers hailing the Führer, he had belonged to the man that would lead them to glory.

Muller stared ahead coldly.

At that moment of intense pressure, he had become as much as a machine as the Heinkel 111 bomber in which he sat. He bore the same dispassionate gaze as one day in 1934, when he denounced his father for helping a Jew escape the murderous intentions of a Nazi street gang.

Only a few miles away, Sidney and Walter stood in their little observation post on Detling Hill, looking aghast at the bomber formation as it traversed their horizon. They could see that a dozen aircraft had dropped out of the main group and were now heading directly towards them.

Their bombs doors were already gaping open.

'Oh Christ Sid, here we go again,' Walter said, as they ducked down behind the sandbag wall.

Sidney reached for the small field telephone beneath the plotting table. He picked up the handset and frantically wound the handle at the front, to charge the line to the airfield half a mile away.

After a few seconds, he hollered into the handset.

'This is the OC. AIR RAID! Take cover. Jerry's right on top of us. TAKE COVER!'

Meanwhile, Walter had raised a connection to Maidstone HQ on his speaker tube.

'Detling OC here. MAIN RAID NOW HEADING DUE WEST,' he shouted above the rising din. 'I repeat due WEST!'

The roar of aircraft engines overhead was joined by the rising wail of the airfield sirens. Both men shrank smaller and smaller in fear behind the parapet, sitting crouched, with their knees almost under their chins.

Walter and Sidney both had their eyes screwed tight shut.

'Bloody Hell....Walt... BLOODY HELL...' Sidney shouted.

Walter couldn't hear him over the ear-splitting roar of German aircraft passing overhead. The first bomb concussions almost shook the two men back up onto their feet.

Two minutes later at the 11 Group command bunker in Uxbridge, the wooden block identifying this raid was moved across the plotting table to Aylesford.

Today's Area Controller reconsidered his options.

His pilots had already flown two or three times each since dawn, breaking the previous daily record of eight hundred sorties.

At this late stage of the day, many of these fighters were now far outside the battle area. With home airfields denied to them by earlier bombing or scattered by the vagaries of pursuit, most aircraft had landed at other aerodromes that afternoon. He had just scrambled four fighter squadrons to counter other German attacks, so there was little left in reserve against the threat now posed by Muller's strike force. Big formations were easy to track, but this particular raid was repeatedly subdividing as it pushed further inland.

The end of the day was always the most challenging time. Losses could not be counted until the later in the evening and by late afternoon it was never clear what, or where, resources were left to counter the enemy.

The raid now heading towards the south of London, placed Kenley, Biggin Hill and Croydon aerodromes under threat, but the Vickers aircraft factory at Brooklands was a possible target too. The whole area offered a myriad of targets and it was impossible to predict where the Germans were heading. Then the Area Controller heard that Hawkinge, Lympne and Detling aerodromes had been attacked. Looking at the plotting table, he decided that he would have to redeploy forces already sent elsewhere.

As the minutes ticked by, the plotting table was covered by more and more markers, as different raids became ever more dispersed across Southern England.

There was no telling what surprise might come next.

Certainly, Major Muller and his comrades were not expecting what happened one minute after their turn over Detling.

As they flew over the village of Meopham, the Dorniers at the back broke away to head for RAF Biggin Hill just as their mission orders dictated.

All thirty of the remaining Messerschmitt fighters went with them too.

Willi Seiler in the top gun position saw them depart, leaving the Heinkels to fly on alone.

'Herr Major, the fighters have gone. They're heading off to the south west. We don't have any cover,' he reported anxiously.

'What did you say Seiler?' Muller replied, his tone suddenly grave.

'All the fighters have left us sir. We don't have any escorts!'

The unease in his voice was plain to hear.

It was an emotion shared by the crews of the other Heinkels, as they too watched the departure of their fighter cover. Equally, the Messerschmitts pilots were just as surprised to see Muller's bombers continue on towards London without them. Within thirty seconds, the distance between the two groups had opened irretrievably wide before anyone really understood what had occurred.

'It's true Herr Major, they've all gone. They're escorting the Dorniers to their target,' Werner Hartmann confirmed, as he watched the other bombers and Messerschmitts diminish from sight. Despite the noise of their engines and the roar of the slipstream, there was a tense silence on the intercom at that moment.

It was just like the silence of their long range radio receiver; something that Willi Seiler had failed to notice ever since they had departed the French coast.

That said, none of the other aircraft of KG1 had heard the urgent coded signal sent to them either. It had been drowned out by atmospheric interference, caused by high air humidity and mist over the English Channel that hot afternoon.

Ever since Stabsfeldwebel Freund received that urgent telephone call and ran into the radio office at Rosières, the 3rd Gruppe communications officer had repeatedly tried in vain to make contact with Muller's raiding force. If the transmission had been successful, Muller would have learnt that his mission had been cancelled, due to a lack of available fighters to escort them to the target. Generalmajor Angerstein's revised instruction had been to join the attack on Biggin Hill, then share the fighter cover back to France. Whilst no-one in the air over Kent knew about this dramatic change of plan, it was plainly obvious that something was now badly amiss.

As the bombers continued towards London, the crew of V4+AJ waited for a decision from their commander. With every passing second, the distance between them and the fighters grew ever greater.

Muller's voice boomed over the intercom.

'All crew…tell me if you can see *any* other aircraft within ten kilometres. Can you see any English?'

Back in the waist gun position, Hans Lehmann scanned the sky.

So did Wilhelm Seiler above, Gerhard Metzger below, Werner Hartmann and Kristian Bauer up front. They probably all wished they had something to report, but at that moment… the sky was clear of danger.

Their brief replies, all in the negative, made the consequence inevitable.

'In that case, we carry on,' Muller informed them bluntly. Calling out to Seiler, he continued. 'Tell the other aircraft that we will complete our mission as directed.'

Muller returned his gaze to the horizon and each of the six men on-board contemplated his own future.

Glad for something to do to break the tension, Willi Seiler ducked down to the radio sets alongside his seat and hailed the crews of the other bombers.

The news he gave them was not what they wanted to hear.

Many of them privately concluded that today's raid was rapidly becoming a *Himmelsfahrtskommando...* a mission straight to heaven.

Chapter 20

The big guns that Betty Vigar had watched being towed down Sidcup High Street yesterday morning, were now positioned in open farmland a mile to the east of Craywood House.

Captain Patrick Cardington of the 1st Anti-Aircraft Division surveyed his half-battery of four Vickers Armstrong 3.7inch heavy guns, and was finally happy that all was in order. Although his men had moaned as they toiled in the summer heat, he had driven them hard to ready the battery for action within just thirty hours of arriving here.

Cardington certainly had his work cut out for him, as his unit had only been formed three weeks ago. Fifty of his men were little more than raw recruits, just out of basic training. They were still getting used to being in the army, let alone the complexities of gun laying and target prediction required of a modern anti-aircraft battery. Fortunately, he had twenty five *Terriers;* older, more experienced men like him from its original Territorial Army formation. Some even carried medal ribbons from the last war. Cardington had built around this cadre of experienced gunners, as young and old worked together to bring the unit up to scratch.

Production of the 3.7 had begun in 1938 and two years later, it was fast becoming the backbone of Britain's anti-aircraft defences. Yet, with thousands of artillery pieces abandoned during the defeat in France, today there were only 650 of the modern 3.7's left to share around. Nevertheless, with obsolete 3 inch and 4.5 inch guns loaned by the Navy, AA Command had managed to muster 1750 heavy ack-ack guns to defend Britain.

This number was completely inadequate to protect the whole country, so they had to be positioned on a priority basis. The South East had the greatest allocation, given the importance of defending the capital and its industry. It was, by no means, an ideal situation, but the best that could be managed for the moment.

Recent raids had prompted a rethink about where to position these precious weapons. The traditional eight gun battery was divided so that more, smaller units, could be spread further. Each gun could fire ten 28lb high explosive shells a minute, to as high as 25,000ft, so a group of four weapons like Cardington's could still deliver a devastating barrage against enemy aircraft. Reliant on traditional manual fuse setting and loading, even a small battery like this needed a contingent of eighty men, split into three watches, to function effectively over any twenty four hour period.

Plans were already afoot to automate the gun's action, to double its rate of fire and dramatically reduce its manpower requirement. The key to this would be an automatic shell loading and fuse setting device, the design of which had been entrusted to a civilian engineering company called Molins. This company specialised in producing high speed cigarette manufacturing machinery, ideal experience on which to draw for the design of a quick firing gun mechanism. By total coincidence, Molin's research facility was based at Ruxley Corner near the huge Klinger Factory, just a few hundred yards away from where Cardington was now standing.

All in all, the large industrial estate at Foots Cray held a far greater importance to Britain's war effort than any local people could possible imagine. Five days previously, a senior civil servant in Whitehall had noticed the common address of these key facilities and, even more importantly, grasped that one was an Austrian-owned company. With great common sense and perhaps a healthy dash of paranoia, he deduced that the Nazis already knew all about what the Klinger factory produced. He placed an urgent recommendation for anti-aircraft protection and yesterday's arrival of the gun battery was the result.

Of course, Cardington had no idea what the Klinger or Molins factories actually made. He just assumed this area had to be important, to warrant the protection offered by his guns, one of Britain's most precious resources at that moment. He was far happier to be emplaced in countryside, compared to their previous position at Danson Park, surrounded by the modern housing estates of Welling and Bexleyheath.

The new position offered a far better field of fire with little housing on three sides, so there was less worry about falling shot when they next fired their guns in anger. Whilst his gunners may have preferred their previous site for its civic amenities, at least they could now see what they were aiming at and not break people's roof tiles with falling shrapnel. They had fired the first practice rounds at midday, a loud announcement of their arrival to the surrounding towns and villages. At least the shell bursts now showered their debris harmlessly over little more than fields for several miles around. The signals unit from Foots Cray Camp had just connected their telephones to the military circuit and as the time approached 5pm, Cardington was awaiting his first test call from the local AA command centre.

The telephone rang.

That was prompt, Cardington thought.

He picked up the receiver and responded with his unit identification.

It certainly was a quick call.

Within seconds, he turned on the spot and hollered at the top of his voice.

'Make ready for action... air raid approaching from the east!'

The men standing around the battery stared at him in confusion.

'Oh, for God's sake...' he muttered to himself.

This time, he remembered to take his silver whistle out of his top pocket and blew on it as hard as he could.

The signal galvanised everyone into action.

They ran here and there to their proper positions... the guns, the ammunition pens, the locator and target predictor.

Captain Cardington watched it all with a fair degree of anxiety.

Chapter 21

In the basement of Anti-Aircraft Command in Maidstone, a switchboard operator was busy phoning her raid alerts ahead towards London.

Now she waited impatiently for a connection to the Bexley, Sidcup and Foots Cray ARP.

In the sky high above her, Werner Hartmann studied the landscape of North Kent rolling out in front of him. Through the haze of grey smog on the horizon, he could just perceive the densely built-up heart of Britain's capital city ahead. As he looked right, he saw the town of Dartford and running through its centre, he identified the main railway line to London.

Referencing the map and photos he had taken from Bauer a minute before, Hartmann saw the A20 road from Maidstone on his left, passing through the village of Swanley. Then he spotted where it broadened into the new autobahn section, a few kilometres ahead. From this waymark, he calculated they were only four minutes from target and started the bombsight stopwatch in front of him. He turned to face Muller in the pilot's seat and signalled that all was well with their current course.

Flipping open the cover of the bombsight, he armed the bomb bay and selected a close salvo release. As lead bombardier, his job was to hit the target dead centre.

'Seiler… tell the other aircraft that we are commencing the bomb-run. Order them to close up tight behind us, we are going to hammer our target today!' Muller called out to the dorsal gunner.

He turned to Bauer next to him, with a look of dis-satisfaction.

'Keep your eyes on the sky. Make yourself useful,' he instructed.

The young pilot made the best of bad situation and tried to look as vigilant as possible. He was glad that he been relieved of the task of navigating for the raid. All in all, it had been a pretty bad day for his fledgling career. The sooner he put today's misfortunes behind him the better, as far as he was concerned.

Behind them in the main fuselage, the radio set crackled with replies from the other aircraft and Seiler reported that everyone understood Muller's instruction.

Bauer turned towards his commander, subconsciously seeking his approval.

Muller gave him a sharp nod and stared ahead.

In the distance he could see hundreds of fat, wallowing barrage balloons tethered above South London. Knowing these generally flew at heights of up to 1500 metres, Muller decided it was time to take the formation down to an altitude about 500 metres above them. It was a dangerous tactic to fly so low, but this was a key component in his recent successes and gave British ground defences far less time to target his aircraft.

This variation from Luftwaffe tactical doctrine had been Muller's private addendum to the official briefing at Rosières. The disadvantage of lower level flight was that if something did go wrong, a pilot had much less height, less airspace, in which to take evasive action or recover a damaged aircraft. However, low altitude attacks greatly improved the bombing accuracy of each mission. In Muller's opinion, this justified the higher risks, even if it raised much disquiet amongst the pilots of the 11th and 12th staffeln.

Muller thought about their target, London Bridge Station, the nexus of railway services from across South East London and most of North Kent. These key railway lines all converged onto a single viaduct, fifty metres wide and ran side by side for the last four kilometres toward the grand station. From the air, the viaduct cut through the confusing sprawl of London's suburbs like a huge arrow pointing towards their target. Just a cat's jump before this was a large public recreational park at Greenwich, bordering a large open heath. Altogether, these were obvious landmarks amongst the dense housing of the city.

Their first waymark was the A20 autobahn at Sidcup.

The reconnaissance photographs showed how it cut cleanly and obviously through the farmland and woods of Foots Cray and Sidcup, conveniently on a heading perfectly aligned to the beginning of the great railway viaduct. All they had to do was navigate to the Sidcup area and then this succession of waymarks would lead them to their target. Muller planned to follow the course of the viaduct right up to the targeted station, so that any bomb creep-back would hit the railway lines too.

This daring raid was a key starting point for the systematic paralysation of British railway connections with the southern coast. Stations at London's Victoria, Waterloo and Clapham Junction and further south, at Guildford, Canterbury and Ashford had all been moved to the top of Luftwaffe target lists in the last 24 hours. The British Army had been stripped of most of its motor transport during the Fall of France. German strategists had correctly guessed that the British were now precariously reliant on their railways, to move any large mass of troops against the coming invasion.

So the Luftwaffe had been told to sever these vital lifelines. Within days, the entire South Coast invasion front would be cut off from meaningful re-supply of men and military resources.

Today's raid would also demonstrate German hegemony over the capital city, for every Londoner, every news reporter, and the whole world to witness. Muller had the nerve for this mission and that was exactly why Generalmajor Angerstein had picked him to lead it. Lesser commanders would have abandoned the task, but Muller was determined to see it through, whatever the cost. His reputation as one of the brightest stars in the Luftwaffe's bomber arm was well-earned and his implicit pact with Germany's Führer offered a greater destiny too.

Now he could see the great capital city ahead, the heart of the British Empire. To Muller it was the centre of a tyranny that had obstructed Germany's true destiny for far too long.

He smiled at the prospect of what he and his men were about to do.

Captain Cardington stood in his command dugout to the right of the four gun emplacements. Next to his position was the huge sound locator, looking like four monstrous gramophone horns, used to listen to and pinpoint targets for the battery's gun-laying.

Its operators called out, to announce that they had a bearing on the sound of approaching aircraft engines. The instruction was quickly passed on to the other emplacements and the guns turned to face the approaching enemy. Cardington surveyed the horizon through his binoculars, until he saw the German bombers approaching through the heat haze. Their distinctive arrow-like profiles instantly identified them as Heinkel 111's. He looked around to the men on the optical rangefinder and saw that they had acquired the target as well.

Now, mathematics would take control.

The typical German raid flew at 16,000 feet at around 200 mph. The warhead of a 3.7's shell took ten seconds to reach this height, during which time the enemy aircraft would travel 900 yards. So the correct vector required aiming ahead to where the enemy aircraft was going to be, by the time the high explosive projectile arrived. Each projectile carried a time fuse and if set correctly, it would explode near the target showering red-hot metal splinters in a two hundred yard radius. The higher the target, the longer it would be in the field of fire, but the less accurate the barrage. If the target was lower, results would be more deadly, but offer less time to engage aircraft before they passed out of view.

Consequently, each gun could engage high flying raiders within a six mile perimeter. However, their great weight meant that they could not track fast-moving targets below 3000 feet and effective engagement radius would be no more than a mile. The men at the observation post would feed the height, bearing and speed data into the electro-mechanical target predicator. Then the calculated firing solution would be passed electrically by cables to a set of dials on each weapon. The gunners followed these dials to hand-crank the required elevation and traverse of the guns, but, in effect, the whole battery was remotely guided by the officer at the target predicator.

Each emplacement had two hundred shells ready for use. By each gun stood a line of loaders, each one ready for the exhausting task of feeding their weapon's ravenous appetite once it commenced firing. The gunners sat alongside each artillery piece and stared at the sky as the tension mounted, whilst each gun sergeant watched the battery commander and awaited his signal to open fire.

It suddenly struck Cardington how peaceful the countryside was at that moment. There was a hint of gentle birdsong on the wind, the caw of ill-tempered crows behind him in the woods.

All was tranquil in the intense heat of that afternoon.

The village of Foots Cray was less than a mile away and he wondered why he hadn't heard the wail of its air raid siren yet. This sense of peace was completely at odds with the tight knot that twisted in his stomach.

A bead of sweat ran down his forehead and into his right eye, blurring his vision. Then he noticed renewed activity at the target predictor as the men there set a new firing solution. In response, the gunners on all four weapons furiously cranked their handles to re-align their gun barrels. Peering through his binoculars again, he could see why... the German formation was rapidly dropping height.

At a rough guess, they were now at only 6,000 to 8,000 feet; less than five miles away and the opportunity to fire upon them was shrinking rapidly.

To complicate matters further, the enemy bombers were flying directly towards the battery and this made the engagement even harder. If the aircraft flew directly overhead, Cardington's gunners would have to raise their weapons' elevation to near vertical to follow them. They would waste vital seconds traversing 180 degrees, to track their targets back down as they escaped from view.

He made a quick mental calculation. The number of shells the battery had time to fire had more than halved already.

Cardington couldn't wait any longer.

He raised his right arm bolt upright.

He brought it down with a chop whilst blowing long and hard on his whistle, his personal signal to open fire.

For the second time in five minutes, Werner Hartmann had an uninterrupted view of impending disaster. At the foot of a wooded hill ahead, he saw a sudden burst of white smoke, as a British artillery position commenced firing.

He turned around towards Muller and Bauer and screamed one word above the roar of the engines.

'FLAK!'

Turning back, he looked at the bombsight stopwatch.

It had not even marked a full minute since they commenced the bomb-run. The second hand moved on inexorably... 51...52...53...54...55...

All hell broke loose.

Raymond was gently dozing on a wooden sun lounger on the patio. Maude had collected the crockery from their afternoon tea onto a tray, when the loudest commotion she'd ever heard assaulted her ears. She turned towards the source of the booming explosions on the other side of the hill. Raymond awoke, utterly bewildered, sat up and joined her gaze towards the dreadful noise.

The crashing bangs continued, multiplied, became utterly deafening and then, he caught sight of explosions high in the sky above Cray Wood.

A split second later, a swarm of huge German aircraft roared into a view over the hilltop, pursued and tormented by a myriad of stinging, black smoke bursts. One aircraft was already veering off to the north, smoke spewing from its left engine. It seemed to scream in agony, as a high pitched wail signalled its rapid descent towards Foots Cray village.

Dumbfounded by the spectacle, Raymond rose to his feet, his waking mind barely able to comprehend what was happening around him. More aircraft roared overhead, veering crazily, disorganised, in ragged formation as anti-aircraft fire continued to explode around them.

Another was struck, with a tremendous explosion.

It banked sharply to the right, rolled over on its back as flames erupted along its fuselage and fell into a steep dive towards St Paul's Cray.

It was certainly doomed to crash.

Maude stood speechless with the tea tray still in her hands, as she watched the first stricken plane plunge towards

Foots Cray. It levelled out and disappeared from sight behind the skyline, leaving a trail of thick, black oily smoke in its wake. Then she heard a strident clattering noise around her.

She looked down to see a piece of twisted, smouldering metal two inches long lying on the flagstones, just a foot away. More came, as piece after piece of jagged metal fragments fell around her.

'Get inside Aunt,' Raymond shouted, as he launched himself like a rugby player into a tackle.

Taking hold of her mid-rift, they plunged through the open French Doors into the lounge.

The tray and crockery crashed onto the stone steps, accompanied by the sound of shattering glass, as the windows were rent by falling shrapnel.

Edward Vigar had put on his overalls ready for his ARP meeting. He finished tying his bootlaces, picked up his satchel, his steel helmet and walked out of the bathroom as the kettle whistled in the kitchen.

Suddenly, the once-familiar sound of heavy gunfire and exploding shells met his ears. Rushing straight through the dining room and out into the garden, he looked towards Sidcup.

A large aircraft was approaching, barely a thousand feet above the ground.

Looking right, he saw the rest of the formation; big fat Heinkels, flying over the town about a mile away, heading towards London. He ran down the garden, past the air raid shelter and tin shed, through the gate, towards his family out in the park.

Ginny and Patricia stood transfixed by the sight of the stricken German aircraft. Half a dozen of the children also stood in awe, about fifty yards away on the grass near the railway line.

Ken had taken hold of Betty and was pushing her backwards towards where Edward stood.

'GET DOWN EVERYONE!' Edward roared.

Albert grabbed Patricia and forced her to the ground underneath him, in a vain effort to shield her from the approaching aircraft.

The Heinkel was now less than two hundred yards away, trailing thick smoke from its right-hand engine.

With absolute horror, Edward saw its belly doors spring open and he glimpsed the cruel, dark core of the aircraft.

Black cylinders tumbled out as it roared overhead.

The bombs whistled over them in a blur and seconds later, Hazelmead Road was rocked by multiple, ear-splitting, gut-wrenching explosions. Then a shower of debris rained down upon the houses and gardens of Lamorbey.

Edward found himself sitting upright on the grass, his ears ringing painfully from the sharp report of the bomb detonations.

He looked through the rising dust cloud and saw that free of its heavy payload, the aircraft was regaining height. The glass canopy of the flight cabin was shattered and one of its large landing wheels hung limply from underneath the burning engine. He watched with grim fascination while the Heinkel bucked and yawed, as its pilot fought to keep control. Behind it, a thick trail of smoke curved across the sky as the aircraft headed east, then slipped from sight below the rooftops.

Edward crawled over to where Patricia and the others lay in the grass.

'She's alright Ted, she's alright,' Albert reassured him.

Patricia sat up, bewildered, deafened by the bomb blasts and they looked to their daughters. Ken had protected Betty too and they were both sitting up now.

Ginny was standing about twenty yards away to their right, staring into space.

The grass around her was strewn with broken bricks.

'Oh my good God, no….' Edward cried out.

He realised the immensity of what had just happened and worse still, what lay just yards in front of his eldest daughter.

He ran over to Ginny and grabbed her by the shoulders to drag her away.

The small body of a young boy lay on the grass, it was little Jimmy, today's Man of the Match.

His head had been pulverised by a lump of flying debris.

'Virginia. Look at me… LOOK AT ME!' he shouted to his daughter.

Ginny's eyes were wide with shock.

Her face was ghostly white.

Looking back at her father, she was a scared little girl again. Then her face filled with rage, she looked up at the sky and screamed out loud.

'You bloody, bloody, bastards. I bloody hate you! Why have you done this? What have we *ever* done to you?'

She began to shake, as an eruption of emotion took hold.

Holding her very tightly, Edward brought her back to her mother, her sister, her uncle.

'Take her inside Pat, take them both inside,' he instructed.

Patricia didn't say a word.

With tears welling in her eyes, she looked towards the little boy's body on the grass. The three women shuffled back up the garden to the house, while the kettle whistled merrily.

Edward realised that Ken was trembling too.

The colour had drained from his face, not so distant memories suddenly resurgent.

'Come on son… we have to do this,' said Edward.

He picked up one of the sunbather's blankets and the two of them walked towards Jimmy's body. Behind them they could hear Albert talking to the other children. They gabbled back in their excitement, uncomprehending of what had just happened.

Then came a woman's voice, rent with fear.

An inevitable, high-pitched scream of raw, utterly irreconcilable anguish followed a second later.

At the gun battery, the men were cheering. The pungent smell of burnt cordite hung on the air and empty shells cases in their hundreds lay strewn about, many still smoking and crackling from their brief, violent time in the gun breeches.

Captain Cardington was pleased with the performance of his men. They had been operational for barely an hour and when thrust into action; they had bagged at least one German bomber and badly damaged a number more. The guns now pointed towards Cray Wood and high above it, black smoke from the last shell bursts was dissipating slowly.

Not bad for a bunch of raw recruits, he thought proudly, while he stared at the drifting smoke.

As the sound of the bomber engines diminished, he heard a number of dull, thumping booms in the distance. He wondered who might be on the receiving end of their explosive payloads.

Bizarrely, he felt his gaze suddenly drawn to the woodland.

It was certainly very old and one tree in particular caught his attention. It was different from the others; it had an immensely wide trunk and thick weary branches that grasped at the sky. Positioned at the centre of a slight clearing on the hilltop, it was surrounded by younger, more naturally formed trees that appeared to shrink back from their brooding, stronger master.

Cardington wondered how many years had passed since this lord of the forest was first a sapling, what other events it had witnessed as the ages passed by. That thought reminded him of a picture he had once seen in a history book, a Victorian illustration of the druids of Ancient Britain gathered in worship around their sacred oak.

He smiled at the comparison.

He considered those mystical old men invoking the tree spirit's power to protect them from a foreign invader, much like he and his men revered their Vickers Armstrong 3.7in gun today.

'No 2 Gun were cracking good shots, weren't they sir?' interrupted Lieutenant Dellow, the young predictor officer now stood next to him. 'They had a fantastic bead on the formation leader… perfectly straddled it with shot, absolutely a whizzbang.'

He spoke as if describing a grouse caught by the crossfire of shotguns.

'Yes they certainly did and...' Cardington began to answer. His reply was cut short by the new sound of a rapidly approaching aircraft.

A German bomber appeared over the crest of Cray Wood, the full volume of its plight suddenly, deafeningly, upon them. Its cockpit canopy was smashed to pieces, its left propeller wind-milling slowly, its wings and fuselage riddled with shrapnel damage. The crippled aircraft cleared the hilltop by barely a hundred feet.

The two British officers instinctively ducked, as they followed the course of the plane overhead.

Turning to follow it, Cardington briefly glimpsed a flailing object plummet from the sky. He watched the Heinkel struggle on for perhaps a thousand yards, before it smashed into open farmland and exploded in a gigantic, thunderous fireball of exploding fuel.

'I say, Sir! That's Number Two for our score sheet today,' Dellow shouted above the din, like an excited schoolboy.

Cardington said nothing.

He was looking at a crumpled figure lying on the grass between the gun emplacements.

It was a German airman, his body perfectly still, horribly twisted and broken. A dozen yards of white silk trailed from his open parachute pack and stirred pathetically in the breeze.

Chapter 22

With their ears still ringing from gunfire, the men of the anti-aircraft battery had much to celebrate as they talked, or rather, shouted excitedly to one another in the aftermath of battle. After the exertions of the last five minutes, the look of relief upon their faces was plain to see.

At No2 Gun, Gunner George Williamson was being singled out for particular praise by his sergeant. He was a bit embarrassed by all this attention, as after all, he was only one of the men that served the gun. He just cranked the gun elevation handle, according to what the dial driven by the target predictor told him to do. Nonetheless, the first shells from his gun had exploded right in front of the lead German bomber, whilst the other gun crews had placed their first shots at least five hundred feet too high to begin with. The raiders had almost passed overhead before the other gunners got the correct measure, to add their own fury to the high explosive storm above.

'That was good shooting,' said Sergeant Jock Hardie. 'As my old Da would say… *yer gae 'em a skelpit lug wi'ya foost poonch.*' His broad smile sat widely beneath his flattened, oft-broken nose. 'The drinks are on me laddies,' he declared.

Williamson glanced at his friend, Gunner Percy Bevin, sitting at the gun traversing control. He shrugged his shoulders and Bevin reciprocated his look of bafflement at their sergeant's comments. More to the point, they both knew that just before their gun fired the first round of the engagement, a strange sensation had filled their hands and arms.

The elevation and traverse handles had moved entirely of their own accord.

Both men had felt their tingling hands gripped onto the control handles by an irresistible force, powerless to stop the weapon from following its own whim. After the first five shells were fired… the tingling stopped and the hand cranks responded normally again.

A few yards away, Sergeant Hardie was basking in the praise given by their battery commander.

Gunners Williamson and Bevin had their own conversation too.

'Bugger knows what was going on there Perce?' said Williamson.

'Spooky if you ask me George,' Bevin replied. 'the effin' handle had a mind of its own… I couldn't let the bugger go.'

Williamson considered the peculiar event for a moment.

'I reckon the boffins have *electricated the mechanicals…* trying to do us out of a job,' he ventured. 'A sparks I know told me that can happen with 'lectric shocks.'

'But if Old Jock wants to buy us a pint, I ain't worried.' Bevin interrupted.

They burst out laughing.

Neither was going to complain about being declared heroes for the day. It hardly mattered what strange force had guided their hands so successfully at the gun controls.

They had fought the invader and fulfilled their duty.

Captain Cardington had given No2 gun crew permission to view the crash site, an honour of sorts, whilst the rest of the battery gunners set to the usual post-engagement tasks.

The dead German airman's body was covered with a tarpaulin.

As the clangs of empty shell cases being piled together filled the air, the two gunners concluded their pact.

'Well *Mum's The Word* then!' Williamson concluded. 'We'd better get a move on, before all the good stuff goes.'

They set off towards the burning wreckage of the bomber, with souvenir hunting in mind. As they walked down the field, Bevin felt the strangest sensation of scrutiny and turned around, expecting to see one of his comrades seeking his attention. Instead, everyone seemed thoroughly preoccupied with their tasks at the battery and he looked up to the hilltop.

He studied the treeline…. one particularly large, old tree caught his attention. Bevin's hands tingled for a moment and he shivered with an unexpected, brief sensation of intense cold.

He turned again and ran after his friend.

There was little merriment at Hazelmead Road. A good fifteen minutes had passed after the attack before people felt safe enough to venture out of their houses. They found that their neat middle-class neighbourhood had been transformed into a total shambles within just a few, short, violent seconds.

Towards the bottom of the road, two houses had been completely demolished by explosions in the street. Fortunately, most of the other bomb impacts had been in the gardens of Lamorbey House, on the northern side of the road and did nothing more than ruin lawns and mutilate ornamental trees. Nonetheless, for five hundred yards, Hazelmead Road was strewn with broken roof slates, house bricks and other debris, spread far and wide by the bomb-blasts.

There were shattered windows everywhere.

Many of the picket fences lining the front gardens had been swept up and dumped in great heaps here and there, like a monstrous game of Pick-Up-Sticks. Yet, by and large, most of the neighbourhood had escaped serious damage.

A crowd of people had gathered outside the pathetic heap of rubble that was previously Mrs Jones' house.

Fortunately, the house next door had been unoccupied, as Mrs Wilberforce had taken her children down to Devon to stay with her aunt, while her husband was somewhere in East Africa with the army. Two houses opposite were blown out at the front, with their main bedroom's flowery wallpaper now fully on show to the world. The two neighbouring properties had been almost completely stripped of their roofs.

There were broken slates and glass scattered all around.

However, no-one knew where Mrs Jones was and they didn't know what to do until Albert, Edward and other members of the Air Raid Patrol arrived on the scene. Their training quickly came into play as they formed a rescue squad to venture into the rubble.

'Will everyone please be quiet?' Edward commanded. 'We need to listen.'

The crowd quickly hushed as Edward and Albert ventured gingerly across the mound of rubble, whilst calling out for Mrs Jones. Although she was by reputation a rather large woman, amidst of tons of piled up bricks and timber, she was the proverbial needle in the haystack now. Fifteen minutes passed by and many onlookers had lost interest and wandered home to tidy up the damage to their own houses, when one of the other wardens, old Mr Althropp, shouted for attention.

'I'SE FOUND 'ER.... SHE'S OOP THE BACK!' he hollered.

Edward and Albert clambered and slipped across the rubble to where the kitchen once stood. The side wall was still standing about eight foot high, topped by a large section of the collapsed roof, surrounded by a mound of broken brickwork. Mr Althropp was pointing towards a tiny mesh-covered pantry window, about a foot square.

They saw a frightened face staring back out at them.

'Mrs Jones, it's Edward Vigar, Chief Warden... are you alright?'

'No I'm not! I'm swuck in the larder an I'b lost me teef,' she replied and promptly burst into tears, relieved that her claustrophobic ordeal was nearly over.

The three men looked at each other and smirked.

'Don't you worry now Mrs Jones... we'll get you out in no time,' Albert piped up.

They set to work and after a few minutes shifting bricks and timbers, a dishevelled and bruised Mrs Jones was helped into the sunlight. One hand covered her mouth, for the sake of her pride. There was a cheer from the remaining bystanders. The Johnsons from next door took her in for consolation and a cup of tea with a shot of navy rum, saved especially for emergencies.

The Sidcup Air Raid Patrol took stock of the situation.

'We need to check for duds Ted. We should get people out of the way until we know it's safe,' Albert ventured.

Old men they were, but their 1914-18 sense of purpose had resurfaced. For the next few hours at least, they were in charge.

'Where the Hell's Ernie?' Edward asked, to no-one in particular.

'Problee lurk'ing round somewherez...' Mr Althropp suggested, with more insight that anyone could appreciate.

He sucked his teeth loudly.

'I'll go and look-see. I am too bloody old for all this foolery 'ere,' he concluded. He walked off towards the ARP office in search of their missing comrade.

Albert and Edward walked onto the street and looked it up and down.

There was shattered glass and ripped curtains everywhere, the road was covered with broken bricks and torn-up fence sticks. Looking up towards the cinema, there was a second, twenty foot wide crater slap bang in the middle of the road. To its right, part of the nave at St Mildred's had collapsed from bomb blast.

People milled about in and out of their houses, standing in their front gardens, chatting nervously, somewhat lost for any real purpose. The war had definitely come to Sidcup and the relief on their faces, that they were still alright, was plainly obvious.

'We had better find the bomb craters... make sure they're all accounted for. It was a Heinkel wasn't it Ted?' Albert asked.

'Yes it was. The damage isn't widespread enough for 100 pounders; they carry thirty or so of those don't they? I reckon it dropped the bigguns...' Edward replied, referring to the latest guidance on enemy munitions.

He thought for a moment, before concluding.

'The 500 pounders... there should be no more than... eight?'

Albert shook his head, as he tried to process the shock of it all.

'Just our luck he chucked them out here, what happened to it?' he asked. 'I couldn't see anything from where I was.'

'I saw it heading back that way, but it was flying low and on fire,' Edward explained. 'I don't suppose it could have made it that far.'

He pointed first towards Eltham, then around, towards Sidcup High Street on the hill above them.

There was a screech of bicycle brakes behind them. They looked round to see that Roger Deacon had arrived, out of breath from pedalling so hard. He had the look of youthful excitement writ large across his face, understandably so, as this was the biggest event in his short life.

'Gosh this is a right mess Mr Vigar… what happened? Was it *Stookers*? What were they after?' he gabbled on, with a barrage of questions. 'I bet it was the railway line wasn't it? I mean… that's really important isn't it? Has anyone been killed? Surely there must be someone dead? '

'It was a big Heinkel, Roger… it was in trouble and jettisoned its bombs, that's all,' said Edward, avoiding any mention of the one certain casualty. 'Now will you calm down please…we have work to do.'

'Yes, of course Mr Vigar. What shall I do, does anyone need rescuing?'

He looked disappointed that there hadn't been any Stuka dive bombers, the most famous of Nazi warplanes.

'We need to set up a cordon first. Get everyone out of their houses and out the way, that's best, until we've checked the gas and water mains. Can you get all the wardens here first Roger?'

The young man made to cycle off, but Edward grabbed him by the arm to ask a final question.

'Have you seen Mr Harrop anywhere?' he asked.

'Oh, he was in the office about an hour ago… he sent me home… for my dinner.' Roger answered quickly.

'Well, go down there and see if you can find him. We need him here, Mr Althropp has gone ahead,' Edward instructed.

Without further hesitation, Roger pedalled down the street, weaving crazily around all the debris.

'Would you mind helping out here for a bit please Bert?' Edward asked. He was mindful that his friend was meant to be on Home Guard duty in Eltham soon.

'I can stay for a while, but I should head off home soon, it's nearly six.' Albert paused, then referring to his Austin 7,

215

continued, 'I had better see what state Bessy is in, I suppose?'

'Can you see how Pat and the girls are for me? Tell them I'll come back as soon as I can,' Edward asked.

Albert nodded in agreement, turned and walked briskly back to the Vigar house, stepping over or around whatever littered his way.

As he watched him go, Edward's thoughts turned to his other friend.

Where's Ernie? I need as much help as I can get.

He looked around and considered a checklist of actions to secure the area.

Edward felt under pressure. Not just because of his job in all this, but also because this was about all his community, his neighbours, his friends, his family.

In sum; absolutely everything and everyone that he held dear.

He spotted their local bobby, Sergeant Bilsborough, picking his way past the bomb crater in front of the cinema. Edward realised that he should confer with him about the situation and waved his arms to get his attention.

The veteran policeman acknowledged the signal and began to walk towards him.

Archibald Sidney Althropp, simply *Old Sid* to his friends, had turned the corner into the church schoolyard.

He heard Ernest Harrop's muffled voice, shouting inside the ARP office.

The sandbag wall had collapsed in a heap across the office doorway and evidently he was trapped. Sid walked round to the other side of the building and looked in through the broken window. He saw his fellow warden looking flustered at the pile of sand bags that had spilled into the doorway, blocking his exit.

216

'Ernieboy… oze 'ere,' he called out, as he rapped on the broken window frame. 'Now don't you panic boy.''

Inside, Ernest looked completely bemused. After a moment, he realised where the voice was coming from and looked around.

'Whyz don't you joos get owt this way, you silly boogger?' Sid suggested.

Ernest came to the window.

'I didn't think of that,' he replied, rather shamefaced.

They knocked out the broken glass, so that he could safely clamber outside.

Ernest's terrible weekend showed no sign of abating.

He had been fast asleep when the bombs dropped and was scared out of his wits in those moments, when he awoke to the sound of Hell and Damnation itself.

Thrown onto the floor by the bomb percussion, he had huddled under the desk knowing exactly why he deserved such persecution. He had prayed to God for forgiveness and absolutely promised to mend his ways.

Ernest had vowed that, henceforth, he would be a good person in return for at least a brief continuance of his miserable existence. A moonlit siren, a violent thuggee's attack, Nazi bombs falling like rain, none of these belonged in Ernest Harrop's humdrum little life. He wished it was tomorrow morning already, so that he could go about opening shop with its dreary, but safe routine. However, when he stepped out into the yard and caught sight of the neighbourhood and its dishevelled state, all thought of his worries vanished.

The deep bomb crater in the road, only a few yards from where he had been snoozing demonstrated he was graced with some good luck after all.

'Oh my God Sid, how bad is it?' he asked.

'Oh bad enough Ernie-boy. Therez 'ouses blown clean up skyward and a fair clutch has haft to come down yet, I'll be sure,' replied Sid. 'It was a 'hole murder of Nazis chucking awt bombs… jus'like seed sown to tillage.'

Old Sid had got rolling with his tale and chattered on.

'Not that I sawz it meself… me and Missus Althropp was making ourz tea and didn't know bugger all abow't, until 'em bombs started thun'dring. I'se went straight under kitch'n table with my Maisie… I dunno whaz good that'n haz dun uz tho'?'

Ernest frowned.

He thought to himself how much Old Sid overplayed his Old Kentish accent at times.

Sid Althropp certainly had seen a lot of things in his seventy five years. As he loved saying, *he cus 'member whatr here'bouts… before t'even waz a Sidcup.*

His heart belonged to Lamorbey as his family had lived there for generations. His father had been one of this area's last tenant farmers, long before it was all sold up for redevelopment. While Sid was sad to see everyone's homes looking so battered, in his heart he would have preferred it if all this had remained as the fields, hazel coppices and orchards of his childhood.

Only seven years before, this place had still been simple countryside. Then the estate developers arrived and started to replace it all with brick and concrete, building ten thousand houses between here and Bexley village. Sid had spent his working life as a cooper with a bit of smithy work thrown in too, keeping his hand in at his old friend Doug Holland's forge at the top of Sidcup Hill. That was a proper way to lead a life, he believed. He didn't care much for this modern age and what so-called progress had brought here today.

However, Ernest was truly dismayed by the devastation around him. He had grown up as Sidcup had grown up, this was his whole world, and the sight in front of him placed his worries into a better perspective for the moment. He visibly rose in stature, to his full height of five foot four inches, and his sense of duty came to the fore.

'Come on then Sid, our community needs us!' he announced, his mood brightening for the first time in days.

Sid shook his head wearily.

'Oh Gawd, here's we goes agen,' he moaned, 'ev'body is 'n such a rush thaze dayz.'

Albert stood outside the Vigar home and took a few moments to collect his thoughts. Miraculously, Betsy had survived the onslaught with only a large dent on the left front wing to bear witness to recent events.

However, like its neighbours, the Vigars' front garden was a complete mess. It looked like it had been hit by a hurricane, covered in debris and Edward's much-prized roses had been stripped of their blooms, returned to winter's barren stalks. Most of the windows at the front of the house were broken or cracked, yet from first appearances, there only seemed to be superficial damage.

Rather than let himself in the back door as usual, he decided that on this occasion, he should seek permission to enter and gently knocked on the front door.

Patricia opened the door.

She looked fairly calm considering the visit they had just received from the Luftwaffe.

'Oh Bertie,' she said, immediately putting her arms around him. 'Why didn't you just let yourself in?'

'I don't know really, it just felt more proper, all considering what's happened,' he explained as he hugged his sister back. As they walked into the hall, he asked more pertinently, 'how's the girls?'

Betty appeared from the dining room with a dustpan and brush held in her hands. Ever the practical one, she had already made a start on tidying up. She rushed towards him, dropping the dustpan in her hurry to hug him too, belying that her nerves were not entirely settled at all.

'Oh it's awful Uncle,' she said. 'Why did those awful Germans have to come here?'

'It was bound to happen one day Betty, it's just that today was our turn.' Albert replied. 'Where's Ginny, what sort of state is she in?'

Mother and youngest daughter looked at each other and both pulled that concerned-looking face with thin lips that people do, when words fail them. They led him into the dining room, to find Ginny sitting at the table with her head held in her hands.

She looked up and revealed the raw face of someone who has been crying a lot and hasn't finished yet. Her hair was tangled, messed up, in contrast to her usual, perfectly groomed appearance. The smattering of freckles across her cheeks that usually hid beneath her makeup had made a rare appearance.

Her complexion was pinched white against her auburn hair. Ginny glanced at Albert and she crumpled into tears afresh. Her lips trembled and a new sob burst out, as she buried her face in her hands again.

Patricia pushed past Albert to comfort Ginny and, looking back at him in the doorway, she gave a slight flick of her head to tell him to leave. He turned to Betty and the concern on her face for her big sister needed no explanation.

'Come on Betty, let's go and have a look outside, it's quite a sight,' he suggested, with forced enthusiasm.

They walked back to the hall and out into the front garden.

'Oh my…' Betty said with a nervous giggle as she surveyed the street. 'It's a terrible mess isn't it? Have many people been hurt?'

'I don't think so. We had to dig Mrs Jones out of her larder though… the only thing left standing of her house, but she's alright. The other houses around have been bashed up too, but I don't know who might be injured.'

Betty broke his flow of conversation.

'I know Jimmy Marsden is dead, I saw it myself. Dad and Ken took him home wrapped in a blanket. I watched them through Ginny's window… it's no use pretending.'

There was a brief silence while Albert chose his words.

'Oh Betty … it's a tragedy that children get caught up in this awful modern war. You too… none of you should be involved,' he declared. 'In my day, as ghastly as it was, at least it was just men in the trenches. I'm so sorry.'

'How is poor Mrs Marsden?' Betty asked. 'Ken seemed to have to almost carry her home?'

'I don't know Betty… she won't be good, will she? Her neighbour took her in…Gertrude is it?' he replied. 'Where's your Ken by the way?'

Betty looked startled by his inference.

'What do you mean *my* Ken?'

'Oh, come on, I saw those goo-goo eyes over lunch!' he joked.

'You did not… stop it Uncle,' Betty replied, her face bright red with embarrassment.

Albert smirked, enjoying the opportunity to tease his niece a little. It was a momentary sliver of normality, in the midst of an extraordinary afternoon.

'It's no use denying it…I expect you'll be married in a week,' he said.

'Stop it. How can you say that, at a time like *this*?' said Betty, with dismay. 'I don't know where he is anyway…after you were at the Marsdens… he just disappeared.'

Albert was confused by that revelation.

'Disappeared… what do you mean?'

'You went off looking for Dad… and he was just… gone,' she explained. 'He didn't come back…it must be half an hour ago.'

'Oh, I expect he's somewhere, helping out.' Albert suggested.

'I don't really care. I'm going to clear up inside, it's a mess everywhere.' Betty replied.

She walked back inside, angry with her uncle.

Albert found himself standing alone on the driveway.

He took stock of the events of the last hour and shook his head in disbelief at the silly, stupid comments he had just made.

Shock does funny things to people… even me, he considered.

In the small ARP office at St Mildred's Church School, the telephone was ringing but there was nobody there to answer its belated air raid warning call.

Ernest and Old Sid had run into Roger by the bomb crater outside and they all walked back up the road, to meet Edward. Roger gabbled away as he walked his bicycle alongside, excitedly discussing every item of damage that he could see. Sid trudged along behind them, lamenting his beef and kidney pudding, now covered in fallen plaster on his kitchen table.

'Where have you been Ernie? Are you alright?' Edward asked.

'I'm sorry Ted. I took cover in the office and had to wait for someone to help get me out.' Ernest replied, embarrassed.

'You cood'av yoozed yer eyes,' Old Sid cut in.

No-one took any notice.

'We need to check the gas and water mains…' Edward continued.

Ernest turned and pointed up the road, towards the Plaza cinema.

'That crater is filling with water, there's definitely a leak there,' he announced. 'We'll need to get to the mains stopcock to shut it off.'

'The most important thing to do first is to count the craters, can you do that Ernie?' Edward explained. 'Take Roger with you…'

'An' whas 'xactly da yoose need me far than?' Old Sid interjected impatiently, getting increasingly bored by the second.

'You can check for gas, Sid. Go up the road and knock at every house and tell people to check for leaks.' Edward instructed. 'If there is any sign, get them outside immediately and tell them to gather…'

He looked around, up the road to where it was clear of debris. '…up there by Augustine Avenue, that seems far enough way. Can you do that Sid?'

'Reckonz so, I can mange sum whiffs of gaz alright,' Sid replied, as he ambled off.

'Well… that's if anybody can actually understand the old coot,' Ernest commented.

All three of them roared with laughter. It felt good to release the tension of the last hour, rekindling a sense of shared purpose, common to many old soldiers.

'Come on Master Deacon…, *lez go lookin' for 'oles*,' Ernest declared, with youthful vigour.

As Ernest and Roger set off on their bomb survey, Edward decided there was time enough to go home to see Patricia and the girls.

He needed to check they were alright and pay a visit on poor Mrs Marsden, to commiserate on her loss. He was pleased that Ernest was back on good form again, especially after his uncharacteristically strange behaviour over lunch. Edward owed a great deal to his old friend, all the way back to when they served together in the last war. His pal Ernie had encouraged him to pick up on the job offer at Ideal Homesteads, met Albert and, through him met the love of his life.

The poignancy of the phrase, *the last war*, weighed upon him. As Edward walked home, he wondered when, exactly, their Great War had been replaced in common parlance by this new conflict.

He took stock of the last few hours.

Even though the sun hung low in the sky, it was still very hot and his clothes were absolutely filthy.

He realised that he didn't smell too good either. The unpleasant aroma was a mixture of dirt, sweat and something… nasty.

More by instinct than anything else, he unbuttoned the front of his boiler suit and was revolted to see that his shirt was now stained dark red. Once his shock subsided, Edward thought about the poor, sweet little boy he had taken in his arms and realised that he was covered with the child's blood. He caught its musky scent, instantly stirring a long-buried emotion, from deep in the pit of his stomach. He recalled blood, gore and noise. He could smell sodden leather, stinking mud, shit, piss and unwashed men. Once again, he felt the ever-present fear of violent death that had accompanied his life in the trenches. Like many of his generation, he'd spent twenty years thinking he had successfully forgotten it all, but in truth, it had stayed with him… always.

He quickly buttoned up his boiler suit, thankful that its dark blue material perfectly hid what had happened. The ARP uniform was well chosen for its purpose. He walked on, determined to get home and clean himself up as soon as he could.

Just as he passed No76, Ken appeared from the grassed alleyway that that led from the narrow end of Chaucer Park. He looked nervous and off-balance, not altogether quite right, Edward thought.

'Hello Ken, where have you been?' he called out.

'Oh… I'm sorry. I had to… to take some time… to myself, I'm sorry.' Ken stuttered.

There was a large damp patch at the front of Ken's trousers.

'I quite understand,' Edward replied, observing Ken's embarrassment with newly found empathy. 'Don't worry about that son… I often did that, back in the last lot.'

Ken's face flushed red, his eyes dropped to the ground.

Edward persisted with his tale.

'Them bloody whizz-bangs exploding above scared the right crap out of me loads of times. I can't remember how often I wanted clean trousers,' he revealed. 'It's fine Ken… it's a terrible thing that's happened here today.'

'Yes Mr Vigar, it was a horrible thing to see,' Ken answered, glad that the subject had moved on from his nervous bladder.

He fell silent, lost for words or purpose, painfully aware that he was really an outsider in the midst of this local crisis.

Edward sympathised afresh with the look of gut-wrenching fear that soldiers have often seen in their comrades' faces.

'Come on son... let's head back to the house. We have plenty of clearing up to do, I bet.'

He briefly placed his arm around Ken's shoulders and gave him a reassuring embrace. He pitied this lost young man. Despite the freshness of their acquaintance and Ken's current jitters, Edward still felt confident that he was a straight sort of fellow.

The young soldier seemed to perk up for this show of fatherly affection.

'That's better... let's be getting on.' Edward concluded, as he walked towards home.

Ken looked towards the park to check that the ghostly vision of the French officer really had gone. It had appeared for just a few moments, amongst all the smoke and falling debris from the bomb blasts and Ken had instantly felt the full terror of his nightmares again. It still persisted in his mind, burrowed deep, lurking, waiting.

He took a deep breath, then another, to clear his head.

Looking down at his flies, he saw that stain was drying, fading in the cloying heat.

Satisfied that he looked reasonably decent again, Ken walked quickly after Edward.

Chapter 23

As dusk settled across Southern England on that September Sunday, for many people it was a time to reflect on another tumultuous day. For most it was a brief calm in the middle of the storm, but for others, fate continued to play its hand.

Maude stood in her lounge, surveying the damage dealt to her once unblemished Grande Salon. She had just swept up the broken glass and went outside, to survey the patio in the twilight of the fading day. Having already gathered most of the shrapnel shards into a neat pile, she decided that this would suffice until she could check again more thoroughly in the morning. She peered through the encroaching darkness and wondered where Raymond had disappeared to, when a flicker of light inside the summerhouse provided the answer. Considering the trauma of the last few hours, she wondered why her nephew would be drawn down there, instead of helping her to clear up the damage inflicted to the house.

As ever, he is following his own whims first, she thought, *rather than helping me here.*

Despite his earlier heroic act, Raymond had quickly reverted to his normal self-centred ways and she couldn't help but wonder about his true motive for re-opening the summerhouse. Initially, she had thought it was just a reaction to her warning about Bridger's Farm, a simple way of placating her. Considering the tremendous effort he was putting into the summerhouse, Maude was now absolutely certain that he was up to something.

Knowing Raymond, that *something* would not be good, or necessarily legal.

She was no fool, her many acquaintances around Sidcup fed her with mostly everything she needed to know about his activities. The letter from the War Agricultural Ministry had only confirmed what she already suspected. The livestock headcount, or more accurately the lack of it, seemed to confirm the many rumours about Raymond's black market activities. Unfortunately, in terms of gleaning more information, despite her ploy of appeasement, he hadn't dropped his guard at all during afternoon tea.

The Nazi air attack had overshadowed everything since.

A lesser woman might have felt frightened following such a close encounter with the enemy, but not Maude. She was well-practiced in her role as the solid foundation stone of the family. She was not going to crack at the first sight of those beastly Germans, who had caused everyone so much heartbreak over the last forty years. Her lifelong friend, Robert Higgins, had taught her much about the German psyche, learnt from spending much of his early life in the land of the old Kaiser.

The son of the great diplomat, Charles Higgins, Robert had spent much of his childhood in Berlin, when his father served as an ambassador to the German crown towards the end of the Victorian era. On his retirement and return to England, Higgins Senior gained a peerage, bought a grand new house in Lamorbey and became a firm friend of Maude's father.

Thenceforth, the Higgins family were ever-present at Craywood House and childhood friendship grew into a deep understanding between Robert and Maude. So much so, that she was devastated by his decision to return to Germany in 1895, to pursue a career in the rapidly developing field of orthopaedic surgery.

Yet despite the distance between them, by frequent letter and occasional visits home, Robert became Maude's most earnest suitor. It would be many years before she knew herself exactly why she would not accept his repeated offers of marriage; that would take the arrival of her beloved Daphne and all that this precipitated. Although Robert was disappointed in his romantic quest, he and Maude remained the firmest of friends over the years that followed. It was the perpetual abstractness of Robert's overseas location that made it possible for the ever-wary and private Maude to trust him as her only true confidante. By expressing their thoughts by regular postal correspondence, in many ways they came to know each other far more intimately, and frankly, than many a married couple would ever do.

By the time war threatened in 1914, Robert had become one of Germany's leading surgeons in the treatment of bone disease and injury. As a true British gentleman, he chose to return to England to join the Royal Army Medical Corps. In this respect, he would serve the country of his birth, rather than the one in which he had spent most of his life. He knew that modern warfare would produce an exponential increase in traumatic injury to millions of fighting men and he had the skills to help them. From military hospitals in France over the next four years, his surgical skills earnt him the gratitude of thousands of British soldiers recovering from mutilations caused by the horrors of trench warfare.

After the Armistice in 1918, Maude was the first person that he called upon on his return home. Discovering the tragedy of Daphne's demise and her orphaned children, Robert willingly gave Maude the emotional support that she so desperately needed. He instinctively grasped the true reason for Maude's deep despair and despite his own romantic disappointment, perhaps because of it, he proved to be her greatest-ever platonic friend. Robert provided the strong shoulder on which a grieving Maude leant, as she began to build a new life for her and her wards. Once he was satisfied that she was able to continue life on her own, he resumed his medical career with a variety of ever more senior posts around the British Empire.

However, like her and she knew, because of her, Robert never married.

It was Maude's second greatest regret that she could never give him what he so desired. She could not help her nature and just as she could never forget her love for Daphne, Robert understood and accepted this. What he could not know, is that Maude was also protecting him from the terrible curse that she believed Cray Wood had placed on her, and anyone that she held dear. Nonetheless, wherever he worked around the world, no matter how long he was gone for, Robert would always come back to Craywood House and Maude.

In 1937, at the age of sixty four, Robert decided it was finally time to retire. As his father did before him, he returned to England and the old family home in Lamorbey. For a few years, hardly two days passed without this unlikely couple spending time together.

All that changed last year, with the outbreak of war with Germany. As Britain lost progressively more and more of its manpower to the military, Robert and his peers were called back to work, to plug the gaps in Britain's medical services. In 1914, Robert had helped his fellow man at the Western Front and in 1940, he was doing it all over again from the Home Front. Maude was so pleased for him, he had been given a second lease of life in what he did best… caring for others.

Even so, one thing didn't change; their absolute commitment to Monday nights and Bridge. They had partnered in this Machiavellian game of cards on and off since their youth and in recent years, built a fearsome reputation in local circles. Maude was glad that tomorrow wasn't her turn to host, as broken windows would never do for her guests.

Even if there is a war on, she joked to herself.

Her least favourite phrase did have some uses after all, she realised with fresh understanding. Considering that Craywood House would host the Sidcup Bridge Club in a few weeks' time, the third Monday of the month as always, Maude decided she would quickly have to get everything shipshape. She prided herself in providing the club's grandest venue and as ever, she had high standards to maintain. There was time enough to affect the necessary repairs and in the meantime, she would enjoy tomorrow night's tournament at Mrs Price's house in Station Road. She hadn't seen Robert since Friday afternoon as he'd been busy at the hospital and she had to admit, she had very much missed his company.

Maude's thoughts were interrupted, when Raymond appeared at her side.

With his shirt sleeves rolled up, hot and sweaty, he was filthy from his exertions in the now darkened summerhouse.

'I've made good progress Aunt Maude! I've taken most of the rubbish out and it's really come up a treat down there,' he said with uncharacteristic enthusiasm. 'You should come and have a look.'

'I'm sure it's lovely Raymond, but really… there are far more pressing matters,' she replied with annoyance. 'You could have given me some help here … clearing up all this broken glass and these infernal objects strewn all over the place.'

'I'm sorry Aunt. Is there anything I can do to help you now?'

'Actually, I'm sure you can,' she quickly responded. 'We need to get this glass replaced, perhaps you can organise this for me? I know it's hard to come by. If we can't get any, we'll have to take it from elsewhere in the house.'

'I could have a word with Vigar.' Raymond replied. 'He's sorting out fencing for me at Bridger's next week… he owes me a few *favours*.'

That final emphasis aggravated her.

'Another one of your nefarious activities Ray-Monde?' she asked.

Seemingly oblivious to the thrust of her comment, or indeed the gravity of what had happened just a few hours before, Raymond continued in the same, carefree manner.

'And look what I have found down in the rose beds,' he announced, pointing behind her.

She noticed that just a few yards from her feet, he had placed a large curved sheet of metal… about four foot long and two wide.

Her curiosity got the better of her and she walked closer to inspect it.

It was burnt and sooty around the edges. In places its green and blue paint had been blistered by tremendous heat and on one corner neatly stencilled letters betrayed its military, foreign origin.

'Oh my gracious, that could have killed one of us,' she exclaimed. 'Where was it exactly?'

'Down there, the third bed from here,' Raymond revealed. 'I'm going to have a good look around tomorrow to see what else I can find.'

Maude looked at the large section of aircraft cowling at her feet. She thought back to the hair-raising moment when the doomed German aircraft roared overhead.

Come to think of it, the whole incident had been extremely strange, she thought. They had only just got back to their feet and gone back outside after the guns finished firing, when suddenly, a stricken German aeroplane flew straight over them, spewing smoke and debris.

There had been a terrible, unnatural screaming noise.

Is it something to do with modern aeroplanes, she wondered, *as their engines are much bigger and more powerful these days?*

The noise had been strange, unnerving; somehow *more* than mechanical.

It had almost been *shrieking…* like a cacophony of tortured voices.

Maude giggled.

It had sounded like the choir at All Saints screaming their heads off, as if they had trapped their fingers in a door!

She started to laugh and she didn't really know why, but it all seemed very funny. Her head was in a swoon, it felt a bit like being tipsy. Just for a moment, those far-off nights of champagne and gin with Daphne came happily to mind. She felt a pleasurable sensation in her loins, absent for many years.

She looked at Raymond.

He was smiling and Maude couldn't remember what on earth she had just been thinking about. She realised that something was wrong with her right hand and looked down to see blood running through her fingers, dripping onto the flagstones.

Utterly bewildered, she looked more closely and discovered a deep gash about three inches long in the flesh of her palm. It was bleeding profusely and only then, painful.

Blood.

She looked down again.

The engine cowling at her feet had a corresponding streak of bright, fresh blood along a sharp, jagged edge where it had been ripped from the German aircraft earlier. Maude couldn't remember trying to pick up the cowling, not even touching it actually.

She came to her senses.

'Oh my gracious, what have I done?' she exclaimed, turned and hurried into the house. She headed for the kitchen, in search of fresh water and something to bandage the cut.

Raymond thought darkly that Maude deserved that wound.

The sun had almost set and night was laying its cloak over the garden, the summerhouse and the woodland that overlooked them all. Even though the evening air was hot and still down in the garden, up on the hilltop the wind had risen sharply. Up there, the trees still caught the last light of the sun, shaking their branches violently in the wind, their leaves jostling with a deafening roar of agitation. He saw a brilliant, billowing flash of white... deep within Cray Wood.

Raymond strained his eyes, trying to catch another glimpse of it.

The wind up on the hilltop suddenly abated and the tree branches settled back down to a more peaceful, gentle swaying. Through a kaleidoscope of shimmering leaves he saw the white flash again... a circle of intense white light.

For a moment, he thought he was looking at the full circle of the moon.

Raymond was confused. The moon had been waning to a narrow crescent of illumination over the last few days. It certainly shouldn't be visible until well after midnight.

He blinked and the strange sight vanished.

The image staring back at Ginny from her bedroom mirror was no longer that of a young girl. Though her eyes were still red from tears and her complexion quite pale, her visage was older, darker, more serious than anything she had ever contrived with makeup.

She had aged years in the last few hours.

Whatever she thought of her outward appearance, on the inside she had lost a great deal of her last innocence today. Under the light of the four light bulbs that her father had fitted around her *Hollywood Mirror* for her last birthday, she studied the dark rings under her eyes. Despite it being nearly bedtime, she took a large blob of foundation cream from her last pre-war pot.

She rubbed it gently across her cheeks and carefully under her eyes.

The slow massage of the precious cream into her skin was just as beneficial to her sense of well-being as it was to concealing her freckles and any remaining evidence of her earlier distress. The gentle pressure of her index finger across her skin was calming, reassuringly familiar as she put her face back on to meet the world anew.

With the little finger of her right hand she rubbed the tip of a lipstick and applied just a hint of colour to her lips. The remainder she rubbed into her cheeks to restore a healthier glow. Of course, with a more plentiful supply of cosmetics, she would have applied so much more, to complete a glamorous effect to hide behind.

Since the war began, even Ginny had learnt to make do with less.

Like many women across the country, she scoured the ever-thinner magazines and newspapers for helpful suggestions on how to manufacture what was now so lacking in the shops. Beetroot gave a good strong colour for rouge and lips, burnt cork could substitute for mascara. Ginny had even read how candle soot could be mixed with petroleum jelly to create a dark eye-shadow. Although she hadn't felt desperate enough yet to try this last recipe, she knew the time would come one day. Even more distressingly, the shortage of alcohols had practically closed down the perfume industry in England and Ginny's last bottle of

Bourjois Soir De Paris, her signature scent, was kept safely put away in her dresser. Now it was only brought out for the most special of occasions, but, on that basis, she had used more than three quarters of it in just the last few weeks.

Ginny might have been more sparing in its use if she'd known that the Bourjois factory had been utterly destroyed by bombing two weeks ago. On the positive side, Betty had already proven to be an absolute treasure in procuring the rarest of feminine necessities from Uncle Ernie's shop. For some time yet, it was likely that the Vigar sisters might retain an advantage over most local girls through their association with Harrop's The Chemist.

Of course, Betty really didn't seem to worry too much about cosmetics herself, as she was so confident in her plain manner.

Unlike me, Ginny thought.

She looked closely at her reflection.

Her nose was just too big and slightly too turned up as always. Her eyes were the wrong shape and as for her chin, oh… where to begin?

Everybody told her that she was pretty, but she just couldn't understand it as, to cap it all, she was just too fat. Ginny had thought that with all the rationing and shortages, she would have been able to shed a few pounds to make her waist slimmer, but it just hadn't happened. Yet, despite what Harper's Bazaar magazine said, in reality, she had come to understand that most men seemed to like a fuller figure… so her big boobs had usefulness after all.

When she looked at her sister, Betty always seemed to radiate a natural beauty that Ginny felt she could never hope to match, no matter how much she tried. To make it even harder to bear, Betty had a confidence and an intellect that Ginny struggled to equal, or at least that's what she believed. Ever since they were children she had felt that Betty was their father's favourite. No matter how much Ginny laughed and danced and entertained the family, tried her hardest to win at everything at school, somehow Betty had always been the apple of Daddy's eye.

This was why Ginny had to try so much harder to be noticed. She firmly believed that as actress Mae West had declared… *It's better to be looked over, than overlooked!*

Tonight, the glitter and glamour of Hollywood movies seemed a million miles away. Stark reality was watching that poor little boy killed, right in front of her.

Despite what they told his mother, Ginny had seen the look in Jimmy Marsden's eyes as he lay there dying, with a large chunk of his head cleaved straight off by a hideous shard of metal. She had run to him, only to watch, powerless to help, as the blood poured out in a brief, pulsating torrent from the gruesome hole in his head. His lips had trembled, he had mumbled in confusion and pain.

Then, he died.

The way his expression just, well, *stopped*… had been utterly shocking.

Ginny had been frightened, but not so much of the Germans, as she knew that danger had already passed. The fear that swelled inside her was actually of *herself,* as never before had she felt such utter anger boil within her. A feeling of pure, uncomplicated hatred for the murderers of that little boy had totally overwhelmed her.

It felt like a rage that would consume her whole.

Yet, Betty just seemed to take it all in her stride. She had even got on with tidying up the house, which only served to make Ginny feel even more isolated in her anguish.

Later on, just before sunset, Ginny looked outside and found that Hazelmead Road had been transformed into a scene of devastation. It was like a movie set from *Gone with the Wind*. Whilst the houses hadn't caught fire as they did in the city of Atlanta, for Ginny, at that moment, it had felt like everything she held dear would soon be lost.

Now she sat at her bedroom dresser, content that she had at least partly restored the beautiful mask that protected her from the world. She tried to cheer herself up by thinking about her promiscuous Moon Bathing, as she preferred to call it. She managed a sort of giggle, but then the lights around the mirror dimmed and robbed her of that brief moment of happiness.

As was so often the case, the electric supply had reduced in response to the need for wartime economy. The filaments of the light bulbs glowed weakly yellow and the room was brought near to darkness under their feeble illumination. Whether intentional or not, it felt like the electricity company had told her that the day was done.

Ginny sobbed in despair.

She needed her leading man, her hero, someone to take her away from all this and keep her safe.

Downstairs, the doorbell rang as if to announce his arrival.

Patricia Vigar stood alone in the darkened hallway by the front door and wondered who could be outside at this late hour.

'Hello, who's there?' she asked warily.

'It's Raymond Delafort, Mrs Vigar. I'm sorry to call at this time, I was wondering if your husband is there? I'm terribly sorry to disturb you.'

After a day like this, Patricia really could have done without a late night caller, especially as she was alone in the house with just the girls. However, she reasoned the matter must be urgent and decided to let him in.

'Please wait for a few moments… I must turn the light out first,' she instructed. She switched off the hall light, pulled back the heavy blackout curtain and unlocked the door. Raymond stood in the porch, ghostlike, his face illuminated by a small torch in his hand.

As ever polite and charming, he continued.

'Is Mr Vigar here, by any chance?'

'No, he's on duty this evening, they've had so much to do after the bombs this afternoon. Can I give him a message?' Patricia replied tiredly.

He looked off-balance, uncharacteristically uncertain.

He clearly had something else on his mind.

'Yes, I'm sorry.' Looking around to add emphasis, he continued, 'I had no idea about all this, is everyone alright?'

'Yes, we're all fine here, is there a message for Ted?' Patricia answered impatiently.

'We had quite a time of it at Craywood,' Raymond replied. 'Bombers flew over the house and several were shot down I think. There's a gun battery the other side of Foots Cray now, but we had no idea it was there until they started firing their cannons.'

'Raymond, it's late, well past eleven, is there anything I can do for you?' Patricia said with growing frustration. 'We've all had a long day and I really should go to bed.'

'Yes, I wanted to talk to Mr Vigar about building matters, would he be here tomorrow?' Raymond continued.

More honestly, he asked.

'Is Virginia alright?'

Patricia pretended she hadn't already guessed the real reason for his presence.

'Yes Raymond, she's fine… I'm fine… we are all fine,' she stated. 'If you call into the yard tomorrow, I expect Ted will be there. Now then, I really DO need to be going to bed.'

She made to close the door, but was thwarted in her escape, as Ginny's voice rang out from the top of the stairs.

'Oh Raymond. Is that really you?' she called.

She ran down the stairs, past her mother in the doorway and threw her arms around him.

'I'm so glad to see you… it's been simply awful here,' she exclaimed.

He held her tightly, with all the dramatic charm of a movie star.

'*I just had to come and find you Virginia*… I was so very worried about you,' he declared with somewhat exaggerated passion.

Patricia was outraged by his blatant opportunism. She doubted that he'd had even the first clue about the bombing of Hazelmead Road until just a few minutes ago.

It was time to put a stop to all this nonsense.

'Well, you've seen her now and it's time we all went to bed,' she said as she pulled her daughter back inside. 'I'm sure you've got somewhere to go on your motorbike. GOODNIGHT Raymond.'

Ginny didn't argue with her mother and stood inside the hall, looking out to Raymond in the darkness.

'Will I see you tomorrow?' she implored. 'Come and meet me at the factory, I have my lunch break at 12.30.'

'Of course I will Virginia, I'll be there for you,' he replied suavely. 'Goodnight Mrs Vigar, I hope we all have a peaceful night.' Raymond concluded, as he retreated into the darkness.

Patricia shut the door and bolted it firmly shut.

Turning to her daughter, she fixed her with the full force of a mother's reproach.

'YOU are going to get yourself into a lot of trouble if you not careful. Now go to bed this instant my girl,' she shouted, without a care for what the neighbours might overhear. 'WE'VE ALL HAD A BLOODY TERRIBLE DAY AND

LET'S HOPE THOSE BUGGERS DON'T COME BACK.'

Her patience had expired to the point of using coarse language, a rare event.

'But you don't understand Mummy…. *I love him.*' Ginny replied, with all the drama of a wronged heroine.

She burst into tears and ran back up the stairs to her bedroom.

'Oh dear God, give me strength,' Patricia muttered, as she followed behind her.

As Raymond walked back to his motorbike, he thought back to when he first met Virginia Vigar that night in Burton's Ballroom. He had quickly calculated that she would be a much tougher nut to crack than the girls that usually satisfied his sexual appetite. It would take far more than a few glasses of port and lemon to get her knickers off.

So he had pandered to her dreams of love and romance, fed by the American films she so loved. The Vigar girl had taken every step that he had carefully laid out for her over the last few weeks.

He considered that if this Scarlet O'Hara needed a Rhett Butler to unlock the gates to her passion, he was just the man for the role.

Ken was lying on the camp bed in the lounge, smoking a last cigarette before he went to sleep. He thought about the overheard conversation and listened to Raymond's motorbike accelerate off down the road.

In the downstairs bedroom, Betty was still awake too.

She thought about Ken in the front room and how disappointingly he had behaved during their crisis this afternoon. Yes, he had protected her when that German plane attacked, but then… *he had run away.*

She had seen the look on his face.

He was just plain frightened and that was not at all what she had hoped for in him.

Betty wished her dad was in the house. She stared at the faintly luminous face of the clock beside her bed. As the minute hand approached midnight, she wondered how long it would be before her father returned home. She thought about her eventful day and how her theory about Ginny's romantic life had been proven correct.

All was silent outside and it occurred to her that she had not heard a single train on the railway line for several hours. Eventually, her mind stopped racing and as tiredness finally came for her, the tick-tock of the clock gently lulled her to sleep.

As it counted out the last seconds of the day, in airfields, aerodromes and countless offices and depots, the people of Britain and Germany's armed forces continued their relentless pursuit of war. Mechanics laboured over repairs to damaged aircraft, clerks counted statistics and compiled reports and exhausted airmen slept like the dead. Both sides counted the human cost of this day and marshalled their resources for the new one ahead.

Despite the six o'clock raid on Biggin Hill airfield by the Dorniers of KG26, the sector control room hurriedly created in the village bakery had been declared operational, just after 9pm.

At half a dozen Luftwaffe airbases across France, the roar of aircraft engines heralded the opening moves of a new strategy. Hundreds of heavily-laden bombers accelerated towards take-off and began their grasping ascent into the dark night sky.

Soon the wings of eagles would cast their shadows by moonlight, as well as in the bright of day.

Chapter 24

The thick, acrid smoke from the burning vehicles billowed around Ken, stinging his eyes.

As he surveyed the scene of carnage around him, his ears rang from the explosions of the air attack, wrapping him in a bubble of shrill, shrieking tinnitus. He wanted to get away from this place, he wanted to run, but his feet felt like lead weights and yet again… he was forced to watch the same sickening drama unfold before him.

He looked towards the ditch alongside the road, where civilians and soldiers had taken cover as the German fighters strafed the column. For many it was the place of their last living moments, their bodies cast into grotesque postures by the bullets and explosions that slayed them. The living and the dead lay side by side as chosen by the lottery of war. While the survivors struggled to comprehend what had happened around them, their elation at their own good fortune fought against the horror of proximity to sudden, violent death.

A dishevelled-looking woman in her thirties was looking towards Ken.

Her expression was rent with anguish, her mouth formed words that were lost in the screaming noise inside his head. She was trying to clamber out of the ditch but an older man, her father or an uncle perhaps, held her back. More than that, he was actually fighting to hold her down and Ken couldn't understand why this could be.

He looked to his left and saw the army lorry in which he had been travelling was off the road, wrecked, almost overturned. It was fully ablaze and strewn around it lay several bodies clad in khaki. One of Ken's comrades sat with his back against a tree, legs out straight, in a pool of blood, his eyes stared back lifelessly.

Oh God… Dear God, why must I see this again? Ken screamed inside his pounding head.

He looked down to his feet and saw they had sprouted dark wooden roots that reached out in every direction, anchoring him to the ground. He watched with dreadful fascination as the wooden growth transformed his legs into a hideous, ugly, gnarled old tree trunk. As the terror of this nightmare took Ken fully within its grip, he cried out for salvation.

The smoke cleared to reveal dead horses, still in their traces attached to a heavy artillery piece. A French officer appeared just yards away, a revolver grasped in his right hand. A young foal lay mortally wounded on the ground in between them and Ken couldn't understand how such a young horse came to be there. Its back was broken and as it writhed in agony; its belly split open and disgorged a bloody mess of glistening entrails upon the road.

Dear God, Dear God… please stop this! Ken shouted over and over.

His eyes would not close.

He could not look away.

He was paralysed, rooted to the spot, an unwilling witness to slaughter.

The French officer raised his revolver and took aim. His face bore an expression of absolute torment; ashen, filthy, his tunic was splattered with blood.

With his left hand, he cocked the weapon, slowly took aim and fired.

Deaf to its report, Ken watched split-second by impossible split-second as the revolver recoiled and the bullet span from its muzzle.

Ken screamed.

The sound poured out of him in a never ending torrent, as if it would draw out from his soul for all eternity.

Betty was awoken by a strange sound coming from outside her bedroom door and looking at her bedside clock, she saw it was 4am.

She wondered at first if it was Dad returning from his patrol, but the murmuring noise came again. It was a man talking in his sleep and she realised it was probably coming from Ken, across the hall in the lounge.

She quickly hopped out of bed and crept over to her door to listen better and as she stood there, it became clear that he was having a bad dream. Every now and then, he shouted out, mostly unintelligible, garbled nonsense, but she gleaned the odd few words. He seemed to be asking, no, pleading with someone to stop doing something.

It wasn't a nice thing to hear.

Her inquisitive mind persuaded her to go out to the hall to hear him more clearly. She carefully opened the door, turned on the light and padded a few steps over to the lounge.

Just as she got there, a blood-curdling scream burst forth from inside the room, loud enough to waken the whole house, the whole street probably.

Without a second thought, she rushed into the room.

The camp bed was empty, the blanket thrown aside and then a scream came again, from over by the bay window.

This time it didn't stop, the scream kept coming. Most people would have turned tail and run out of the room, but for some reason, Betty knew instinctively that this situation posed no danger to her. The noise was one of utter fear, not anger or malice.

By the light from the hall, she saw Ken huddled on the floor, curled into a ball just like a baby.

'Ken it's alright. Wake up Ken, you're quite safe,' she said, crouching next to him.

He looked up at her and spoke with pure terror.

'Am I dead? Oh God… AM I DEAD?'

Then he recognised her and grasping where he really was, burst into tears and sobbed.

Betty had never ever seen a full-grown man cry before and the sight touched her heart. She felt that he was a good person, but something truly, terribly, awful had happened to him. Without even thinking, she sat down and put her arms around him.

'Please Ken, it's alright. You're safe here, it was a dream that's all,' she reassured him.

Ken looked into her eyes.

As confusion slipped from his face, calm slowly began to replace his fear.

'I'm sorry Betty, I've let you down. I'm so sorry,' he sobbed.

Patricia's voice cut through the moment.

She was standing in the doorway.

'What's happening, what's wrong?' she asked firmly.

'He's had a terrible nightmare Mum,' Betty explained.

Patricia walked over to the couple huddled on the floor, to see for herself.

'I'm so sorry, Mrs Vigar,' Ken managed to splutter, utterly ashamed at the predicament in which he found his waking self.

Patricia knelt down.

Like many wives of her generation; she took it all in her stride, as for every old soldier, there is often a wife well-practised in dealing with night terrors. Even though Ken was a relative stranger, she had seen this all before.

'Come on, let's be getting you up,' she suggested gently. 'You need to walk around a bit, if you feel able.'

Ginny's voice joined the drama.

From the top of the stairs she called out, half asleep, anxious.

'What's happening, is it an air raid? Do we need to go to the shelter?'

'Elizabeth, go to your sister, I'll deal with this,' Patricia instructed her youngest daughter. 'Put your dressing gown on too.'

As a slight sense of normality returned, Betty's bravery slipped away. She left the room, to go upstairs and explain everything to Ginny.

Patricia looked at Ken, who now sat shamefaced and embarrassed.

'I think we could all do with a cup of tea. Come into the dining room whilst I get it on the go,' she continued. Then she gently led him by the hand, out of the lounge.

Patricia heard the turn of the back door lock and Edward walked into the kitchen, just as she arrived from the dining room.

He was about to hang up his satchel and helmet, when he noticed the harrowed look on her face.

His look of puzzlement begged an answer.

'There's never a dull moment in this house!' she replied.

Chapter 25

Lit by dawn's first glimmer, Ken sat alone in the Vigars' garden, listening to the birdsong which heralds a new day. Reflecting on his circumstances, the conclusion wasn't favourable.

He knew that he wasn't right in himself and the stigma of shell shock weighed heavily upon him. A large part of his memory of his last days in France was entirely missing, but the more frightening aspect was how small, terrifying details kept coming back to him through the same recurring nightmare. It had got to the stage that he didn't want to sleep at all, for fear of what the next dream would reveal.

Even when Ken was awake, he was plagued by sudden, shocking flashbacks, triggered by all manner of random things. The flare of a smoker's match, the slam of a door, even laughter could make him flinch like a reflex reaction to an electric shock. These memories came as split-second bursts of images, some strange, some disturbing, but never with enough context to make any proper sense. He could not ever hold these revelations long enough to fully grasp their meaning. It seemed there was a profound reason why his subconscious had blocked out so much of his escape from France and he was especially fearful of what this meant.

What horrors were being hidden? Ken considered, over and over again.

More immediately, he was terribly embarrassed by his behaviour in front of the kind family that had taken him into their home.

Having considered the options, Ken had decided it was time to leave the Vigars and sleep rough until his leave was over. He would take to the woods again. Just as he had done in France when fleeing the Germans and more recently, at the beginning of his home leave. This time, he wasn't going to consider returning to the camp at Foots Cray. For all he knew, these would be his last few days of freedom before the war reclaimed him. The whole country was anxious about the coming invasion and Ken knew that he would literally be in the firing line when the Nazis came.

He couldn't think beyond that, no-one did anymore.

Ken thought of where he had spent his first night of leave and what a mistake that had been. Instead of providing peace and calm, the smothering atmosphere of absolute isolation in that hilltop woodland had only served to darken his mood. After a night of troubled sleep beneath a great old oak tree, he had awoken to a view of a large stately mansion in the valley below. Surrounded by formal rose gardens, the grand house clearly belonged to a rich family, reinforcing Ken's feelings of mental and material inadequacy. This had spurred him on to get away from there as fast as possible on that Friday morning.

Yet, his chance meeting with Betty in Sidcup High Street had completely raised his spirits. It was his first encounter in months with someone normal, outside of army life and buoyed by conversation with a pretty young woman, he'd found the courage to go and see his family in Bermondsey.

He should have realised that his step-mother, Bertha, would not welcome him there. Ken was not of her blood and her disdain for him had not abated, even though he was now a full-grown man. *Oh look what the cat has dragged in*, she had announced sarcastically, before telling him there was no bed for him in her house. When he appealed to his father for support, Albert Kendrick just shied away from confrontation with his wife. That was not to say that Albert was a coward. Far from it, as in the trenches of The Great War he had acted with great valour and been awarded the Distinguished Conduct Medal. At war's end he returned broken by the horror of it all, a pale shadow of his former self. To have a father with such a credential for gallantry and such a sad conclusion, made Ken's anguish at his own fragile sanity even harder to bear.

After the row with Bertha, Ken fled the house with his kitbag and no plan as to what to do next. He had wandered to London Bridge Station and took a train back to Sidcup, as Foots Cray Camp seemed to be his only remaining refuge. However, Ken's had mood lifted once more on that journey out of the city. As he stepped onto the platform at Sidcup, he spotted another, quiet, out-of-the-way place that could be his home for a while.

Unfortunately, sleeping in the bushes by the railway line, overlooking a small public park, had conjured yet more disturbing sights that night. Ken had seen very strange things going on and awoke the next morning, full of anger and wondering which was madder, him or the world around him. He recalled what Betty said about her uncle, the man that had been kind to him at Eltham Palace in early June. Deciding to try his luck with someone who had shown simple charity before, Ken went in search of Albert Culpepper. The offer of a bed overnight was followed by Sunday dinner with the Vigars and despite his troubles; Ken had found brief happiness in their company.

The air raid had ruined *everything*.

Smoking another cigarette, Ken heard noises from the kitchen. He looked round to see that Patricia had awoken again, for the second time that morning. He felt embarrassed, knowing that the moment was close when he would have to talk to her.

'Are you ready for another cuppa?' she called from the back door.

He jumped to his feet and decided it was time to broach the subject, to get it over and done with.

'You have all been so kind… and leave you all alone… I'm going to pack my kitbag…' he spoke his lines rapidly, just as he had been rehearsing for the last hour, but not necessarily in that order. 'I'm so sorry… for what happened earlier Mrs Vigar… I've imposed enough on you already... I really must go.'

Patricia just looked back and smiled.

'Oh no you won't! You owe us hard labour for your board and lodging young man,' she replied. Then, in a loving, motherly fashion that Ken had so little experience of, she continued. 'You don't get off the hook that easily.'

Ken was bewildered by her response and meant to argue.

Patricia's facial expression stated that this would not be a good idea.

'Let's sit in the garden with our tea and have a little chat,' she said, closing the matter.

Ken tried to draw on his cigarette and realising that it had gone out, he looked for his matches. He checked his right trouser pocket and then, on the left. Instead of a small cardboard box, his fingers felt something unexpected.

Retrieving the mystery object, he was utterly puzzled to see an acorn nestling in the palm of his hand. He recalled his night under the old oak beside that grand house and shuddered.

Repulsed by the thought of it, he hurled the acorn across the garden. Ken suddenly felt better for that brief, energetic action. Embarrassed by such an irrational act, he looked at Patricia. Without saying a word, she smiled back at him, her eyes laden with sympathy.

To escape her gaze, Ken checked his wristwatch. It was now 7.15am and Sidcup was utterly peaceful. Not a sound of a single aircraft echoed across the clear blue sky, not a single train could be heard along the railway.

Whilst the air still carried night-time's chill, the sun had risen well above the horizon and its touch was already hot to his skin.

In the huge underground command bunker at RAF Uxbridge, the heart of 11 Group's mission control network, the day had started worryingly slowly.

After sunrise crept across the battlefield, no Luftwaffe activity was seen by either RDF or the Observer Corps for nearly two hours. Not a single Luftwaffe reconnaissance flight had been spotted over Southern England and soon the reason became obvious. The early morning mists cleared quickly as air temperatures rose rapidly, indicating that Monday 2nd September 1940 would be an exceptionally fine and hot day.

The high altitude Junkers 86 had taken off in twilight from an airfield in Belgium, to slip across the sea and follow the sunrise to Margate at 6.14am. As it traversed the southern counties, its crew found that the cloud cover that usually obscured so many targets was this morning, completely absent. Apart from high level, wispy cirrus clouds way above the aircraft, the observer in the Junkers surveyed a completely uninterrupted view. On his wireless set, he tapped out a brief broadcast and his coded message reported ten tenths visibility, from the curve of one distant horizon to the other. Luftwaffe High Command had been handed thirteen hours and thirty three minutes of perfectly clear weather, to take full advantage of before sunset.

On the other side of the Atlantic Ocean, the United States had narrowly escaped the ravages of a hurricane moving up its eastern seaboard. The British Isles would not be so lucky, as a man-made onslaught started to build upon its shores.

Just after 7.40am, operators at several RDF stations watched an enormous return signal grow on their display screens, indicating a huge conglomeration of aircraft gathering over Calais. Ten minutes later, the first wave of a hundred raiders was spotted crossing the North Foreland of Kent heading for the Thames Estuary. Fighter Command sent just four squadrons in pursuit, holding its main strength in reserve.

This would prove to be the correct decision for the moment.

While Edward Vigar caught up on his sleep after yesterday's exertions, the rest of the family resumed their routine. Patricia had made a start on the laundry and badgered both the girls to set off for work on their bicycles.

Ginny generally avoided cycling as much as she could.

She took to walking her bike the last few hundred yards up the steepest part of Station Road, as Betty slogged on ahead. Reunited at the police station, they coasted down the high street and parted company at Harrop's. Betty waited outside for Uncle Ernie to open up and Ginny carried on down Sidcup Hill towards the Klinger factory.

She arrived just before 8am, but instead of her usual journey to the first floor offices, Ginny was redirected to the production floor. She was given a set of overalls and shown to the changing rooms, to shed her now-redundant summer frock.

Everything in Ginny's world was changing at an alarming rate. As she stood at the production line, surrounded by the heat and noise of clumping, huge machinery, she was on the verge of tears as everything familiar and reassuring was stripped away from her. Following the harrowing experiences of the previous day, she quickly fell into a state of utter despair.

Some of the workers were quite friendly to this new girl, but she couldn't really take it all in, as a stern supervisor gave her a bewildering set of instructions for her new role. The coarser types of women working there took great pleasure in reminding Ginny of her fall from grace as a management secretary. By mid-morning, she was utterly exhausted and quite frightened by what was happening to her. Whereas her sister would have taken a more stoic approach, this was not part of Ginny's impetuous personality. She could only see that she had been thrown into a cauldron, with little hope of escape.

Fortunately, she saw one familiar face when Mabel Smith's older sister, Grace, made an appearance at the morning tea break. She was a supervisor in the next section, responsible for the cleaning and oiling of small parts prior to assembly. Noticing Ginny's distress, she came over and reassured her that everything would fall into place within a few days. She would try to get Ginny moved to her department, where the work was a little easier.

Back at home, Hazelmead Road had become quite a tourist attraction.

Hundreds of commuters found themselves without any London-bound service at the station that morning and news soon travelled about the terrific bomb damage to be seen just around the corner. In the absence of any transportation to work, many people took the opportunity to gawp at the bomb craters around the demolished houses and feel lucky that the Nazis hadn't called on their own homes yesterday afternoon. By 10am, trains were running up and down the line as far as Blackheath but no further, as the large junction at Lewisham Station had been heavily bombed.

There was quite a bit of conjecture amongst the commuters as to why Lewisham had been picked out for special attention, as the bombers could easily have gone on to attack the even bigger stations like London Bridge, Waterloo or Charing Cross. Most people thought that the barrage balloons or RAF fighters had scared the Germans off.

The reality was that it was a simple case of mistaken identity by a leaderless unit in the heat of battle. Nonetheless, with the railway lines destroyed at Lewisham, the train services of three suburban lines could no longer connect to the city. Every bus in South East London was full to the brim and bus stops hosted long queues of people, waiting patiently for their ride to work. Some held up cards with their destination written upon them and passing cars and lorries filled whatever space they had with anyone that wanted a lift to work. The most ardent saw that this situation would take days to resolve and went home to get their bicycle, if they had one, or simply walked the long miles into town.

Major Horst Muller's mission may have failed, but dropping 26 tonnes of bombs on a sprawling city like London was guaranteed to cause devastation somewhere. Six hundred and sixty four houses had been damaged, twenty three Lewisham residents were killed and eighty two injured. Tens of thousands of people were prevented from getting to work properly, costing the economy 400,000 man hours of lost productivity over the next few days.

This was just one raid by less than twenty aircraft, on a day that the Luftwaffe had flown over 900 sorties. Whilst only a minority of these missions ever fully achieved their key objectives, the incidental, cumulative damage to British industry and its defences was impossible to comprehend.

As the lunch break at Klinger's was called, Ginny went into the washrooms and stared at her face in the mirror over a basin. She saw a thick smear of black oil across her right temple. She shuddered, recalling the uncomprehending look on Jimmy's face as his life faded away.

Tears welled in her eyes as she tried to wash the dark stain from her skin. No matter how hard she rubbed with soap and water, it stubbornly refused to dissipate.

'Not so grand now are you, Miss La-di-da?' One of the burly women called out from behind her, to a chorus of laughter from her cronies.

Something snapped inside Ginny and she turned to confront her tormentor.

'Just… just… *fuck off* and leave me alone!' she shouted into her face.

Ginny ran out of the washroom, intent on finding some sunshine by which to eat her sandwiches and plan her escape.

As she walked out into the yard, her saviour was already waiting at the factory gates, on what seemed to be a perfectly quiet summer's day.

Any such calm would be shattered over the following hours as the Luftwaffe threw its full strength into the assault. By now, Fighter Command and its leaders stood on the brink of chaos, as the telephone lines between Dowding, Park and Leigh-Mallory rang red hot.

In this perfectly clear weather, the Luftwaffe was finding and attacking its targets with deadly accuracy. As 11 Group was being overwhelmed, Leigh-Mallory sought permission again and again to launch all of his fighters at once, in his *Big Wing*. Dowding held him back, evermore fearful of the consequences of making an irreversible strategic mistake at this critical juncture. Park was fully occupied trying to parry each German thrust, so the last thing he needed was 12 Group's aircraft running amok over his territory, adding to the confusion. Whilst the RAF commanders argued, they would certainly have been surprised to have known that their adversary was also suffering a crisis of indecision.

After a month of battle the RAF had not been defeated, yet it did now appear as if the battle had reached a turning point.

Over the last week, Fighter Command had been losing aircraft at least in equal rate to the Germans and both sides knew the Luftwaffe would win such morbid arithmetic. Furthermore, German pilots sensed that the quality of RAF flying was in decline and Luftwaffe intelligence reports confidently declared that the RAF's strength had fallen below 200 fighters. However, through subterfuge and round-the-clock factory production, the British actually had 690 combat fighters in service that day.

This gap between fiction and fact would profoundly skew Luftwaffe strategy. The greatest irony was that with such a high proportion of its strength called to combat every day, RAF fighters were rarely on the ground when Luftwaffe aircraft arrived to bomb or photograph them. In Poland and France, the element of surprise had won the air battle over the first few days for the Germans, destroying most of their opponents' aircraft before they even took off. This time, the British knew they were coming and had already dispersed their forces across a myriad of hiding places. Consequently, German fighter pilots wanted to focus on hunting down British fighters in the air. They believed that the bombers should be the lure, not the actual instrument of victory, to draw out the RAF's last Spitfires and Hurricanes… served up ready for destruction.

In theory, the Luftwaffe had an overwhelming advantage in the sheer quantity of experienced fighter pilots at its disposal. Yet without drop tanks, their Messerschmitts didn't have the range to chase British pilots to their doom. No-one in Germany knew, or cared about, the importance of these disposable fuel tanks and no priority had been given to their production. Besides, there were only small profits to be made from manufacturing such simple pieces of equipment.

Even so, Goering's instincts told him that the key to victory was to kill the men inside the RAF machines, not so much destroying the planes themselves. He understood that any combat pilot took a year to train properly. If his pilots could kill their expert British counterparts quicker, their raw replacements would be easy quarry. The proof of this was that after the great air battle was over; RAF statisticians would determine that just 16 of their most experienced pilots had, between them, shot down over 200 German aircraft.

Yet of all British airmen shot down over England, only a third were killed outright. The rest escaped by parachute, either wounded or immediately able to fly again. A week earlier, Goering had asked fighter ace Adolf Galland whether British pilots should be shot from their parachutes, but fortunately for them, a sense of chivalry was still upheld by most Luftwaffe pilots in 1940. Galland declared that he would consider it an act of murder and the subject was dropped. If they had both known the fate that awaited German cities in just a few years' time, they might have acted far less honourably that day.

Meanwhile, the commanders of the two Luftwaffe air fleets in the battle, Generalfeldmarschals' Hugo Sperrle and Albert Kesselring, completely disagreed about the true state of affairs.

The former argued vociferously to continue the pressure on RAF airfields, as he was more attuned to the advice of his fighter pilots like Galland. However, Kesselring put greater store in the intelligence reports and chose to believe that Fighter Command was already on its knees.

As a former army officer, he regarded airpower as a tactical weapon for the support of land warfare and this belied the reason for the Messerschmitt 109's short range. The aircraft's design had traded size for higher performance at the expense of fuel capacity. This mattered little in its intended function to use on forward airfields to leap-frog alongside the army's rapid advance.

However, thrust into the role of long range escort fighter over Britain, the little Messerschmitt could not meet these new expectations. The jagdgeschwaden were losing just as many pilots from running out of fuel, as they were in combat. Such was their frustration and fear of the English Channel that they had taken to calling it *The Sewer*. No matter which strategy was employed, the fundamental failing in the German case for victory was the inadequate range of its high performance fighters.

Kesselring was increasingly mindful of the shrinking timescale left for the Wehrmacht's Channel crossing. He was impatient to commence the next phase, the destruction of London's communications and supply routes to the forthcoming invasion front. He proposed that the time had come to seal off South Eastern England from the rest of the country. Goering listened to all the arguments. Although his instincts leant towards Sperrle's wish to maintain pressure on RAF airfields... he had the added burden of reporting directly to the Führer.

Adolf Hitler wanted results and had run out of patience.

Furthermore, German public opinion was incensed by the RAF's apparently indiscriminate bombing of the Reich. This was the first ever time that German cities had been attacked from the air and the attendant outrage was completely disproportionate to the meagre weight of bombs dropped. Fearful of losing political capital, both with his peers and the German people, Goering found himself backed into a corner. Under this immense political pressure, he decided it was time to attempt the much vaunted Knockout Blow. He wanted an all-out attack, to strike as soon as possible.

Goering had convinced himself that the impact of this blow might topple Churchill's government or give the Wehrmacht the necessary conditions to launch the invasion. At the very least, he hoped the British would be forced to throw their scant fighter strength into the fight and his Messerschmitts might yet prevail.

In short, it was a three way bet and Goering didn't hesitate to tell his Führer what he knew he wanted to hear.

Chapter 26

When Edward Vigar finally awoke late that morning, he was especially grateful for his profession as a small-time builder. One of the advantages of being his own boss was that he didn't have to clock on and off like most paid workers. With only five hours sleep since he returned home in the early hours, he still felt mentally and physically exhausted by the aftermath of yesterday's air raid.

As he stirred from sleep, he thought over the previous day's events and, on balance, was pleased with how his community had coped with adversity.

Incredibly, poor little Jimmy Marsden had been the only fatality of the attack. Whilst a number of people had been injured, they had suffered no more than cuts and bruises. Even Mrs Jones, whose entire house had collapsed around her, had escaped more or less unscathed. To cap it all, one of her neighbour's children found her false teeth in the remnants of her larder. Bar a missing molar on the bottom plate, she could now face the world with confidence again. Before going on guard duty in Eltham, Albert had fetched Dr Barnard from his house in Station Road to sign Jimmy's death certificate, so that funeral arrangements could get underway. Sergeant Bilsborough had managed to get a telephone call through to Bexley Police Station and from that, Mrs Marsden's sister had been brought over to join the family in their grief.

Even Old Sid had proven up to the task. He successfully sniffed out a ruptured gas main down by Augustine Avenue and evacuated all the residents thereabouts, with a lot of shouting and waving of hands. The gas was turned off at that end of the road and, finally, everyone was allowed home just before sunset. The water mains had taken a bashing too. There were puddles welling up all over the place, giving the Water Board engineers lots to fix over the coming days.

All in all, the Sidcup ARP had fulfilled its duties admirably and Edward was proud of his men. Fortunately, the Nazi bombs had mostly fallen, to little effect, in the garden of Lamorbey House. The last one impacted a hundred yards short of the Plaza... so Dad's Palace had made it through the ordeal too.

Edward lay in bed awhile contemplating all of this a little more, until the rasp of the lawn mower in the front garden aroused his curiosity. He couldn't be bothered to unclip the blackout blind and stumbled downstairs in his pyjamas, to be presented by a most unexpected sight. Whilst Patricia was in the midst of her usual Monday washday routine, the girls had long since gone to work and it was Ken that had been mowing the lawns.

Patricia smiled sweetly as he entered the kitchen.

Looking out to the back garden, Edward could see the grass was already cut out there.

Ken appeared with the last of the cuttings for the compost heap and looked hot after pushing the mower up and down. He emptied the grass box and stood upright to rest his back for a few moments. Seeing how sweaty Ken looked, Edward recalled just how heavy army trousers were in the heat. He was pleased to see that the young soldier was still here as, after his arrival home, Edward had left that decision up to Patricia. It was her house and if Ken's antics were too much to bear, of course, he had to go.

Edward would later find out that his wife had watched that young man in the garden for a full thirty minutes that morning, before finally talking to him. Despite the drama of the early hours, she had taken pity on him again. Not least because of her memories of their early years of marriage, when Edward had struggled with his own night demons of wartime horrors.

Ken walked back into the kitchen.

'Hello Mr Vigar, you're up then? I hope I didn't wake you with the lawnmower?'

'No… not at all,' Edward lied and then continued, 'so are you fit enough for real men's work?'

Ken looked utterly puzzled.

'I'm going to teach you the joys of rendering this morning,' Edward continued. 'You and I have got a job to do… *at the Palace.*'

Patricia smirked at the look of bewilderment on Ken's face.

John Fellowes stood by the Rolls Royce limousine and watched Madame Maude storm across the yard at Bridger's Farm.

Within a second of opening the door for her, she had set off like a greyhound let loose from its trap at the races. He was relieved that her wrath had been turned upon someone else for a change. Actually, he had the feeling that he was rather going to enjoy what would happen next.

They had arrived just before 11am and Maude immediately set to a tour of the premises, moving from building to building in her quest for information. Over the last five minutes, John had seen her mood darken with every step

He decided it was high time to employ his usual strategy to keep himself out of harm's way and went to the boot of the car. He took out a small bucket, filled it with water from the tin can he kept there as well, soaked a wash-leather and started to polish the car's bodywork.

As long as he was working… he would remain invisible.

John had turned up for work that morning planning to lose himself in the garden for a few hours as usual, but instead Maude had instructed him to prepare the Rolls for a journey. The destination hadn't surprised him, given snippets of conversation he had overheard during the preceding weeks. Like most servants, John heard and saw a lot of things about the Delafort family and could draw his own conclusions about their affairs quite successfully. He had seen this one coming for a long time and was increasingly hopeful that Mr Raymond's undoing was nigh.

Maude's voice boomed across the yard and he looked up to see that Samuel, the youngest of Mr Cameron's sons had arrived to greet her. Although they were too far away to be heard clearly, the look on the lad's face pretty much confirmed that he was *getting a right good bollocking*, John thought with a wry smile. Then he felt sorry for him, as he recalled that Samuel was a slow and dim-witted boy and probably had no idea what Maude was raging about.

At first glance, the farmyard looked much like any other, with the cottage on the right and the other sides bounded by three large wooden sheds, for livestock and machinery. Looking straight ahead towards the pastures and orchards all seemed neat and tidy, but something was missing.

It struck John how quiet it was here today.

He realised the absent element was the sound of all the animals he would expect to hear on a busy farm.

Maude and the young farmhand went inside the cottage and John decided it was safe enough to take a look around for himself. He strolled over to the pig shed and found about twenty porkers there, looking happy enough. Yet from his last visit earlier in the year, he would have expected to have seen at least a hundred fattening up to provide the nation with chops, ham and bacon. He walked back out to the yard and saw Maude and the boy marching across the first field, no doubt in search of his father or even more importantly, Mr Raymond.

John took his pipe out of his pocket and charged its bowl with fresh tobacco.

Once alight, he sucked at it thoughtfully.

He did a quick count of the sheep in the fields and estimated that about sixty ewes and lambs were in sight and smiled to himself again. Back in March he had seen at least that many pregnant sheep, so there should be almost twice as many of their offspring as well by now. Given the value of black market meat, he surmised that probably half of the new lambs had never made it past Easter. Fancy restaurants and hotels in London would pay twenty shillings, ten times the ration price, for an illicit leg of spring lamb for their rich diners. By adding in the missing pigs and God knows how many other fiddles… all in all, Raymond must be pocketing an absolute, ill-gotten fortune.

Well, as sure as eggs are eggs, he thought, *Madame Delafort won't stand for this.*

More to the point, she wouldn't want her nephew going to prison either.

By now her voice could be heard bellowing again, at Mr Cameron presumably, from somewhere behind the cottage.

John puffed away on his pipe for a few minutes more and enjoyed the late summer heat as he learnt against a stone wall. Every now and then the deep thump of explosions echoed from far away, to remind him that all was far from well. The blue sky was covered by contrails left by aircraft pursuing their deadly tasks.

His thoughts returned to the war, never far from anyone's mind these days. The talk of Foots Cray pubs last night had been Sidcup's brush with the Nazi invader and he fancied taking a look at the bomb damage himself, when he got a chance. He felt lucky that his little village was far too insignificant to ever warrant any attention from the nasty Hun.

Maude appeared from the cottage doorway with a face dark as thunder.

She walked briskly towards John.

He stood to attention.

'Fellowes... take me to Mr Burridge immediately,' she barked.

John noted that in Maude's opinion, her solicitor deserved a formal title, yet he did not. He watched her adjust the bandage on her hand with a little discomfort, then took his cue to open the rear passenger door for her to alight.

He closed it firmly behind her.

Taking his place in the driver's seat, he was safely separated from his employer's rage by the glass cabin partition. For his own part, he was disappointed not to have seen Mr Raymond get the stripping down he deserved. John puffed his cheeks, exhaled with disappointment, started the engine and slipped the clutch, then got the vehicle under way.

As they drove out of the farm, he decided to head towards the Welling Way, then across to Blackfen and up past Lamorbey to the solicitor's office in Sidcup High Street. That way he might get a glimpse of all the bombed houses he had heard so much about.

As they drove along, he weighed up Maude's next move.

It certainly made sense to bring her trusted legal advisor into consultation about the brewing scandal Raymond had precipitated. Furthermore, as it was a Monday, Dr Higgins would be arriving for dinner later, as was their routine before Bridge Club. John could see that Maude was gathering her cabal of most trusted advisors to plot a way out of this situation. *As sure as eggs are eggs*, he thought again, *the old battle-axe would find a way to wriggle out of this one.*

John shook his head gently and exhaled again with resignation.

As much as he would love to witness Raymond's fall from grace, he knew that it would probably never happen… considering the influence that Madame Maude wielded around here.

After a late breakfast, it had taken Ken and Edward over forty minutes to walk just 150 yards to the cinema, as they negotiated their way through all the sightseers surveying the bomb damage.

Edward's habitually-carried ARP helmet and satchel had brought him plenty of questions from everyone on the way. John Topham, a famous local photographer, spotted them and insisted on recording the pair for posterity against the backdrop of devastation. Then they were further delayed by shopkeepers seeking advice about blast damage to their premises. Apart from smoke damage, the front of the Plaza was pretty much unscathed, its glass doors having been boarded-up since the outbreak of war. It was well past 11am by the time they eventually walked around the back of the cinema. Edward was anxious to get started, before Roger Mellard, the manager, arrived. However, the dismal sight that greeted them made it obvious that no builder's work would be done there today.

A huge pile of collapsed scaffolding lay at the base of the wall that Edward was meant to be repairing.

The rendering here had first started to crack about three months ago, but it had been a low priority for Mr Mellard at first. With much wider events to worry about, a few fractures in the cement coating across the back of the building held no great importance. That is, until a twenty by five foot long section fell off last week, near to where children from the adjacent flats were playing and he accepted that something had to be done. This huge, new building had taken several years to properly settle on its foundations and Edward had been in and out many times, to fix snags, here and there.

Now, he was confronted by a much bigger problem.

He had spent a week, on his own, erecting wooden scaffolding up the sixty foot high wall so that he could repair it, only now to see it all collapsed in a heap at its base.

Ken and Edward walked closer to survey the damage and its likely cause, when they saw a huge brick chimney stack lying on top of the pile of broken timbers and planks. A quick glance at the roof of the adjoining flats highlighted the thirty foot tall stack's absence from its rightful place.

A middle aged lady with her hair in curlers appeared on the steel stairway that led from the flats.

'A right racket that made yesterday when it came down, I thought my ceiling was going to collapse and kill me!' she shouted out.

'When did all this happen?' Edward asked.

'When that Nazi flew over of course,' she paused for effect. 'There I was… screaming for my life and that bomb blew up over the other side and shook everything up.'

She straightened her housecoat, self-importantly. 'You should see the state of my flat… cracks everywhere, windows broken and my doors won't shut properly now. It shouldn't be allowed… that's what I say,' she declared indignantly.

'Are you from the landlord?' she added as an afterthought.

'No, I'm the builder hired to sort out this wall,' Edward responded.

He realised that the job had got a lot bigger, as a patch of render about fifty foot wide and twenty foot tall had also fallen. Given the chronic shortage of building materials, this job would have to change from repair to stripping off the rest of the wall instead.

Either way, it was now a huge piece of work for Edward alone. Mind you, there would be a good amount of money in it for him now; with lots of labour to charge for, but no materials cost... a small-time builder's dream job.

'Are you sure you're not from the landlord?' the woman asked more pointedly. 'Renie's place is just the same, someone should be sent to fix it all up.'

'Really, I'm not, Madame. I'm just here for the cinema.' Edward explained.

She didn't look too convinced, but faced with two denials there wasn't much else to be said. Disappointed by his response, she turned and walked back up the stairs to her flat.

Once she was up at her level, she called out one last time.

'IT SHOULDN'T BE ALLOWED!' she shouted angrily. 'If you see the landlord... make sure you tell him that Mrs Dockwell isn't happy.'

Then she disappeared from view.

Ken looked at Edward.

'It shouldn't be allowed,' he said, mimicking the irate woman.

Edward shook his head.

'Maybe she should have a word with Mr Hitler too?' he suggested, with a laugh.

Ken walked over to the heap of fallen timbers. It stood about twenty feet high, as each level of Edward's scaffold had collapsed on top of another under the huge weight of the chimney stack.

Edward joined him and the pair stood together, surveying the damage.

'I guess I won't be learning about rendering today, Mr Vigar?' Ken concluded.

Edward thought things over and made his decision.

'I'll have to take my time to sort this mess out. I'll tackle it later in the week,' he replied. 'Today… I think you'll be learning about country fencing instead Ken. Let's go down to my yard and get the van.'

They set off for Vigar's Builders Yard, down by the station sidings.

As they walked, Edward talked about what he loved about his profession and why it could suit a young man like Ken. It felt to Ken as if he was almost being interviewed for a job. Their conversation was broken, first by the deep sound of heavy explosions far away and again, minutes later, by the drone of many aircraft engines. They looked up and saw thirty Hurricanes and Spitfires heading south.

Conversation turned to the air battle presumably taking place somewhere down in Kent. Just as they approached the yard, the grand old Delafort Rolls Royce passed them by.

Edward caught a glimpse of Madame Maude in the back, looking as inscrutable as ever. The high-pitched warble of the siren up at the police station filled their ears.

'Oh for God's Sake, we'll never get anything done at this rate,' Edward exclaimed in frustration.

They both surveyed the sky.

There wasn't an aircraft in sight now, just those ever-present contrails marking their passage.

'Shall we push on?' Ken asked.

'Yes… let's get moving,' Edward replied and they hurried along.

As Edward and Ken headed over to Eltham, a huge raid of over 250 German aircraft was approaching the Kent coast at Margate.

Park ordered all of his squadrons back into the air, as he didn't want to be caught napping again. He wanted everything thrown at this formation, before it split up into smaller groups and became impossible to track across the battle area. Unfortunately, the British fighters were bounced by over 70 Messerschmitts near Sheerness and the bombers slipped by, to split into their different mission groups.

By 1.30pm, the sky across Kent and Surrey became a tangled confusion of marauding fighters and inbound and outbound Nazi bombers. One airfield after another was bombed, as the German fighters protected their larger brethren from RAF interference, but at a heavy cost to themselves.

The British fighters were just returning to their bases to refuel and re-arm, when, once again, the call to scramble was sent out from Fighter Command's sector stations. Yet another attack of over 200 aircraft appeared on the RDF screens and many of these raiders were making their second visit to Britain this day. The aircrew of both sides shared their exhaustion as, time and time again, they flew into combat.

In particular, the German bomber crews were being stretched beyond their limit. Their sorties would often be three times the duration of the fighters, as they had to fly across France to assembly points, even before embarking on each foray across the Channel. Combined with the escalating frequency of night missions, the bomber crews of the kampfgeschwaden were being called into a twenty four hour battle and the strain was becoming unbearable.

None of this was apparent to the people of England as the crash of battle echoed far and wide. Wherever there was an airfield, there seemed never to be a moment's peace and quiet, whether it was from the roar of Hurricanes and Spitfires taking off, the drone of approaching raiders, or the rasp of machine gun fire high above. It looked like the

Germans were finally getting the upper hand, as British fighter losses mounted rapidly through the afternoon.

Later that evening, squadron reports on Dowding's desk revealed that 33 RAF fighters had been lost that day, 20 pilots killed or seriously injured and all but two of 11 Group's aerodromes bombed.

The commander-in-chief's eyes welled with tears, as much from exhaustion as emotion, as he fretted about how much longer *his brave boys* would survive.

Chapter 27

Much earlier that day in Queen Mary's Hospital in Sidcup, a German airman had awoken in bed thankful to be alive, even if at the price of being marooned in enemy territory.

A short while after waking he had dared to lift his head, to take a cautious look around the ward. It was early morning and the sunlight was feeling its way past recently opened curtains, to reach out across the other patients as they slept. The beds, scant furniture and medical equipment all had a foreign look to him. He saw that the room was formed from a long wooden hut about twenty metres long, with the unclad boarded ceiling rising to the roof apex. From the rafters hung a long line of electric lamps and just two had been left on through the night hours, to cast a dim yellow glow upon the ward. He sensed that this was once a military building, but had long since donned civilian garb.

The German's head throbbed painfully.

His right leg felt a whole lot worse.

Looking at the plaster cast stretched out in front of him, he considered that the pain was a small price to pay in return for his life.

By his bedside sat an old soldier, perhaps sixty years old, who bore an expression of bored antipathy towards his charge. Beside him, the German's uniform jacket hung from a steel surgical stand along with his blood-stained trousers, cut fully open along one leg, for all to see.

Without his uniform, clothed in hospital pyjamas, the German felt entirely stripped of his identity and utterly lost in a foreign land. Despite his fatigue, he was on edge. The adrenalin-fuelled life that hallmarked his existence until just a few hours ago would take a while to subside. Looking around the room, the beds were all occupied by civilian patients and two were awake already, staring back at him with a mixture of curiosity and ill-feeling. He didn't understand what they said to each other, but through sign language and gestures he tried to express his thanks for their kindness. He wasn't altogether sure whether they understood him, but he felt better for trying.

Thinking about the previous day, he could remember the take-off from Rosières, the flight across the sea, minor actions; the routines common to any combat flight.

Yet after that, everything was very confused.

He remembered beginning the bomb-run and next, he recalled lying in a grassy field, racked with pain. He remembered voices, shouting, British soldiers, being poked hard in the ribs with a rifle, being carried into the back of a small truck.

More pain… then he passed out.

Sometime later he awoke in a small prison cell, just as two stern-faced men in black uniforms opened the armoured door with a crash. When he saw the gnarled wooden truncheons hanging from their belts, he was thrown into absolute terror.

Despite the agony of his broken leg, he had tried to crawl into the corner of the cell for protection and pleaded desperately for his life. However, after a lot of shooshing and palm-raising by the Englishmen, he calmed down a little. Only when a canvass stretcher was brought into the cell did he fully accept that they were not going to beat him to death after all. After that it was all a blur again, until he properly woke up in this hospital bed thirty minutes ago.

The old soldier looked at him with growing interest, now that his captive was fully awake. After a while, the frostiness between adversaries thawed a little. The guard smiled and produced a packet of cigarettes. The German gratefully took one but, after a few puffs, his head swam so badly that he had to lay his head back on the pillow.

He stared at the ceiling and collected his thoughts again.

New images came to him. He saw the interior of the bomber, bucking and rearing like a wild animal. He recalled terrific noise, smoke and fire, someone shouting at him and then a ghastly feeling of falling.

He shifted in his bed a little, his groin and chest felt bruised and painful. He remembered the violent wrench of the parachute harness, then hitting the ground with agonising impact.

Suddenly, a voice spoke to him in perfect, if somewhat old-fashioned German. Its tone suggested an older man and the airman made to lift his head to look at its source.

'Good morning. No, don't get up, not yet at least. I want you to lie perfectly still,' the voice instructed with authority. 'Fortunately for you, I spent a fair part of my youth in your homeland and acquired modest skill with *Deutsch*… so we can have a little chat.'

'Thank you Herr Doktor,' the German replied, as he stared at the ceiling.

'Now then, you've had a blow to your head,' the voice said quietly. 'You have a mild concussion…as well as breaking your right leg, but I'm sure you are well aware of that already.'

A pencil appeared in front of the airman's eyes.

He tracked its tip left and right and up and down, as instructed by the kindly voice. Hands felt expertly across his limbs, up and down his body.

Satisfied by the lack of any adverse reaction, the doctor spoke again.

'Well, you seem a lot more together now, shall we try sitting up?'

He said something in English.

The soldier rose slowly from his chair and helped the airman to sit upright in bed. Without changing the blank expression on his face, he sat straight back down.

The airman looked to the German speaker on his right.

He was an elderly man in a white medical coat, in his late sixties probably, perhaps older. Although seated now, he looked to be quite tall, but lean and wore small, round horn-rimmed spectacles. His silver hair was neatly parted and he sported a flowing, old-fashioned moustache. In sum, he carried an air of great authority and wisdom. The doctor looked back at the airman with the non-judgemental expression of someone who had a long career dedicated to the care of others, whatever the circumstances.

Given the reasons for his predicament, the German felt ashamed.

'I'm very sorry Herr Doktor. I'm sorry that… we… I… have come here to…' he began to apologise, but he could find no more words.

'Yes, quite.' Robert Higgins responded courteously, but firmly. 'Well there's *nothing* more to be said on that subject.'

The airman glanced nervously at the old soldier.

His lack of reaction seemed to confirm that he was oblivious to their conversation in German.

'Now then, you have a broken tibia,' Robert continued. 'It was a compound fracture, rather nasty actually.'

He paused.

'So you were brought straight into surgery on arrival, but fortunately the blood-flow to your foot had not been compromised.'

Robert thought for a moment, to find the correct word in German.

'The *narcotic* from surgery will make you feel fairly poorly for a while longer and then there's your head injury. As far as we can tell, it was only a mild concussion, no fracture, so you will have a bad headache for a few days. You may experience memory loss, confusion, sickness, blurred vision and tiredness in any, or all combinations. If these symptoms worsen, you must tell someone immediately. I have written all this up in your notes, they will go with you to your next destination.'

The German took a while to take in this barrage of information.

'Will I recover well, Herr Doktor?' he asked.

Robert looked over his patient's medical notes upon a clipboard and considered his answer.

'I can see no present reason that would prevent a full recovery, however nothing is guaranteed and you will be wearing that cast for two months. It'll be quite a task to get your full fitness back after that.'

His expression took on a more serious look.

'Unfortunately, with a severe injury such as this… your leg may never be quite as it was before,' he explained.

'Thank you for your help, I am grateful,' the German replied with relief. Starting to think about his future, he then asked, 'where will I be sent after here?'

'I couldn't possibly tell you young man. Not allowed to, but actually I don't know anyway,' Robert replied. 'The authorities will wish to question you before you are interned… you are *their* property now.'

The notion of captivity was starting to dawn upon the German. He was no longer a free man, if his life in Luftwaffe service could ever have been called *free* that is.

Robert stood up and made his farewell.

'Well, take care of yourself young man. Goodbye.'

Impulsively, the German reached out and caught Robert's arm.

'Herr Doktor… have you seen any of my comrades here?'

Robert considered his response.

Deciding it held no great security significance he bent down and spoke in a low voice.

'I'm sorry. I understand that you were the only survivor from your aeroplane. So… you should be grateful.'

He walked away, leaving the German airman to mourn the loss of his comrades.

Stabsfeldwebel Freund stood in the kitchen of Horst Muller's billet, in the village of Meharicourt.

He had just finished packing the major's personal effects into his travel trunk and would take them back to the airfield. There they would be held for a few days, in the slim hope of his reappearance. Failing that miracle, they would be sent back to his family in Germany, along with the possessions of thirty six other airmen that had failed to return or died from their injuries, as a result of yesterday's second mission.

Of the nineteen bombers despatched on the raid, only ten had returned here intact. Six Heinkels had been shot down over England and a seventh had crashed three kilometres short of the airfield, killing all on-board. Two more had landed at airfields closer to the coast in a pretty poor, shot-up state. At least one of those was likely to be a write-off, from what Freund had overhead in the operations office.

By all accounts, the mission had proceeded well at first, despite the foul-up over the fighter cover. Then it was mauled by British fighters. The ever-resolute Major Muller had carried on regardless, but it seemed now he had paid the greatest price. His aircraft dropped out of formation after receiving extensive flak damage and had not been seen since. Another had taken hits and crashed within just a few seconds. Whilst the remainder of the staffel did go on to attack the target, Freund doubted that the tremendous cost had been worth it.

Heads will roll over this, he thought. *But not many heads hang around here for long anyway.*

Gefrieter Amacher dragged the major's trunk out to the staff car.

Freund knew he had many hours ahead of typing up reports on yesterday's raid, but at least his calculations for fuel and munitions were going to be a lot simpler from now. The roar of aircraft engines from the runways reminded him that it was business as usual, as the rest of the gruppe prepared for battle anew

The two men lifted the trunk onto the back seat of the car and got into the front. As they drove back to the airfield, both of them privately wondered what sort of man would be sent as Muller's replacement.

Albert Culpepper was standing in the street outside his timber yard, when the familiar sight of Edward's blue van appeared. It crossed the junction of Eltham High Street and the Well Hall Road that led down to the station, and pulled up next to Albert.

He was surprised to see his good friend appear so unexpectedly and walked over to the kerb. Ken stepped out of the passenger door. Edward appeared from the other side and walked round to greet him.

'What are you doing out here Fingers? I thought you'd be having your nap,' Edward joked.

'Looking at *that*,' he replied, pointing upwards.

In that moment, Edward and Ken both became aware of all the people that had also stopped on the street and joined their skyward gaze. Away in the distance, perhaps a mile or so to the north, a single aircraft was flying erratically, about 5000 feet above the town. It seemed to be ambling, drifting, climbing momentarily and banking to one side, then the other.

Broadly speaking, it was flying in a wide circle around the neighbourhood. Its distinctive humpback fuselage identified it as a British Hurricane fighter, the cockpit canopy was wide open and to all appearances… the pilot's seat was empty.

'Oh my good God. How long has this been going on Bert?' Edward exclaimed, now as astounded as the other onlookers around them.

'About fifteen minutes I reckon. I was in the office pottering around and I heard the engine overhead,' Albert replied. 'It's flown over about a half a dozen times I think. Christ knows what's going to happen to it?'

'It's going to crash, that's what,' Ken joined in, matter-of-factly.

They all stood together and watched it with dreadful fascination. Rationally speaking, the prospect of a three ton, pilotless aircraft tearing around should have sent everyone scurrying to take cover. Instead, everyone just stood by, in awe of the peculiar event.

'You wouldn't have thought it possible with modern aircraft, would you Bert?' Edward mused out loud. 'Those old stringbags in the last one did that sort of thing… but they were just like kites floating around… compared to that monster up there.'

The Hurricane wandered south and disappeared from sight below the roof tops. Everyone waited for the sickening crash of impact, but it didn't come. The ghostly fighter had taken itself off somewhere else, to extend its existence for just a while longer before its inevitable demise.

'Maybe the pilot is still in it and has woken up?' Albert replied hopefully.

None of them would ever know.

Twenty minutes later, the fighter from 253 Squadron, that had only flown down from Scotland three days earlier, ended its brief life by diving into an apple orchard in Keston. It crashed six miles short of Kenley aerodrome, having nearly made it home. Its pilot would take a day to return to base, having parachuted from the stricken aircraft over Gravesend, eighteen miles away. He never suspected that his badly shot-up aircraft had that much life left in it. Fortunately, no-one was hurt by the crash and the pilot flew again within hours of his return.

After the errant Hurricane disappeared from view, everyone waited to see if it would make a dramatic reappearance. When five minutes passed without a further sighting, most people lost interest and resumed their afternoon's activities. Edward explained to Albert that he was looking for timber good enough to sort out fence repairs at Bridger's Farm, so they all walked into the yard to see what might be found. The two older men walked up the stairs to the office to get the kettle on the go. A brew of tea was required before anything could proceed.

Ken waited in the open-air section of the yard. He recalled his two previous visits, after he escaped from France and, more recently, when his visit on Saturday led to an overnight stay here.

Looking around, it was obvious that wartime restrictions were now having their effect on business. The pens and racks contained little new timber since his first visit, but now there were huge stacks of rough, salvage wood. It was mostly old floor boards and roof timbers, a lot of it blackened by smoke.

Albert came down the steel staircase with a two tin mugs of tea, with Edward following close behind with his own drink.

He must have read Ken's expression.

'Not what it was… not by a long shot son,' Albert said, as he handed him a mug.

'I guess it's hard to get now that everything is rationed, Mr Culpepper?' Ken replied.

'Everything is restricted,' Albert revealed. 'Imports have completely dried up since the war began. Shipping is needed for other things I guess. I'm much like a small shopkeeper now and I can only sell if people have the proper paperwork.'

He continued sadly. 'Practically all that I can get is only second-hand. You can guess where that is coming from…and more and more each day. I suppose I'll get by… only myself to keep now.'

Ken felt sorry for Albert. He had gathered from conversation over Sunday dinner that he was a relatively recent widower.

Edward cut in, to change the subject.

'So, Bert… what can you find me for Bridger's?'

Before Albert could reply, they were deafened by the throaty roar of an aircraft right above their heads. It was so loud, they all ducked instinctively. It felt so close that they might be pulverised by the sound alone.

Most of their tea was now spread across the cobbles.

'JESUS H CHRIST! Is that Hurricane back?' Edward shouted.

They all looked up, to see a thick trail of black smoke stretched right across the sky, only a few hundred feet above them. Then they heard the clatter of boots across the stones behind them.

Young Bob Taylor had run in from the street.

'It's a Jerry Mr Culpepper,' he shouted excitedly. 'A real proper Jerry and it's on fire. I think it's going to crash!'

Chapter 28

Shortly after midday, a single formation of 250 German bombers and fighters crossed the South Coast at Hastings. Throwing everything into the fray, Keith Park scrambled eleven RAF fighter squadrons and a gargantuan air battle quickly developed over eastern Kent.

Park had little left in reserve.

The Luftwaffe was targeting his airfields with venom, but was also going after key aircraft factories in earnest as well. Just after 1pm, a bad situation for the British got a whole lot worse, as another raid of over 200 aircraft was seen approaching from France. This time, 12 Group was ordered to send in more and more fighters in support of Park's squadrons. Fighter Command was being drawn into the gigantic air battle of higher and higher stakes that Dowding had long-feared.

At his headquarters at Bentley Priory, Dowding watched the evermore crowded plotting table with increasing anxiety. He recalled the frenetic air battles at the worst moment above the old Western Front. When the Germans broke through in 1918 and began pushing the British army back to the sea, the Royal Flying Corps had almost bled to death before the rout was turned.

The memory of this had stopped him sending more RAF fighters to France in June, but now he wondered if he had only really delayed an inevitable fate. The Germans had already near-destroyed Britain's home army and seemed poised to deliver the same fate to his beloved Fighter Command.

Raymond Delafort was blissfully unaware of the forces gathering against him, or his country, as he headed for Craywood House.

As he tore down Sandy Lane, accompanied by the chugging roar of his motorbike's engine, he just couldn't believe his luck with Ginny's misfortunate reassignment to drudgery at the factory. There couldn't have been a more timely contrast between her new, dreary situation and the life of status that a union with the Delaforts appeared to offer.

Of course, he hadn't the slightest intention of actually fulfilling his implied promise to walk her up the wedding aisle. Virginia Vigar's long term future was of no concern to him. All he cared about was how much fun he could have with her in the present, so her tears were easily stemmed by his false declaration of love.

He had to admit though, when her eyes opened wide, she really had looked the most beautiful woman in the world to him.

Raymond laughed at his fleeting sentimentality.

He returned to the absolutely delicious thought of what was nestled inside her knickers. It seemed that tonight would be his best chance yet, to savour that pleasure for real.

He pulled onto the gravel drive of Craywood House, drove across to the garage and discovered that its doors had been left open.

The garage was empty.

It seemed there were no bounds to Raymond's good fortune that afternoon.

With Aunt Maude out of the way for the time being, he would be free of any more difficult questions about the farm. He certainly had quite a tight schedule to meet. First, he would finish arranging the summerhouse, the thought of that made him laugh again and then he would quickly return to Bridger's. There he would clean and polish the motorbike, get something to eat, dress up and be ready at the Plaza cinema by 7.30pm.

He set to work with all the enthusiasm of a small boy who has been offered an extra special treat in reward for his labours.

Two musketeers, a soldier and a young home guard rushed outside in search of the source of the dramatic noise overhead. There they were joined by the shopkeepers of Eltham and their customers on the pavement too. Everyone could hear the aircraft's engine misfiring somewhere above and a trail of thick oily smoke hung over the high street.

As they craned their necks, a Messerschmitt 109 shot overhead, only a few hundred feet above them. Its right landing wheel was fully extended, yet the other was tucked up in the left wing, advertising that something was wrong with the aircraft's mechanical systems. It turned westwards momentarily and climbed a little before belching a thick clump of smoke, accompanied by a throaty bang from somewhere within its engine.

With a lurch, it banked sharply northwards and pulled round in a circuit behind the opposite parade of shops.

The left-hand wheel started to lower down.

'He's going to try to land it!' Ken exclaimed.

'There's only one place round here he can get that thing down... behind the palace,' Albert responded. 'I'll get my rifle... let's go after him.'

Before anyone could say a thing, he ran back into the yard and headed towards his office.

'What shall we do?' Bob asked, bewildered and excited all at once.

'You heard the man... Let's capture a Nazi!' Edward responded.

Albert ran back out onto the street with his home guard Ross rifle in hand and they all piled into the Vigar Builders' van. Edward revved the engine, while Bob clambered in the back and Albert sat in the passenger seat. Ken stood outside on the running board, clutching the open door as the vehicle set off.

'Here he comes again,' Ken shouted and indeed Albert's prediction seemed correct.

The German fighter completed a circuit around the town and now, a thousand yards distant, flew towards them with its engine misfiring and belching even more smoke. It was heading south towards King John's Meadows behind Eltham Palace, about 500 hundred yards away.

The little blue van tore up to the crossroad and lurched around the corner, narrowly avoiding collision with a horse-drawn milk cart. Bystanders began to run behind it in pursuit, also wishing to witness the extraordinary arrival of their enemy. The van tore down Court Yard, slowed sharply at the Moat Bridge and then turned a sharp right down the narrow lane, to skirt along the perimeter of the fields.

They arrived just as the Messerschmitt set down and bounced across the uneven meadow at breakneck speed. It seemed that the pilot had managed to land his aircraft safely, when its left wheel juddered and partially retracted. This sudden movement threw the aircraft briefly back into the air, spinning a half loop, before it came crashing down on its back and skidded to a halt.

Edward gunned the van down the lane for about seven hundred yards and then slammed on the brakes. They jumped out and ran part-way across the grass towards the over-turned aircraft.

Then they stopped.

No-one knew what to do.

The Messerschmitt was lying upside down, with the sky blue of its underwing camouflage facing the sky. Its left wing had taken the full force of the impact, bent and half-twisted backwards, to now prop up the fuselage about one foot off the ground. All was suddenly quiet, apart from the tinkling of hot metal somewhere within the engine bay.

They heard the muffled sound of the pilot shouting.

He was alive, but trapped. Hanging upside down in his harness, his head and shoulders were visible through the steel-framed glass canopy, which he had swung only half-open until it wedged against the ground, preventing his escape.

The reason for his anxiety became only too clear, as the stench of aviation spirit filled the air.

Ken could see fuel leaking out of the ruptured underfloor tank, now above the trapped pilot. It was dripping down inside the cockpit and over the German, as he pounded against the canopy with his left fist, in a desperate attempt to force it further open.

'Oh my god, the poor sod, is there anything we can do?' Edward said, echoing everyone's thoughts.

To compound the awfulness of the moment, the canopy glass shattered and they could hear his shouts with full clarity. The German had found his pistol and used its butt to hammer and break the thinner side glass.

Still upside down, he managed to push the metal frame of the weakened canopy back a little more.

He squeezed his head, shoulders and one arm free… but then stuck fast.

So he took to using his free arm to push against the side of the fuselage, as everyone heard his feet kicking desperately inside the cockpit. They couldn't understand his panicked words, but it was obvious that he was pleading for help.

'We must do something!' Bob implored his comrades.

Only a madman would go anywhere near the crashed aircraft, which was now, to all purposes, a ticking bomb.

Then it happened.

The leaking fuel had run across the grass to the front of the aircraft. Something hot inside the engine bay made contact with the fumes rising around it.

With an almost entrancing whoosh, the fuel ignited.

The flames rose rapidly around the engine and dark smoke started to billow in the air.

The pilot wailed with fear and then stopped. They all looked on with dread as the young man reached out to grab his pistol and point it towards his head.

'I can't watch this,' Edward said. 'Nor should you, Bob.'

He grabbed the teenager's shoulders and wheeled him around.

But, there was no gunshot.

Ken and Albert watched in horror as the pilot continued to hold the shaking gun to his head. Even as the flames licked around the canopy and crept inside the cockpit, the young man couldn't pull the trigger. Such was his instinct for survival, even as his screams became shrill beyond measure; he just couldn't take his own life... not even at this most obviously desperate moment.

Through the drifting smoke, Ken saw the French artillery officer standing some way behind the crashed aircraft.

The twisted body of a child lay at his feet.

Ken could see the utter anguish on the man's face, as he raised his revolver.

Now, he knew what he had to do.

He grabbed the rifle from Albert's shoulder, pulled the bolt back, pushed it forward to load a round and released the safety catch. Ken took aim and fired his first bullet at the screaming German pilot fifty yards away.

He reloaded, fired, repeated this once more and the screaming stopped.

Albert looked at Ken, dumbfounded.

'It was the right thing to do,' Ken said and handed the weapon back.

He walked back towards the van.

A number of people had arrived at the top of the field and looked on in bewilderment at the now-blazing Messerschmitt. Albert looked at the rifle for a few moments... then slung it back over his shoulder.

Turning towards Edward, he spoke first.

'It was the right thing to do.'

'Yes Bert... it was.' Edward replied.

Edward put his arm around Bob, who looked back at him with confusion, unable to fully comprehend what had just happened.

They watched the blazing aircraft for a few minutes, as the enormity of what they had witnessed sunk in. They turned the backs on the tragic scene and began to slowly walk back to the van.

As Ken sat on the grass watching the others approach, he looked at the smoke drifting across the meadow.

The spectre of the French officer was visible for a moment again.

The child with black hair stood alongside him now.

The smoke billowed across them and they were gone.

In that instant, he understood what his nightmares, those whispers, had been trying to tell him... ever since the night he slept under that great, old oak tree in the woods above that grand house.

In that isolated, mournful place, it had crept into his mind, his spirit and drawn out his memories, previously buried, too horrible to confront. Ken had feared its intent, but now he realised that it brought salvation for his sanity.

As he stared at the burning aircraft, Ken shivered and thought about a horrific day on a war-torn road in France. He remembered the woman screaming at the sight of her son lying in the road, dismembered, disembowelled, shrieking in agony.

The boy was beyond all hope of help, until the sharp report of the French officer's pistol shot put him at peace.

Now Ken understood that it truly was the right thing to do.

He felt a profound sense of relief.

No... a better word was *release*, as he looked at his new friends and smiled.

Chapter 29

Stabsfeldwebel Freund waited patiently as a Fiesler Storch light aircraft deftly landed at the airfield's western perimeter, well away from the main runways. With its incredibly short take-off and landing capability, the remarkable little Storch fulfilled many roles within the Luftwaffe and Wehrmacht and today, this one was providing a fast taxi service between KG1's three airfields.

Freund watched the Storch trundle across the grass towards him and when it was just 50 metres away, the pilot cut the engine. With a display of panache, he swung the aircraft around with the last of its momentum, so that his passenger could dismount directly in front of Freund.

The mystery visitor clambered out of the plane and unloaded a large leather-faced box, the sort that was often used to protect cameras or scientific equipment. He introduced himself as Major Ahrens and instructed that the box be carried with extreme care. As Freund walked him to the staff car, he noted the brown-edged collar tabs on the officer's jacket. This signified that he was a radio communications specialist.

They exchanged simple pleasantries as they drove across the airfield, but the major didn't give anything else away.

Freund considered why the aircrews returning from this morning's raids had been held back from further operations and ordered to rest throughout the afternoon. The tired airmen had readily accepted the offer of much-needed sleep, taking to their camp beds as soon as they had been fed.

Considering all things together, Freund concluded that this officer was here for the special briefing that was scheduled for 9pm that night.

As they pulled to a halt outside the main offices, Major Ahrens insisted on carrying the mystery item into the building himself. Freund returned to his own office, none the wiser for what all the fuss was about. That is, until Gefreiter Fischer handed him a new set of logistics orders for the 3rd Gruppe's next mission.

Now this did warrant close attention.

They had to fuel and bomb-up all forty two remaining bombers at Rosières for a single mission together.

Three significant facts leapt off the page.

Take-off time was set for 10.30pm that night, only 25% of the payload would be high explosive bombs and the rest would be made up of incendiaries, delivered earlier that day.

Freund's mind raced with all the possibilities yet again.

Whilst a few of the gruppe's aircraft had flown night missions over Britain before, they had been relatively minor nuisance attacks, rather than major assaults. However, a raid on this scale, at night, potentially heralded a significant change in tactics, especially as incendiary bombs were used against towns and cities, not airfields.

Freund reasoned that the major's box held the key to this new conundrum.

He noted that all the navigators had been ordered to gather an hour before the main briefing. Putting it all together, he guessed that the mystery major was here to instruct on a new radio technique. Such matters were always shrouded in secrecy, so he decided to concentrate instead on the Herculean logistics task expected of him. He sat down at his desk, reached for his cardboard folder of past mission calculations and began his arithmetic.

Freund was correct.

Major Ahrens was on a whistle-stop tour of local bomber airfields to deliver training on a new, top secret technology.

The real reason for the Luftwaffe's peculiar night missions over England, first detected by British RDF back in May, had been to test a revolutionary navigational device. Those solitary aircraft had been sent to specific places, to check that special radio beams aimed from Western Germany and Denmark did indeed converge over a designated location.

This ingenious system codenamed *Knickebein*, the Crooked Leg, sent a Morse Code-like radio beam that aircraft could follow for hundreds of kilometres, even in the pitch black of night. The on-board radio operator would listen for the constant tone of the correct path, but would hear dots if the aircraft strayed left or dashes to the right. From this, he could order course changes to the pilot, until he reacquired the centre tone. A second radio beam was transmitted to intersect the first, just where the aircraft should start its attack run, typically one minute before bomb release. So even dense cloud cover, on a moonless night would no longer prevent German bombers from finding their goal with an unprecedented accuracy of about 500 metres. In comparison, their British counterparts wandered around blindly over Germany, often missing their intended targets by ten or twenty miles.

The really clever part about Knickebein was how it utilised the well-known Lorenz blind landing equipment fitted to all German bombers and occasionally installed in British aircraft too. Despite the large number of crashed German aircraft in English possession since the start of the battle, the Knickebein secret hid inside the Lorenz receivers unnoticed for several months. British intelligence services heard many references to the mysterious code word, but for a long time had no clue as to what it referred to.

One day, a captured Luftwaffe radio operator was overheard joking about Knickebein to his comrades... *They'll never find it you know.* This confirmed that this *it* was real, physical and there to be found, somewhere within the realm of radio.

Encouraged afresh, British air crash investigators renewed their efforts and finally cornered their elusive quarry. They realised that many German bombers' Lorenz sets had been tuned to an unusually high sensitivity, capable of detecting a signal sent over very long distances, thereby revealing their true purpose.

On the night of the 21st of June, an RAF search plane was sent aloft with a specialised receiver and, by sheer good fortune, detected the fabled Knickebein beam. It followed its path until the crew heard a second, intersecting bomb signal and realised that they were directly over the Rolls Royce factory at Derby. This was the sole production plant for the Merlin engine that powered all of the RAF's Hurricanes and Spitfires.

The profound shock of this discovery spurred immediate action. British radio scientists quickly developed a way to broadcast crude radio interference, to obscure the guidance signal within the beams. This was at best only a stopgap. The beam was still a broad indicator of direction for an enemy raider to follow, even if its pinpoint accuracy was obscured. The chief scientist on this project, Reginald Jones, proposed a method whereby British transmitters could broadcast extra dots and dashes on one side of the Knickebein beam. If it worked, this would trick the German bombers to veer away from the true path, in effect, *bending* their beam.

This new military science was in its infancy and tonight would be a test run for Jones' new theory. Whilst the intended target might be protected, it could be at the cost of leading the raiders onto another unsuspecting British town nearby. However, this was the price of war, as the visible conflict in the skies was joined by a new, hidden form of warfare by electronics in September 1940.

Unbeknownst to the British, German radio scientists had anticipated this new arms race and already taken their next step, with Knickebein's successor, *X-Geraet*. This was a greatly more sophisticated, purpose-built system and far harder to defeat. Major Ahrens had one of the precious devices in his leather box and was here to explain its operation. He would also reveal how others like it now equipped aircraft of an elite Luftwaffe unit, KG100, whose job was to fly ahead and use this specialist equipment to pinpoint their targets. Ordinary bomber crews would still need their Lorenz sets to get reasonably close before British jamming disturbed the Knickebein signal. By then KG100's pathfinders would already have marked their destination with incendiary flares... a fiery beacon to guide them to target.

Tonight would be the turn of the Rosières aircrews to practice this new technique on an unlucky English town.

Ernest Harrop's safe and insignificant day in the shop had nearly drawn to a close. Relishing every moment of its humdrum normality, the day flew by in stark contrast to the terrifying events of his weekend.

He had walked downstairs at 6am this morning; much earlier than usual, such was his eagerness to resume his predictable life. Mabel and Betty arrived an hour and a half later and the routine of customers, sales and gossip sped the hours away. Everything felt as it should be and even the distant booms and drone of aircraft held far less concern for him now. Ernest had even enjoyed a tingle of excitement when he looked up Mabel's skirt as she stood up the ladder to reach a top shelf. However, the thrill of seeing the back of her thighs instantly evaporated as his memory of Friday night made sharp again. Ernest had renewed his vow to mend his perverted ways, but a few hours later, it already felt like a hard pledge to keep.

He was rather proud of his efforts after yesterday's bombing attack and had basked in the praise it fostered, given by so many of the ladies that visited his shop today. They had heard all about the terrible damage inflicted on the residents of Hazelmead Road and how the courageous ARP had come to everyone's rescue.

It was good to have men like Mr Harrop around to protect them, they said and everyone agreed that Sidcup had had its brush with the war. Lightning was unlikely to strike twice in such an unimportant little town. Unfortunately, none of them could know that such a sentiment would ring so very hollow, so very soon.

As 5pm drew close, such was the breadth of Ernest's happiness that he told the girls to go home early. He'd heard them talking about a trip to the pictures, so he said they could leave promptly, to give them more time for their tea and to get their *glad rags* on. In contrast, Ernest was looking forward to a quiet night locked safely indoors with his French postcards to keep him company. Mabel had certainly perked up at the news of the early finish, as she had spent most of the day looking unwell, complaining of a poorly stomach *after eating something iffy*. She was out of the door like a shot and Betty almost had to run after her to remind her about their cinema date.

That was odd, Ernest thought.

When he had heard them talking earlier, it had sounded as if Mabel wasn't keen on the cinema trip. Then again, if she was unwell, it would be understandable.

'Is she alright?' he asked, as Betty walked back inside.

She hesitated for a moment before framing her reply.

'I think so, ladies matters Uncle, you know…'

'Well you be on your way young lady, I know you have big plans for this evening,' he replied, feeling bighearted at that moment. 'I'll be fine here, tidying up… before I close up.'

Betty went down the back of the shop to get her bicycle from the yard and Ernest went to the shop counter. He'd been looking for a specific ointment for Mrs Rogers, the vicar's wife at St John's. The only place he hadn't yet searched were the drawers under the main counter. He got down on his knees to better pull out the heavy bottom drawer, when the bell on the door tinkled, to signal another customer entering the shop.

He looked up quickly and nearly had the fright of his life.

A huge figure loomed in front of him, silhouetted against the sunshine streaming through the shop front.

Ernest actually wailed out loud at that moment, believing that his terrible assailant had returned, like the Devil incarnate.

'Mr Harrop, I'm sorry, I didn't mean to frighten you,' Ken apologised.

Ernest knelt there frozen in terror until Ken moved to one side and the sunlight illuminated him more fully.

'Oh well…you shouldn't creep up on people like that Kenneth.' Ernest said by way of explanation, as he stumbled to his feet. He tried to regain his composure. His heart was racing wildly and he felt light-headed from the shock and reached out to steady himself.

'Is Betty still here? I haven't missed her already have I?' Ken asked. 'Are you alright Mr Harrop?'

He was puzzled by the state of the man in front of him.

Before Ernest could answer, Betty appeared from the back, wheeling her bicycle down the passageway.

'Here I am. Who wants me?' she said excitedly, although she already knew the answer.

'Me.' Ken replied simply. Then he smiled the widest, happiest smile that Betty had ever seen.

Somehow he was transformed.

He stood taller, straighter, more confident and cheerier than at any time since they first met.

Betty beamed back at him.

She was sure that everything was going to be alright.

She just *knew* it.

Chapter 30

Patricia felt as if she was standing amidst absolute pandemonium, as all the members of the Vigar family arrived home together on that Monday evening. Dinner was still only half-prepared when Edward, Ken and Betty appeared at the back door, all gabbling away, thirteen to the dozen. They all stood right in her way, in the middle of the kitchen, talking excitedly of Hurricanes and Messerschmitts and plane crashes.

Virginia burst through the front door. She declared, self-importantly, that she was filthy dirty and must have the first bath, as she had *the most important evening planned*. Although Betty pointed out that the dirtiest person really should go last, this fell on deaf ears as Ginny turned for the bathroom. When Patricia eventually got Edward to slow down and start from the beginning, she discovered just how eventful his afternoon had been. He recounted the story of the ghostly Hurricane fighter and the tragic tale of the trapped German pilot.

'Did he suffer terribly Ted?' she asked.

'It was quick,' he answered.

There was an awkward silence.

Ken and Betty made a tactful exit towards the front room, while Edward continued with his story. He explained how they had waited for the police to arrive, completed an incident statement and stayed until Albert mustered a Home Guard detail.

By then, the wreckage had cooled down enough for an ambulance crew to retrieve the pilot's remains and take them to the mortuary. Finally, he explained about what had happened to his scaffolding behind the cinema and that all in all, no work had been done to earn any pennies for the family today.

'Terrible times Ted, you really can't tell what each day will bring now.' Patricia replied and deftly changed the subject. 'Little Jimmy's funeral is set for Wednesday… we should all go to that.'

Edward responded in the simplest way possible.

He took her in his arms and kissed her.

They stayed like that, cuddled together, until Betty burst into the kitchen, a few seconds later.

'What's for tea, Mum?' she asked excitedly. 'Come on…it's nearly six o'clock, we have to get our skates on.'

'Mutton leftovers, mash and Dad's runner beans… if that's alright with you Madame?' Patricia replied.

'Good… 'cos I'm famished.' Betty exclaimed.

She hurried to the bathroom and started to bang on the door.

'Ginny! Ginny! Leave the water in and hurry up… otherwise I'll blow the door down!'

She hurried into her bedroom to get undressed.

It was time for Ken to speak.

'I think I had better make myself scarce… whilst the ladies are in their boudoirs,' he said with a big grin.

'You look a lot happier young man.' Patricia noted.

'I'll get Betty's bike out of the van and give it a once-over,' Ken responded, as he walked out the back door. 'It needs a clean and a bit of an oiling I think.'

He had a noticeable spring in his step.

'Ooooooooh!' said Patricia, raising her eyebrows. 'I take it you picked Betty up from Ernie's and your dirty old van is outside then?'

'Yes, My Love.' Edward replied, knowing full well that she wouldn't really be embarrassed by its presence. 'But I'll drop it back at the yard later… the neighbours won't see it outside for too long.'

'Well make sure you do Mr Vigar… we have standards to maintain,' she joked. They kissed again, accompanied by the sound of Betty's fist pounding on the bathroom door again.

Yet it didn't quite drown out the racket of Ginny singing *On The Good Ship Lollipop*, very, very badly.

Edward and Patricia looked at each other and burst into laughter.

Ken appeared from the back yard.

'I can't see Ginny's bike… it's the red one isn't it?' he asked. 'I thought I'd give that a polish too… I can only see your black Swift in the shed, Mrs Vigar.'

Patricia thinned her lips and joined Betty outside the bathroom.

'Where's your bicycle young lady?' she shouted. 'Have you left it at the factory *again*?'

'Sorreeeeee Mother.' Ginny answered. 'I took the bus home.'

'You will be sorry… if you don't stop hogging the bathroom,' Betty piped up.

The lock snicked open. Ginny strode out in her silk dressing gown and wafted up the stairs, like a Hollywood starlet.

In the kitchen, Edward exchanged glances with a smirking Ken. Edward shook his head slightly and concluded with just one word.

'Women!'

Elsewhere in Kent, the great air battle had continued as a fifth wave of bombers crossed the South Coast at 5.15pm, intent on pounding airfields again. However, the people of Sidcup carried on their small-town life, blissfully unaware of the titanic struggle taking place all around them.

Near Maidstone, Detling aerodrome was hit yet again.

Walter Camp and Sidney Worsell were finally relieved from a second day of duty. They headed home, shouting at the top of their voices, both of them deafened by events, but glad to have made it through another harrowing day.

Practically all of 11 Group's airfields had been hit and as a parting shot, just before 6pm, RAF Hornchurch in Essex received another visit from the Luftwaffe. After this, the fighting petered out and the battle area soon emptied of aircraft from either nation. Their commanders awaited reports from their forces and whilst Dowding and Park had much to worry about, Goering was positively ecstatic with the progress apparently made today.

It was amazing how one day's fine weather had made such a difference. Although the Luftwaffe had lost thirty one aircraft, it was reported that the RAF had fared far worse in the air and on the ground. Once again, the reduced number of bomber interceptions boded well and the Luftwaffe had enjoyed a relatively free rein to pursue its goals.

Goering had much to celebrate as he prepared for a strategy conference convened for the following morning. Yet, if he had been the sort of man who looked at the detail, he would have focussed far more intently upon the rapidly accelerating loss rate of his fighters. Goering was a big man with big ideas and left the small things for his subordinates to deal with. However, none of them rushed to highlight that his mighty Luftwaffe had lost a staggering 37% of its entire combat strength in recent months. Instead, Goering focused on how grandly he would announce his new strategy to the Luftflotte commanders tomorrow.

It was far easier to fantasise about the terrible fate that he had planned for the British, than deal with the inconvenience of their continued stubbornness.

Robert Higgins pulled up on the drive at Craywood House and was pleased to see Maude waiting to greet him at the front door.

From the look on her face, he could tell that something was wrong. He saw the bandage on her hand and walked quickly across the gravel.

'Oh my dear, whatever have you done?' he asked with concern.

'Oh… Robert this is nothing, I cut myself in the garden that's all… there are much bigger troubles to deal with,' Maude replied with a smile.

She took both of his hands in hers and neither spoke for a moment.

'I'm glad that you are here now,' she concluded.

They walked inside and headed for the dining room, as Maude explained the detail of her family crisis. As they ate, she revealed her findings at Bridger's Farm and Mr Cameron's defensive finger-pointing. Then she moved onto her conversation with Godfrey Burridge, his view on a possible criminal prosecution and potential seizure of the farm by the War Agricultural Executive.

Finally, she aired her solicitor's practical suggestions, given through loyal support of the family over many years, good and bad.

Robert loved to see Maude so animated and thought how radiant she looked this evening, even in the midst of such problems. She appeared so alive, positively glowing and his mind cast back to their younger days.

He considered how their lives could have been so different.

Nonetheless, here he was, ready to help the woman he had always loved and together they would find a way to avoid the impending disaster.

Robert took it all in. His analytical mind started to weigh up the options, their ramifications and possible outcomes.

By the time they had finished eating their meal, it seemed to him that every option led to an outcome that Raymond wouldn't like at all.

Barely had the last knife and fork been put down, before Betty and Ginny whipped everything off the dining table and rushed it all into the kitchen. The washing up was completed in record time, without the usual argument over who would wash or dry.

As the plates and saucepans clattered into the cupboards, Edward drank the last of his beer and then Ginny reappeared. She snatched the empty glass from his hand and took it to the kitchen.

'Blimey, anyone would think they were in a hurry,' he joked and looked across to the clock on the mantelpiece. He spoke loudly, to tease his daughters again.

'Five to seven? Oh dear, but I've got a few more jobs for you to do yet.'

'Oh, leave them be Ted.' Patricia chided.

'Go on girls, off you go,' he relented, feeling his wife's disapproving glare.

Betty and Ginny rushed from the kitchen to their bedrooms, to complete their final preparations for the evening ahead. Ken stood up and walked to the mirror above the fireplace. He took up his forage cap and perched it at a rakish angle on his head. Satisfied with his reflection, he wheeled on the spot and stamped his feet to attention.

'All present and correct Soldier?' Edward asked in an officer's tone of voice.

'Yes, Sah!' Ken replied.

'Yes, Sah!' The girls repeated in unison from out in the hall.

'Come on Ken… we have to go, the programme starts at half past,' Betty declared.

Ken looked for permission from his superior officer.

With a nod from Edward, he went to the hall and the girls giggled as they all went to the front door.

'Now be careful. Listen out for the siren and come straight home afterwards,' Patricia called out.

'And no *funny business*,' Edward added.

'Oh Daaaaaad….' the girls replied, in chorus again.

The youngsters made their way outside.

Just as Ginny was closing the front door, she turned and looked at Patricia.

Love you Mum, she mouthed silently.

Then, she was gone.

'Well… we didn't even get a kiss,' Patricia lamented as she walked back to the kitchen.

'I know, too grown-up, and too excited about the pictures. That's all,' Edward consoled her.

Patricia's face darkened for a moment.

'They will be alright tonight, won't they?'

'They'll be fine… Jerry won't bother with us again, anytime soon,' he replied. 'There's nothing here for them, I'd say we had our one and only visit yesterday.'

'Well, we had two sirens this afternoon, at lunch time and about half past four,' Patricia revealed. 'I was surprised you let them go tonight, actually?'

Edward look puzzled.

'I thought you had said it was alright?'

'But I thought you had,' she replied.

They both realised that assumption had carried events.

'They'll be alright I'm sure… I'll keep an eye on things,' Edward reassured her. 'First peep of the siren and I get straight down there and get them out, remember… I am Chief Warden.'

'At least Virginia won't be on that Raymond Delafort's motorbike, now *that* is dangerous,' Patricia continued. 'Remember, he was round here late last night. That was really odd. Did you see him today… he said he wanted you to mend some windows?'

'No, Love, I didn't get over to Bridger's, did I?' Edward reminded her.

'I expect he'll turn up sometime,' she pondered. 'Anyway, I told Virginia that on no account should she get on that motorbike… have you seen the way he charges around on that thing?'

'Don't worry… they're only down the road. Ken will keep an eye on them both,' Edward replied.

They sat in silence for a moment. Patricia rose from her chair, walked to the French Doors and looked out into the garden. The sun was low in the sky now and her attention was caught by a cloud of midges dancing in the warm evening air.

Lost in thought, she stared at the frenzied mêlée of tiny flies, so redolent of the greater human drama played out daily in the skies above.

Like Mother Fox that once stood on a woodland hillside, Patricia worried about the future and what it would mean for her family.

'I hate this bloody war,' she murmured.

Ken, Betty and Ginny walked quickly down Hazelmead Road. They had all linked arms, with him in the centre, thoroughly enjoying the attention of the two sisters.

Up ahead, a large queue of people was already snaking back from the Plaza, well past the shops. As the happy trio drew close, they could see what had caused the big attraction tonight.

As well as the murder mystery that had been showing for the last week, the billboard declared that Arthur Askey's hilarious new caper, *Charley's Aunt*, was starting tonight. Normally new runs began on Sundays, but the cinema had been closed by yesterday's bombing. So an extra-large crowd was gathering in anticipation of the new feature opening this evening.

'Hello playmates!' Ken called out, mimicking the comic star of the film.

'Ay thang yooooo,' the girls gave Arthur's catchphrase reply.

All three burst out laughing.

Betty noticed something pinned upon Ginny's dress, revealed as she loosened her coat.

'That's Mum's diamanté broach,' she declared accusingly. 'Does she know you have that?'

'Oh Fiddle-Dee-Dee Betty,' Ginny replied. 'Don't you worry… she won't mind.'

As ever… what Ginny wants, Ginny gets, Betty thought.

She decided to make no more of the matter.

Betty was more interested as to why Ginny looked especially anxious to get to the cinema so quickly.

'And who are you looking for?' she teased.

'Mabel of course, you said seven, but it's nearly ten past,' Ginny replied.

'I'm sure Mabel can cope,' Betty declared. 'That's…*if*… she is coming.'

Ginny suddenly looked somewhat off-balance.

'What do you mean… if…?' she asked.

'Oh, she wasn't well again today,' Betty replied. 'To be honest, I don't think she's up to it.'

They walked past the huge bomb crater, now roped-off like a cricket pitch in the middle of the road. Ginny looked even more uncertain, but then a big smile broadened on her face as she spotted Mabel outside the cinema.

'Cooo-eeee!' she called out and trotted over to where Mabel stood amongst all the other queuing people. She noticed her school friend was not alone, Mabel's big sister Grace was with her.

'Hello Grace, how are you? I haven't seen you in ages,' Ginny joked, as she transformed into her usual excitable, gregarious, larger-than-life character and gave them both a big hug.

'Better for being out of Klingers,' Grace replied. 'Good job I heard about Charley's Aunt, as otherwise, Miss Grumpy here wouldn't have come out tonight.'

'How are you feeling dear?' Ginny asked Mabel. 'Still a bit poorly?'

'I'm fine thank you, absolutely fine thank you,' Mabel replied defensively.

Before she could continue, Ginny had snuck herself in with them in the queue and started to gossip away with Grace, her new best friend.

Ken and Betty crossed the road to join them, but then the tall handsome soldier caught the attention of Grace. She was a lady much of the same flirtatious nature as Ginny.

'Ooooh look at you,' she said with exaggerated delight, much to Betty's annoyance. 'Well, go on... introduce me!'

Ginny seized the initiative and introduced Ken. Before he knew it Grace was all over him, with Betty pushed to one side.

'Excuse me ...you can't just barge in front like that,' a short man, standing behind them interjected.

'Oh yes we can.' Ginny answered cheekily. 'We are war-workers and have top priority.'

'I don't see what that would have to do with it?' continued a disgruntled-looking John Fellowes. 'We've been waiting for twenty minutes already and….'

'Oh steady on… let's not get in a tizz,' Ken interrupted, trying to calm the situation with this irate man and his wife. 'We'll go to the back now. We were just saying hello to our friends… come on Betty, let's get to the back.'

He grabbed Betty's hand and they briskly walked off.

'Hang on, I'm coming too,' Grace piped up and rushed after them, intent on pursuing the nice soldier she had just met.

Now alone with Mabel, Ginny turned and lowered her voice.

'I have a little favour to ask of you darling,' she said in conspiratorial fashion.

Mabel just knew there was going to be a catch.

At a German radio station just south of Boulogne-Sur-Mer, it was now 8.15pm, Continental Time. Code-named *Mont Violette*, this was one of eight new Knickebein transmitters recently set up along the western coast, to support the original stations at Stollberg in Denmark and Kleve in Western Germany. Tonight would be its first operation in earnest… to guide a major raid deep into English territory.

The technicians needed to carefully switch on each part of the apparatus, to ensure that every component was properly warmed up to produce a good, clean signal beam later on. Having considered British jamming attempts over the last month, their new strategy hinged around using a number of stations to transmit decoy beams to false destinations. Only KG1's raiding force would know where to intercept the true signal and then follow it… to where KG100 would illuminate their real target.

At Rosières airfield, the navigators had completed their instruction given by Major Ahrens and awaited the arrival of their flight comrades. The rest of each bomber's aircrew started to congregate in the mess tent, in preparation for tonight's main mission briefing.

An air of expectancy hung over the young airmen, a shared anticipation of the new adventure that lay ahead. It would be a test of their airmanship, pitting them against the dangers of long distance flying in the pitch black of a moonless night. Their sense of excited trepidation was well-founded, knowing that the hazards of misadventure in darkness far outweighed anything to be feared from the paltry British night defences. Nonetheless, the cloak of night would be a welcome protection from the daylight onslaught of RAF fighters. Across the airfield, the fuelling and bombing-up of each aircraft was nearing completion and Stabsfeldwebel Freund sat impatiently in his office, anxious to complete his arithmetic for the night.

The technicians at Mont Violette were pleased with the newly-installed equipment and decided to begin a test transmission. For just sixty seconds, the radio beam travelled across the English Channel and onwards towards the Greater London area. With a few adjustments, it stabilised correctly and then they turned the signal off, denying their British counterparts any further warning. All was now ready for 11pm, local time, when they would transmit on full power.

By then, the bombers from Rosières would be passing overhead, ready to be led to their rendezvous over tonight's target.

Maude and Robert took their dinner plates and dishes down to the kitchen and stacked them neatly by the sink in the scullery. They would be left there for Mrs Tedbury to deal with in the morning, as their conversation had greatly delayed their departure for the Bridge Club. Robert went back upstairs to start his car, leaving her to finish tidying up.

The kitchen was unusually hot and stifling.

Maude felt herself swoon for a moment and she realised that she didn't feel well at all. No doubt the upset of the last few days was taking its effect, as she certainly wasn't getting any younger. Her hand throbbed painfully as if to underscore her thoughts. She looked at the bandage and decided that she must ask Robert to take a look at the wound later. Her head swam again and she reached out to the door frame to steady herself. Marshalling her strength, she shut the larder door, went over to the steps that led up to the hall and turned off the light.

Maude looked into the absolute darkness of the basement kitchen and thought of Raymond. She felt depressed, overwhelmed by the gloom of her surroundings and the feelings she harboured about her nephew.

She heard a voice call out for her from upstairs and, just for a moment, she imagined it was from her beloved Daphne. Maude often fancied that she could hear her dead lover laughing in the next room, or sometimes, catch a glimpse of her in the corner of her eye, trying to brighten her mood. Of course, it must be Robert, telling her it was time to go.

She went upstairs, but he wasn't there.

Maude took her jacket out of the cloak cupboard and put it on, picked up her hat and walked to the mirror to position it, just so. She stared at her reflection and it struck her how careworn her expression had become. She pinched her cheeks to try and restore a little colour to her face, but that only served to pain her wounded hand again. She looked down at the bandage and saw a small, dark spot of blood make its appearance through the linen.

Blood.

Maude knew she had to make a decision, one that her conscience had been wrestling with since returning from Bridger's Farm. Godfrey Burridge and Robert's advice had been all sensible in a normal, modern sense, but she had to be absolutely sure of a way to protect the farm. She had to be certain that the family would escape the scandal precipitated by Raymond's stupid, greedy actions.

She imagined how her father would have responded to this crisis; by donning those ridiculous white robes that he, Charles Higgins and their peers had fashioned for their silly mystic society in those long gone, Victorian times. Off they would have gone; to pay homage to the ancient spirits they believed resided in Cray Wood. The younger Maude had refused to be drawn into his mystical beliefs and after that frightening childhood night in the summerhouse, repudiated his foolish pagan notions utterly. She had her mother to thank for her firm, devout belief in Jesus Christ, Our Saviour, and had chosen the sunlit path instead.

Years later, Maude was tempted again, when she laughed and danced with Daphne, who saw no harm in the illicit physical pleasures they enjoyed. Yes, Maude revelled in the sensuality of their lovemaking, but she did not completely escape her sense of Victorian modesty. In contrast, libertine Daphne ran deep into the woods and shed her clothes, to skip naked and unashamed, around the heart of their modern-day Eden. She laughed and sang in jubilation, but Maude could not allow herself to emulate her lover's erotic celebration of Cray Wood.

As Josiah had warned on his death bed, there is a price to be paid for ignoring the source of such great benefaction. Daphne's horrific death amply demonstrated the scale of retribution taken on Maude for ignoring Cray Wood's call. She clung to her Christian faith and emerged from mourning, determined to extinguish the dark forces that she sensed nearby. Even though she doubted her own sanity for even half-believing her father's final, senile ramblings, she had surrounded the Cray Wood with high wooden fences to seal it off from the outside world. Yet even this physical safeguard proved insufficient... as she discovered on that awful day of blood.

Even today, she could not escape the horror of finding young Raymond beneath the huge old tree with that poor little puppy, brutally slain, its throat slashed open by that wicked army knife.

Like a scene of pagan sacrifice, Raymond stared back with a feigned innocence that only briefly belied the pure malice in his eyes. Of course, Evangeline never found out what really happened to her birthday pet that year, as Maude hid the awful truth from her by declaring that it had run away to find its mummy. As distraught as the little girl was, it was infinitely better than knowing the dog's real fate, at the hands of such a wicked brother. Maude spent the next twenty years trying to protect Daphne's daughter from harm. Evangeline thrived, carefree and unblemished and was now far away... and safe.

Maude looked at her bandaged hand again and thought of the copious amount of blood she had spilt on the flagstones yesterday. She realised that Raymond had tricked her into giving the blood offering again. She recalled the unearthly screams that accompanied the crashing German aircraft yesterday. The very same agonised wails that echoed from the woods as Daphne drew her final tortured breaths in 1918.

Maude felt humiliated by her inability to stop the progress of Cray Wood's power, how the suffering created by this new kind of war overhead, was somehow feeding its appetite below.

It seemed that her father's deathbed revelation about the spirits of Cray Wood was true after all. Perhaps she should heed his terrified warning about the final, horrific price that they demanded for their patronage. She remembered how frightened he was of what awaited him in the darkness.

Maude reached a decision.

It was time for Raymond to leave.

She had kept him here long enough and she was so tired of this responsibility. The world could have him… for better, or probably for worse.

Maude imagined him on a far-away battlefield like his father, somewhere that the most unpleasant aspects of his nature would be put to better use. All the reasons she had kept him away from peaceful society, were now exactly what was needed in wartime.

She hoped, no, she prayed that Raymond's departure would break the curse upon their family. She wished that Cray Wood had called that burning German aircraft down upon itself, to end everything in a final, terrible conflagration.

Maude wondered if she was going mad, just like her father before her.

She heard footsteps behind her.

'There you are,' Robert said, as he walked in from the drive.

'There was no need to shout earlier you know, Robert,' she replied. 'You knew I was in the kitchen.'

Robert looked puzzled by her comment, but no matter, it was time for them to depart.

They had to be at Mrs Price's for drinks at 7.30pm and battle would commence an hour later.

Chapter 31

Roger Mellard inspected the foyer and once satisfied that everything was ready, he signalled for the front doors to be unlocked.

Peter the doorman, or more accurately, Roger's lanky nephew in an oversized uniform, pulled all the doors open wide and their customers flocked inside.

Roger loved the atmosphere of evening performances, especially when it was the beginning of a new run. He had watched the new film earlier that afternoon to check its print integrity and in his opinion, *Charley's (Big Hearted) Aunt* was a real cracker and would be very popular. He had certainly laughed his socks off at various stages of the plot.

The title's reference to Askey's nickname certainly demonstrated his star status above straight-man sidekick, Rupert 'Stinker' Murdoch. Ever since the success of their *Bandwagon* radio show, over the last few years they had become two of the nations' most favourite entertainers.

Despite the forced optimism of the newsreels, the war situation was inescapably grave and everyone needed a bit of cheer to lift their spirits. So Roger had decided to move *Busman's Honeymoon* to the first showing, saving the best until last. It was at the end of its run and half the audience wouldn't turn up until halfway through the programme anyway. Nonetheless, the air of expectancy amongst the customers was so tangible you could almost touch it in the air, as the foyer quickly filled with the hubbub of excited conversation.

As usual, Roger's wife, Minnie, was in the ticket booth and quickly surrounded by a throng of people, but she was a safe pair of hands with this most important task. Imogen at the refreshment counter attracted as much attention despite, perhaps because of, its meagre fair. If anyone wanted to buy a Kia-Ora orange or lemon drink, they had to get in quick before tonight's allocation was gone.

Happy that everything had settled down nicely, he quickly walked through the crowd to the back of the foyer. He reminded his usherettes, Florence and Rose, to check everyone's tickets carefully, to make sure that no-one tried to sneak into the balcony with a stalls ticket. Then he trotted up the wide, sweeping staircase and through the private door to the projector room, to check on Edgar White's progress there.

Edgar was the single most important reason they were still in business today. Ever since the early 1900's, he had plied his trade as a projectionist through the silent era into the talkies. The three, monstrously complicated, projection machines and their huge electrical switchboards took quite a bit of handling and certainly Edgar knew them inside out. His other virtue was that he was well beyond call-up age and remained at his post, long after the rest of Roger's staff had gone to war. It was all a far cry from their pre-war heyday, when the Plaza opened for business with twenty three staff dedicated to delivering the ultimate, modern entertainment experience.

The projector room was already stiflingly hot.

Edgar was well used to it and had already got the first two twenty-minute reels of the murder-mystery cued up on neighbouring machines. When the first reel ran out, the second was ready-focussed to carry on in its place, he could add the third reel to the first projector, then the next on the second machine, until the movie was finished. The third machine was set up for the shorts; local advertising and the latest Pathé newsreel that had arrived at lunchtime.

'All good here Edgar?' Roger asked.

'Yep, we're all set, despite this bloody heat,' Edgar replied.

'Why is it so hot in here?' Roger enquired. He stared up at the ventilator fans in the ceiling, which were humming away at full pelt.

'Summer time, innit? But I can't get that bloody door open,' Edgar replied, nodding towards the fire exit. It would normally be wide open on such a hot night.

Roger went over to the metal door and pulled aside the blackout curtain.

He pushed on the release bar which clicked back as expected, but the door itself stubbornly refused to budge, no matter how hard he pushed against it. Looking above the steel frame, an ominous crack ran up the wall and it was clear to see that the metal lintel had buckled, firmly pinning the door in place.

'Oh my word… this doesn't look good, it must be from that bomb across the road yesterday,' Roger commented.

'Yep, I reckon we're going to boil in here tonight,' Edgar grumbled.

Roger thought for a moment.

After today's heat the auditorium was going to get very hot, especially with the big crowd in tonight.

He went to the door leading to the balcony landing and propped that open with a large fire extinguisher, to give Edgar some respite. He made a mental note to tell the girls downstairs to open the other fire exits to let the cooler night air in, but only after all the tickets for the second performance had been sold.

Managing the ambient temperature was always a problem in a building of this size and at full capacity, over 1500 people could enjoy its entertainment. The summer was not such an issue, but the coming winter would be another matter entirely.

Fortunately, Roger had husbanded the fuel oil for the central heating plant in the basement and the early spring had allowed him to use it sparingly. The storage tank was still half full with about 5000 gallons left, but there would be little chance of getting any more of this precious fuel delivered in wartime. He would have to make it last. There would be plenty of winter nights ahead when the audience would have to keep their overcoats on.

Well it isn't perfect, but it'll do, he thought.

It was certainly better than being closed down, as they were when war first broke out. Initially, the government prohibited large assemblies of people, fearing the danger to them if caught during any air raid. However, it was soon realised that providing entertainment to a worried nation was of far greater importance. The pragmatic solution had been the distribution of a short movie reel to be shown during any air raid alert, announcing that *People may leave, if they wish to do so.* In Roger's mind, nothing better demonstrated British resolve than the small number of people that ever left the cinema when he displayed that message.

'Oh that's better,' Edgar shouted over the hum of machinery, as he felt the room start to cool a little. 'Cheers boss!'

'I had better get downstairs and help with the tickets. I think we'll have six or seven hundred in tonight.' Roger replied from the doorway and was off, back down the staircase.

Yes, it was going to be a good night at the Plaza.

The foyer was full to the brim and already people were filing into the stalls or upstairs, to the higher-priced balcony seats.

As he made his way through the crowd, he was passed by Ginny and Grace chattering way, with the ever-faithful Mabel in tow.

Chapter 32

Betty and Ken laughed as they ran hand in hand down the street, away from the cinema.

Just fifteen minutes before, the evening had not been going well from Betty's point of view, with Grace Smith perched on Ken's arm as the queue inched forward. Betty had been dismayed to find that her night out was being hijacked by Mabel's flirtatious sister. Ginny had been nowhere in sight, no help from her, as usual.

By the time they reached the ticket booth, Betty had just about given up all hope of being alone with Ken, but fate came to her rescue. They had just bought their tickets, when Ken realised that Charley's Aunt was on the later showing. As Ginny and Mabel appeared through the crowded foyer to join them, Grace was distracted by their arrival and Ken quickly turned to Betty.

'Why don't we skip the first film and come back later?' he asked.

Betty barely had time to nod her agreement, before Ken grabbed her hand and dragged her back to the front doors. Grace looked on with disappointment to see Ken escape her grasp, as he waved at her and the other two women.

'See you later playmates! We'll come and find you,' Ken shouted and with that, he and Betty had hurried outside.

As they made sure of their escape by running down the road towards Halfway Street, Betty thought to herself how different he was now, compared with the early hours of that day.

She felt herself swept off her feet by this young man and her soul felt alive, glowing with his attention.

After about fifty yards they came to a halt and, out of breath, they looked at each other and burst out laughing again.

'You are so clever Ken! That was hilarious… did you see the look on her face!' Betty said excitedly.

Without a moment's thought, while still keeping hold of his hand, she darted up on her tiptoes and kissed him on his mouth.

As her heels touched the ground again, Betty's mind reeled at what she had just done. She just couldn't believe it had happened and looked back at him, utterly lost in his eyes.

Very slowly, very gently, he placed his free hand on her cheek and they kissed again. Betty didn't want to let go, not now, not ever and she reached up to touch his hair.

They kissed for a third time, slowly, lingering a little longer. They held each other like this until both sensed it was time to stop and then, stood facing each other. They held hands in silence, enjoying the feeling of the step they had just taken.

Ken spoke first.

'Well… what to do now, Betty?'

Betty blushed, bringing her full beauty to the fore. She stood before him, radiant with the thrill of this new-found experience.

'Let's talk and talk and talk!' she replied.

As they revealed their life's story to each other, the fun times, the sad times, their hopes and dreams, they walked onwards and onwards. Stopping occasionally to kiss, more than an hour had passed by before they even knew it. They found themselves well past Halfway Street, almost round the back of Eltham at Avery Hill, nearly two miles away from the Plaza.

They turned and started to walk back towards Lamorbey, happy that they had the same amount of time alone together, all over again.

The sun had set and by now, twilight was rapidly turning to the dark of a moonless night. As they walked in the cool air, the stars made their first appearance and the night-time scent of flowers added to the perfection of the moment. The closer they got to their destination, their conversation dwindled to a comfortable silence and Betty still had a firm hold of Ken's hand.

On the final few hundred yards before the cinema, they walked slower and slower, until they stopped to kiss again.

Just ahead was The Carpenters Arms.

Betty looked at her new beau and made a decision.

'I don't want to go back. It's well past nine now, we've probably missed the beginning. We can see it tomorrow night… can't we?'

Ken didn't give a hoot about the film.

With only two days leave left, he wanted to spend every possible moment with Betty.

'Will you take me to the pub? I've never been…' she suggested.

'I think a drink to celebrate is very much in order,' he replied with that huge, endearing grin. 'Although, I do have one condition…can I have my hand back for a bit?'

'It's decided,' she replied, 'but you'll have to keep me hidden from prying eyes. I'm under age you know!'

It really was proving to be a night of new experiences for Betty Vigar.

Meanwhile, Mabel Smith sat alone in the stalls feeling pretty miserable.

True to form, her sister had found another soldier to chat up, one of a group on a short pass from Foots Cray Camp.

Grace had disappeared into the back row before the first feature and then Ginny had deserted her as well... when Raymond Delafort appeared ten minutes later. Now they too were back there, canoodling in the darkness, no doubt.

Ginny had made her swear to secrecy and, under Raymond's smug gaze, Mabel was powerless to stop her making a terrible mistake.

So Mabel sat alone, with only her friends' hats and coats to keep her company in the busy auditorium.

Up on the screen, the main feature had just begun.

Arthur and his playmates were setting up the jolly wheeze of the title, whereby he would don women's clothing to impersonate his friend's aunt. Set in an Oxford university, a wizened old college porter that bore a striking resemblance to local legend Old Sid Althropp, was exacting his price for participation in their japes. He wanted 10 shillings each time to see no evil, hear no evil or to speak no evil. Mabel wouldn't be getting thirty bob for her silence about Grace and Ginny's antics and she decided to make the best of a bad lot.

She sat back in her chair and within a few minutes, she was fully immersed in the film and laughing as loudly as everyone else around her.

At Rosières airfield, the mission briefing was drawing to a close. A large map board showed the route by which they and aircraft of other bomber groups would congregate, before picking up the correct Knickebein beam pointing across the English Channel.

The target had been revealed; a key war factory amidst a workers residential district and, most importantly, why correct unit order had to be maintained in the bomber stream. The leading staffeln were loaded with high explosive bombs to take the roofs off of buildings, to open them up ready for the deluge of incendiary sticks that following aircraft would drop. The aircrews started to leave the tent and headed for trucks waiting to ferry them to their aircraft across the airfield. The men were excited and a little anxious, given their first involvement in a new type of raid tonight.

The change in ordnance revealed an obvious change in Luftwaffe strategy for the battle, underscored by the arrival of the munitions train that had pulled up on the perimeter of the airfield that afternoon. Whilst tonight's flyers had rested in their bunks, every other man at Rosières had been pressed into the exhausting task of unloading two hundred metric tonnes of incendiary bombs, delivered directly from Germany. As enormous as this job had been, it would replenish their stockpile adequate for only half a dozen missions. As the young flyers went to their bomb-laden Heinkels, Stabsfeldwebel Freund was just as busy with what felt like an equal weight of paperwork that night.

As the airmen clambered aboard their aircraft, they thought that, perhaps now, the end of the campaign was finally in sight. Excited by their daring mission, these men thought little for the consequences of their actions tonight. All they wanted was to get the job done and force the British to see sense and accept Germany's rule of Europe. The escalating use of incendiaries also marked a change in the focus of Hitler's anger. Attack by fire would be a blunt and indiscriminate weapon against English people in their homes. Such was the Führer's frustration with the lack of progress against Britain's military machine.

He had expected the British to have long since sought terms for peace. His focus was already turning eastwards towards Soviet Russia and his present ally of convenience, but true ideological enemy… Joseph Stalin.

In the midst of Hitler's current battle, a British Avro Anson communications aircraft was flying along the South

Coast of England. Inside the small twin-engine aeroplane, an engineer from Reginald Jones' research team listened intently on a captured Lorenz set. He was searching for any trace of a Knickebein beam crossing the coastline that night.

The aircraft was patrolling a circuit between Hastings and Folkestone, when he heard the tell-tale dots and dashes tone over Dungeness. He told the pilot to turn the Anson into the beam's path and they homed in on the continuous tone at the centre of the signal, just as a German bomber would. The Anson followed its lead inland to gain a compass bearing on its direction. This beam was pointing across Kent towards London or, more specifically, the vital commercial docks in its eastern quarter and beyond into the heart of England.

The operator radioed his findings on to the scientists at the jamming transmitters below… so that the beam-bending experiment could begin.

Having listened to dance music on the wireless for an hour or so, Edward and Patricia Vigar seemed to be enjoying their usual routine of evening relaxation.

However, appearances can be deceptive.

As 10pm approached, Edward went outside to their tin shed by the back door, for the third time in twenty minutes.

Ostensibly, he was keeping himself busy with little chores. It was just an excuse, to escape the heavy blackout blinds of the house, to listen to the night more clearly outside. For the first time today, he heard the sound of a goods train travelling at speed along the railway embankment, bound for London. Edward took this as a sign that bottlenecks up the line were now being cleared.

Despite the Luftwaffe's best efforts, British determination had overcome adversity yet again.

As the noise of the train receded, the silence of the night returned and Edward strained to hear anything out of the ordinary. Whilst the air battle had raged somewhere every day for the last three months, the evenings had been a welcome respite, with little here to interest Nazi bombers in the darkness. ARP training taught how night-time limited attacks to targets near easily identifiable features, mostly coastlines or rivers. This underscored the importance of the blackout, to deny the enemy any chance of navigation inland and certainly this had proven correct so far. Yet, he did wonder how the newspapers could proclaim devastating RAF attacks over Germany, in the same darkness that blinded the Luftwaffe.

Nonetheless, solitary aircraft would be often heard from time to time hereabouts and the Germans did bomb in penny packets by night, at random places across the country.

With this in mind, Edward couldn't help but feel a little bit anxious whilst his daughters were out of the house. Yesterday's excitement had reminded everyone just how unpredictably dangerous life in wartime truly was.

A voice penetrated the darkness.

'Ted… why don't you go down and have a quick look?' Patricia asked.

'Ooh you made me jump.' Edward lied as he turned to face his wife, who had just slipped out of the kitchen door to find him.

'Look… I know you're anxious and that makes me anxious too. Go and have a look,' she replied.

By the faint light that still spilled from beyond the horizon, Edward could see the worried look on Patricia's face. It didn't matter which one of them had been the first to fret, the subject had now been aired.

'You're right, Love. I'll take a wander down to the office and see how things are.' Edward decided. 'Roger and Old

Sid are on duty again… they'll know if there's much happening.'

With the exception of the occasional clanks and bangs echoing across the landscape from that far-away train, all was silent around Sidcup.

'Yes, you go… you'll feel much better… and so will I,' she revealed. 'The pictures will finish in an hour or so and hopefully they'll come straight back. Then we can all get to bed.'

She planted a big kiss on his lips. 'Go on you… have a good natter with your cronies,' she concluded.

They walked back inside and shut the kitchen door, so that they could turn the light back on. Edward walked into the hall, picked up his satchel and tin helmet and let himself out the front door.

'See you later, Love!' he said and then, he too was gone.

Patricia nipped upstairs to get her nightie and came back down to have her bedtime wash, whilst she waited for her family to come home.

Betty and Ken sat close together in a corner of the pub, well away from the shouts and cheers of darts players in the public bar. Here in the snug, people could hide themselves away and as he talked, she looked on his fine, handsome features and drank in every detail.

Betty listened to each word and every nuance of how he spoke. She watched every mannerism, she noted the shape of his eyes, his nose, his eyebrows, she revelled in the small details of the beautiful man that she had fallen in love with.

She wanted to know everything about him and as he talked about his childhood, she realised that it had been a stark opposite of her own happy upbringing. He had never known his real mother and had been raised almost like an orphan, by a quiet and withdrawn father and stern, cold step-mother. She was coming to realise that, to coin a popular phrase, he needed the love of a good woman to make him complete. Betty was certain she was that woman and as their conversation flowed... time ticked by.

The darts match next door had finished and the public bar was much quieter for it. The banter between players was replaced by a gentle murmur of conversation, as closing time approached. When the landlord called for Last Orders, the bell he rang seemed to call time on Betty and Ken's conversation too.

Both fell silent. Their thoughts moved from present, to the subject they had skirted around for the last three hours... their future.

'Will you be my girl Betty?' Ken asked.

She was overwhelmed by the immensity of the decision.

Far beyond the normal considerations of any relationship, in wartime such a commitment had far-reaching consequences. No-one knew what each day might bring. Ken would be gone after Wednesday and sent anywhere in the world in service to the country. He might be gone for months, years even, before they were together again... if ever.

Tears welled in her eyes.

Instantly crushed by their implication, Ken looked crestfallen,

'Yes Ken! Yes... I will be your girl... always!' Betty declared, as she cast away the sadder possibilities of what the future might bring.

She had put trust in her instincts and her heart pounded with approval.

'Really? Do you really mean it?' Ken asked, his spirits soaring from their momentary crash of disappointment.

'Yes, I really, really do...' she replied as she smiled.

Ken's hand reached out across the table to hers, knocking over his empty pint glass with nervous clumsiness.

He righted the glass and reached out again.

They held hands across the table and nothing more needed to be said.

Back in the stalls at the Plaza, Mabel was thoroughly enjoying her evening, quite contrary to her earlier expectations and disappointments. On the big screen, Arthur and his wacky chums had been quite the tonic after all. The mood in the auditorium was happy and gay as the film drew towards its climax.

Arthur's ruse was uncovered and he fled across the university campus in a madcap fashion that had the audience roaring with laughter. He made it back to his private rooms, stripped off his ladies clothing and instructed his friends to burn the evidence.

Then he jumped into bed to claim illness as his alibi.

The tall chair in the bedroom slowly swivelled round, revealing the Dean of the University.

He had heard everything.

In the auditorium, all fell silent as the audience waited to hear what he would say… you could have heard a pin drop.

Down in the basement of the cinema, a whisper of a click signalled that the Rheinmetall Type 17 electric-clockwork fuse of a SC250 high explosive blast bomb had completed the time delay set by an armourer at Rosières, two days before.

It had ticked away, unwitnessed, for 27 hours and 21 minutes since it fell from Horst Muller's stricken Heinkel yesterday afternoon. Six of the aircraft's eight silos had released single 250kg bombs, but the seventh silo had been short-loaded with only two lighter SC50's, to allow for the weight of the extra crew member, Kristian Bauer. This had provided Ernest Harrop with his predicted total of eight craters, when he counted up around Hazelmead Road yesterday evening.

From the eighth silo, the ninth bomb had fallen unseen and unaccounted for, at an angle of 45 degrees from the steeply-banking aircraft.

It had punched through the base of the tall chimney stack above Mrs Dockwell's flat and onwards, through Edward Vigar's scaffolding, penetrating the cinema's basement wall and finally, came to a halt alongside the central heating plant. The chimney stack had keeled over onto the scaffolding and brought it all crashing down in a huge heap of broken timbers, to perfectly hide the impact crater left by the bomb, before it gouged its way into the building.

This bomb had come out of a munitions factory in Frankfurt only ten days before and was considerably more powerful than any previously supplied to the 3rd Gruppe of KG1. The rapid use of bombs during wartime now allowed the German chemicals industry to utilise more powerful, if less long-lived, combinations of explosives. Based around the traditional Amatol-TNT mix, the inclusion of one tenth of Hexogen raised the *brisance*, the shatter effect, by an impressive 30%. The increase in explosive power delivered by Hexogen went a considerable way to compensate, kilo for kilo, for the shortcomings of German bomber payloads. An additional aspect of this new explosive mix was its much higher incendiary efficiency. This particular bomb had sat perfectly cradled by twisted pipework, above thousands of gallons of heating oil that had leaked into the Plaza's basement from the storage tank outside.

The fuse activated the detonator, which in turn, fired the bomb's 160kg main charge. In this perfectly combustible atmosphere, laden with heavy oil fumes… the resulting explosion was of quite extraordinary violence.

Within the auditorium, the Dean was about to frame his words of accusation towards Arthur when the air, the walls, the floor and the seats quivered for a millisecond.

The bomb blast erupted, as the detonation over-pressurised the basement with an immense production of combustion gases. The pressure wave punched through the floor of the auditorium and carried a dozen rows of seats upwards with their occupants still in place and burst through the roof of the cinema. Simultaneously, the walls of the building bulged outwards for a few extra milliseconds, until the catastrophic rise in air pressure caused the structure to shatter. The final, even more terrible, effect was how the inclusion of fuel oil vapour briefly magnified the fireball to a temperature of 1500 degrees Fahrenheit. The super-heated blast threw a magma-like wave of burning oil in every direction.

The shockwave shot through the ground towards The Carpenters Arms.

It travelled upwards through the feet of Ken, Betty and the other customers to jolt them violently, as tables and chairs jumped and glasses and bottles crashed to the floor.

In the opposite direction, the ground shock reached Ted, Roger and Old Sid to shudder the ARP office and passed by, onwards to the Vigar home.

As Patricia walked out of her bathroom into the hall, the concussion felt like a dull thump under her slippered feet. The following air blast shook everything within a thousand yards, accompanied by the thunderclap of detonation.

Mrs Dockwell had been next door at Renie's making cocoa. As their end of the apartment block collapsed into the shops beneath, their deaths and six of their neighbours were mercifully instantaneous. Forty three people had shared their fate within the cinema, killed outright by the tremendous blast. They were the lucky ones, as Millie Mellard had sold five hundred and thirteen tickets that evening. It hadn't been a full house by any means, but was a good turnout and consequently, a tragic number for that Monday night at the Plaza. Of those people sitting directly above the epicentre of the explosion, twenty two were instantly vaporised, whilst the rest were blown through the roof, torn apart into grisly pieces. The front of the auditorium was engulfed by the fire-flash and then a large part of the roof and balcony seating came crashing down.

Seconds later, the screaming started, as the survivors came to comprehend what had befallen them. Long afterwards, heroic tales and many far less so, would surface about what happened that night. Some people helped others to escape the inferno, whilst many were left to burn to death, trapped in the wreckage of the blazing picture palace.

Ken and Betty gathered their wits and with the other people from the pub, rushed out onto the road to be presented by the fiery glow of the burning cinema.

They joined a throng of people emerging from houses along the road. Some stood to gawp at the spectacular sight, whilst others rushed towards the conflagration, driven by an instinct to help their fellow human beings.

The young couple ran the three hundred yards to the cinema and were confronted by its shattered, rubble-strewn frontage as a host of bewildered, injured people started to clamber out of the ruined foyer.

Many stumbled over the debris alone, while others helped each other in small groups, but most bore a look of abject terror at their situation. Then, the air raid siren on the roof of the police station began its mournful, oscillating, high-pitched wail.

On the eastern side of Cray Wood, Captain Cardington had mustered his men to the guns, prompted by a telephone call from Anti-Aircraft Command. He knew that their gunfire, guided only by their sound locators, would be next to useless. They were unable to see any aircraft in the darkness, unable to estimate the height of this large air raid, first detected by RDF, then heard by Observer Corps stations after it crossed the Kent coast twenty minutes ago.

The rising noise of oncoming aircraft engines seemed to be on a path between him, the Klinger industrial area and the town of Sidcup. Cardington would have no choice but to fire his guns blindly, in the vain hope that they might score a chance hit, or at least disturb the enemy formation.

At Lamorbey, fire had taken hold of the cinema.

Pulsating columns of flame stabbed hundreds of feet skyward, a fiery beacon visible for thirty miles in every direction.

The sky flashed vivid yellow and crimson... just like the target flares carried by the aircraft of KG100.

Thick smoke and noxious fumes from burning fuel oil billowed around everyone outside the Plaza.

To add even more terror to that moment, the drone of approaching aircraft could now be heard.

Now came the reverberating crash of distant gunfire, as Cardington's battery commenced firing.

As shell bursts flashed high above, the booming drumbeat of hundreds of bomber engines raised the cacophony of noise to a deafening crescendo.

Betty looked around in bewilderment.

Her quiet, innocent, little town had become Hell itself.

She caught a glimpse of her father on the far side of the crowd.

Hand in hand, she and Ken pushed their way towards him, through the mêlée of running, terrified people.

When Edward saw Betty, he hugged her tighter than anything he had ever held in his life. He looked at her frightened face, bathed in the flickering glow of the cinema inferno and then looked skywards.

Resigned to their fate, all three of them simply waited for the shriek of falling bombs.

Yet, they did not come.

The bomber stream continued its inexorable journey overhead, towards the rendezvous with its pathfinders above another unsuspecting town, a hundred miles away.

As the roar of engines diminished... Betty, Ken and Edward came to realise that they had been spared.

Patricia's anguished voice called out.

She stood behind them in her dressing gown, breathless, panting, having run down Hazelmead Road in her bare feet.

'Where's your sister, where's Virginia?' She screamed. 'Oh God, *where* is my daughter?'

Raymond Delafort appeared from out of the chaos.

His clothes were torn and filthy, his face was bruised and raw, blood poured from a deep wound on his forehead.

'She's in *there*... Mrs Vigar. I'm so sorry, she's still in there,' he replied.

'Now this is not the end. It is not even the beginning of the end. But it is perhaps, the end of the beginning.'

Winston Churchill

Epilogue

Ginny's ordeal continued. She awoke in the darkness yet again and, gripped by panic, she fought for breath. She lay, pinned down, her face forced into the filthy earth. She recognised the salty taste in her mouth afresh and gagged, repulsed by the thought of the blood that had so nearly drowned her.

She screamed.

Ginny screamed again and again, until what little breath she had was exhausted and she panted as her head swam. She could barely move any part of her body, such was the oppressive weight bearing down upon her. Driven to the point of hysteria by this nightmare made real, her mind struggled to comprehend her situation.

Ginny knew that she was lucky to still be alive, that much was true.

She could remember watching the flicker of the cinema's projectors in the darkness, then something just too horrible to contemplate further, an immeasurably loud and painful explosion inside her head. She recalled falling, plunging downwards into utter darkness. The passing of minutes, hours, perhaps days was impossible to measure and in her delirium, brief moments of her life cascaded through her mind.

She felt the thrill of the motorbike ride with Raymond, and then she was running through fields of long, tall summer grass with a handsome lad from the Boys Home. Her laughter from that moment brought her to a childhood Christmas, as she and Betty giggled with fascination at Uncle Albert playing the spoons. She sat at her typewriter at work and then, she was twelve years old again, singing and dancing on the stage at school with Mabel and Grace Smith. Their happy, innocent voices sang *On the Good Ship Lollipop* as memories swirled around her, with no context of time, order or place anymore. Finally, just one image came into focus and she saw Little Jimmy.

The five year old boy lay at her feet, mortally injured by bomb shrapnel, his tiny life slipping away to another place.

He looked into her eyes and smiled.

Ginny was determined not to follow after him.

She heard a confused, pained-wracked murmur in the darkness.

'MABEL? Is that you, Mabel?' Ginny screamed in desperation.

'PLEASE HELP ME!'

But there was no reply.

This story continues
with

A CHORUS OF MERLINS

3rd September 1940. The RAF faces imminent defeat, Nazi Germany masses an invasion fleet and Britain stands at the brink of calamity. Fighter Command's leaders battle with politics on the ground, as the Luftwaffe storms overhead.

In Sidcup, people reel from the aftermath of the devastating bomb attack. The Vigar family search desperately for their missing daughter, Ginny, whilst the upper-class Delaforts are drawn into the sinister world of the black market. Fighter pilot Dickie pursues beautiful Evie, while soldier Ken tries to win back heartbroken Betty.

Yet nothing is at it first appears, as a dark web of blackmail, greed, betrayal and murder snares everyone within its grasp.

From the author

I can remember the exact moment that I first thought of writing the story that became *Waiting for Moonlight* and its sequels. It was a Sunday evening in 1997, when as a new father; I had proudly taken my wife, first child and my parents on a trip to the seaside.

On the way back we had called into Brenzett Aeronautical Museum, a former RAF station, since turned into a collection of salvaged relics from crashed aircraft from the Battle of Britain. This quiet little place, on the Romney Marsh between Rye and Folkestone had been at the frontline in the Second World War. As I reflected on the success of the trip and the fascination which I held for the objects in the museum, I dreamed about writing a novel one day. It was nearly twenty years before I actually did anything about it.

I was born in 1966 and as someone far cleverer than me once said, I was part of the 'Airfix Generation'. The war was something that felt like only yesterday and it had shaped my parents, their peers and the whole of British society. As I grew up, their principle reference point was *The War* and everything else was categorised as either 'before' or 'after'. So my early years were schooled in innocent admiration of what people like them went through.

My parents were in their seventies by the time of that daytrip and in keeping with most of their generation, they preferred to define their lives by what they had achieved since the conflict. My father, Jeff, died the following year when he was 76 and my mother, Joan, five years after him, aged 80.

However, as Dad approached his last days he started to talk 'about the war' and Mum had plenty to contribute too.

He had been one of the BEF, a survivor of the Lancastria disaster and she had served in the Admiralty. Both of them had eventful lives during that period and the anecdotes, few and far between when I was a child, began to flow. Like many ageing people who suddenly feel the advance of time more sharply, they wanted to get it off their chest. Both of them wanted, needed, to tell me what it was like. It might be regarded as a cliché, but it's true nonetheless.

My older brother, Keith, and my sister, Ann, grew up in the post-war era of austerity and recovery, so they knew what Britain felt like as it rebuilt itself. They told me about their childhoods, learning how to shake off the shadow of that awful thing over their shoulders, how they looked towards a brighter future.

After my parents were gone I got on with my life, worked hard and raised a family that grew to three children. I was 'doing my bit' as that wartime generation used to say. As the rigours of bringing up a young family passed, I started to reflect on what my parents had told me. Whilst they had left it too late to tell their tale themselves, I thought I might try for them. Bit by bit, I started to build a story that might capture the essence of what they endured.

Another key aspect of my upbringing was the broad range of people that I met at our family home. Dad was an international businessman and he loved to throw parties for colleagues and friends. I remember relishing every moment of a punch-up that broke out at a party when I was eight years old. In spite of a Polish-sounding surname, one of Dad's friends had let slip to another that the air force he had served in was actually the Luftwaffe.

Make no mistake; Waiting For Moonlight and its sequels are predominantly fiction. I have taken historical reality and changed it for dramatic purpose. Although Cray Wood, Hazelmead Road, St Mildred's, the Plaza cinema and Muller's staffel are products of my imagination, much of my story is inspired by real places, events and people. If you want to take a look for yourself, a good place to start is the Bomb Sight record for Sidcup.

My mother's friend, Sheilia, grew up in Welling and watched the Battle of Britain overhead, providing me with plenty of insight into life during the 1940's. She dodged falling shrapnel, saw the sky lit red by a burning city and watched a Messerschmitt crash-land in a field near her home. I have also drawn from sources on the other side of events. Rosières-en-Santerre really was the headquarters airfield of KG1, one of the principle Luftwaffe bomber groups in the battle over England in 1940. Karin, the German wife of one of my dad's work colleagues, once shared her harrowing first-hand account of the bombing of Hamburg in 1943. I wanted to give a sense of balance in my writing, from both sides of the conflict. Whilst history is prone to revisionism, I've tried my best not to be naively judgemental of either side in that period of horrific conflict.

So I hope I've done justice to the people that inspired my story. If I have succeeded in giving voice to just a fraction of what they wanted to say, then I'll be happy.

I'll let you be my judge.

My final thanks go to my mum's sister, my utterly fun-loving, completely bonkers Auntie Queenie. Not that she could comprehend it at the time, but her teenage dance in the moonlight became the key reference point for my tale.

Clive Jefferys
London
September 2020

To speak with the author, or receive updates about further publications, take a look on Instagram @clivejefferys or feel free to email: talktome@cejefferys.uk

Printed in Great Britain
by Amazon